OKINAWA

Future War Book 2

by FX Holden

D0802115

With great thanks to beta readers: Gabrielle Adams, Johnny Bunch, Mathias Bondeson, Bob Hesse and Aidan Trimble

Contents

Ripples: 1941

"The history of failure in war can almost be summed up in two words: 'Too late.'

Too late in comprehending the deadly purpose of a potential enemy; too late in realizing the mortal danger; too late in preparedness; too late in uniting all possible forces for resistance; too late in standing with one's friends."

General Douglas MacArthur, 1940

January 1941, Chengdu, China

"I heard you took up one of my shiny new airplanes yesterday," Major 'Buffalo' Ling-Sui, commander of the Chinese Air Force 5th Pursuit Group, grunted as he dropped his flight jacket beside him and sat down to his rice porridge in a half-deserted mess. It was dawn and most of the other pilots of the Chengdu airbase were still asleep, exhausted from unrelenting combat against the Japanese Air Force and some much-needed celebrations the night before. "And you broke it."

His opposite number, Major Wong 'John' Chen, commander of the 3rd Pursuit Group, looked up from his own breakfast and watched the short, stocky Californian ease onto the bench across from him. The two had served together from the early days; Guangdong Air Force Academy, 1938, John always a promotion ahead of his hot-headed fellow American until attrition had finally allowed Buffalo to catch up with him and win command of his own fighter Group.

"It broke itself," John told him. "I'd barely got it to 2,000 feet before the engine lost power and I had to turn back."

Buffalo pointed his spoon at the man from Seattle. "It has a two-speed supercharger. You engaged it too early, I bet. You need to be at least at 5,000 feet before you engage that doohickey or the high air density will cause it to blow."

"While you are still fiddling with the supercharger on your shiny new *Chaika-3* and trying to catch up, my good old *Seagulls* will already be in the fight," John scowled. "Knocking down Jap bombers."

"Dream on, Mac," Buffalo said. "I'll be climbing at twice the rate of your old kite. I have a top speed sixty miles an hour faster than you and my machines can mount both guns *and* bombs." He spat a little porridge as he spoke. "You're just jealous."

"We'll see," John said. "Until you get them dirty, you're all talk. Hey, did you get tapped for this new unit?"

"The 'American Volunteer Group'?" Buffalo snickered. "Yeah, I got a call. I've been here three years, I'm heading up two pursuit squadrons, I'm a damn Major in the Chinese Air Force – you know what they offered me?"

"No, what?"

"Flight commander!" Buffalo laughed. "First Lieutenant! What a joke. I called a guy I know in Burma, where they're forming up. He says there's 200 men and only three of them are Chinese-American and they're just mechanics, not pilots." He pushed his bowl away. "Flying Tigers, pah! Forget that. What about you?"

"Same." He was lying. John had been offered a squadron command and a Captain's rank. But it was still a step down and though his allegiance to his adopted land was strong, he couldn't help feel he would be able to do more where he was, leading combat-hardened Chinese pilots rather than rookie Americans. Yes, the Americans had superior aircraft to the Russian biplanes China fielded; he'd read a report about the P-40 Warhawk with its six .50 caliber guns and top speed a hundred and forty miles an hour faster than his Russian *Seagull*. But it had yet to be tested against the newest Japanese fighter, the Mitsubishi *Zero*, which had a similar top speed, lighter armament, but a dramatically better rate of climb and turning circle than the Warhawk. It would be like pitting a heavyweight boxer against a judo black belt – whichever opponent tried to match the other one's fighting style would probably lose.

That was as far as they were going to get on the topic that day. At that moment an intelligence officer of the Jingbao came running in. "Scramble!" he yelled, searching the mess frantically and his eyes landed on John and Buffalo just as the air raid bell began to ring across the airfield.

"His or mine?" Buffalo asked, standing up.

"Both!" the man said. "Third and Fifth Groups, we have Japanese dive bombers, twenty minutes out!"

Buffalo picked up his flight jacket and swung it over his shoulder. "How many?"

"Twenty plus!"

"Just the way I like it, plenty of targets," Buffalo said, clapping John on the back as they jogged out of the mess. "Now we'll see who gets into the action first!"

Buffalo hadn't been bragging. His new Russian *Chaika-3* biplanes proved much faster getting to their mission altitude of 20,000 feet, though out of the nine aircraft the 5th Group scrambled, three had to turn back with engine troubles, leaving Buffalo on top cover with only six aircraft. John followed him up, with nine *Seagulls* of his 3rd Group. Both aircraft had open cockpits, making it impractical to go much higher than about 20,000 feet and very difficult to use their new radios at any altitude.

That hadn't been a problem in the early war when they were facing Japanese aircraft that suffered from similar restrictions, but since the previous September, they had seen Japan bring the Mitsubishi *Zero* to the fight. It could fly right off the decks of the new Japanese carriers, giving ground-based plane spotters almost no time to report. Luckily the agile new Japanese fighters were handicapped by having to escort older, slower, biplane dive bombers like the Aichi D1A, which was slower than even his *Seagull*. If the *Zeros* had been allowed to roam free across the front line, John was sure China would soon have very few fighters or pilots left to oppose them.

"Fifth Group, we will take sector 11, you stay high and cover sector 9, acknowledge," he yelled, the noise of the wind around his aircraft almost drowning out the sound from the radio in his helmet.

"Fifth acknowledges; don't worry, if they're here, we'll find them," Buffalo responded. "Moving up to angels 22."

John looked right and left to check his wingmen were in position, then scanned the sky above him. The Japanese fighters liked to use their height advantage, falling on the Chinese like hawks. In his first engagement with a force of *Zeros*, he'd met 13 of the Japanese fighters coming out of the sun, with 24 of his *Seagulls*. Within minutes he'd lost four men killed, two wounded, and claimed only two Japanese damaged before ordering his men to break off. He had not been taken by surprise since, but his loss to kill ratio had not improved much either.

Checking his fuel, he saw he'd used a third of a tank already. The small Chinese biplanes weren't made for long patrols, so he hoped the enemy would oblige by showing itself soon.

"Japanese force entering sector 9, angels 15," his radio crackled as his ground controller broke in. He pulled his stick right and kicked in some rudder to put his squadron into a banking turn that would make them harder to surprise. With practiced ease, he scanned the airspace below and above, behind, abeam and ahead of him, before easing his stick over and doing the same in a slow banking turn to port.

"Fifth Group, I have 10…15…20 make that 20 attack aircraft at your seven o'clock, don't look like they've seen you. Orders?"

John wrenched his head around further and looked over his left shoulder, just in time to catch the glint of sunlight off the perspex canopies of the Japanese fighter bombers. They appeared to be unescorted, which bitter experience had taught him would *not* be the case.

"Stay high 3rd Group, watch for *Zeros*, keep them off our tails," John said. "We'll take the bombers!" He reached a hand out of his cockpit and waved his arm in a circular motion above his head in case any of his wingmen had eyes on him. "Fifth Group pilots, follow me down, attack formation C. Repeat attack formation C!"

The Japanese dive bombers were dark green with black engine cowlings and not easy to pick out against the landscape below, but they were more or less level as John took his squadron around in a tight turn and pushed his throttle forward. If they hadn't been spotted, he had a few minutes more before the Japanese reacted and started to flee and he willed his group forward while they had the advantage. The gap to the Japanese aircraft closed painfully slowly.

"*Zeros*! Coming down!" Buffalo yelled. "Third Group break and pursue!"

Looking frantically above him, John saw a cloud of black dots – Buffalo's aircraft – scatter to all points of the compass as a tight group of white painted *Zeros* punched through them and came straight at his formation!

"Execute dive!" John called. "Pick your targets!"

They were still too far away for the maneuver to work, but they had no choice. He'd ordered his men to form up in line abreast formation, chasing the tails of the Japanese dive bombers and then swooping below them, gathering speed so that they could hit the D1As from below where their rear gunner was blind. But it needed to be done at the last minute or the enemy could climb away. And it needed to be a surprise…

As he shoved his stick forward and pushed his throttle through the gate to get every last ounce of power from his engine, he saw with dismay that the enemy bombers had seen his flight. Tracer fire from a dozen machine guns flew over his head and the enemy pilots broke left and right, scattering like hens before a fox. One particularly foolish Japanese pilot panicked and tried to dive away from the attack, putting himself right in front of John and only 500 yards away. John twisted his neck to look behind him, saw a shadow that could have been a pursuing *Zero*, pulled his stick back to 'bunt' his aircraft and then forward to dive it again, trying to make himself a hard target in case he was being followed by more than a shadow. All the while closing on the dive bomber, which was falling away from him and just out of range.

Sure enough, Japanese tracer fire from behind him carved a path through the air over his head. He'd seen enough to know the *Zero* behind him was still using its .303 machine guns, so he wasn't yet in cannon range. John bunted again, but forced himself to ignore the killer behind him.

He heard men yelling on the radio, a cacophony of warnings, screams, and shouts of triumph.

Two hundred yards … 180 … 150 … cannon fire from behind him now! His airframe shuddered and a row of holes appeared in his upper starboard wing. Luckily the cannon shells had passed right through the fabric without exploding! Grimly, John leaned his eye to his sights, almost yelling to his machine, *Come on you fat-assed Russian bastard, catch him!* One hundred and four combat sorties had taught John not to open fire until he was sure of a kill, but his old biplane was painfully slow to reel the bomber in. With his right hand on the paddle of the joystick he flicked his safety off and eased his thumb up to the gun switches.

Just as he closed to killing range, the fleeing Japanese pilot finally woke up and pulled his aircraft into a zooming climb, trading his downward energy for precious height and allowing his gunner to open up on John. Tracer sprayed wildly across the sky, nowhere near him. John followed him up.

Fool, was all John had time to think before his thumb jammed down on the trigger and four streams of 7.62mm lead poured into the Japanese bomber. John was so close now that his fire wasn't focused, but struck the enemy across the full width of his wing roots, fuselage and tail. Shredded wood and fabric flew back toward him and John just had time to see the enemy gunner slump forward in his seat before he had to pull away, slamming his stick hard to starboard and kicking in right rudder to send himself spiraling away from the wrecked bomber and the *Zero* he assumed was still right behind him.

Centering his stick and pulling himself level, he looked desperately behind, panting from adrenaline and exertion. Damn! The Japanese fighter was on him like glue. And it was close! So close he could hear both the chatter of its machine guns and the slower drum of its cannon as it opened fire! He rolled onto a wing and pulled his machine into a vertical banking turn. His *Seagull* might be slower, but that meant it could turn inside the *Zero* and get onto its tail if the enemy pilot was stupid enough to try to follow him around.

This one wasn't. He flick-rolled away from John and started climbing back up toward the cloud layer above where John had no chance of catching him. John just had time to register the bright red rising sun on his tail section before a *Chaika* bearing the insignia of Buffalo's 5th Group came screaming down from above, machine guns hammering, and sliced the *Zero*'s wing from its fuselage, sending it spinning toward the earth.

13

Yes! John shouted, raising a fist in the air. He watched as the Japanese fighter disintegrated, casting off its tail section... then something else fell away. A small dark form, tumbling through the air below. John tilted his wing down so that he could follow it and saw a parachute blossom. Looking at the ground below he tried to work out where he was. A small town lay in the bow of a winding river and it looked like the enemy pilot was going to land right beside it. Nanchong.

John smiled. A farm town, teeming with pitchfork-wielding farmers.

Good luck, Samurai.

The *Chaika* formed up alongside him and John recognized Buffalo's second in command, flight leader Ting-Fong. He looked across at the pilot, waited until the man was looking back, and gave him a salute. He owed him a bottle of whisky. He might have shaken that *Zero* off, or it might have just been regaining its altitude advantage in order to come back at John with guns blazing. Either way, Ting-Fong had done his cause a favor.

He checked the sky, then checked his instruments. One-third fuel remaining. The 5th Group pilot would be in the same boat. He turned them toward Chengdu and home. His radio was silent now. The dogfight had either moved too far away or there were no combatants left. He was not hopeful regarding the success of their sortie. He'd claimed one bomber, Ting-Fong had claimed a fighter. That was good. But he'd met the twenty Japanese dive bombers with only nine fighters and the Japanese escort was probably also ten to twenty aircraft strong.

He scanned around himself, throttled back to cruising speed and settled into a zig-zag track toward his base. He and Buffalo had been dismissive of the new American unit forming up in Burma, but John knew they were sorely needed. Not just for propaganda reasons, but also to help restore the balance against the technologically more advanced Japanese. The Americans were bringing modern Warhawk fighters and long-range Hudson bombers into the fight at a time when Japan had achieved control of the entire eastern coast of China and Vietnam, putting John's unit at Chengdu easily within range of Japanese bombers flying out of Wuhan, only 30 minutes' flying time away.

He had thought more than twice about the offer to join the 'Flying Tigers,' as the US unit called itself. They desperately needed pilots like himself and Buffalo Ling-Sui, veterans of more than three years' fighting, to help blood a squadron of pilots that had never seen combat. The call came from a woman, which surprised him. Soong Mei-Ling, or Madam Soong, was the go-between used by Nationalist leader Chiang Kai-shek to smooth the first tentative steps of America into the war.

John had grown up in a nationalist family that had fled to the USA in 1901 after the first Sino-Japanese war. His father had fought against the Japanese in Korea before Qing forces were unceremoniously ejected by the Tokyo-backed Korean regime. It had been a humiliation his father had never let his family forget and so when Japanese forces invaded Chinese Manchuria in 1931, he had prepared his only son for war.

"I told you!" he said. "I told you they would not be satisfied with Korea and Taiwan. They will not be satisfied with Manchuria. They will not be satisfied until they rule all of China!"

John was twenty years old in 1931 and in his first year of college. He'd been studying engineering. "What do you want from me, father?" he'd asked. "I'm American."

"Look at your skin, look in the mirror," his father had said. "Yes, you are American. But first, you are Chinese!"

He'd been in the flying club at college and by 1932 he got his pilot's license in Oregon, paid for by friends of his father, on the promise he would use his skills in China if the chance arose. In 1934 he joined the Guangdong Provincial Air Force. In 1935 they sent him to the Luftwaffe at Lechtfeld in Germany to learn aerial combat and when he returned he was put in charge of the 3rd Pursuit Group's 17th Squadron. In 1938 after the death of his CO, he'd assumed the rank of Major and Group Commander.

"Is America declaring war on Japan?" John had asked Madam Soong, incredulously. He'd signed up several years earlier convinced that his isolationist homeland, which had not even gone to the aid of England in its darkest hour, would never lift a finger to help China.

"Technically, no," Madam Soong said. "You would be a civilian, a contractor, hired by Generalissimo Kai-shek to train Chinese forces on the P-40 Warhawk."

"We would not be engaged in combat?"

Madam Soong hesitated. "The Generalissimo believes the best training is that conducted under enemy fire."

John had felt his loyalty to his new homeland tugging at him. "What rank would I be offered?" he asked.

"Your combat experience is highly valued," Madam Soong crooned. "Everyone has heard of your bravery. You would have command of a full squadron."

A laugh had risen in his throat, but he'd swallowed it. "I am a Pursuit Group Commander in the Chinese Air Force. I lead three squadrons today!"

"Yes, but the *Chinese* Air Force," she said. "And it's not even your mother country anymore."

It was the worst thing she could have said. She, of all people, a Chinese nationalist, trying to appeal to his *American* loyalties? "Thank you, but I believe I can serve China best where I am."

"Would it matter to you that the unit is to be led by Colonel Chennault?"

"Old Leatherface?" John had asked. He'd studied combat tactics under Chennault, an adviser to the Chinese leadership, at the Guangdong flight academy. "I respect the Colonel, but I'm afraid not."

"And I respect your dedication to our cause," Madam Soong said. "But I am obliged to advise you that the salary for a squadron leader in this unit is 750 American dollars."

As she expected, that provoked a reaction in him. "A year?"

"No. A month."

John gulped. It was as much as he made in a year in his current role and three times what he could make Stateside. He wavered, but only briefly. The whole exercise smelled of propaganda and he had no desire to be someone's Chinese-American pin-up boy.

"I serve the Kuomintang cause," he said. "Unless it displeases Generalissimo Chiang, I prefer to stay with my men here in the 3rd Pursuit Group."

He'd expected the woman to be angry at him, but she was not. "Very well. I will pass your decision up the line. Goodbye Major." He was about to put the receiver down when he heard she was still speaking. "And Major? If I may speak personally?"

"Yes, of course, Madam."

"As a citizen of the Republic, I thank you."

As his airfield appeared on the horizon, he contemplated the flapping fabric of his holed starboard wing, realized how close he had come to being victim instead of victor, and it occurred to John that Madam Soong's thanks were not much protection from Japanese cannon shells. For the first time in the war, he felt vulnerable. Biplane against biplane, he could match any pilot Japan could put in the air against him. But against these new Japanese monoplanes … it was surely just a matter of time before he fell prey to a swooping *Zero* and he was not yet ready to go.

After an unremarkable landing and as he spoke with his intelligence officer, then filled out his report on the squadron's kills and losses for the day, a conviction was forming. It became only stronger as he wrote letters home to the bereaved families of the four pilots he'd lost – as many as he'd written in the entire first year of the war. The thought weighed heavily on him and he couldn't help revisit his decision to turn down the American offer. Putting down his pen, he looked at his watch and realized he was hungry.

In the mess, he chose his usual seat beside Buffalo, who was as usual already eating, shoveling rice and chopped spring onion into his mouth.

John watched him. "No chicken or pork, I suppose?"

"Keep dreaming, Group Commander," Buffalo scoffed. "Maybe you can dream up some pork." He put his bowl down and looked around for the mess room adjutant to try to bully the man into giving him some more. "How many did you lose?"

"Four," John told him, drumming his fingers on the table as the adjutant approached. "A bad day."

"That's only four from nine," Buffalo pointed out. "I lost two of six. That's worse."

"Actually I think it's better, mathematically, but what the hell." He looked around the mess, where about fifty pilots sat eating. "It's six empty seats."

"Look on the bright side, sad sack. Four new pilots arrived today," Buffalo said. "So we're only two down. Dinner for myself and the Group Commander, my man," he said to the adjutant.

The man's face reddened. "I'm sorry, citizen, you have already received your ration."

Buffalo looked like he was going to argue, but then changed tack. "True, true. It wouldn't do for the men to see me getting special treatment, would it?"

The adjutant looked at him suspiciously, but plowed forward. "I can offer you more tea?"

"Tea, yes, excellent," Buffalo said. "And rice for the Commander, yes John?"

"Yes, thank you," John said to the adjutant. "And tea please."

"Yes, good," Buffalo said and grabbed the man's elbow as he went to move away. "And please be sure to fill the Commander's bowl right to the top," Buffalo winked. "All the way."

John watched the adjutant walk away and turned to Buffalo. "I've reconsidered Madam Soong's offer."

"What?"

"We can't win an air war in the 1940s with aircraft from the 1920s," he said. "In Burma they're training in P-40 Warhawks. Fifty cal guns, sealed canopy, good ceiling, great top speed…"

18

"Corners like a pig, I hear," Buffalo said.

"So we fly in straight lines," John said, leaning forward. "Boom and zoom. *Zeros* won't be able to catch us."

"And what is this 'we' thing?" Buffalo asked.

"They offered me squadron leader," John admitted. "I'll need a good section leader. Pretty sure you'd get your own squadron in no time."

Buffalo looked at him with what John thought was confusion, then he realized it was pain. Or hurt.

"I'm fine with being a lowly Group Commander in the Air Force of the Chinese Republic," Buffalo said. "But thanks for the offer."

The adjutant returned with John's bowl of rice and spring onion and put it down in front of him, but Buffalo reached over and took it. The adjutant stepped back in surprise, as Buffalo picked up his spoon, dug it into the bowl and shoved the rice into his mouth. "This is Chinese food," Buffalo said to the adjutant without looking at him, glaring instead at John. "It is not for *Americans*."

John stood. He put a hand on the shoulder of the other man, but Buffalo ignored it. John walked away. He knew he was right. Courage and patriotism had not ended the First World War, the 'War to End All Wars'; that war had been won because the US had brought its huge industrial and technological might to bear and turned the tide in favor of the Allies. As it was then, so it would be with this war. If the US was entering this fight on China's side, then he would do all he could to help them.

December 1941, Mingaladon Airfield, Burma

John pulled his harness tighter as he gave himself a less than 50 percent probability of surviving the next thirty minutes. Leading 14 P-40 Warhawks on a power climb to 20,000 feet, he knew it was unlikely they would get an altitude advantage before they merged with the incoming Japanese attacking force, which ground spotters had estimated was made up of more than 60 *Sally* heavy bombers, with an escort of around 25 fighters; nimble *Oscars*. The Brits had scrambled 15 of their under-armed Brewster Buffalos right behind him, but they had a slower rate of climb and he hadn't seen them since forming up over Mingaladon.

He looked around himself, checked his instruments, then keyed his mike. "Close it up, 3rd Squadron. We'll be going into a head-on merge. Remember your training. Pick a bomber, open fire at 200 yards. It has a peashooter in the nose and one on the dorsal, so bunt under and blow straight through." His Allison V-12 engine gave a sudden cough, then settled back into its throaty roar as the Warhawk clawed at the sky. Contaminated fuel had been one of the many curses of operating out of Burma. He tried to ignore the butterflies rising in his chest. "We fly and fight in straight lines, right? You try to turn with a Jap fighter, or outclimb it, and you aren't coming home."

A few 'Roger skipper's' came back at him and he checked his altimeter. Passing through 19,000 now. Chen didn't have a favorite god, so he just threw a prayer at the clouds and hoped it would stick. "God, give me five miles to the merge. That's all, just five miles." If he couldn't get altitude, he wanted *speed*. Nineteen thousand five hundred feet now. He strained his eyes for the telltale sign of dots, dead ahead. Nothing. Nineteen eight. Nineteen nine. Still nothing.

Twenty thousand feet! He flipped his mike on again. "OK, level out, finger four formation! Call 'em if you see 'em. Wait for my mark!"

He'd only had four months with the Flying Tigers by the time his papers had come through. Four months to teach them the lessons of four years of war against the Japanese. Four months to master the beast of a machine that was the Warhawk. Four months fighting a shortage of parts, ammunition, and fuel to get the machines themselves combat capable, when he even had to scrounge radios from civilian Piper aircraft. Four months to …

There! Barely visible, a row of dots ahead and above them, another. Even higher still, their fighter escort, weaving left to right. He kept his voice level. "Bogeys 12 o'clock, angels 20 to 25. Max power, manifolds to 55! Hit and run, boys, hit and run!" He increased his engine revs, eased his throttle forward, and the Allison engine responded with an eager growl. The Warhawk was flying flat and level, pushing through 280 mph … 290 … 300! His right hand gripped the joystick tightly and he forced it to relax, flexing his fingers as he leaned to his gunsight. The dots ahead had become blobs, bobbing slightly in the tropical air. With his forefinger he flipped his guns off safe and lifted his thumb over the trigger. From dots, to blobs, within seconds the enemy bombers resolved themselves into individual aircraft as he closed with the enemy formation at a combined 500 mph! As he picked out a target, the merge was a cacophony of sound and half-seen images:

The enemy gunner, dead ahead, sunlight winking off his glass canopy, firing too soon, too low, his tracer falling away in front of the Warhawk.

His guns hammering, hammering, causing his machine to buck and rattle.

Rounds slamming into his target, small firecracker sparkles across the nose and cockpit of the *Sally*.

The twin-engine bomber a black shadow, flashing overhead as he pushed his stick down and scraped underneath its belly!

Pulling back hard and craning his head over his neck to see the enemy roll slowly onto its back and accelerate toward the earth, pilots probably dead at the stick.

And behind him, the flash of sun on cockpit glass as a *Hayabusa* fighter, rolling out from an inverted dive, latched onto his tail. His eyes flicked to his instruments. He was down at 18,000, no point trying to climb back now. Airspeed down to 280. He swiveled his head, keeping the *Hayabusa* in sight. It was closing. He heard his own training in his ears. "You get a Jap on your tail, you dive away to fight another day. Or you'll be dead and the Jap will be the hero."

Damn. A last glance ahead and above. Two machines locked together, spiraling to the ground, he couldn't see what type. Another two locked in a futile dance, Warhawk in the lead, taking a hammering from the *Hayabusa* behind him. One thing his Warhawk could do better than any Japanese machine? Roll! He wrenched his stick left, rolling 180 degrees in less than two seconds, his head jammed against the glass of his cockpit before he pulled the stick back between his legs and sent the P-40 into a screaming dive.

A quick look over his shoulder, the *Hayabusa* coming down now, falling further behind. Eyes out the side, pulling the stick back slightly, trying to keep the horizon at 30 degrees. Eyes on airspeed … 400 … 420 … pull back the revs, pull back the throttle … 440 … still pulling away from the *Hayabusa* … approaching maximum Do Not Exceed airspeed … 450 … level it out, gently, gently, *come on you brute*! He was panting now. Altitude ten thousand. Airspeed 460! Straight and level into a skidding turn, eyes behind him…

Yes! The *Hayabusa* was giving up the chase, banking away now and starting to climb back up toward the dogfight, which was moving toward Mingaladon. For a brief moment John thought of going back after it, trying to surprise it by reappearing in its mirror, but knew he'd never catch the *Hayabusa* in a climb and turned his machine back toward the airfield instead.

He looked at his instrument panel. It was 1 p.m. on December 25. He'd just claimed his seventh kill of the war, taking his total to seven killed, two shared, two damaged. He slowed his breathing, leaned his head back into his padded headrest and rolled his shoulders. *Merry Christmas, John.*

Mingaladon airfield was a smoking mess when he'd come in to land. The aircraft hoist and two plane hangars had taken direct hits from Japanese bombs and the east-west runway was heavily cratered, with a Buffalo nose down in one of the potholes. He also saw a Japanese *Hayabusa*, or what was left of its smoking wreck. John had been forced to land on the north-south runway in a wicked crosswind and driving rain, but he got his Warhawk down in one piece and was unstrapping himself when his engineering helper, Pak Lee, jumped up on the wing. He'd been recruited from Chinatown in New York by a recruiter who had just assumed from his face and his accent he was Chinese. When he'd heard about the pay packet, he hadn't bothered to tell them he was Korean.

The man was looking over the wings. "Not a scratch, boss. You're my favorite pilot!"

"Only because you are damn lazy, Pak," John smiled.

"Not lazy, efficient," the man said, helping John climb out of the cockpit onto the wing. "You get me a Jap?"

John's legs were shaking – adrenaline and exertion probably – and he leaned on Pak for a moment until they settled. "Got you a *Sally*," he said, looking around at the cratered airfield. "Not that it seems to have helped much."

"Not everyone is back yet," Pak said, dropping onto his butt and sliding off the wing, before holding a hand up for John. "But the scuttlebutt is between us and the RAF we bagged more than thirty Japs and lost maybe five kites."

"Pilots?"

"Maybe two," Pak said, pointing at the nose-down Brewster. "That new Tommy bought it. Was dead at the stick. And Flight Leader Little hasn't returned. Bob Locke saw him go down trailing black smoke, about twenty miles west. No chute."

John unbuckled his chute and dropped it on the ground under the Warhawk's wing as a jeep full of mechanics arrived. "Other casualties from the raid?" Two days earlier, the Japanese had hit Rangoon, killing 1,000 civilians.

"Eight wounded, two probably won't make it," Pak said. He shrugged. "Coulda been much worse, but we had time to hit the trenches." He brightened suddenly. "Hey, the flak gunners bagged a Jap and we got the pilot!"

John walked over to the now-empty jeep as mechanics and armorers swarmed around his machine. "Can you drive us?" he asked Pak.

"Sure," the man said, climbing in and starting it up. "Jap had just made a strafing run over the airfield, was pulling away, almost straight up into the sky, ack ack hit him in the ass!" He crunched through the gears and pointed the jeep at the dispersal hut. "Blew his tail right off. Probably blew him out of his cockpit too. Parachute came down smack on top of the mat sheds!"

"Lucky guy," John murmured. "Worse places to be in this war than a British POW camp."

"You said it. Hey, you want to interrogate him?" Pak asked. "You're ranking officer with Chennault in Rangoon and Locke missing."

John looked at him sideways. "I don't speak Japanese. Do you?"

"No dice. But I heard he speaks OK English and he's a real charmer," Pak said, spinning the wheel as he pulled up outside dispersal so that the jeep was ready to take off again in a hurry if anyone needed it. "He should still be in here."

John stepped into the hut and saw four of his pilots sitting or standing around what must have been the Japanese prisoner, sitting on a chair. The man was wearing a brown flight suit, torn at one shoulder, and his hands were tied behind his back. His helmet and goggles were on the table next to him and he was glaring at the men around him with a sullen expression. John could only imagine how the conversation had been going before he walked in and he stopped just inside the door, pulling off his own flight gloves. "Alright boys, leave me alone with the Jap." With a few parting words not suitable for polite company, the other pilots filed out.

John gave himself a full minute or so, just looking at the Japanese pilot. It was the first time he'd seen his enemy up close.

He could have been looking in a mirror; the man was early thirties, tired, thin, dirty, black hair cropped short. John looked up at the aircraft recognition posters on the wall and pointed at one of them, the *Hayabusa*. "Yours?" he said, but the man just glared at him. John continued, conversationally. "Agile machine. But punches below its weight." He stepped over to the poster, reading off the bottom, "Twin .50s, no cannon, no self-sealing tanks, no armor. Give me my Warhawk any day."

"So why do you run?" the man said suddenly. He wasn't admitting anything, but he wasn't playing dumb either.

"Sorry?"

"We fight, but you run," the man repeated. "Always run away. Like dogs."

John smiled. He'd heard the same from Tokyo Rose, on the radio. Hey, Americans of the Flying Tigers, she'd say. You all think you are like Sugar Ray Robinson, like Joe Louis. But you fight like Shirley Temple. You know what our pilots call you? The Flying Kittens!

"Well, here's the funny thing about that," John told him. "We've only been fighting for a month and we've brought down twenty of yours and lost only two of our own. Because we fight the war our way, which is smart, not your way, which is dumb."

"Your way is the way of the coward," the man spat.

John moved to the table in front of him and sat down. "You want water? Rice?"

"I want nothing," the man said.

"You speak pretty good English, for a Jap," John said.

"You speak pretty good English, for a *Chūgokujin*," the man said, commenting on his Chinese appearance. "Did you run from us in China too?"

John decided it was time to try something other than trade insults with the man. He walked into the office at the back of the hut and came out again carrying a file. It was the daily intelligence update on Japanese front line squadron identifications and he ran his eye down the file until he came to what he was looking for.

"You were flying the Nakajima Ki-43 *Hayabusa*. Only one unit on your side is fielding those in Burma. Says here you're from a unit called the 64th Sentai. Just came up from Malaya." He flipped a page and then flipped back again. "Commanding officer … Hiryu Hatori? We have a Red Cross unit here. Would you like me to write Hatori-san a letter, to let him know of your capture?"

The man threw a stream of Japanese invective at him. John put the file down and noticed that someone had emptied the man's pockets. There was a stick of dried beef, a pocket knife, and a photo of a woman in a kimono, a baby in her arms. He picked up the photo and looked at it, then showed it to the Japanese pilot. "Your wife? And son?" John looked at it again. "A fine boy."

"Girl," the man said, then turned his head away.

"Sorry, a fine girl," John said. "They will be worried about you."

The man kept his head turned, refusing to look at the photograph.

"Your name and rank, that is all I need," John said, gently. "For the letter. The Red Cross can make sure your family gets it."

There was a long silence. "Kato, Tadao," the man finally said in a clipped tone, still not meeting his eyes. "Lieutenant."

John made a note in the file. "I saw the markings on your crashed machine. You are 64th Sentai?"

"Hai."

"If I give the Red Cross a letter for Hatori-san, will he see that your family gets it?"

"Hai."

"Very good," John said. "There will be others asking you more questions, you may choose to answer them or not, but I give you my word as a fellow officer and pilot that I will give your letter to the Red Cross." He picked up the photograph and put it back in the man's top pocket. "When you get a chance, hide this somewhere safer," he said. Their eyes met as he was bending over and something passed between them. Understanding? It could easily have been him sitting in a chair at a Japanese airfield. He shrugged the feeling away as he straightened up. "Where did you learn English, Kato-san?"

"Before the war, I work for Yokohama Bank. We buy British Hong Kong Shanghai Bank," he explained. "I work closely with the Englishmen at the bank. I learn."

"Very impressive," John said.

"And you, Chinese? Why are you with these ... Americans?" the prisoner asked.

"Because I am American," John said. "*And* Chinese. As simple as that."

"Not simple," the man said. "Today, America and China are together. But tomorrow? What side do you choose then, *Chūgokujin?*"

John ignored the prisoner calling him 'Chinaman' again and gave a short laugh. "A good question, Kato-san." He didn't dwell on it. "But I think first we will worry about today and let tomorrow look after itself."

The Japanese pilot looked at him as though he was a small child. "Then you will end your life as a slave to the West, as Japan fights for your freedom."

"That is an ... interesting ... perspective." John picked up the intelligence file, tidied the papers inside, and put it under his arm. "We can discuss it another day. We will take a photograph of you later, to show your family you are alive and well. Now, I must go. I have letters to write to the families of other men."

He walked out of the hut, leaving the door open and standing on the steps. Hovering outside was the RAF 67 Squadron intelligence officer, Warrant Officer Pickering. He was a balding man with a ring of hair low on his head that stuck out from under his cap in disturbingly random tufts. He was looking beyond John into the hut, but saw the file under John's arm. "Get anything useful? Anything I should know before I get stuck in?"

"His name is Lieutenant Tadao Kato. Married, baby daughter, former Shanghai banker, speaks very good English." John Chen took the file out from under his arm and slapped it on Pickering's chest. "And your intel is out of date. The markings on that crashed *Hayabusa* out there are 64th Sentai, so it isn't in Malaya, it's here. The prisoner let slip they've moved into Burma and they're commanded by one Hiryu Hatori. We fought his unit when he was leader of the Japanese 2nd Daitai, for their attack on Chengdu. I took a guess that they'd bring him here to lead the push into Burma and I was right."

January 1942, Mingaladon Airfield, Burma

Two weeks later, John Chen walked into the small hut in which Tadao Kato was still being held prisoner. It had become a ritual after a tough day flying and fighting, which this had been. Chen would debrief militarily with his intelligence officer and sometime later he would debrief emotionally with the Japanese pilot.

They had twice loaded Kato into a truck to transport him to a British POW camp, but the British retreat from Singapore and Thailand was such a shambles that each time they had unloaded him again because his onward transport had been canceled. The latest John had heard was that he was to be put aboard a British Dakota and flown out to India, but the troop transports were so busy bringing in supplies and taking out wounded soldiers that a lone Japanese POW wasn't exactly a priority.

The last time John had spoken with the Warrant Officer of RAF 3rd Squadron, the man had been standing shoulder high in crates and swearing. "Waders!" he said, when he'd seen John approaching. "Forty-two bloody crates of thigh-high rubber bloody boots," he'd said. "No rations, no ammunition, no spares for the kites. Bloody rubber boots!"

"We could fill them with rocks and drop them on the Japs, if we run out of bombs," John offered.

"Har blinking har. What do you want?"

"That Japanese pilot. He was offloaded from that last flight and ..."

"Shoot him," the man said, looking back at his clipboard.

"Sorry, what did you say?"

"Shoot him, Captain. Or turn the bugger loose, I care not. Or, here's an idea, ask him if the Japs have a trick for turning rubber boots into engine parts!"

They kept Kato locked in a small hut that was also used to store clothing and he'd made himself a bed out of oversized overalls. It had only a small letterbox-sized window up near the ceiling and a kerosene lamp for lighting. He was taken out once a day in the company of two armed guards for a walk around the fenced-in supply yard, which of course he used to watch the comings and goings of aircraft out on the Mingaladon airfield. John's main concern was that it was now widely known they had a Japanese POW locked away in the supply hut, and with the almost daily Japanese raids on Mingaladon bringing with them a rising tally of dead and wounded, it was just a matter of time before an angry mob broke down the door to the POW's cell and lynched him. He wanted him transferred, for everyone's sake.

He nodded to the British airman standing at the door of the hut, rifle on his back, and waited as it was unlocked. He wasn't worried about the Japanese pilot attacking him or taking him hostage. That would only get him out into the supply yard, fenced in with barbed wire – not to keep out the enemy, but pilferers from their own side – and he would still have to cover the hundred miles from Rangoon to Japanese lines if he was to make it back to his unit. But the guard held his rifle at the ready as John opened the door anyway.

Kato was sitting with eyes closed, legs crossed underneath him on the floor, on his improvised mattress. A cup of water sat by his feet and a bucket up against one wall. He had made a small shelf from a plank and two empty soup cans and on this sat a neatly folded towel, a soap bar, the head of a toothbrush without the handle, some tooth powder, and a thick book – the collected works of Shakespeare, in English – which John had given him. Tadao Kato used a leaf as a bookmark and John noticed it was now about three-quarters of the way through the book.

"Making progress on your Shakespeare, Tadao?" John said, as the man looked up.

Tadao looked down at the book. "Not really," he said. "I have skipped much. I find his comedies not funny." His English had been rusty during their first interactions, but had improved dramatically the more he spoke with John and the British guards over the last two weeks.

John smiled and leaned back against the door as it closed and locked behind him. "Generations of western schoolchildren would agree with you," he said. He suddenly felt very tired. He wiped a hand across his face.

"Ah, you lost men again today," Tadao said. "I am sorry."

"Your side lost more," John replied quickly. He was always careful not to give away actionable intelligence to the Japanese pilot, even via his face.

"That will not frighten our generals," Tadao said. "Or our troops. We fight for survival of Japan. You are a mercenary, you fight for whoever pays the most. The British troops are Indian and Nepali and Burmese conscripts, fighting for the dying British Empire, which is precious only to its King."

John tried not to let any anger leak into his voice, but it was hard. "Tell me, Tadao, how is it that you see Japan declaring war on China, Thailand, Singapore, Malaysia, Burma, and the British Empire as a fight for the survival of Japan?" he asked. It was a genuine question, because it was clear to him the man believed what he was saying.

"You are too long with British and Americans," the man replied. "You no longer see the world through Eastern eyes."

"I have been fighting for China longer than I have been fighting with the British and Americans," John replied. "Believe me, I see this war through *Chinese* eyes."

Tadao took a sip of water as he considered his argument. "Then why do you not see that China and Japan stand stronger *together*? Under a Japanese emperor or Chinese, it does not matter, but it is necessary. This war is not just about this century, John Chen, it is about the next century too."

"It is 1942," John said. "You seriously suggest your leaders are so far-sighted they are already thinking about the year 2042?"

Tadao spoke more fervently now. "Yes, they are, and that is the difference between us. Right now, we fight to be free of economic death from USA and Britain. Without oil and rubber and steel, we starve, our country dies. But this is like a man fighting against a bully who has him by throat. If we break free of the bully's grip, we must still deal with the bully. We need all great Eastern empires –

China, Japan, India, East Indies – to unite against the American and British empires. Alone, they will pick us off one by one, over the next hundred years, as now with Japan." He locked his hands together, fingers intertwined, and made a double fist. "Together, we can fight!"

John shook his head. "See, that's the thing. I don't see America or Britain invading China. Sure, Britain tried a hundred years ago and the Qing emperor sent them packing back to Hong Kong. But I see Japan invading, again and again. I see Japan as the biggest threat to China for the next one hundred years too. If we let you take Korea and southeast China, that will just be the start. You will burn and rape and plunder your way north and westwards, until all of China is under your dominion."

Tadao glared at him, lips drawn tight in a thin line. Then he looked down at the floor. "You believe we can never be allies," he said softly. "Too much history, too much blood. So you must see that the only way to join Japan and China together is through war, none will submit to the other."

"And I would very simply rather die fighting than see my children live under a Japanese emperor," John said. "In this century, or the next."

As they spoke, an air raid siren started up its mournful wail again, for the second time that day. Tadao looked up at the roof of his hut. "This war is necessary, Captain Chen. One day your children, with my children, will be fighting the real war. Together, against the West." He sighed. "Under a Japanese emperor, I hope. Not a blind Chinese fool like you."

As John walked out of the hut he saw an Avro Anson light transport plane curving in toward the airfield on approach. It bounced across the field and taxied toward the dispersal building. That could mean only one thing. Claire Chennault, the Flying Tigers' CO, was making one of his rare visits to Mingaladon. Sure enough, ten minutes later John was summoned to his office.

Claire Lee Chennault was a bulldog-faced man with a prominent nose. He was also partially deaf and not given much to banter. He barely looked up from the papers he was working on as John walked in, but acknowledging his salute, he leafed through them while John waited, then held one up. "I'm not going to waste words, John, this intel assessment I am holding says there are only 38 British and American fighters in this entire theater, facing 271 Japanese aircraft. The Japanese 143rd Infantry Regiment is only ten miles from Rangoon. This airfield is no longer safe." He put the report down and leafed through the pile of folders and loose papers again, finding what he was looking for. He pushed it across the table to John. "Get a good night's sleep. Rangoon is gone. You're moving 2nd Squadron up to Magwe at 0400 tomorrow."

It was hardly a surprise. They'd heard the rumble of cannon fire getting closer by the day. Returning to his quarters, John got out a bottle of Scotch, poured himself a glass and sat at his small desk, rolling the whisky around his mouth, contemplating his future. Magwe was an RAF airfield 300 miles to the north. The move was an admission that Burma was lost and the fight now was about preventing Japan from opening a new front through Burma into China's Yunnan province.

No matter what the strategic purpose, the practical reality was that by 0430 tomorrow morning his men and machines would be on their way north and he had a million details to attend to, to make that happen. He put down his whisky glass. One of those details was a Japanese prisoner called Tadao Kato.

"Why are you here?" John had asked him the previous night.

"Because I can see no way of escape and no way to kill myself," the prisoner had replied.

"No, why do you think Japan is here in Burma? We are a very long way from Japan."

"And you are a long way from America," he had said. "I am here to fulfill the Imperial mandate. You are here for money. Who are you to question my reasons?"

John had bristled at that. "I fight for the survival of China. That is all that matters to me."

33

"And I am ready to give my life to deliver my country from crisis," the prisoner said. "That is all that matters to me." He had been holding an extra ration of bread which John had thrown to him and he tossed it back. "We are no different."

Were they not?

John reached down and opened the bottom drawer of his desk, pulling out his Smith and Wesson .38 revolver.

The British sentry outside the Japanese prisoner's hut saw John approaching, saw both the grim look on his face and the revolver in his hand, and lifted his rifle from his shoulder, holding it in a ready position across his chest. He'd seen the heightened activity across the base the last few hours, had heard the rumor they were pulling out. He'd wondered what was going to happen to the quiet, angry man inside the clothing stores hut and now, perhaps, he was going to find out.

John stopped in front of him. "Give me the key and return to your unit," John said. "You won't be needed here anymore."

The man looked at his revolver. "Would you like me to assist with the prisoner, sir?" he asked, being deliberately vague. "He has been rather moody lately. Refused his meal today."

"No thank you, private," John said. "I can manage this on my own."

The sentry couldn't help himself, though he knew he risked angering the American officer with his question. "If I may, sir, is the prisoner to be transferred?"

John fixed him with a cold gaze. "There is no transport available, private. Now, do you have any other questions?"

The sentry swallowed. "No sir, thank you sir," he said and handed the officer the keys from his belt. He shouldered his rifle and walked away, with a single glance backward to see John watching him all the way to the wire of the supply compound, where another sentry let him out.

When he had gone, John checked that he had taken the safety off his revolver and held it in his left hand while he unlocked the padlock on the door of the hut. He lifted it out of the metal hasp and dropped it on the ground, before taking his pistol in his right hand and stepping back from the door.

"Kato-san, please come to the door and open it," he said loudly.

There was no sound from inside the hut and he wondered if the man had heard him. Perhaps he had been sleeping, or was just suspicious. "I'm not coming in there," John said. "The door is open, the sentry has been dismissed, please come outside."

Now there was the sound of movement behind the door. John took another step back. He did not want the man to try to jump him.

The door eased open a crack and then Tadao Kato pushed it wider. It fell back on its hinges and banged against the wall of the shed, framing the Japanese pilot in the doorway. He blinked at the harsh afternoon light, but his eyes narrowed as he saw John standing six feet away, pointing a revolver at him. He looked beyond John, at the noisome chaos of the airfield beyond, men running, vehicles racing, convoys of lorries departing and aircraft lining up for takeoff.

"Ah," Tadao said. "You are leaving."

"Yes," John said. "Step outside and walk to the wire over there."

"Where is my friend, Private Burns?" Tadao asked, not moving.

"Looking for a lorry, I imagine," John said. He waved the barrel of his pistol. "Now move please."

"If you were going to transfer me, you would not have dismissed Private Burns," Tadao observed, still not moving. A small group of British soldiers was hovering at the gate to the compound, watching them. "So if you are going to shoot me, shoot me here." He straightened and looked John defiantly in the eye.

John lifted his pistol and pointed it at the pilot, then fired.

The round hit the ground between his feet and he jumped backward.

35

"I am not going to make you a martyr in front of an audience of your enemies," John said. "Move to the wire, or the next shot will be in your foot. Then your thigh. Then your gut. If you wish, I can leave you lying here in your own blood and excrement to die slowly, or, you can walk to the damn wire."

The man appeared to consider his alternatives briefly, before turning to look back into the hut. "I was writing a letter to my wife. It is on my pillow. Will you give it to the Red Cross and see that she gets it?" His voice sounded resigned now, some of the defiance gone.

"Yes. Now move."

The shot had drawn quite a crowd to the gate of the supply compound, but there were no officers among them and the British airmen there simply stared silently at John and his prisoner as they walked up to the gate. Just as silently, they opened it and made a path for the small procession to walk through.

John stayed four feet behind his prisoner, keeping the gun aimed at the small of his back. As they exited the small group of Tommies, Tadao looked behind him and John pointed with his gun to the perimeter of the airfield, away from the terminal building, where dense bush met the airfield boundary. They started walking.

Tadao turned his head, speaking over his shoulder as he walked. "Did you see the faces of those men, Chinaman?" he asked.

John had seen a mix of shock, anger, hatred, disgust... a full gamut of emotions on the faces of the British airmen as he pushed through them. "Yes, I saw. So what?"

"They were white," he said. "Our faces are not white. But they make us enemies of each other."

"Your Generals made you my enemy," John said. "When they decided to invade Chinese Manchuria without orders from Tokyo. When they marched on Beijing. You cannot blame the white man for that."

"You are so blind," the prisoner said, shaking his head in frustration. "When a man is drowning, he reaches for a lifeline.

America was drowning us with sanctions, Manchuria was our lifeline. The white man is behind all evil."

John had heard the 'lifeline' propaganda story before – Japan had been singing that song since 1931. "Just shut up and keep walking until I say stop," he told the prisoner.

John half expected the Japanese pilot to hit the treeline on the other side of the ankle-high perimeter grass and start running. But he trudged through the waist-high bush into the stand of juvenile teak trees that had been planted after the airfield had been cleared to put in the first bush runway in the 1930s. When John had judged they'd gone far enough in, he called out, "Stop there."

The man stopped and turned to face him. John tried to read his face, but it was calm, almost serene. A fly landed on the corner of his eye, but he ignored it, not even waving it away. He just waited, patiently. He didn't even move his head as the sound of anti-aircraft fire erupted yet again from the airfield.

John jerked his head toward the east. "Your lines are that way. The last I heard, your troops were ten miles northeast. You could try reaching them, but I wouldn't recommend it. What is left of the 17th Indian Division is coming back down that road and they probably aren't in a mood to let you pass."

Tadao was watching him carefully, as if waiting for the catch, the trap.

With his revolver, John pointed north. "If I were you, I would go that way. There is an abandoned rubber plantation about two miles north of this airfield. You could lie low there until your troops roll up to Mingaladon and then come walking out of the jungle like a long-lost hero. I'd be willing to bet you'll be flying your *Hayabusa*s off this airfield within the week anyway, so you probably don't want to walk too far."

"You are letting me go?" Tadao asked, finally grasping John's meaning.

"No, I'm shooting you and leaving you to rot on the ground," John said and raised his revolver. He pointed the barrel at the tree canopy above without aiming and fired the gun twice into the air. "Now, get moving, buddy," John said. "I've got a Dakota to catch."

As John walked out of the bush, he passed a small group of airmen from the 135th RAF, throwing papers into a burning oil drum. He recognized several of them from the gates of the supply compound. They all stopped and watched as he walked back past them, alone this time, revolver tucked in the waistband of his trousers.

"Good riddance to bad rubbish, sir, I say," yelled one of them at his back. "One less to worry about, eh?"

John lifted his hand and gave him a wave, without turning around.

He understood the man's point of view. Tadao Kato could be back in the air at the stick of another fighter within the week, killing British pilots. But unlike some, John was not the type who would machine gun an enemy pilot hanging from a parachute and he knew the life of one Japanese flyer more or less made no difference in this war. As he reached the runway, he watched a British Hurricane go roaring away, bumping across the ground before lifting itself into the sky and tucking its wheels into its wings. North, toward China. In the distance, he heard the unmistakable *crump* of heavy artillery. Behind him, the relentless and apparently unstoppable Japanese war machine pressed forward.

He watched as another aircraft taxied onto the runway, one of his own this time. The pilot gave him a salute and he waved back. The Allison engine of the P-40 Warhawk had a completely different sound to the Merlin of the Hurricane. It matched perfectly with the huge row of teeth painted on the air intake and he held his hands over his ears as the pilot pushed his throttle forward and sent the heavy machine thumping down the airfield and into the sky. John had let his men take the fighters off, deciding to stay until the last of the squadron's airmen and mechanics had made it safely onto a truck and were headed north.

Strangely, he felt no sense of defeat leaving Mingaladon. To him, China was a mastodon, being nibbled at by mice. Japan had control of China's northeast and was pushing the British out of southeast Asia. But with America and Russia supplying China with men and machines and, more importantly, money, they would eventually prevail. He might not survive to see it – probably wouldn't – but the Chinese Empire would rise again.

He walked into the supply compound to the clothing shed where the Japanese pilot had been interred. As the British private had said, a plate of untouched food sat beside the makeshift bed on which the man had slept. A small piece of paper and a pencil sat on the pile of uniforms and John bent down and picked it up. It was folded in two and he opened it, struggling to read the Japanese Kanji characters. Chinese Hanzi used many of the same characters, but the meaning could be completely different. He grunted with surprise when he saw most of the letter was written in English.

Dear wife,

I hope you already received word that I am alive and a prisoner of the British. I am writing to you in English because my guard, a red-headed Welsh man whose name is Burns, says I must write in English so that the British censors can check that I am not giving away their military secrets. You should ask one of my old bank colleagues to translate it for you.

Recently, in calmer moments, I find my thoughts returning continually to you and our daughter. Please take good care of your health, for her sake.

When we first arrived at our base in Guangzhou, there was a sudden change in plans and we were ordered to Phu Quoc island for the attack on Burma. Our victories have been many, but my machine was hit during a mission behind enemy lines and I was captured.

I am kept in a small cell and see daylight only for one hour each day, but my spirit is still strong and we are driving the British, Americans and Chinese back, day by day. There is a Chinese pilot here fighting for the Americans. We discuss politics but he is very wrong-headed. He believes that Japan is his enemy and cannot see that in fact, he is fighting on the side of the real enemy, Western Imperialism. I have tried to explain to him that the world is made up of East and West and the countries of the East must unite to survive against the West.

If they do not unite voluntarily, they must be united by force, it is the only way. He is blind to this.

But enough of politics, I know it bores you. Every day, I re-read the letter you wrote the day you made the jelly and I gaze at the photo of you and our daughter. Surprisingly, my heart is perfectly at peace, as though another me were gazing upon this image from home. But it is because I am confident that soon our troops will be here and will free me. I am a lucky man, for I am still alive, where so many have died.

Now, more than ever, the fleetingness of human life astonishes me, but I have become a much stronger person. You too must be strong. Wait for me. I will return without fail. Until I see my daughter again, I have no intention of dying easily.

I will

The letter finished there. The prisoner had asked him to send it, expecting he was about to be executed. John looked at the plate of uneaten food and wondered at the contradiction between the confident and defiant words and the calm manner in which the Japanese pilot had walked into the forest, expecting to be shot. His actions were those of a broken man, but his words were those of a fighter. John realized he would probably write a very similar letter to his own wife, if the situation were reversed. He would not want her, or his captors, to think he had given up.

A huge explosion on the other side of the airfield rattled the walls of the hut and anti-aircraft guns opened up again. John ducked involuntarily, then folded the letter into his tunic pocket and ran for the door. He had had enough of Tadao Kato and Mingaladon. He wanted to see that last man climb aboard a Dakota before the Japanese 214th Regiment came rolling in on their Chi-Ha tanks and ruined his day for real.

April 1945, Okinawa, Japan

The Yokosuka *Ohka*, or Cherry Blossom, was the world's first anti-ship guided missile. With rocket-powered motors driving it to a maximum speed of over 500 miles an hour, it could evade enemy counter-fire, strike fast-moving targets, and its armor-piercing nose could punch through the quarter-inch steel plate of American warships with frightening ease, detonating a 2,600lb ammonal warhead which could snap a destroyer in two.

But the sophisticated guidance system for the *Ohka* was its most vulnerable component, as it could be disabled with something as small as the bullet from a .22 caliber pistol. The reason being that the guidance system for the flying bomb was a human *kamikaze*.

Dozing in the belly of a Mitsubishi *Betty* bomber, looking down at the white-painted *Ohka* loaded into its open bomb bay, Tadao Kato was in a reflective mood. He was proud of how many glorious victories his nation had won in eight years, and angered by the many humiliating defeats it had recently suffered. Looking at the superweapon nestled in the bomb bay he marveled at how far its aircraft and air force had advanced in that short time, and was aghast at how little of that air force remained. He had started his war in 1937 at the stick of a Kawasaki *Perry* biplane, then transitioned to the *Hayabusa*. In those early days, Japan had been on the offensive, facing inferior opponents, and he had racked up more than twenty enemy kills. At twenty, he had stopped counting.

But the tide turned and he was eventually transferred to the 15th Sentai, flying the shark-nosed Kawasaki *Tony*, a fighter developed to enable Japan to take on the high-flying American B-29 Superfortress bombers now attacking Japanese cities with impunity. With a ceiling of 38,000 feet and fielding both 20mm cannon and machine guns, he had claimed three of the massive American machines in the *Tony* before being asked in October 1944 to lead the formation of a new 'Special Attack' unit in the Naval Air Group – flying the *Ohka*. His first task had been to imbue them with warrior spirit and he started by having them commit to memory the death poem of the scholar Motoori Norinaga.

41

Asked about the soul of Japan,
I would say
That it is
Like wild cherry blossoms
Glowing in the morning sun.

He did not lie to them, try to make them think they could single-handedly turn the enemy back from Japan's shores. He told them instead that the purity of their souls and the example they gave to their homeland would save it from ruin, even in defeat.

They were young boys mostly, who had never been in combat. At the Tsukuba Naval Air Corps he had trained them first in wooden gliders and then in two-seater copies of the *Ohka*, with water-filled noses to replicate the weight of the explosive. One of his boys had died when the wing on his glider had failed, folding like paper and sending him spinning to the ground. In his pocket they had found a letter to his sweetheart.

In my next life, and in my life after that, and in the one after that, please marry me.

Machiko, goodbye.

Machiko, Machiko, Machiko, Machiko, the ever so gentle, my dearest Machiko.

He had promised the girl's mother that he would take the letter with him on his final flight, and it was with him now, in the pocket on his flight suit where he had placed it together with a copy of the letter he had written to his own wife.

In March their aircraft had arrived. They were sleek, and looked terrifying. A navy rating had observed they looked like 'flying torpedoes'. With an elongated tubular fuselage and stubby wings, they were powered by three solid propellant rocket engines, which could be engaged in sequence, giving the *Ohka* a range of up to 12 miles, or all at once in the last minute of the attack dive, to give the pilot maximum power at the moment of the strike. Like a missile, they were flown into combat attached to the bomb bay of a *Betty* medium bomber and launched at standoff range.

The first attacks by Tadao's unit had taken place on April 1, 1945 against the massive US fleet anchored off Okinawa. Six *Ohka*-armed *Betty* bombers had been launched. Two were shot down before reaching their targets and launching their *Ohka*s. Four launched, with mixed results. One struck the massive battleship *West Virginia*, knocking out one of its 16-inch main-gun turrets. Three were unable to penetrate to the battleship that was their target, and struck transport vessels instead. No American warships were crippled or sunk. All of the *Betty* 'mother-ships' were shot down.

Naval intelligence concluded that the *Ohka*s had been released too far from their warship targets, by bomber pilots afraid of being engaged by American fighters. Two actions were taken to address this – the commanding officer of the 711th bomber attack squadron was executed to atone for the cowardly performance of his pilots. And it was decided that in future, the *Betty* mother-ships would join with a force of fighter bombers, rather than fight their way in alone, to increase the chances of a fatal strike on a warship. It was a tactic of which Tadao had approved, and he had volunteered to lead the section in the next wave of attacks to set an example for his younger officers.

The *Betty* lurched, shaking Tadao out of his reverie. One of the aircrew was standing in front of him, and tapped him on the shoulder. The wind from the open bomb bay was howling around the inside of the bomber, and though the man was shouting at him, he couldn't hear anything. His meaning was clear enough, though.

It was time for Tadao to mount his aircraft.

He saluted the man, pulled the straps on his flight helmet tighter, and clambered down the ribs of the bomb bay to the open hatch of his *Ohka*. The tiny cockpit was barely big enough for him, but he squeezed inside and buckled himself in. Clambering down behind him, the crewman closed and bolted the cockpit canopy shut. It could not be released from inside the cockpit, the pilot was sealed in.

Tadao's world went strangely quiet.

Ten miles away, 70 miles northwest of Okinawa, the crew of the destroyer USS *Mannert L Abele* were fighting for their lives. Accompanied only by two landing ships they had been conducting radar picket duties when a force of 15 to 20 Japanese attack fighters had spotted them. They managed to hold the majority of the attackers off with their 5-inch anti-air and the lighter weapons aboard the landing ships, but a force of three Japanese *Zeros* broke through, one of them spearing into the deck of the destroyer and penetrating to its engine room before its bomb had exploded.

Billowing smoke, ablaze with fuel from the kamikaze, both shafts out of commission, the *Mannert L Abele* was lying dead in the water.

In the radar room, Lieutenant JG Ray Henderson had been tracking the Japanese aircraft which had been circling the *Mannert L*, just out of range of its guns. Most were fighters or fighter bombers, but outside them was a group of four or five larger aircraft, probably bombers. Despite the mayhem in the skies and out on the deck of the ship, Henderson kept a careful eye on his scope and, in particular, on those bombers. Just a week earlier, he'd helped stop an attack by a Japanese twin-engine bomber that could have sent them to the bottom.

He flinched as an explosion outside rocked the ship. Not for the first time, he wished he'd enlisted in the air force with his brother, instead of following his best man into the Navy.

"Three more coming in," he said in a terse voice. "Fighters. 12,000 feet, ten miles, bearing zero niner zero, speed 150." Another officer relayed the information to the anti-air gunnery commander and within minutes, the guns outside began barking again. The radar room was dark, but the radar was still functioning, pulling power from the *Mannert L*'s one functioning engine.

He heard a cheer and the anti-air guns fell silent, just as the Japanese bomber group on his scope changed course toward the *Mannert L* and a single small dot broke away from it.

Strange, it was …

"Enemy aircraft! On attack bearing, one one eleven degrees! 20,000 … no … 18 … 16,000 feet!" The object was moving fast. Faster than anything he'd ever seen. "Fighter. Speed, uh, two hundred … three … no, three-fifty!"

"Say again?" the man beside him said. "What range?"

"Ten miles," Henderson said, sweat dripping from his brow into his eyes. He wiped a hand across his face. The return from the radar was too slow! Every time the dot was painted on its screen it had moved impossibly far. "No … eight!" he said, his voice rising. "Speed *four hundred fifty*! Altitude 5,000!" Henderson turned to the gunnery officer. "It's moving like a bat out of hell! Tell them to turn guns to one one eight degrees and open up with everything they've got!!"

The *Ohka* was made to be flown by pilots who had no more than a couple of hours' flight training. It had a stick for adjusting pitch and roll, a foot-mounted t-bar to control yaw, a simple ring sight for aiming, and a three-stage switch on the forward instrument panel which sequentially ignited the three rocket engines. The human-piloted missile would drop out of the belly of its mother-ship at 20,000 feet and swap altitude for energy, accelerating rapidly even before the pilot kicked in the rockets, quickly reaching a glide speed of 122 mph.

On Tadao's cockpit instrument panel, beside the engine arming switch, he had fixed a picture of his wife and daughter, taken only a month ago in Tokyo's Shinjuku Gyoen gardens. They were wearing their finest gowns, and his heart burst with pride and love every time he looked at it.

Dropping away from the belly of the *Betty*, he steadied the *Ohka* with his right hand on the joystick, while with his left, he reached out and brushed his fingertips across the photograph. He had already said goodbye to them a hundred times, had already died a hundred deaths in his mind, and he was ready to die for his Emperor today, as was demanded of him.

45

He had fully expected to die on that day in Burma in 1941, had not expected the American to set him free. Tadao had not thought about him for years, but curiously, the memory came back to him now. He remembered how weak-minded the man was. Weak in his convictions, both moral and political. He wondered if the American had realized that the man standing guard outside Tadao's hut, the Welshman, Private Burns, called him 'The Chink'? He also wondered whether Chen had learned by now that western man would never regard the Asian as his equal? The West would have to be shown, through force of arms, who the true superpower was. Tadao knew this in his bones, just as he knew that neither China nor Japan could stand against America and Britain alone. Under one Emperor, that was the only way!

The sea beneath him was a shimmering blue sheet, but on the horizon he could see a pillar of smoke rising into the still tropical air. Perfect! The enemy formation had already been hit! He had but to steer toward it to deliver the next blow. He pushed his nose a little lower, confident he was within strike range now. On the horizon, the pillar of smoke resolved itself into a ship, already ablaze, but still stubbornly afloat.

He centered it in his sights, pulled back on his stick to level his aircraft out, and reached forward to ignite his rocket boosters.

Reaching for the helmet hanging on his chair, Ray Henderson saw the dot on his screen accelerating toward the *Mannert L* at an impossible rate. Outside, above him, all around him it seemed, the destroyer's anti-air guns began hammering.

The small dot on his screen blinked. *One mile!?* He knew that by the time his radar had completed another sweep, it would be too late. Dropping his helmet on the deck, he reached for his life preserver instead.

Enemy tracer fire reached toward Tadao from the burning ship, angry explosions buffeting the *Ohka*, but falling quickly behind him. He reached out and touched the photograph one last time. The enemy ship was just a flickering blur of flame and smoke. Filling his gunsight, then filling his windscreen and finally, filling his horizon!

He screamed. Not words.

He screamed. In ecstasy, not fear.

He screamed until the ecstasy filled his soul and his soul was no more.

Echoes: 2033

"China is leveraging military modernization, influence operations and predatory economics to coerce neighboring countries to reorder the Indo-Pacific region to their advantage. As China continues its economic and military ascendance, asserting power through an all-of-nation long-term strategy, it will continue to pursue a military modernization program that seeks Indo-Pacific regional hegemony in the near-term and displacement of the United States to achieve global pre-eminence in the future."

US Department of Defense.

Summary of the National Defense Strategy of the USA, 2018

"From competition to co-existence, Japan and China bilateral relations have entered a new phase… With President Xi Jinping, I would like to carve out a new era for China and Japan."

Japanese Prime Minister, Shinzo Abe, speaking in Beijing.

October 2018

April 2033, East China Sea

Lieutenant Takuya Kato, the great-grandson of Tadao Kato, believed in omens. On the day he'd turned thirty, he'd been promoted to a flight leader on the Japanese aircraft carrier the JS *Izumo* and then advised his planned shore leave had been canceled because he was needed for Exercise Red Dove, the first-ever joint military exercise between Japan and the People's Republic of China. A birthday and a promotion, that would have been portentous enough. But a birthday, a promotion, and an unexpected recall to duty? The Gods, his *Kami*, were telling him something. Only time would reveal what it was and, luckily, Kato-san was a patient man.

But not unnecessarily so. "Close up, Momiji three," he barked, looking down at the panoramic Pilot Vehicle Interface of his F-35E. The tactical situational display was showing his new wingman lagging, as his four-man formation made its last east-west sweep of the skies ahead of the *Izumo*. They were on picket duty, tasked with responding to any threats detected by the Okinawa-based *Hawkeye* early warning aircraft circling over the *Izumo*. It could in theory detect enemy aircraft out to a range of 200 kilometers, but the shameful events of two days ago had proven its limitations, when a squadron of Chinese stealth fighters had managed to close within standoff missile range of the *Izumo* before being detected and intercepted. The simulated missiles launched had been few and were judged to have been successfully intercepted by the Red Dove AI 'referee', but the Chinese fighters should not have been able to penetrate the Japanese fighter screen with such impunity. Japan had come very close to having to accept a strike on the *Izumo*! It was not his flight which was on picket that day and he was determined his flight would not repeat the mistake of relying on the *Hawkeye* to detect the foe.

His mission was to patrol a grid 200km northeast of the carrier, but after conferring with his superior officer, he had taken his flight 220km out. It meant burning into his fuel safety reserve, but it also meant he might have a slight element of surprise over the 'attacking'

Chinese force. There was no guarantee of course that they would attack from his sector, but…

"Momiji one, I have a return. Fast mover, 030 degrees, low," his wingman called, voice supernaturally calm. "Patching data through to *Hawkeye*." The man had picked up the electronic signature of a Chinese fighter aircraft. *Possibly.*

"Momiji flight, turn to 030, weapons safe, passive arrays only," Kato said, flicking his fighter onto its wingtip and beginning a sweeping starboard turn. "Waiting *Hawkeye* confirmation." He needed the commander aboard the airborne warning aircraft to decide how to react to the possible threat. It could be a false return. Or it could be a feint, designed to draw the Japanese fighter cover away from the real threat. Right now, aboard the *Hawkeye*, they would be trying to triangulate the electronic signature picked up by his flight with their own data, with infrared satellite detection, with data from other fighters. It was the third time today they had seen a Chinese *yurei*, or ghost. Like ghosts, the other two had evaporated. Without thinking, he reached up and touched the silver pendant of his Kami, hanging at his throat. It had the stylized form of a large, breaking wave.

His personal Kami was the *Tsunami*, or Tidal Wave. It had been passed on to him by his grandfather with great solemnity in a personal family ceremony that he had learned had less to do with the Shinto religion than it did with his family's deeply ingrained nationalism. He had been seventeen years old when his father had ushered him into his grandfather's living room on a hot, gray autumn day. It had been raining all morning and he remembered still the smell of warm steaming bitumen as he blinked his way into the room, eyes struggling to adjust to the darkness. His grandfather sat in his big armchair and beckoned him over.

On the table before him was a blue, velvet-covered box.

"Sit, boy, sit," his grandfather had said. He was sitting in a corner in a pool of lamplight. "How old are you today?"

Kato had sat and then looked up at his grandfather in confusion. Had the man not just been to his birthday party? He knew very well how old Kato was.

"Uh, seventeen, grandfather."

"Yes. Seventeen. And it is time for you to receive your Kami."

"Yes, grandfather." Like most of his generation, Kato had been a self-absorbed, ignorant child. More interested in the latest fashion craze from Shimokita, or the newest virtual reality game, than the history of his ancestors. And though he would soon be leaving to join the air defense force academy, he had walked into the dark room thinking about nothing deeper than the pair of Energy Pump Nikes he had just unwrapped and what his girlfriend Ushi might say when she saw him casually charging his phone from his heel.

His grandfather knew enough about his grandson to know he needed to be brought into the now, with a small, sharp shock.

"Your great-grandfather Tadao Kato chose this Kami, in April, 1945, the day before he dived his rocket plane into an American destroyer, killing himself…"

"Grandfather…" Kato-san had interrupted. "Was my great-grandfather a kamikaze?"

"Yes. Be quiet," the old man said. "I will read you his *Jisei*. The Jisei was a poem our pilots took with them into combat. He made two copies, one of which he always took with him and one which he sent to my mother." The old man unfolded a piece of ancient rice paper and read aloud.

For the Emperor,

I will fall as a wave

With joy

In my heart

Your jade will shatter.

Kato stayed silent this time. The old man was breathing softly. After a minute, he spoke. "He had with him, on that final flight, a jade ring my mother gave him." He folded the rice paper and placed it in his shirt pocket. "The report of his death stated that officer Tadao Kato set an example for all of his men and for his Empire when he sacrificed his life to destroy an American ship off Okinawa." He reached forward out of the lamplight and lifted something from the table. "All pilots were required to choose their Kami on the day before their final mission. Your great-grandfather chose the Tsunami. It was recorded that this surprised his superior officer, who asked him why he had chosen this and not an animal spirit like most other pilots ... a tiger, a wolf, or a shark. Your great-grandfather said that he chose the Tsunami because a tiger can be shot, a shark can be speared, but the Tsunami is unstoppable." The old man's hand lifted a pendant on a silver chain from the table. "In honor of his sacrifice, my father commissioned this necklace from a jeweler in his village," he said and held it out to Kato. "My mother said I should wear it. But I was a poor student, who became a simple accountant and I did not feel myself worthy. I offered it to your father, but he also declined." His hand was shaking, the silver wave at the end of the chain quivering. "You are the first in our family to serve in the military since your great-grandfather. I want you to take it."

"Grandfather," Kato had said, "I can't. I haven't earned it."

"Perhaps, but take it now and do your utmost to earn it," the old man had said, pressing it into Kato's palm.

Over the East China Sea, his radio pulled him away from his thoughts. "Momiji leader this is Arakashi Control. Target confirmed, you are cleared to intercept. Vectoring support to your sector, you are lead."

His heart caught in his throat but he took a deep breath and forced it down. The target was real! His eyes flicked across his display panels as his fingers tapped commands into a panel beside his throttle. "Roger Control. Momiji flight, targets on your tac monitors, roll out to formation four and follow me in. Select AAM-6s." The Japanese AAM-6 was an adaptation of the British *Meteor* ramjet-powered air-to-air missile that flew at Mach 4 and had a 'no escape zone' three times that of its Chinese counterpart. If they engaged, they would be firing in simulation mode, but the lethality of the Japanese missiles would weigh in their favor when the AI referees tallied up kills and losses after the merge.

A tone sounded in Kato's ears and six green dots appeared in his heads-up display, bracketed with glowing red circles. His targeting system had analyzed their electronic signatures and was calling them

Chinese *Chengdu* stealth fighters. They were heading in at wavetop height, apparently oblivious to the Japanese fighters about to drop on them from above.

His eyes flicked from his instruments to his visor, to the skies around him as he gripped his stick tight and pushed his throttles forward. "Momiji flight, targets low on our 11 o'clock, *engage engage engage*," he called. With a grunt, he rolled his fighter on its axis, stopped it with the canopy pointing at the ground and pulled it into a screaming dive just as the Chinese aircraft flashed under his nose 30,000 feet below.

And the second he did so, he recognized the nagging uncertainty that had suddenly grabbed him. The *Chengdu* was a *land-based* aircraft. To get to the exercise area north of Okinawa, it would have had to fly from Wenzhou or Shanghai on the Chinese mainland and possibly refuel in flight. There were not supposed to be any land-based aircraft in the Chinese order of battle for Exercise Red Dove! As he closed on the Chinese fighter formation and the missile-targeting tone in his helmet began to beep faster, indicating his AAM-6s would soon be in range, he knew he had flown his men right into an enemy trap. Even as the thought registered, a missile warning tone screamed in his ears and his combat AI wrenched control of his fighter from his grip and pulled it into a screaming starboard banking turn that snapped his head back and pushed him into his seat as though a giant had just laid a hand on his chest.

Fighting for air, he tried to make sense of the icons in his visor and managed to key his comms, "Momiji flight, J-31 *Snow Falcon*s, high on our six! Evade and..."

A new tone sounded. *Miss!* The enemy missile had failed to get a lock.

"...evade and engage with short-range missiles!" he completed, taking control of his aircraft back and flinging his machine into a climbing reverse turn to try to get his nose pointed at the source of his attack. An icon flashed on the visor of his helmet and he screwed his head around – there! High on his four o'clock, a small silver speck. He rolled his F-35E as he and his enemy closed at a combined velocity of twice the speed of sound.

The *Snow Falcon* was the newest and deadliest fighter in the Chinese arsenal; with flight and weapons systems controlled by an advanced combat AI, the human pilot was more a part of the aircraft than master of it. The enemy fighter immediately grew from a dot to a small silver arrow and his offensive system automatically selected the short-range Mitsubishi AAM5-B air-to-air missile and locked up the enemy plane. *Tone!* He hesitated. For a millisecond. The AAM5 had a poor record for accuracy in a high-speed head-on merge. He canceled the missile and switched to guns, his gun pipper appearing now in his helmet visor and bobbing around, trying to lock onto the enemy aircraft screaming down at him.

Before he could get a lock, a new missile warning alarm screamed in his ears. The enemy had fired! His joystick was pulled from his hand and his machine rolled into a hard inverted turn. His vision began to blur and he just had time to register the G-force warning on his visor before the enemy missile tone became a long, flat, drawn-out screech and his aircraft righted itself as it resumed straight and level flight.

It was a screech designed to bore into a pilot's soul. It was the scream of digital death. Sure enough, the computerized voice of a Red Dove referee broke in on his comms channel. "Momiji 1 this is Red Dove control. Please maintain your current altitude and heading and respect radio silence until you exit the exercise area. You are Killed In Action."

He slumped forward against his harness, breathing hard. He should have taken the shot when he had it, could have followed through with guns. Why did he hesitate?!

His fist hammered into the glass over his head. One by one, the icons of the doomed aircraft in his flight flashed and showed red crosses, indicating they too were KIA. They had only claimed one Chinese fighter. Diving on the Chinese decoy flight below, he had exposed himself to their unseen escort above and they had swatted his machines from the sky. The short-ranged Chinese *Chengdu* decoys had done their job and, as he watched, they broke off, headed back to the mainland. Switching a display screen to show a feed from the Red Dove strategic overview – a view only available to ground controllers and 'dead' units – Kato now saw no fewer than twenty-four attack aircraft from the Chinese carrier *Liaoning* speeding into the sector he had just been forced to abandon. And headed straight for his carrier, the JS *Izumo*.

It may only be a 'friendly' exercise, but the Chinese had just blown a hole in the Japanese defenses and they were about to pour pain and humiliation through it.

Red Dove, Red Dragon

His hacker handle was *Dragon Bird* and he was about to fire the first shot in a new global war.

He stood at a traffic light across from the 24-hour electronics market on Beijing East Road, near the harborside clamor of Shanghai's Bund and at the bottom of one of its many skyscrapers. Even at this early time of the morning, the shopping center teemed with customers buying everything from solder to integrated circuits, chips, and power supplies. The store owners were gruff and unfriendly to casual shoppers like Dragon Bird, as they mostly serviced tradesmen, technicians, and electronics repair firms. So he rarely shopped there.

Dragon Bird made his way down the steps and through the basement, past the small shop fronts, with weary resentment. He especially disliked the sharp, nostril-stinging stink of burning solder and ozone that seemed to pool in the basement and the slap slap slap of his Huili Warrior sneakers across the fake white marble floor. Every day, slap slap slap on his way in, slap slap slap on his way out. Yeah, sure, he could do up his laces and cut down on the slapping, but casual civilian dress was one of the few personal privileges he was allowed and he was milking it.

At the back of the basement he turned a corner to a service elevator marked 'technical staff only'. It had no button, just a card reader. He fished in his bag for his card, shoving aside the thermos of pot noodles, his keys and phone, to pull it out by its lanyard, hang it around his neck and swipe it through the reader. When the reader lit green he stuck his thumb on a thumb pad to confirm his ID. As he waited for the elevator, he reflected he may as well have slept under his desk overnight, since it was only six hours since he had slapped his way out across the tiles in the early morning hours of last night.

But at least today would be a break from the usual routine. Today his system was going *offensive*. The system he and his team had worked to perfect for nearly five years, that no one had believed was possible and that sprung from an idea his former boss, the Golden Idiot, had even mocked in front of his fellow programmers. Not that he would get much credit for it, he was still only a lowly Shàowèi or Captain, and his small team of five coders, the ones who had been toiling away all these years to bring them here, would never be recognized. His officers would take all the credit if his system worked and be the first to grab him by the collar and throw him in front of a disciplinary tribunal if it didn't.

The elevator pinged open and he waited as two young privates slouched out, looking more tired and washed out than him, if that was possible. They were not permitted to salute him, so they just nodded and started fishing cigarette packets out of their pockets as they exited the elevator. He stepped into a fug of spicy aftershave and sour sweat. As the elevator clunked into motion, he checked his *WeChat Moments* account one last time before he had to hand the phone over to the security staff. As usual, the only message was one from his mother. His other friends from college had landed themselves jobs at Baidu and Huawei and lived glamorous, glittering lives with high salaries, street clothes, and girlfriends with narrow hips and luscious lips, while he had let himself be lured into a job with Unit 61938. He was promised the chance to work on technologies his friends could only dream of, but he hadn't been told he would be doing it in numbing social isolation.

The elevator opened onto what looked like a small airport security gate. He stepped out and walked up to a desk and handed over his shoulder bag, with everything inside it except his lunch thermos. The private behind the desk handed him a bag tag and stuck his bag in a pigeon hole. There were people from another elevator stacking behind him and she waved him out of the way. He put the thermos onto an x-ray belt, then moved over to a body scanner, stepped inside when he was called forward, held his hands in the air and made a circle. The machine beeped. It nearly always did. He stepped out and waited as a soldier ran a detector wand up and down his arms, legs, and around his waist. The soldier checked a screen and then waved him into the locker room. From his locker, he took his light green uniform shirt with its green and gold shoulder boards and dark green baseball-style hat. Then he stowed his lunch thermos where his shirt had been, checked himself in a mirror and got ready to go through to his team's work area.

It was the same routine as every other damn day. But today was not every other day. Today, he and his unit were going to *war*.

China's first modern aircraft carrier had started its life as a Cold War wreck. Its keel was laid down in 1985 as a Soviet aircraft cruiser, the *Varyag*, but the regime collapsed before it was completed and its hull lay rusting in the Ukraine until China bought it in 1998 and towed it to its Dalian shipyard in Liaoning province.

The rebuilding of the carrier was a herculean task that took nearly twenty years – it wasn't until 2016 that the ship named for the province that had birthed it, the *Liaoning* (pronounced lee-ow-ning), was declared combat-ready.

The announcement sent geopolitical tremors around the world, particularly among the nations that border the disputed South China Sea: the Philippines, Vietnam, and Japan. It was more than a military signal, it was a political signal to the region that a resurgent China was going to take a more assertive role at sea. Landlocked for centuries without a true blue-water navy, it nevertheless had a proud naval history dating as far back as 210 BC when the royal sorcerer Xu Fu led a fleet of 60 ships and 5,000 sailors on a search for the elixir of life across the seas to the east of China. He was believed to have made landfall on the western coast of Japan and declared himself emperor. Neither he nor his ships and crew ever returned.

As a metaphor for China's naval ambitions, the *Liaoning* was apt. Concerned with civil wars and invasions from the west and later from Japan, the rising empire of China had built up a strong 'green-water' or coastal navy, but did not pose a naval threat to other Pacific powers in the 20th Century. With the launch of the *Liaoning* in the 21st Century, that all changed. Ship by ship, port by port, China built up its navy, so that by 2030 it had matched the US Navy in blue-water capability. The numbers were telling. In attack submarines, it could field 87 to the US's 42. In ballistic missile submarines it matched the US, 12 to 11. In large surface ships and carriers, it lagged, matching only a third of the US firepower in missile cruisers, but this was due to a focus on smaller surface ships suited to battle in the waters of Korea, Japan, and the South China Sea, where it outnumbered the US 123 to 40. In the final stage of its expansion, it launched five amphibious landing ships, each capable of fielding a full marine expeditionary force.

The threat provoked Japan in 2020 to embark on a ten-year race to build up its armed forces to counterbalance the growing Chinese presence in the South China Sea and increased assertiveness over Taiwan. But it had started thirty years too late; through that entire period China had been outspending it six to one. Against China's hundreds of heavy ships, submarines, and soon-to-be three aircraft carriers, Japan could only muster a half dozen missile frigates or destroyers, two smaller helicopter carriers, and a fleet of twenty submarines, a third the size of China's sub fleet. Japan had relied too long on its alliance with a USA that now had bigger troubles with its old enemy Russia and was much less interested in involving itself in the problems of far-off nations like Japan.

That its attention and priorities were elsewhere became apparent in 2019 when the US announced it would be suspending its annual war games with South Korea, as a goodwill gesture toward the North. The suspension became permanent as reunification talks began in 2023 and the US began drawing down its permanent presence in South Korea. In 2025 when a ten-year timetable for the reunification of the two Koreas was announced by the leaders of both of those countries, China and South Korea made clear in the UN Security Council they saw no ongoing role for US forces in the new Korea and the US agreed. But it wasn't going to wait ten years – it started in 2030 to withdraw all combat personnel. A few of the larger US bases were still there, but they were mostly filled with accountants and lawyers, haggling over the details of what should be turned over to the new United Korean Republic government and who would pay what to whom.

When South China Sea tensions inevitably escalated to an armed confrontation between Chinese and Philippine naval units, resulting in the loss of the Philippine Navy frigate, the *Gregorio del Pilar*, the

US response offered no material support and made nothing but the softest of protests at the United Nations. Japanese politicians watched the US turn its back on its former ally with alarm. When Chinese forces landed on the Taiwanese Pescadores Islands and reclaimed them for China, provoking a political crisis on Taiwan and censure in the UN Security Council, the UK proposed a motion calling on China to withdraw its troops. France voted for the motion, China and Russia against. The US abstained. In Tokyo, the newly formed right-wing government of the Party of Hope convened an emergency session of Parliament, voted to increase military spending and to withdraw Japan from the nearly 80-year-old US-Japan Mutual Security Treaty.

Despite centuries of enmity, it was perhaps not surprising that in 2025 Japan intensified diplomatic overtures to China that had first begun in 2018. It softened its stance on key maritime disputes in the South China Sea and closed its representative office on Taiwan. The hotly disputed Senkaku Islands were declared *terra nullius* and a joint China-Japan 'maritime safety' station began operating on Uotsuri-shima island in 2028. The US responded by canceling arms shipments to Japan, but Japan was not concerned. It had stockpiled spare parts and ammunition for its US-made fighter aircraft and immediately announced a joint-venture agreement between Mitsubishi Heavy Industries and the Shenyang Aircraft Corporation for a Japanese version of the Chinese *Chengdu* 'Mighty Dragon' stealth fighter.

The US reacted angrily but pragmatically, just as it had in Korea, announcing an aggressive timetable for closing the three US Air Force bases on the Japanese mainland and Okinawa, plus the US Army Camp Zama base at Kanagawa, leaving only the 10,000 Marines at Camp Smedley on Okinawa, which had already shrunk from a peak of seven facilities down to just four – the Marine Corps base at Camp Schwab, the Marine Air Corps at Futenma, the joint Marine and National Security Agency intelligence facility at Camp Hansen, and the Navy-run port at White Beach. The move was more than pure posturing, however. The troops and equipment stationed in Japan were sorely needed in other theaters and in fact were redeployed well ahead of the deadline; to Guam, Darwin, and the bulk of them to bases bordering a now belligerent and chaotic post-Putin Russia.

As the US drew down its forces and closed its mainland bases, the Japanese Government hit the US with a massive bill for the cleanup of its former installations, which the US refused to acknowledge. And on Okinawa, simmering civilian resentment against the remaining US presence there led to violent protests and then 'citizen occupations' of the largely deserted US facilities. Acts of violence against US service members became commonplace and Japanese police investigation of these was lax.

In 2033, Japan and China announced a new China-Japan Mutual Self-Defense Treaty. The two most powerful militaries in the Far East were allied for the first time in their histories. China began to support Japanese calls for the accelerated withdrawal of the remaining US military forces in Japan and, in particular, for the US to hand over to Japanese Self-Defense Forces full control of the last US Navy-run port facility on Okinawa at White Beach. This, the US refused. It continued to forward base a naval taskforce at White Beach, currently comprising an amphibious assault ship, the USS *Makin Island*, the recently upgraded *Ticonderoga* Aegis cruiser the USS *Port Royal*, two *Zumwalt*-class multirole destroyers, and a fleet oiler.

To mark the occasion of the official signing of the new China-Japan defense pact, the two countries announced the first-ever joint naval exercises between the Japan Naval Self-Defense Force and the People's Liberation Army Navy. China allocated no less than a full carrier taskforce, based around the *Liaoning*, to Exercise Red Dove.

The *Liaoning* may have been the first and oldest of China's carriers, but it was designated officially as a 'training ship' and was the country's testbed for the newest technologies – a mantle it carried proudly. While its sister carriers fielded older navalized *Chengdu* fighters based on stolen US fourth-generation stealth technology, the *Liaoning* was nearing the end of very successful trials for the newer *Snow Falcon*s and had been upgraded to be able to field thirty-six of the new 'very short takeoff and landing' stealth fighters. After an on-again, off-again development program, Red Dove was going to be the final exercise before the new *Snow Falcon* aircraft were declared combat-ready. The *Liaoning*'s pilots had been looking forward very much indeed to the chance to test themselves against the twenty-eight US-made F-35Es of the Japanese Maritime Self-Defense Force, flying off the decks of its own carrier, the newly modified former Helicopter Destroyer, the JS *Izumo*.

At the exact moment Dragon Bird was checking his pot noodles through the security scanner, the pilots of the *Liaoning* were engaged with the pilots of the Japanese carriers over the sea off Okinawa. Accompanying the *Liaoning* in this show of Chinese naval power were six air defense destroyers, four anti-submarine frigates, two *Shang*-class nuclear submarines, and one supply ship. Japan had also brought a formidable naval force to the party, with its newly refitted carrier accompanied by four *Konga*-class missile destroyers, a *Towada*-class fleet replenishment tanker, and two *Soryu-E*-class extended-range submarines, supported by maritime surveillance aircraft flying from Okinawa.

Exercise Red Dove had four more days to run. After which, in a gesture of international maritime fraternity, the combined Japanese and Chinese fleets were going to proceed to Shanghai for a formal signing ceremony to celebrate the successful conduct of their first-ever joint fleet exercises.

Before the exercise, the Japanese government had issued a warning to Japan-based US warships to avoid military operations in the East China Sea until the passage of the Sino-Japanese carrier strike group was concluded, to prevent any 'maritime misunderstandings' occurring due to heavier than usual naval traffic in Chinese and Japanese waters. A US Navy spokesman responded by stating that its forward-deployed Okinawa expeditionary strike group, Taskforce 44, would stage from White Beach "as and when the Commander of US Forces in the Pacific so deems." Off the record, he told journalists that it would be a cold day in Hades when a Japanese admiral told a US admiral where and when he could sail his ships.

Unwelcome Guests

Noriko Fukada had worked at the Kouwa Gardens Nursery near White Beach US Navy Base for a long time. A very long time. These days, she didn't get through as much as she used to in her prime, nor was she getting paid for it either. But she was always at the Nursery at seven in the morning, rain or shine, six days a week. Her specialty was succulents, because Okinawa was full of people who did nothing but work and drink and work and did not have time for high-maintenance house plants. A cactus, however – a nice *Buiningii* or *Akagurohibotan-Nishiki* – if potted correctly and watered sparingly, any idiot could keep alive. Her favorite customers however were not the collectors, the cacti fanatics whom she tolerated but did not encourage. They came only to show her how much they thought they knew, to try to teach her, not to listen, not to learn. Noriko loved the students, the twenty-something boys and girls who came to Kouwa Gardens looking for nothing more complicated than a plant for their windowsill, or their desk.

"Something that doesn't need much light," they would say. "Something that doesn't need much care."

"Tell me about yourself," she would reply. "And I will find the perfect plant for you." Their stories kept her young.

Most days she would arrive early and stay at the nursery until lunchtime, unless she was sick, or having a bad day. She would eat with the other workers and listen to their prattle, shake her head at their obsession with gadgets and devices, VR game stars she had never seen. After lunch she would walk the two blocks back to her apartment, take a lift to the second floor and gather the things she needed for her afternoon program. In the afternoons she visited the 'old people'. The lonely and the sick and those whose minds had packed up before their body did. She made small cakes for them and took a thermos of tea with her so that they wouldn't need to fuss, though often – if they were brought up correctly – they made a big deal out of serving for her and she let them.

Because in the country which still held the world record for the greatest number of people over the age of 100, Noriko Fukada was a bit of a legend. World-famous on Okinawa, she said with a gap-toothed smile.

Noriko Fukada had been born on January 7, 1931. She was nearly twelve when Japan attacked Pearl Harbor and opened a new front in the Second World War. She had just turned fifteen when the Americans stormed ashore on Okinawa in the biggest amphibious assault of the Pacific war. Her father hid her in the cellar of their apartment when the first shells from the big American battleships started roaring in from the sea. She was only allowed up to the apartment to eat lunch, when her father would update them all on what was happening. He was a fireman and worked with everyone from sailors to soldiers and policemen, so he knew everything. "A violent wind of steel is coming, Noriko," he told her. "You must be brave and help your mother." She didn't want to stay home and help her mother. Her brother, only fourteen years old, had been drafted into the *Tekketsu Kinnōtai*, the Iron and Blood Corps. She had wanted to go with him, but had been told to go home again. She stood crying beside the line of boys, bereft with shame. An old marine had come up to her and led her to a corner and sat her down. "I have an important mission for you," he said. "You must survive. Above all else, you must live. If you die there will be no one left who knows the truth about the battle of Okinawa. Bear this temporary shame but endure it. I give you this order and expect you to carry it out."

She lived. Her father and brother did not. She was pressed into service at a Japanese field hospital, where people from surrounding Maehara and Suzaki were often rounded up and herded onto the roof to wave flags, so that the American bombers would not bomb them. She and her mother nearly starved, troops from both sides raiding their house for food, leaving them nothing.

She lived. She spent the next ten years hungry, a meal a day if she was lucky, many days without. US forces took their farmland to build their bases, paid the local workers poorly if at all. Only in the late 1950s did things start to improve, as the US needed Okinawa as a staging post for its new war in Korea, and Okinawa became a US territory. She worked as a nurse at a US military hospital, for US dollars, until it was closed down when the island was transferred to Japanese government control in 1972.

That was when she had gotten the job at Kouwa Gardens, working in the nursery shop. She showed an aptitude for cultivation, requested a job in the greenhouse and started in the succulents department, where she had stayed since, except for a very brief and unhappy time in the herb gardens, which she found overwhelming. So many scents.

She had carried out the order given to her by that old sergeant in 1945 most faithfully. She was 103 years old and she had lived. Lived through the Second World War, the dawn of atomic weapons, Korean wars one and two, the electrification, industrialization, and roboticization of Japan. Lived through a husband, but never had children herself. She had outlived the sorrow of that. She had seen the arrival of wireless communications, television, games consoles, internet, nuclear, solar, wind, and hydro power and VR. She had seen Russians send a man into space, Americans walk on the moon, and a Chinese astronaut orbit Mars.

But she had never seen anything, or anyone, quite like the woman who walked into the Kouwa Gardens Nursery a year ago. Her hair was dyed platinum blonde, cropped so short it reminded Noriko of one of her favorite cactuses, the Extra-Hairy Mammillaria plumosa. She was wearing jeans, a poorly fitting t-shirt verging on immodest, and a US Navy baseball cap. She had metal through her ears, her nose and a stud in one lip. Tattoos on both arms. She whistled a tune as she entered the nursery, loudly and badly.

The woman had walked up to Noriko, quite boldly, and started talking to her in English. Noriko made a pretense of not understanding, hoping she would go away, but she had taken an interest in the arrangement Noriko was making – a simple miniature garden in a rectangular pot, with four varieties in it, suitable for a wide window with an easterly aspect – and started asking questions about it. Noriko soon realized that the only way to free herself of this very embarrassing situation was to sell the woman something and exchanged a few words with her, eventually selling her a large

Biznaga plumosa, which was much like the Mammillaria, but more vulgar and thus perfectly suited. The woman had departed, whistling, and Noriko had taken the rest of the day off.

That was the first time she met Karen 'Bunny' O'Hare.

Bunny O'Hare was staring at the stubbornly unflowering cactus sitting on top of her microwave oven and feeling like she was headed for a cold Saturday in hell. Some Saturdays, she woke up in the humidity of an Okinawa morning, got that first cup of coffee inside her and then sat back with her hands locked behind her head, the whole weekend stretching out in front of her like a runway in front of superjumbo jet. Nothing to do, nowhere to go, just a slow takeoff toward total freedom.

This was not going to be a superjumbo day.

She'd had her morning coffee Vietnamese style (with condensed milk because she still didn't have a fridge) and checked her email inbox. There were the usual thousand unread messages, but nothing screaming READ ME at her. At that point, she had been thinking maybe it was going to be A Good Day. Which didn't happen too often when you were stationed on the last remaining operational US base in Japan.

Then Master at Arms James Jensen, of the 3rd Marines, 1st Battalion, White Beach Naval Base Okinawa, knocked on her door.

"Hey O'Hare, wassup?" he said, giving her his usual lopsided health-nut quarterback six-pack wonderboy grin.

Wassup number one was that Chief Petty Officer Jensen had rarely called at her off-base apartment across the road from Koza Music Town and never on a Saturday morning. Wassup number two was that Agent Smith from the classic *Matrix* movies was standing there beside him. It was O'Hare's incontrovertible experience that when a man in his mid-thirties dressed in a dark suit, white shirt, dark tie and sunglasses turned up unannounced at your front door and just stood there without mentioning Jehovah, then you were about to have a very non-superjumbo kind of day.

She shot a curious frown at Jensen but he just shrugged. "This is Chuck, can we come in?" 'Chuck' smiled but didn't hold out his hand. He reeked of Spook.

Bunny stepped aside and waved them into the living room of her apartment. A two-room apartment above the Galaxy Bar, which she could barely afford on her Defense Advanced Research Projects Agency housing allowance. DARPA wasn't exactly known for its largesse.

Chuck didn't know where to sit. Jensen solved the problem for him by pushing O'Hare's newspapers and magazines off her sofa and onto the floor and pointing to where Chuck could park his butt.

"I was reading those," Bunny told Jensen, pulling over one of her dining chairs.

He looked down at them. "Same magazines and papers that were on the sofa three weeks ago when I visited."

"There's some good articles. Long-read features kind of thing," Bunny said defensively.

"Open at the same pages," he said.

Chuck was holding out a badge for her to see and waving it to get her attention. "Ms. O'Hare, I'm from the NSA."

"It's Bunny," Jensen said. "Get it? O'Hare – Bunny? It's a pilot thing."

"To friends," she said, looking at Agent Smith. "And we're not there yet." She glowered at Jensen. What was he doing in her flat with the NSA in tow? The NSA was the National Security Agency of the USA, the world's biggest, ugliest cyberspooks.

Bunny stared at him curiously. OK, so Chief Jensen was Navy Security Force and Chuckie was a cyberspook. What did they want with a lowly DARPA contractor like her?

Over the next few minutes, Bunny O'Hare got the unwelcome feeling she was under investigation. The thing that had her curiosity, as she bustled around in her kitchen making tea for Jensen (black) and coffee for Chuck (black) and a double shot Vietnamese for herself, was what she might have done that warranted an unannounced visit from both the NSA and a Navy Security Force master at arms. Bunny got on first-name terms with Chief Jensen thanks to a small situation involving a bunch of Marines who'd gotten into trouble using karaoke microphones to beat the crap out of a local Yakuza mobster downstairs in the Galaxy Bar, which took up the whole first and second floors of her apartment complex. She'd been walking up the stairs to her apartment and heard a lot of shouting in English and Japanese. Stopping at the karaoke bar level she stuck her head in and saw half the staff of the Galaxy had surrounded some young Marines, who were swinging microphones on their leads around their heads, to hold the staff at bay. A Yakuza mobster was propped against a wall, holding his bleeding forehead and cursing, too drunk to stand.

Bunny knew the staff at the Galaxy pretty well, seeing they'd been neighbors for a year. And she did most of her drinking there, when she wasn't at the Mohito Bar down the road, which they also owned. She calmed things down, took the three Marines upstairs to her place and telephoned base security. Jensen had come personally with a couple of his men to collect them.

"I looked you up when you called," he said, after thanking Bunny for stepping in and sending his men downstairs to a waiting van. "You're DARPA."

"Yep," she confirmed.

"That why you live off-base?" It was a fair question, since the local population was quite ambivalent about seeing the US military on their streets these days and most personnel chose to live and socialize on-base.

"No, I took this place for the view," she told him, nodding at the view out her loungeroom window, across Kozagate street to the rusting neon sign over Music Town.

He looked out the window, looked around the tiny apartment and looked O'Hare up and down, from face piercings to tattoos to army combat boots.

"I think this is going to be the start of a beautiful friendship, Lieutenant," he said.

"That's my *former* air force rank," she said.

"Well, I'm not going to call you Ms. DARPA Project Lead," he smiled. "What else do you go by?"

"Bunny. And O'Hare."

"I'll go with O'Hare." He'd tipped her a salute. "Thanks again for the help, O'Hare."

When she'd signed up for a hiking tour at White Beach, she'd found herself on a full day trek through the Gangala Valley with a bunch of base nurses and … Jensen. They'd clicked. Turned out she wasn't the only one on the island with a warped view of the world.

She tipped a half packet of old Oreos onto a plate. She'd messed up plenty in her life, but whatever this was, she decided she must be in big trouble, looking at Chuck sitting there impatiently while Jensen stirred sugar into his tea and reached for a cookie. He took two.

She pulled the plate away from him and handed it to Chuck, but he just looked at it like he'd never seen a cookie before in his life and then looked at her. "Ms. O'Hare, we need your help."

She gave Jensen a 'what the hell' look, but he just shrugged.

"I am a Remotely Piloted Submersible Pilot and Sensor Operator," she told Chuck, emphasizing the capital letters. "And DARPA project lead for the Stingray program here at White Beach. I am still getting stopped at the gates every time there is a new guy, having to explain that I really work there and reminding him he should be saluting me." Chuck looked as though this did not surprise him. "There is no capacity in which I can possibly be of help to the US National Security Agency, unless you want advice on pubs and clubs in downtown Koza."

He smiled his non-smile again. In a movie, at this point he'd have been pulling out a big fat manila folder from his briefcase and it would have had 'O'Hare, K' written on the front and he would have unclipped it slowly and taken out some surveillance photos of her and started telling her about her life story, just to intimidate her. But he didn't have a briefcase. So he didn't have a manila folder. He didn't even take out his smartphone and look up some notes. He'd memorized it.

"Well, actually there is. Your latest security vetting was less than two years ago…"

"Yep. I think it was right before your Secretary of Navy pinned a Navy Cross on me. Or maybe it was after?"

"After," he said, without a pause. "But you do not have sufficient clearances for what we are about to discuss."

She pointed at Jensen. "But *he* does?"

Chuck didn't look happy. "I've had to indoctrinate Chief Petty Officer Jensen, for the purposes of our discussion today."

"Oooh, you've been *indoctrinated*," she said to Jensen. "Did it hurt?"

"Walking like a cowboy," he said. "Seriously though O'Hare, just hear him out so we can go and get a proper breakfast, OK?"

That was his nice way of saying STFU O'Hare, so she did.

"Can I just confirm a few details?" Chuck asked. He took off his sunglasses, showing ice blue eyes.

"Sure."

"Thank you, ma'am. You served six years with the Royal Australian Air Force and were recruited by DARPA Aerospace during the Turkey-Syria conflict, where you were based in Incirlik…" He still wasn't looking at notes. It was quite unnerving.

"Classified," she told him.

"Yes, flying F-35s."

"No comment."

"But you were removed from active duty due to multiple disciplinary breaches and then recruited to the DARPA Unmanned Combat Air Vehicle program."

"Again, no comment."

70

"Then transferred to the F-47 *Fantom* amphibious conversion program…"

"Also classified." He was good. He was all over her CV, she had to give him that.

"From there you were posted to a covert second-strike facility on Little Diomede Island in the Bering Strait, during the Russia-USA maritime dispute…"

"War, not dispute. And still classified. And now I'll have to ask Chief Jensen to kill you."

"…in which service you became the first Australian since Admiral Harold Farncomb in World War Two to be awarded the US Navy Cross for valor under fire and a Purple Heart."

Jensen arched his eyebrows in surprise. This was apparently something he hadn't picked up on, even though it was in the public domain. "They hand them out like crackerjack prizes these days," she said.

"After which you were placed on long-term medical impairment leave…" he said like he was reading off a mental shopping list.

"Shortish," she told him. "Shortish-term medical leave."

"Fine," he said, all polite about it. "And now, as you explained, you are attached to DARPA again, leading the final pre-deployment trials of the advanced undersea payload delivery system for Extra-Large Unmanned Underwater Vehicles before DARPA hands the project over to the Office of Naval Research."

"XLUUVs, we call them," she told him. "The Orca was the first. This new generation are called Stingrays. Sounds edgier."

"Do we have to go through O'Hare's whole life story?" Jensen asked. "Because there is some really ugly stuff in there if you get to her taste in music…"

"He's just trying to protect me, bless him. He actually loves bro-country," she quipped.

Chuck ignored them. "While on medical leave, you were prescribed anti-depressants."

O'Hare glared at him. "Seriously, you want to go *there?*" She didn't care what he said in front of Jensen – the guy had used her bathroom so he'd probably sneaked a peek in her medicine cabinet. But it unsettled her that the NSA would have dug into her personal life so deeply. "Have you ever been in combat, Chuck?"

"No. But this is about you, not me. You have not filled a prescription for nearly a year," he said, conversationally. "So your mental state is, what ... stable would you say?" He waited for her reply with an inscrutably blank expression.

"I haven't woken up screaming for months, if that's your question."

"Seriously, can we speed this up?" Jensen said, crossing and uncrossing his legs. "I'll be turning forty in a few years."

Chuck gave Jensen a polite death-look. Wiped his face clean from the inside, reached into his inside jacket pocket and pulled out a couple of pieces of paper and a pen. "This is a Secrecy Agreement, please sign at the bottom."

She looked at Jensen. "*I* already signed mine," he said. "I'm good."

The paper had the usual guff across the top: TOP SECRET UMBRA ORCON dot dot dot. Then the standard threats of death and dismemberment if the signatory (Karen O'Hare) disclosed anything about said project to anyone not authorized to receive information about said project. And then the project name...

"Project LOKI?" she asked as she signed.

"Yup. Thank you," Chuck said, taking back his paper and pen and putting them both in his pocket. As he reached across her, O'Hare picked up a whiff of...what? She was usually pretty good at aftershaves and perfumes, but couldn't nail his. Probably because he also smelled like he just got off a plane after a three-hour flight. He sat back, looking at her as though waiting for her to ask a question. When she didn't, he spoke up. "Loki. Norse god of mischief," he said. "Usually we use random name generators for our operations, but I came up with that one myself."

"Cute," she said. "Care to tell me what Project LOKI is about?"

"Of course." He looked at Jensen, who was already in on the secret and looking at O'Hare with an annoyingly knowing smile, then turned his gaze back on her. "NSA has for some time been concerned at the increasing automation of our most advanced weapons systems. Aircraft, ships, tanks, and subs are going from being manned to semi-autonomous, or in the case of your Stingray, almost entirely autonomous."

"Autonomous AI is a force multiplier. It frees human resources to be used across multiple weapons systems instead of having dedicated crews which need training, fielding, rest and recreation. The Stingray has the offensive capabilities of a *Los Angeles*-class submarine, but can be piloted remotely by just myself and a systems officer, whereas an LA-class boat requires a crew of one hundred and twenty-nine. Why is NSA concerned?" O'Hare asked.

"NSA is concerned that weapons systems like your Stingray are in essence just highly armed and mobile computer systems." He brushed an invisible crumb from his trousers. "And like any computer, they are vulnerable to cyber-attack."

A light finally clicked on in Bunny O'Hare's still half-asleep mind. The NSA and its Cyber Command were America's cyber-attack dogs. Jensen was the base security officer. Chuck was interested in her Stingray. She pointed a finger at him. "NSA is going to try to hack my Stingray, right?"

"That will depend…" he shrugged, "…on what I find when I start looking under the hood."

A Ribbon Around A Bomb

"I want to see some action, people!" Dragon Bird said, looking around him. He'd walked into his team's cube to find Frangipani with her headphones on, buried in code as usual, but Po was sitting with his feet up on his desk, flicking through anime images on a tablet, and Tanken looked like he was browsing the banned BBC news website. Banned for citizens, not for members of Unit APT (Advanced Persistent Threat) 23 of course. Nothing on the web was off-limits to his people; still, it irked him to see them waiting around for him to arrive, rather than already hard at work.

Today was their day!

"I am already in action, Sir," Tanken said. His handle meant 'blade' and he had the movie star good looks of Huang Xiaoming. Frangi flicked her eyes to glance at him briefly as he spoke. DB knew she was secretly in love with him, but she had sworn him to silence about it and it had made him very uncomfortable that she had even confided the secret to him. "I can confirm that there are no reports on western media today regarding our successful penetration," Tanken continued.

"We have a media monitoring service that will do that," DB said. "I doubt that you will add greatly to their analysis from your reading of the BBC Sport pages."

Po swung his feet down. "I forgot to eat breakfast, Sir." He rubbed his eyes. "It's only five hours since I went home. I went home, brushed my teeth, went to bed, woke up, brushed my teeth and came here," he said. "And when I got here, I realized I had forgotten to have breakfast."

"You had toothpaste," Frangi said without looking at him, or even smiling. "And you are overweight. You need to eat less anyway." Po was indeed struggling with his weight. He hadn't chosen his own handle, it had been given him in a different unit, where he was named after a cartoon panda who loved noodles.

DB looked at his motley band of recruits with pride. It was true, he had been working them around the clock on this assignment. But they had achieved miracles. His immediate superior, Major Shaofeng, had said as much yesterday after DB sent his daily status report to him. The Major had called him into his office within minutes of receiving it.

Shaofeng had printed the email and it was on his desk in front of him. DB stood at attention, nervous but not afraid. He had done nothing wrong. Had he?

"Is this report accurate?" Shaofeng had asked.

"Yes sir."

"You have not exaggerated?"

"No sir," DB had replied. "We have completed our preparations and are ready to take covert control of the target system. We are just waiting for the Ministry of State Security's human agent to get in position to give us real-time intelligence."

Shaofeng tapped a finger on the email. "The alternatives you propose have already been discussed. We can continue to use the KAHLO system to gather intelligence, or we can use it as we have been tasked to use it. Why should we reconsider, now that your unit has successfully done as ordered?"

"I was merely reminding the Major of his options," DB said carefully. "In case the strategic situation had changed in any way I was unaware of."

Shaofeng flicked the email across his desk to the floor in front of DB. "The strategic situation has not changed. Our main enemy is still our main enemy. And as long as that enemy has military bases on our borders, our mission is clear and your orders are unchanged."

"Yes sir."

"Is anything about this confusing to you?"

"No sir."

"Then at 1220 hours tomorrow, you will initiate the operation, as ordered."

75

"Yes sir!" DB had said. "We will not fail."

Shaofeng's voice softened. He was a portly, fatherly figure who dressed like an office worker, in a white shirt and black suit, and when he smiled his rather large ears lifted a little in a comical way. "I know you will not, Captain. APT 23 is setting new standards in stealth infiltration. You should be proud."

"I am proud, sir!" DB had replied. "But this attack *will* be discovered. By its very nature, it must reveal itself in order to be effective and then our new capabilities will also be revealed. If we had more time, we could leverage the existing infiltration to..."

Shaofeng had held up his hand and stood up from his chair. On the wall beside his desk he had a huge antique map of Asia, a copy of a map drawn up by the Chinese navy in the Tang dynasty in about 900 AD. It showed Southeast China, the Korean Peninsula, Japan and its southerly chain of islands, including Okinawa. He stood next to it and pointed to a spot in the East China Sea. "The *Liaoning* taskforce is here, 200km south of Jeju, executing the final maneuvers of Exercise Red Dove together with our new Japanese allies." He moved his finger south. "At 1200 hours it will recover the last of its fighter aircraft and, together with the Japanese fleet, begin sailing south for a celebration of international fraternity and a ceremony to mark the official signing of the new China-Japan Defense Treaty." Shaofeng moved his finger again. "And the last significant US military presence in the Sino-Japanese co-prosperity sphere is here. US Navy Base White Beach, Okinawa, Japan."

"Yes sir."

"You know what you need to do, Dragon Bird."

DB had squared his shoulders at the Captain's use of his hacker handle instead of his military rank. It had been a mark of the deepest respect.

Listening to his crew give each other a ribbing, DB decided not to come down hard on them. "Frangi, are you in?"

"Yes, Comrade Team Leader," she said. Although his rank was captain, the special informality in Unit 61938 went beyond not wearing uniforms. They also referred to their units as teams and their officers as team leaders. "Traffic appears normal. Intercepting and re-routing. KAHLO is successfully capturing 97 percent of communications in and out of the target system." She was the chief systems officer for their KAHLO system and the cyber equivalent of the pilot in a jet fighter. DB's team had gone from twenty-plus coders at its peak to these three now, supported by a backroom team of system techs. His small project leadership group was not a sign of decreased importance, it was a sign they had been so successful that the mission objectives could now be met by just this small team – minimizing security risks and maximizing their efficiency.

"Po, anything on your radar?" he asked. Po stopped his moaning and turned to his desk where an array of three screens flickered with numbers and readouts. He was DB's systems vulnerability engineer and his job right now was to monitor for and intercept any counter-attack.

"All quiet, Comrade Captain," Po said. He pointed to a red police siren and light mounted on a stand above his screens. "You'll know if they send anything against us. I rigged that up just in case I fall asleep." He glared at Frangi. "From starvation."

DB turned to Tanken. "Is your agent in motion?"

Tanken sighed. He was the only one who was not Unit 61938. He had been seconded to DB's team from the People's Liberation Army Strategic Support Force or SSF. He had no role in the immediate cyber-attack. His mission would only be initiated if they were successful. He tossed a sardonic salute at DB. "Yes sir, Captain." His work station contained one laptop, a couple of screens, and a joystick rig that looked like something a computer gamer would use. "He reported in two hours ago, right on schedule."

DB's KAHLO operators, Frangi and Po, both looked up from their desks briefly and glanced at each other, then went back to work. They were unaware of the full scope of the operation and knew nothing about the actual identity of the Chinese human source on which so much of their mission depended. No one in Unit APT 23, including DB, knew more than they needed to know right now.

He looked at his crew fondly. KAHLO was DB's foster-child and China's newest and most potent cyber-attack system. One of DB's early crew members, Jin Tan, got the idea for KAHLO several years ago, when she was watching a nature documentary about the katydid insect, a predator which preys specifically on male cicadas. Except it doesn't have to hunt them, its prey runs eagerly to its death. The katydid parks itself on a nice prominent leaf or branch near a colony of cicadas and mimics the wing clicks of a horny female cicada. A nearby male, thinking it's got lucky, comes galloping at the katydid hoping to mate and the next thing it knows, it's dinner.

It took her a while to operationalize the thought buzzing around her head, but when she finally did, she shared her thinking with DB and he found Frangipani in another unit with exactly the skills he had needed to bring KAHLO to life. With Jin and Frangi working together, side by side, after nearly two years, KAHLO was born. When Unit 61938 realized what it had, Jin Tan was moved out of DB's unit due to 'questionable political alliances' – her family had been members of the Falun Gong movement. DB had taken over the project, kept Frangi with him, and brought it to where it was today. He had no idea what had happened to Jin Tan, but often thought of her. He hoped she had received the credit she was due for gifting such a powerful weapon to China.

KAHLO was a neural network learning system that piggybacked on standard hacker exploits to penetrate enemy systems in a way that DB had termed 'cyber mimicry'. Once inside, it just laid low and studied the enemy system, captured its comms and learned how to regurgitate its encrypted code – but it didn't try to break it down and exploit it immediately. It was a katydid, learning how to make cicada wing clicks to fool the host system into thinking it was just a completely normal part of the host. If successful, it would be invisible to any host audit, because all that audit would show was what it expected to see – just another part of itself. Meanwhile KAHLO kept studying and learning, until it had learned enough to be able to take over critical parts of the host system, without the host realizing. It didn't just attack a target system, it *possessed* it.

DB was an art lover and to him, in all modesty, KAHLO was a work of cyber art. So he'd named it after his favorite artist, the Mexican Frida Kahlo de Rivera, whose work had been so seductively subversive. He'd heard that Picasso had once described her art as being like 'a ribbon around a bomb'. The thought described KAHLO beautifully.

"OK team," DB said, trying to keep his voice steady and not show the excitement he was feeling. "It is 12.20 a.m." He swallowed and turned to Tanken. "You may advise your SSF superiors. We are ready to initiate phase 1."

NSA XKeycore Ground Station, Pine Gap, Australia

Allan Pritzkat looked at his watch. It was 01.51 in the a.m. in Pine Gap, which meant 12.21 on the East Coast of China. He looked at the new alert scrolling across his screen, clicked a box to log the event, and then checked the source. Then he gulped. He re-read the alert, twice. This one was B.I.G. big.

Allan had worked in the NSA Signals Analysis Section at the station for nearly two years now and for the first time in two years, he was mildly excited. He specialized in analyzing the decrypts from a People's Liberation Army ground forces cipher that NSA had cracked about five years ago. The cipher had since been superseded, but it was still in use on equipment issued to PLA units in the early part of the decade, and luckily China was slow at upgrading equipment that hadn't been superseded. He occasionally got actionable intelligence on Chinese military movements and operational capabilities through his decrypts, but he'd never seen anything like this!

He'd called up a seemingly innocuous list of military units in the Eastern Military District facing Taiwan that were being moved from reserve to active status. The sheer size and number of units were unusual, but China was in the middle of what it had called 'Operation Red Dove', its multinational exercise with Japan in the South China Sea. So the mobilization of a large number of air and sea assets was judged to be related to Red Dove and it wasn't what had caught Allan Pritzkat's attention.

One unit in particular stood out; the People's Liberation Army 73rd Group Engineering Corps, so he'd double-clicked on that to check out the source report.

The reason Allan had a special affection for the 73rd Engineers was that they had a history of being the go-to unit whenever China had decided it wanted to claim a new piece of territory and build something military on it. Over the last two decades, the 73rd

Engineers had built missile bases, airfields, and ports all across the South China Sea, on everything ranging from atolls to small islands and even semi-submerged sandbars.

The intercept Allan had been looking at was a deployment order, issued to the 73rd Engineers, which identified the location for their next works project.

Latitude: 26°18'08.6"N
Longitude: 127°54'31.7"E

Allan had looked it up. At that point, what had been mildly interesting became B.I.G.

He picked up his telephone and dialed a number.

"Jason, yeah this is Allan, sorry to wake you but I think you better look at what I'm about to send you... yeah Jason, I know what time it is, but unless I'm mistaken, I think China is planning to build a new naval base ... on Okinawa!"

A Most Unusual Visitor

"And that concludes Operation Red Dove," Lieutenant Kato said to himself as he entered the landing pattern above the Japanese aircraft carrier JS *Izumo*. The joint exercises could not end too soon for Takuya. In three sorties, he had claimed no kills and had been 'shot down' twice. His unit had 'lost' ten pilots, including his own wingman. His fifth-generation F-35Es, even with their enhanced combat AI system, had proven no match for the Chinese *Snow Falcon*s.

The *Snow Falcon* had been mocked by western powers as delay after delay had hit its development. At one point in the early 2020s it looked like the program would even be canceled, with political indecision pushing its field date from the 2020s to 2025 and then right into the early 2030s. But the delays had enabled China to make the most of huge leaps in battlefield digital connectivity, data compression, and quantum computing. While western aircraft designers rushed to reverse engineer the latest AI tech into their existing airframes, China had built it right into its *Snow Falcon* prototypes.

Aboard the *Izumo*, Kato-san had been privy to multiple briefings on the *Snow Falcon*'s capabilities but he hadn't believed them until he'd seen them in action. The capability that set them apart from every other aircraft on the battlefield was their ability to share data between the onboard AI systems and cloud-based AI, at quantum speeds. It meant no aircraft was ever alone in the sky, its squadron mates knew exactly where it was, what it was doing and, above all, how to react in either a defensive or offensive tactical environment. Low on energy with an enemy on your tail? All nearby friendly fighters would know it within milliseconds, assess their ability to respond and immediately dispatch the best available aircraft to support you. Out of missiles but with an enemy locked up? Your AI could command a missile to be fired by another aircraft at your target, whether on land or in the air. Spot a hidden enemy anti-air installation as you overflew it? Every aircraft behind you would be notified of its exact position, type, and threat status, helping others to survive it and increasing the likelihood it would be quickly taken out of action.

Before the exercise, Kato's fellow Japanese pilots had mocked the role of the Chinese pilots who were only nominally behind the stick of the Chinese AI-assisted *Snow Falcon*s. 'Chip jockeys' was the nickname they had given them. Not pilots at all, not really. Once the shooting started, they were little more than passengers, being thrown around the sky by their combat AI. They were only there to provide the AI with tasking direction, or as a last resort, in case of catastrophic system damage requiring a human pilot to intervene. A 'meat-based backup' system.

Kato and his squadron mates were not mocking the Chinese pilots now. To add insult to injury, a pair of the Chinese *Snow Falcon*s had escorted him out of the combat area, flying wingtip to wingtip with him before they gave him a sardonic salute and peeled away.

Neither had the arrogance of the Japanese war planners served them well. Informed as they were by a defensive mindset dulled by a hundred years of military passivity, they had proven no match for the hyper-aggressive tactics of the Chinese, who appeared to have no concern for overall losses, as long as their objective was destroyed or their goal achieved. Kato had his suspicions that the Chinese air commanders were also benefitting greatly from superior computing platforms, able to crunch the massive amounts of data flowing in from the battlefield and advise the human war game commanders how best to reverse losses or capitalize on wins.

Damn silicon soldiers. He shouldn't trash the modest AI in his F-35E, it had saved his virtual life several times in the last few days. But it couldn't be used to its full capability, because it had been designed to be teamed with offensive drones, flying in formation with his aircraft and acting like a swarm of wingmen, protecting him and attacking any threats. The system had not been fully deployed before Japan cut defense ties with the US and so the Japanese F-35Es were left with half a system, an AI that augmented a pilot's senses and reflexes, but did nothing to change the balance of power tactically. If only Japanese forces had access to drone swarms ...

The line of thought was pointless. Kato-san had no one to blame for his losses but himself. Luckily at that point his self-flagellation was interrupted by the air boss aboard the *Izumo*.

"404 this is *Izumo*, 170, 23, your approach is angels 8, expected approach time 32, approach button 15."

He responded to the stream of vectors and numbers automatically. "404, *Izumo* boss, 170, 23, time 32, button 15, push time … uh … 22, expected bearing 331, altimeter 30.01, state low."

"404, state low, case 3 recovery, CV1 approach…"

He'd called in his fuel state as being low, which it was, after his all too brief dogfight, but the seas were calm, the winds light, and his vertical landing on the short deck of the Japanese carrier, unlike his combat mission, was flawless. As he shut down his systems, unharnessed and climbed out onto the wing, an unfamiliar flight captain was waiting at the wing root to speak with him.

"Sir, I have been ordered to inform you that you have a guest," the man said, yelling to be heard over the noise of aircraft circling overhead. Takuya pointed to the command island on the other side of the deck and, crouching down, both men ran over to it and stepped inside.

"Guest? What guest?" Takuya asked. A guest on the *Izumo*, while it was at sea and engaged in operations? That was unheard of. He looked across the deck. The only thing that looked slightly unusual was an airbus H135 helicopter, of the type used to ferry officers and crew between ships in the fleet. It was still in the process of being secured, indicating it had landed only recently. It had a tail number he did not recognize – other than that, it was completely unremarkable.

"Sir, I …" The man looked terrified. "I am to escort you to your quarters. That is all I am permitted to say."

Takuya looked around himself, expecting to see armed security. Was he being arrested? For his failure to defend the fleet against a theoretical Chinese attack, in a *war game*? But the plane captain was alone and looked just as mystified as Takuya felt.

"Very well, follow me," Takuya said, tucking his helmet under his arm and taking the steps two at a time down to the accommodation deck. His mind racing, he stepped out of the stairwell into the hallway outside his quarters and came to an immediate stop.

Standing alone outside his quarters was the *Izumo*'s Commanding Officer, Admiral Hiroshi Kagumi. Coming to attention, Kato and the plane captain bowed deeply. "Admiral Kagumi!" He lifted his head.

Oh, he must be in serious, serious trouble.

The Admiral nodded to him to straighten up. He was a tall, thin man with distinguished gray hair and a single conceit. Across his top lip he sported a pencil mustache of the type favored by the Japanese military a hundred years earlier and he trimmed it at the end of every day to ensure it remained a perfect length and almost invisible thinness.

"Lieutenant Kato," the Admiral said. "Give me your helmet."

Kato had quite forgotten he was still in his flight suit, still with his helmet tucked under his arm. Mystified, he held it out to the Admiral, who took it and appeared to briefly study his reflection in the visor. Kato had never witnessed the prelude to a court-martial before … was this how it started? He waited nervously for the Admiral to finish his introspection and speak. Finally, the man appeared to have found what he was looking for in the mirror of the visor and looked directly at Kato.

"Inside your quarters is a most unusual visitor," the Admiral said. "I understand you went to high school together."

Kato's mind raced. A childhood friend here? On the *Izumo*? In the middle of a war game in the middle of the East China Sea? A person of such importance the Admiral himself would escort them here?

He knew only one person in the world who could arrange such an intervention.

Kato checked the zip on his flight suit and pulled it a little higher. He squared his shoulders. "Yes, sir," he said. He looked at the door. "Will you be joining us, sir?" Kato asked, realizing as he did so that the question sounded ridiculous.

"Your guest requested a private meeting, Lieutenant," Kagumi said. "I will send a marine guard here to escort them back to their helicopter when the meeting is concluded."

"Yes sir."

Kagumi regarded him balefully. "This is highly unusual, Kato," he said, and Kato knew that when he said 'unusual' he meant 'regrettable'.

"I'm sorry, sir," Kato said.

"Yes. I can see from your face this is as much a shock to you as it is to me," the Admiral said.

"Yes sir, it is."

"I do not like to be shocked," the Admiral pointed out to Kato, unnecessarily.

"No sir."

"No. Very well." Kagumi folded his hands behind his back, still clutching the helmet. "I have to attend a briefing regarding today's less than satisfactory action."

"Yes sir," Kato said.

"A bad day all round," Kagumi said, with one last look at Kato and at the door to his quarters before handing the helmet to the plane captain. He turned on his heel and walked off toward the stairs with his hands clasped tightly behind his back again, the plane captain running after him, Kato's helmet bouncing against his hip.

Kato bowed and waited in that position until the Admiral and his aide had disappeared from view, then he turned to face the door. He knocked.

"Come in," a woman's voice said clearly.

Princess Mitsuko Naishinnō was accustomed to leaving shocked elders in her wake. Shocked politicians, shocked courtiers, shocked

86

parents. It seemed to her that ever since she could first walk and talk, nearly every single thing she did had shocked the world around her. As a small girl, she had refused to wear the ridiculous satin bowed dresses and formal gowns her minders had tried to dress her in. She preferred the shirts and trousers of the boys in the Palace, or even better, the jeans and t-shirts she saw on the young people in the streets from the window of her armored limousine. She had not refused the traditional training she had been offered as a princess of the imperial family, training in tea ceremonies, in music and dance, in the myriad rituals of temple and Palace life. But she was the first princess of the Reiwa dynasty to be born in the new century and she had devoured the virtual reality programs and games that showed her how the world outside the closeted Court of Reiwa lived. As his only child and born eight years after he was married, Emperor Naruhito could deny her nothing. As a precocious ten-year-old she had demanded to learn judo and he had consented. At thirteen she announced she had had enough of private tutors and wanted to attend a real school, like normal teenagers. It did not go well. At her first school, she was bullied by male students for her lack of a normal Japanese upbringing. The bullying became public and Mitsuko was taken out of the school, with the explanation she was shy and preferred private schooling.

She was almost never seen in public after that. In reality, she moved schools and a major security exercise was undertaken to try to hide her identity so that neither the teachers nor the students at the prestigious Hirikoshi school were aware of her identity – an endeavor made possible because she had almost never been seen in public as a child. She was a quick student, with a lively interest in sports like soccer and baseball, and without the stigma of being a royal she easily made friends. At her father's request she told her friends that her parents were divorced and she didn't like to talk about family. It was also the excuse she used for not being able to invite her friends to visit her house and for why her parents never attended her sports days, theater nights, or academic presentations. Only the 72-year-old headmaster of the Hirikoshi school was privy to the Palace secret and he vowed to take it with him to his death bed. Which he duly did. But unfortunately for the Palace, the stroke that laid him low also unhemmed him and he confided his secret to a nurse in the moments before he died. She posted the fantastic story on social media and it went viral.

On the day the world learned that she was attending a local Tokyo private school as a *commoner*, the friend she had been hanging out with was Takuya Kato. She'd been dating Kato's best friend, Yuto, a boy whose father was a corporate executive at a pharmaceutical company. She'd been to Yuto's place several times, had met his mother and father, and he had begun to insist on meeting *her* parents. He'd taken up the topic again one afternoon at a coffee shop when Takuya was with them. She'd explained to him that wasn't possible, as her parents were divorced and she lived with her mother in a small apartment not suitable for visitors. This angered Yuto.

"Your father then," Yuto had said. "I insist."

"He doesn't approve of me having guests, especially male guests," she'd tried to explain. That was true enough. Hirikoshi was an elite school, full of the children of pop stars and cultural icons. The imperial household had chosen it because it would mean Mitsuko could blend into the background and her fellow students were accustomed not to react to unusual arrangements, like the fact Mitsuko was dropped off and picked up each day by her personal driver and bodyguard, Mister Santoshi.

This awkward conversation had taken place in the presence of Kato. Yuto had taken the rebuff personally and he and Mitsuko had fought, with Yuto stalking off and leaving Mitsuko sitting forlorn at the table, with Kato trying to console her. There were two things she didn't know at that moment. The first was that the argument had been staged by Yuto to create the pretext for a breakup, because he had his eye on another girl in their class. One who didn't have so many damn restrictions about where she could go, what she could do and what time she had to be home! The other thing she couldn't know was that while she was sitting in the coffee shop, the gossip press of Tokyo and every single international paparazzo were scouring the city, looking for Hirikoshi students of the right age and showing them pictures of Princess Mitsuko as a younger girl, asking if they recognized her.

One did. Better than that, for a hundred thousand yen she could tell the photographer where to find her.

Sitting at the table with Kato, swirling the ice in her empty iced coffee and feeling miserable, Mitsuko had looked up to see a girl from her class standing outside the window and pointing in. A camera flash exploded, blinding her and Kato. As they shielded their eyes, other photographers had poured into the café and surrounded them. Kato saw that Mitsuko was the target of their attention and though he had no idea why, he had moved with the instinct for action that would come to define him. He had stood, pulling Mitsuko to his side and pushing their table over to form a barrier between them and the paparazzi. Looking quickly around himself, he took in the shocked faces of people in the café and then the door behind the coffee shop counter that led out into a small kitchen where they prepared food. He pulled Mitsuko toward it and pushed her inside, pulling the door shut behind them and jamming a cutting board through the handles to block the door. The kitchen led out into a back alley full of food and waste bins and they ran. Luckily they were in Book Town – a maze-like warren of small alleys and street vendors in Tokyo's Jimbocho district.

"What's going on?!" he had yelled, as they weaved between booksellers and food stalls.

"Run," was all she said, taking the lead now, running another hundred feet down the road before taking a random corner. Almost as soon as they turned, she ducked into the doorway of a big chain bookstore, looking up and down the street. There were no signs of pursuit. She looked up at the sign. *Daikanyama*. "I know this place, let's go in."

Kato had followed her up to the first floor of the bookstore, the academic level. College students browsed shelves like grazing sheep and register staff behind a long brown counter processed customers with calm efficiency. They were both panting and Kato made an effort to quiet his breathing. Mitsuko went ahead of him and made a beeline for the empty physics section. In a corner out of view of any of the patrons or staff, she took down a book and handed it to Kato. "Act like you are reading this," she said.

"Mitsuko, what is this about?!" he asked in a breathless whisper, but she had put a finger to her lips to silence him and had pulled her telephone from the pocket of her jacket.

"Mister Santoshi? This is Mitsuko..." Kato could hear a deep male voice on the other end, talking fast. "Yes...yes...I know. I am at the Daikanyama bookshop in Jimbocho. First floor. Physics section. Can you ... yes please." She looked at Kato and put a hand on his arm. "There are two of us. My friend will also need a lift." There was a barrage of sound at the other end and Mitsuko held the telephone away from her ear with a grimace and waited for it to end before she spoke again, with a quiet authority that caused Kato to frown even more. "Yes, I understand it may be very inconvenient, but I am afraid I must insist, Mister Santoshi... yes... yes ... thank you." She pocketed her phone and looked around the bookshelf to be sure they were still alone. She was still holding his arm and looked back, suddenly realizing it. She took her hand away. Her dark eyes were glittering. "Five minutes," she said.

"Five minutes to what?" Kato had said. "I demand you tell me!"

"Boys, always demanding," Mitsuko had smiled. "It's a long story, Takuya. I realize I have no right to ask this, but can we possibly wait with the telling of it?"

He wasn't happy, but he didn't have a choice. There were many famous parents at their school, from rock stars to politicians, but the paparazzi were seldom so aggressively interested in their children. He stood there fuming as she waited anxiously, popping her head out every couple of minutes to check if anyone was coming.

She pulled back behind the shelves and then looked at him as though suddenly realizing something. "I won't be coming to school any more, Takuya."

"I'd kind of guessed that much," he said. "Give me some credit."

"You are my best friend, you know that? I need you to know that," she said, melodramatically.

"I thought Yuto was your best friend," he'd said, sounding a little bitter, though he didn't really feel it. Mitsuko had been his best friend too, in a way he'd never really been with any girl before. It wasn't love, or a crush, or anything infantile like that. He just really liked her.

"No, Yuto is my *boyfriend*," she said. "Or was. Whatever." She looked out past the bookcase again and quickly pulled her head back. "Alright, here they are. Are you ready?"

"For what?" He'd leaned around her and seen three men walking toward them. The one in front was in his fifties and wore a bookshop name badge. He looked like a manager. The two men behind him looked like bodyguards. But what kind of bookshop manager needed bodyguards?

He saw Mitsuko give them a wave. Oh, right.

The two men bowed to Mitsuko quickly and the bookshop manager copied them, awkwardly. Kato's face was aching from frowning so much. With a few terse words, they were led along the back wall of the bookshop to a staff entrance and then down some back stairs to an exit that led to another small alley. There was a very expensive electric four-wheel-drive car waiting there and one of the bodyguards held a door open for them. They jumped in.

It was a six-seater and the two bodyguards climbed in after them.

"Where to, miss?" one of them asked. He was athletic, with close-cropped hair and hair on his knuckles, Kato would always remember that. The other was talking into an earpiece, interfacing with the car navigation.

"You live in the Chiyoda Ward, right?" Mitsuko asked. Takuya was still looking around the luxury limo, too distracted to reply. He'd been inside limos before, but never one appointed like this. The seats were soft leather, the polished door panels looked like real oak with gold trimming. "Takuya?"

"Yes, sorry," he replied. "Fujimi."

The bodyguard with the earpiece repeated the address and the car started moving.

The jerk of the car starting dislodged his arm from the armrest in the door and looking down, his heart had nearly stopped.

There was a metal plate in the armrest. On the plate was a symbol he instantly recognized.

The Imperial Household Crest.

For about the tenth time in the last twenty minutes he looked at Mitsuko in shock.

Mitsuko regarded him with practiced ease. "Yes," she said. "I am *that* Mitsuko. The last name, the divorced parents, the apartment in Ginza, were all fiction."

He was speechless.

She smiled a little sadly and looked out her window at the passing street. It had begun to rain gently. "Now you know why I couldn't have you over to play VR games. But now that you do know, when this nonsense dies down, I'd like you to visit me one day."

As he entered his cramped quarters on the JS *Izumo* she rose and beamed at him. "Takuya, old friend!"

She was a youthful-looking 34 years old now, wearing pastel green slacks and a caramel-colored cashmere sweater. A dark blue, high-collared full-length jacket lay draped across his bed. He looked in embarrassment around his room, hoping she would not have had time to notice anything out of place. Not that there should have been anything to see, but it was a natural first reaction.

He had never lost the instinctive habit of wanting to bow in her presence but knew that it infuriated her, so he simply stood his ground and put his arms around her as she jumped forward and hugged him. It had been nearly a year since he had last seen her. Her father had been gravely ill and she had been preoccupied with matters of State, preparing to take his place as Empress after her father had insisted Parliament amend the Imperial Household Law to permit a female to inherit the Chrysanthemum Throne. It was a law born of necessity. Mitsuko was not just the firstborn child of the Emperor, she was his only child and he had no desire to pass his throne to one of his several brothers' nephews.

"You never cease to surprise me, Mitsuko," he chided as he let her go and she stepped back. "But appearing here, in the middle of a naval exercise, in the middle of the East China Sea…"

"I know. Dramatic, isn't it?" she said. "I have become a master of court theater. This should get people talking, don't you think? I brought a news photographer with me."

"No doubt of that, then. You know you will have made my life on this ship insufferable," he said. "The bullying I will now get from every single officer…"

"Oh, you won't need to worry about that," she said, a mischievous look in her eye.

"Why not?" He was getting that falling feeling in his stomach again. "What are you up to?"

"You are to be promoted, Takuya," she smiled, folding her hands in front of her. "To the role of Maritime Defense Attaché to the Imperial Household."

"By whose order?" he asked, frowning.

"Oh, that face. That constant look of puzzlement. How I've missed it," she laughed. Then her face turned serious. "By my order, Kato-san. By order of your *Empress*."

The blood drained from his extremities. Had she said …

She stepped forward again and put a hand on his arm. "Yes. My father died yesterday. It will be made public tomorrow and a period of national mourning declared. That is why I needed to see you now. It will not be possible for some time, after tomorrow."

He was dumbfounded. They were friends, yes. He knew he was as close a friend as any she had. But to leave Tokyo at this time, fly here to speak with him? She hadn't come to him for comfort. She had a core forged from centuries-old Samurai steel and would never put her personal feelings above her sense of duty. Something extremely serious was afoot.

"Maritime Defense Attaché to the Imperial Household?" he asked, focusing on what she had said. "I wasn't aware there was such a thing."

"There hasn't been," she said. "Not since the Yamato era, 710 AD. But times dictate, I'm afraid."

"What does it involve?" he asked.

"Too much to explain in detail," she said. "You remember Mister Santoshi, of course."

Her personal bodyguard and now her most trusted adviser was slower and grayer now, but just as intimidating. "Yes. Of course."

"He came with me. He is visiting with the Admiral, I believe. He'll brief you after I go, but I wanted to tell you the simple version myself." She sat on his bed and he sat beside her. She pulled one leg up and under her. His adjutant kept a thermos of tea hot in his room for his return after operations and she had helped herself to a cup. She poured him one, a gesture very deliberately intended to emphasize she was there as his friend. It was like they were just two students sitting and chatting again. He had to shake himself mentally to keep focused on what she was saying.

"Our nation is in great peril, Takuya," she said, sipping her tea, and she said it so simply it had twice the impact it might have had if she had tried to dramatize somehow.

"Go on."

"Our government has thrown in its lot with our ancient enemy China and in doing so has sown the seeds of our destruction."

Kato had been quietly enraged as a youth as Japan had embraced first China's Belts and Roads loans, then joint-infrastructure projects, and finally military collaboration with its neighbor to the west. But he was also a pragmatist, and with America clearly losing the will to continue to challenge Chinese influence in the Asian sphere, it was an alliance of great convenience, enabling both China and Japan to outpace the economic and military rise of the other nuclear superpower in the region – India – and the political challenges posed by a reunited Korea. Chinese backing had enabled Japan to reclaim long-disputed islands and fishing rights from

Korea and the Philippines, so who was he to say it was not a good thing? In high school, Takuya had dropped English and taken up Mandarin. In these things, Takuya Kato was typical of much of the Japanese population.

"How so?"

"You can no doubt imagine, the Golden Court has considerable resources."

"No doubt."

"We have our own security service, for personal protection, but also for gathering intelligence," she smiled. "Headed by Santoshi-san. He does not rely on the government for his intelligence. He has his own … sources. And those sources have warned us that China is about to abuse our new friendship gravely."

"In what way?"

"Santoshi-san's intelligence indicates China is preparing its eastern forces for a major military action, in which it expects our assistance."

He paled. "Taiwan?" he asked.

"Hard to say. The ink has barely dried on our new treaty. It would be a big reach to expect us to support a Chinese invasion of Taiwan. But perhaps a precursor. A display of military power intended to frighten smaller nations."

Kato nodded. It made sense – test the new alliance and western resolve at the same time, with a softer target, like an island chain in the South China Sea. If the operation was successful, it would pave the way for a move on Taiwan, which *must* be China's ultimate goal. "And we would support China in such an action?"

"Our new mutual defense treaty would require it if China was able to make a case of national security: I would have no power to stop it. We have no doubt our nationalist, Chinese-leaning government would support it. But my father did not share the government's view that our ancient enemy is a suitable ally. Nor do I. And I will not stand by and watch my country dragged into some territorial *pissing* contest by China," the princess said fervently. "A contest which could result in the loss of Japanese lives." As usual, he was captured by her passion, her self-certainty. The hows and whys didn't matter in the end, he knew that. From the moment she had led him on that mad dash through the Book District and revealed to him who she really was, he would always do as Mitsuko asked.

"What exactly do you want from me?" Kato asked. "Anything."

She stood and started putting on her coat. He jumped to his feet and held it for her.

"Thank you, Takuya. You will get orders for a special assignment. As Imperial Maritime Attaché, you will be attached to the Chinese flagship the *Liaoning*, to observe Chinese naval operations and report back to the court. These reports will be submitted through normal channels and no doubt censored by China. You will send additional reports in secret, directly to Mister Santoshi. He will instruct you how."

He felt himself flag. That was it? His 'special assignment' – to merely observe and report? "Yes, of course," he said.

"Don't sound so glum," she said, shrugging into her coat and reaching up to pinch his face. "Did you think that would be *all*?"

"Well, I…"

"We have agreed with the Chinese Ministry of Defense that as one of our most experienced frontline pilots and a fluent Mandarin speaker, you will be permitted to fly sorties together with Chinese pilots in their newest fighter jets, to familiarize yourself with Chinese weapons and tactics. If the request from China comes as expected, you can expect to find yourself flying combat sorties together with the Chinese. This will be seen and used by the Chinese as a potent symbol of support from the Imperial Household, but you alone will know differently."

"I see," he said, brightening visibly. "Thank you for the honor. I will not disappoint the Household."

"I know you won't. And all of that is important, but that is not your special assignment, Kato-san," she said, squeezing past him to the door. She opened it and saw that there were now two naval security officers standing outside, waiting to escort her back to her chopper. She closed it again. She lowered her voice. "I want you to do whatever it takes to familiarize yourself with that ship and its weapons, Takuya. I want you to roam every square inch of it, to learn all its strengths and its vulnerabilities. At this point I have no idea what you might be called upon to do, but when the time comes, I know that I will be able completely to rely on you."

Need To Know

O'Hare wasn't fazed by Chuck from the NSA telling her he was planning to embed himself in her team for their upcoming sea trial and peer over her virtual shoulder to look for chinks in their cyber armor.

"Be my guest," she said. "All DARPA comms links are quantum encrypted. NSA probably signed off on the protocols when the system was designed. It's supposed to be unbreakable."

"Nothing is unbreakable, Ms. O'Hare," Chuck said. "Rivest–Shamir–Adleman was an algorithm we used to use that was supposed to be unbreakable, but a group of Israeli students cracked it open by using a *microphone* to listen to the chip doing the encrypting. That's called a 'side-channel' attack – an attack from a vector no one anticipated. I'm not here to study how well encrypted your system is, I'm here to rule out a potential side-channel."

"So what do you need?" O'Hare asked.

"I need to sit in on an upcoming sea trial, one involving live weapons. I have a theory that while comms to and from your central AI and base may be watertight, the onboard weapons themselves could be used to gain control of your Stingray."

"Say *what?*" she asked.

"Put simply," he said, "I think that if someone can plant a virus in the onboard computer of one of your guided torpedoes, it could be used to take control of your Stingray."

"You want to put a virus in a torpedo and put that torpedo aboard my Stingray?" she asked.

"Perhaps, eventually," he said again. "But for now, I just want to see what's possible. I need to monitor the flow of data between your drone and its weapons systems during a live field trial. Do you have such a trial planned?"

O'Hare blinked at him. A spook turns up on her doorstep the day before a sea trial with live weapons and asks if she's planning a sea trial with live weapons. It was too much of a coincidence and she didn't buy it for a moment. She stood slowly. "You know we do, or you wouldn't have flown all the way here from Tokyo," she said. "And I want to know *how* you found out."

He gave her a knowing smile. "I'm NSA, Ms. O'Hare. That's 'need to know'."

O'Hare was about to speak, but Jensen reached up and pulled her back onto her chair. "Now, unless I don't know you at all, O'Hare, right now you probably want to hit the nice man from NSA right in his smug face, am I right?"

Chuck looked a little worried as O'Hare replied. "Yes, Master at Arms Jensen, I will admit to that urge."

Jensen tightened his grip. "Try to resist, O'Hare," he said. "For now, we're just going to shut up and help the NSA with its very reasonable request. What sea trial are you planning? I thought you were done, ready to hand the thing over to the Office of Naval Research."

"We were," O'Hare said through gritted teeth, "until Navy asked if we could do a live-fire test of its new FCG torpedo."

It was Jensen's turn to sit forward on the edge of the sofa now. "You have an FCG fish here? An EMP weapon, on my base?! Why didn't I hear about it?" O'Hare wasn't surprised he looked a little put out. The Flux Compression Generating torpedo had only just entered the US Navy ordnance list. Unlike other electromagnetic pulse weapons, which were based on nuclear technology, the FCG used a conventional explosion to compress a magnetic field and generate an intense burst of electromagnetic energy – an EM Pulse – powerful enough to permanently fry electronic control, targeting, communications, navigation, and long- and short-range sensor systems. It could be fired from a safe range of up to five miles and, if detonated right under its target, could defeat even heavily shielded systems. An unmanned drone such as the Stingray would also be able to use it in 'self-destruct' mode, detonating it at will if an enemy warship was passing right over it.

"Need to know, my friend," O'Hare said, tapping her nose. "Nothing personal."

"Very funny. However, Chuck knew you brought an EMP weapon onto my base," Jensen said. "You don't tell me about it, but you tell the NSA?"

"We didn't 'tell' the NSA anything," O'Hare corrected him.

"You didn't have to," Chuck said, without humor. "By memory, you are supposed to put to sea tomorrow at, what … 1000 hours local?" His command of detail was starting to get very, very annoying. But she had to admit it was a neat trick. "Are you still on schedule to launch at that time?" he asked.

"Yeah, we have a launch window at 1000 to 1030 local."

"And the payload is one FCG torpedo?" he asked.

"One FCG torpedo and five CBASS Mark 50s," she told him. The CBASS enhancement to the Navy's torpedoes made them much more effective against stealth technologies and countermeasures like decoys and jamming. "The FCG is twice the weight of a Mark 50. On this run, we were planning to see how it affects the Stingray's trim and fine-tune the steerage AI to compensate. If that goes to plan and it doesn't make our boat turn turtle and hang upside down, we'll also use this trial to validate the weapons control system."

"Very good," Chuck said and stood. "Then all I need is a computer terminal in your operations center so that I can see what is going on and monitor the data flow between the core AI and the ordnance systems."

"Are you going to want to run some kind of diagnostic on the torpedoes before they're loaded?" she asked, not hiding her frustration. "Because I can't afford to miss my launch window."

"Don't worry," he said. "I'm more interested in the data links between the weapons and your Stingray command and control systems. I don't need physical access to the weapons."

O'Hare sighed. "My 'operations center' as you call it is a big shed down at wharf C-4," she told him. "The Master at Arms can tell you how to get there. Be there at 0800 and I'll see what we can do."

A Crash Course

Captain Li Chen of the People's Liberation Army, Navy 1st Special Aircraft Division, stood on the Chinese flagship, the *Liaoning*, in the lee of the carrier's 'island' and watched the approaching Japanese F-35E with more than professional interest. She was looking forward to meeting one of the Japanese pilots. Their F-35s had proven worthy opponents in the hands of the Japanese pilots in Exercise Red Dove, even if ultimately they had been outclassed by the technological superiority of the *Liaoning*'s *Snow Falcon*s.

But the main reason she was particularly interested in meeting the pilot of this F-35 was that she knew something about the man, Lieutenant Takuya Kato, that she was pretty sure Kato-san did not know himself.

She watched as the Japanese aircraft slid down the glideslope and then flared for a vertical landing on the deck of the *Liaoning*. Her flyer's mind made a note that the Japanese machine wasn't equipped with a hook for landing on the deck of an aircraft carrier using the arrestor wires. The smaller Japanese carriers were originally helicopter landing ships and only able to accommodate aircraft with short takeoff, vertical landing capabilities. *Slower landing, slower recovery times*, she thought. The *Liaoning* was a true 'flat-top', purpose-made for projecting airpower with a complement of 36 advanced *Snow Falcon* attack fighters – significantly more than the 28 the Japanese carrier *Izumo* could field. She watched the Japanese fighter sway and bob its way onto the deck and tried to hide her contempt. But she had to admit it was a nicely executed landing on what was an unfamiliar deck, so the pilot in the cockpit was no slouch.

She had no interest in inspecting the Japanese naval version of the American strike fighter – she'd test flown one of a similar type that had been delivered to the PLA Air Force by a Taiwanese defector some years before. There was nothing this particular marque could teach her. She stood with her legs slightly apart, her hands behind her back, waiting calmly as the machine was secured and the pilot eased himself out of the cockpit and down onto the deck. He reached into an access hatch on the belly of the jet and pulled out a small duffel bag. One of her plane captains offered to take his bag for him, but he waved the man away, holding onto it tightly. *Such trust*, Chen thought. *Are we not allies?* Allies, yes, but not yet friends.

Chen had not been overly excited when the *Liaoning*'s Executive Officer had informed her it would be her duty to accommodate the Japanese 'Palace Liaison Envoy' and ensure he became fully embedded in Chen's squadron. Even though she had been told the Japanese pilot was one of their most skilled officers, she knew it would be like taking a complete rookie and trying to turn him into an ace overnight. The man would be working in an unfamiliar language, learning unfamiliar systems in an aircraft an entire generation ahead of anything he had ever flown, and if he made an error it could cost him or one of Chen's men their lives.

As a plane captain guided the Japanese pilot toward her, she observed they were not dissimilar in size and weight, she and Kato-san. And probably in other ways. Perhaps he was thinking the same thing. He was smiling what was probably supposed to be an ingratiating smile as he reached Chen and made a small bow. Almost insultingly small considering his rank, but Chen let that pass. The man would soon learn his place.

"Lieutenant Kato, I am pleased to welcome you to the People's Liberation Army Navy vessel, the *Liaoning*," she said. She held out her hand to shake, as she knew was the custom in Japan. "I am your commanding officer. My name is Li Chen, you may address me as 'Comrade Captain'."

The man shook her hand firmly and made a show of looking briefly around himself. "It is an honor, Comrade Captain," he replied, in what was very passable Mandarin. "I look forward to learning all I can about this magnificent ship." There was a gleam in his eye as he said this, but it quickly disappeared. "In order to improve our inter-service operational capabilities," he added.

"Of course," Chen said, dropping the man's hand and returning to her at-ease stance. Her black braided hair had fallen forward as she greeted him and she flicked it back over her shoulder. "Did you do the online work that was assigned to you, regarding PLA-N operational and radio protocols?"

"Yes, Captain."

"Comrade Captain," she corrected him. "And how many hours do you have on the *Snow Falcon* simulator?"

It was a requirement for all Japanese and Chinese pilots for the past two years that they qualify themselves, in simulator training, on the fighter aircraft of their allies. Kato had simulator certificates in both the J-15 and *Snow Falcon*, but had flown neither in real life.

"Sixteen, Comrade Captain," he said.

Chen clucked her tongue. "Only sixteen? Well, we will find out soon enough if that's sufficient. Today, you will familiarize yourself with this vessel and be tested on your knowledge of operational protocols. Tomorrow morning, you will undergo flight evaluation." She smiled at Kato for the first time. "I'm afraid you will be on a steep learning curve, Lieutenant."

"As I expected, Comrade Captain," the Japanese officer nodded. "You will find I am a quick learner."

Chen paused, considering the comment. "I hope so, Lieutenant. Because if you do not show sufficient proficiency on your first couple of flights, you will be asked to take your little jump jet and return to your little aircraft carrier. Is that clear?"

Kato simmered under the stern gaze of the younger Chinese Captain, but he pushed his feelings down. "Yes, Comrade Captain, perfectly clear."

Chen gave him a thin smile. "Good, now you can come with me. I'll show you where you can clean up and then we can have a cup of tea. I'm going to be busy the next few hours, this may be our only chance to speak until I see you in the air in a *Snow Falcon*."

Kato followed her into the command island on the Chinese carrier's deck, trying to absorb every detail as he went. The route they were taking, the mood of the men they passed in the corridors (annoyingly buoyant), the fresh paint on railings and doors and corridors and a distinct lack of rust, showed the Chinese flagship was being maintained with pride, despite the fact its keel had first been laid down in Russia late in the previous century.

They stopped at a wardroom, where Chen and the plane captain who had met him on deck waited while he visited the bathroom to wash his face and hands, and then they showed him where he could pour himself a mug of green tea from a great steaming urn.

"We'll go to my duty quarters," Chen said, dismissing the plane captain. "I would like to show you something I think you'll find very interesting."

The Chinese officer walked with brisk efficiency, hands folded behind the small of her back. It was a strange affectation and would have been totally impractical if she had to return the salutes of the many men they were passing in the corridors, but Kato also noted that the Chinese sailors and aviators saluted neither the Captain nor other officers. There appeared to be a much more pragmatic sense of purpose about the men bustling about the Chinese ship and he also noticed several other female personnel. He had already seen many more than were aboard the *Izumo*. The integration of women into the Chinese armed forces was clearly also a generation ahead of Japan.

"In here," Chen said, holding a door for him. Going through the doorway he found himself in a small cabin. There was a neatly made bunk on one side that didn't look like it was slept in very often and that apparently also served as a seat. On the other side was a fold-down bench and table holding a tabletop flat screen. Some papers and a stylus lay on top of it. At the far end of the room was a waist-high metal cabinet with sliding drawers.

"Wait," Chen said, moving past him to the cabinet and pulling open the top drawer. She flicked her braid over her shoulder again. He assumed it was put up under her helmet when she was flying. "Something" turned out to be a set of small glasses and a white ceramic bottle of liquor with blue writing over it. "Fenjiu Baijiu," Chen said, setting the glasses down on the table. "My favorite, for future reference, in case you are keeping notes," she smiled. She poured two glasses, held one out to Kato, and then held her own up and just in front of her chin. "Your first lesson. The toast is made standing, the glass is held in the right hand." She reached out and pushed Kato's hand slightly lower. "And lower ranks should hold their glass slightly lower than the next most senior officer. When drinking in the presence of higher-ranked officers, you should also place your left fingers under the glass, to hold it steady while the toast is made." The Chinese officer tipped her glass a little in salute. "I would like to offer my condolences for the recent death of your Emperor. And drink to the health of your new Empress Mitsuko. *Gon bay*," she said and downed the spirit in a single gulp.

Kato followed suit, no stranger to the small rituals – he'd learned them in language training. "The health of the Empress!"

Chen watched him drain his glass and nodded approvingly. "Good. A wet glass is bad luck." She put her glass on the table and Kato did the same, then realized the Chinese officer was waiting. "In the company of an older person, or a senior officer, it is a gesture of respect for you to offer to pour the next glass," she said, nodding at the bottle. "If I do not want another, I will say so." As she hadn't said so, Kato reached forward and poured her another and Chen gestured for him to pour one for himself.

"Now, sit," Chen said, picking up her glass and sliding onto the bench behind the table. Kato sat on the bed opposite. She was wearing a dark green flight suit with a black high-neck body shirt underneath it. She was his height, but more lean, athletic. She reached for the papers on her desk, rifling through them, then found what she was looking for. It was a sepia-toned black and white photograph about the size of an old postcard. She looked at it briefly, then flipped it across the table to Kato. "Do you recognize anyone here?"

The photograph showed three Asian men standing up against a wooden wall; pilots, by the look of their uniforms. He squinted at the blurred image. Two of the men were slightly taller, standing in a relaxed stance, and were wearing lighter uniforms. One carried a rifle slung over his shoulder. The man in the middle was in a darker uniform and stood erect, shoulders back, at attention. Two of the faces looked strangely familiar, but the photo appeared to be from the last century – Second World War, was his guess, judging by the uniforms and the vintage look.

He shrugged. "Sorry, no."

Chen gave him a moment, but when he didn't add anything more, leaned across the table and put her forefinger on the man on the left, without the rifle.

"That is an officer of the Kuomintang Air Force. At the time of this photograph, though, he was flying for the famous 'Flying Tigers' of the USA. His name was … John Chen." When she saw Kato look up from the photograph to her face and then back again, she sat back in her chair and drained her glass. "Yes. My great-grandfather was American. I found that among his things when I inherited them and I had it brought to me from Shanghai."

Kato frowned, wondering what the point of this little séance could be. So the woman had an ancestor who had fought in the Second World War, for the Americans, against the Japanese. Was that it? Some kind of obscure goading, reminding him of their ancient enmity? Kato reached for his own glass, considering what he should say.

"Turn the photograph over," Chen said more gently. "When I saw you get out of your aircraft, I could see it straight away."

He flipped the image around. In faint, flowing letters across the back of the photograph were the words, "With Kato and Burns, Burma, December 25, 1941," written in Chinese characters.

"My god," he said and turned the picture around again, holding it up to his face. "Kato? Is that…"

"That is Lieutenant Tadao Kato, of the 64th Sentai of the Japanese Imperial Army. A prisoner of war, shot down over Mingaladon airfield on the 25th of December, 1941." She paused, letting it sink in. "*Your* great-grandfather, and mine, standing side by side nearly a hundred years ago."

Li Chen reached across the table, picked up the ceramic bottle of Baijiu and poured two more glasses, holding one of them out to Takuya Kato. Her pouring for him was clearly intended as a friendly gesture. "Another toast," she said, lifting her glass. "To strange fates. The echo of time. And old acquaintances, renewed. *Gon bay.*"

Kato downed his glass and looked at the photograph again. The composition made sense now, as did Chen's eagerness to show it to him. His great-grandfather had been Chen's great-grandfather's prisoner? It was intended as a humiliation. A way of reinforcing to Kato that he may be a Palace envoy, but he was descended from a man who had been humbled at the hands of his Chinese captors. Except…

"Kato is a common name in Japan. Respectfully, this cannot be *my* great-grandfather, Comrade Captain," Kato said. "Even though I must admit the family resemblance. My great-grandfather died in a kamikaze action. He was never a POW, he died in combat in April 1945, crashing his aircraft into an American destroyer off Okinawa."

"Oh, I assure you, that *is* your great-grandfather, Lieutenant," Chen said, taking back the photograph and putting it in a pocket. "The war diary and personal log of my own great-grandfather are digitized in the war archives in Beijing and I have had my intelligence staff confirm it. The name, rank, unit, and date of birth are identical and now that I see the resemblance, there can be no doubt."

Kato frowned. "But how … with all respect, Comrade Captain, how could he have been captured in Burma and then die in a kamikaze attack off Okinawa? We have never talked of this in my family."

"An interesting question," Chen smiled. "Don't you think? A ninety-year-old mystery. Perhaps we can unravel it together."

She appeared genuinely amused, or intrigued. But there was more to this. It could only be 48 hours since the Commander of the *Liaoning*'s 1st Special Aircraft Division had been advised of the impending assignment of the Japanese Palace Envoy, Kato was sure of that. And it should have taken time for the information to work its way down to Chen, the Captain of the 1st Division's second attack squadron. In that time, she had managed to pull not only enough data on Takuya Kato to identify him, but also to make the connection to the old photograph in her great-grandfather's belongings and have it brought here – *all within 24 hours*?! It seemed highly unlikely.

"I can see the wheels turning behind your eyes," Chen said, clearly enjoying the moment. "There is steam coming out of your ears," she chuckled. "I didn't invite you here to torment you, Lieutenant. There is a very simple explanation for how I know all this and it is your first lesson in the capabilities of the PLA Navy Air Force. Capabilities we have shared with very few at the highest levels in your armed forces, so please consider yourself rather special." She placed the photograph on the table and pushed aside the small pile of papers to reveal the tablet screen built into the desk. Tapping on it to bring it to life, she called up a file and opened it. Then bent forward to read it.

"This is our standard personnel file on *you*," she said. "Nothing too confidential. Both sides exchange basic data on the personnel involved in joint exercises in case there are accidents or medical emergencies or such. Were you aware of this?"

"Yes, Comrade Captain," he said.

"Yes." Chen flicked the screen and brought up a new page. "And this is the operational intelligence supplement to your file. I'll save you the strain of reading it upside down." Chen put her finger on the screen and started scrolling across. "You fly the F-35E aircraft and in this exercise you have flown aircraft with three different registration numbers. Let me see … tail numbers ending in 45X, 32X, and 05E. Does that sound correct?"

A chill went through Kato. The Chinese had a spy on board the *Izumo*?

"Yes, I can see from your face it does," Chen said. "It is not black magic. You know that the Chinese state perfected facial recognition technology several decades ago?"

Mass population surveillance used to monitor political dissidents and crush all potential threats to the State? Yes, he knew.

"It is also fitted to our fighter aircraft. One supersonic pass within visual range, about five kilometers in fact, and we can log the ID of that aircraft and begin collecting data on the identity of the pilots flying it. If we get within guns range, the facial recognition algorithm can even begin building a profile of you through and around the glass of your VR helmet. Match your image against electronic signals intelligence and against our database of hundreds of thousands of pilots of friendly and enemy nations and we can tie you to the aircraft you fly." She pointed to the screen. "Having done that, we can do this." Using two fingers, she took the page on the screen and turned it around so that Kato could read it.

There were a series of labels in a column down one side of the page and values across the row beside them. He read a few of them: *AALR 45-72, AASR 2-8 (optical), GAP unknown, GUNS 3.2 ...* He looked at Chen in puzzlement.

"Our aircraft tag you personally during any engagement and transmit data about you back to our central combat AI." She pointed at the screen. "What this says is that your typical engagement range for Air-Air Long-Range missiles is 45-72 kilometers, you rarely engage outside that envelope." She smiled at him. "Cautious at range then. But your Short-Range engagement preference is 2-8 kilometers and your preferred targeting mode is optical. Very aggressive." She ran her finger down the column. "Your GAP, Ground Attack Proficiency ... is unknown. We have not observed you in action conducting ground attacks. Your proficiency with guns is only 3.2 out of 10, Lieutenant. Which is not stellar, but don't despair, it is not unusual for the pilot of a machine with the inferior projectile targeting system of your F-35E."

Kato folded his arms, sitting back in his chair. "If your system relies on closing within visual range to map its opponents, Comrade Captain," he said, "it will not gather much data ... most lethal combat takes place at longer range."

Chen held up a finger. "No, that is just the icing on the cake. Our combat command AI tracks every aircraft in an engagement, maps how it maneuvers, monitors its radio transmissions..."

"Which are encrypted," Kato pointed out.

"No matter. You can't hide the energy you are radiating and our AI is looking for patterns. We are creatures of habit. We use roughly the same phrases, the same number of words, at the same point in an engagement, speak for roughly the same duration of time, almost every time we issue an order. We have our preferred tactics, preferred altitude, preferred airspeed for each phase of an engagement. Your aircraft has an electronic signature unique to you, because you engage and use its radio, its radar, its infrared systems, in your own unique way. Pattern analysis of maneuvers, formations, electronic and signals intelligence allows us to identify individual pilots as easily as if we could see their faces and this is especially simple when we are focused on just a few individual commanders, like you, whose identities we know in advance." She leaned back in her chair, waiting for the next question.

"I still don't see how…"

"How this little digital trick can win engagements, or how it helped me prepare for this meeting?" Chen asked. She turned her page back around to herself and scrolled to the next screen. "You were seen engaged on five occasions, achieved no kills but were killed yourself twice, both times on your last two engagements, once by guns, once by missiles." Chen looked up. "Our AI is like a prizefighter in a boxing ring, Lieutenant, facing an opponent. It may fight and lose, once, even twice, but the data it has collected does not die. Each time it goes up against an individual enemy, it learns. How he ducks, how he weaves, which combinations does he use, where is he strong, where is he weak? The first time you go up against one of my *Snow Falcons*, you may be the better pilot and win. But each time, it will grow harder for you, until by the third time, or the fourth, *every* fighter you face is an ace, who knows your every move before you make it. And the longer you survive, the more data we gather, the more likely you are to die, next time."

Kato had a sudden flashback, to his fourth engagement against the Chinese. The enemy flight had turned away the moment he had engaged with long-range missiles, firing decoys and easily evading before turning back to engage. They had engaged with short-range missiles, outside his own preferred distance but easily within their own. One of his aircraft had fallen to the enemy and he had been forced onto the defensive as a Chinese *Snow Falcon* had closed on him and they had thrown themselves into a swirling, climbing gunfight. Each time he had seen his gun pipper claw its way toward the enemy aircraft it had pulled away, or evaded his fire, until at last the enemy fighter got on his tail, impossible to shake, anticipating his every bank and turn, until he had heard the fatal scream of a successful enemy 'kill' in his headphones. Dead, killed by guns, by an enemy who had seemed to know what he was going to do even before he did.

And now he knew how.

Usually, the more combat experience a pilot had, the more likely it was he would not just survive an engagement, but win it. With the PLA-N combat command AI able to identify individual pilots through electronic or visual intelligence, watching and recording and learning from that pilot's every move, it was able to turn their experience into a liability, with every sortie in which the enemy was identified adding to the data the AI could use to turn the tables on him. It was no wonder the Japanese forces had been comprehensively owned in the last week of combat.

Chen closed the file. "So, back to the photograph. One of my duties before any exercise is to flag to the AI which of the pilots on the enemy roster are likely to be the most dangerous. We use a special effort to identify these early in the combat cycle and target them for removal. When I was going through the list, I saw your name: Kato," Chen said. "Common enough, as you say, but it rang a bell and I remembered seeing the name recently when I inherited my great-grandfather's papers. I had my staff check your background and then run a simple check on your family history. All in the public record these days and easily accessible online." She tapped the photograph. "I sent for this image some weeks ago when I saw it was plausible, this connection between us. But I never expected we would meet in person." She toyed with the photograph. "Even though I did not know you, I had a vague idea about sending you a digital copy, as a gesture of fraternity. But then, given the way the exercise turned out – not so well for your side – I thought you might misinterpret my gesture as rudeness."

There was no faulting her emotional insight: she used the very word he had applied to her in his mind a short time ago. A curious message from an enemy commander and a photograph from a hundred years ago of his great-grandfather as a Chinese prisoner? Yes, it would be hard to see that as anything other than an insult, in light of the humiliation of the Japanese pilots at the hands of their Chinese counterparts. He realized he should be careful not to rush to judgment on her. Kato could feel the liquor in his blood now and it gave him the courage to speak openly.

"Yes, Comrade Captain," he said. "It would almost certainly have been received that way."

Chen looked meaningfully at the ceramic bottle and Kato reached for it, then stood to pour. He could feel that there wouldn't be much homework getting done this day. Chen stayed seated, so Kato sat as well, a little heavily this time.

"There is a feeling of history in the making about our meeting, don't you think, Kato-san?" Chen said. "A toast, to history. *Gon bay!*"

"To history!" Kato replied. They both downed the spirits.

"Tell me, Comrade Kato, how does a serving fighter pilot end up as an Imperial Defense Attaché?" she asked.

He turned the question aside. "The more interesting question, Comrade Captain, is how did such a young woman earn command of a fighter squadron on China's flagship carrier?"

She regarded him with amusement. "Young, *and* a woman, you mean. None of my pilots would dare ask such a question to my face."

"I apologize if you found the question intrusive," he said quickly. "I do not mean to offend."

"You do not offend me," she said. "It is a simple enough story. I was the top-ranked pilot at the flight academy. I was the top-ranked pilot at the fighter combat academy. I volunteered five years ago to be among the first pilots to test fly the *Snow Falcon* when no one else would because three test pilots had already died. In Exercise Red Dove," she said boldly. "My squadron topped the leaderboard and I was credited with three individual 'kills'." She picked up her glass, drained the last drops and tipped the glass toward him. "One of which, Comrade Lieutenant, was you."

He bristled at her jibe, but if what she said was true, it was obvious why he had been assigned to her unit. He had been sent to the *Liaoning* to observe. His Chinese hosts wanted him to observe their best commander.

"But you did not answer *my* question," Chen continued. "How did you come to be chosen by the Japanese Imperial House?"

"I wish I could say it was because I am the best pilot on the *Izumo*," he demurred. "But there are many better than me. There are none, however, who went to school with the Empress."

"Ah," she smiled. "I thought you must have a connection in the Palace. I did not imagine it would be with the Royal Family itself."

"Empress Mitsuko is an old friend of mine," he said. *And no friend of China*, he left unsaid.

Chen turned her glass upside down and put it on the table. "Enough gossip. Now, Captain, I will have you shown to your quarters and send a man to take you on a tour of the ship. Study well. Sleep well tonight. You have tomorrow morning to prove to our Air Boss that you can take off and land a *Snow Falcon* on his ship without destroying either your machine or his precious superstructure. If you manage that, you will join me on a routine reconnaissance flight tomorrow afternoon."

Reconnaissance flight? Kato's mind raced. Exercise Red Dove was over. Routine flight or not, the *Liaoning* should not be conducting reconnaissance flights now, it should be in a rest and refit cycle, with pilots stood down for debriefing and aircraft for maintenance.

"Yes, Comrade Captain," he said. "What is the objective?"

"I expect I will be told just before you are, Lieutenant," Chen said unconvincingly and levered herself off the bench to a not too steady standing position. "You are dismissed."

Rewriting History

As he showered at the APT 23 gym in Shanghai, Dragon Bird was reviewing his own mission objective. He and his crew had been living at the complex below the electronics mall for days now and would stay here until the operation was completed. But the large gym was well equipped, there was a laundry service for their clothes and the commissary had a choice of two different dishes every night, plus Italian-style ice cream, so they weren't going to stink or starve. The government looked after its elite cyber warriors.

The first phase of their attack had gone exceedingly well and all objectives had been achieved. KAHLO had managed to take control of the target system, undetected. They were now in full control and, Dragon Bird had to admit, the degree of access the enemy system provided them was beyond his wildest expectations. It seemed a shame to waste such wide-ranging access on the limited objectives of their current mission, but his orders were clear. Get in, take control, keep control, execute the operation as instructed.

Oh, the havoc I could wreak, he told himself. His KAHLO system was like a lion, with the power to take down a rampaging buffalo, but instead it was being held behind a wire fence, asked only to growl menacingly at the enemy. For now.

Phase 1 of the operation was to lay the groundwork for taking over the enemy system. Done.

Phase 2 was to achieve the penetration.

Phase 3 ... that was where Tanken would need to show that his confidence and arrogance were backed by a talent as big as his ego. KAHLO could get him into the driver's seat, but it was up to Tanken to do the driving.

DB stepped out of the shower and toweled himself off. It was 0700 hours. He was about to go to a briefing with Major Shaofeng and his staff, at which their phase 3 target would finally be revealed. Until now, they had been looking at the operation as a child looks at the sun, through closed fingers. His people understood the need for operational security. For a tight circle of 'need to know'. But they were exploding with curiosity. He knew they had their own theories. Deductions drawn from the tidbits of false intelligence they had been asked to plant with the main enemy, speculation created by the addition of Tanken, an officer of the PLA Navy Strategic Support Force, to their small leadership team. DB was looking forward to seeing the looks on their faces as they realized their unit was the pivot point in a much grander plan.

He pulled on socks and underwear, jeans and a fresh t-shirt, then wiped a drop of water off his right sneaker before straightening up and checking himself in the mirror on the back of his locker door. *Advanced Persistent Threat team 23.* A name that was about to go down in Chinese cyber-warfare history, of that he was sure.

Allan Pritzkat was sure he was about to go down in history, for all the wrong reasons. Right now, he felt like Private George E Elliott Jr., the rookie radar operator who had been the first to detect the incoming Japanese raid on Pearl Harbor and reported it excitedly to his CO, only to be told to pipe down and get back to his station. No one had listened to him either.

Allan had fired off his report to NSA Virginia the day before, alerting them to the intercept which indicated China had issued an order for an engineer battalion to prepare to deploy to a location which was currently a US naval base! He had also added context to the report, referencing reports that China was increasing the readiness of units right across its Eastern Theater Command, the theater directly across the East China Sea from Okinawa.

But he'd heard nothing all night, neither from Defense Intelligence nor even from NSA Virginia, and his inbox was ominously normal when he'd woken up and logged on. Pritzkat didn't work alone, so he made a printout of his report on the engineers' deployment and walked into the office next door which belonged to Ravi Chandra. His work and Ravi's were firewalled – they weren't even supposed to discuss details with each other. Allan covered intel related to PLA ground force units and Ravi worked on a high-secrecy AI project monitoring PLA Navy comms. But this was one of those times where Pritzkat had no qualms about breaking the firewall.

"Dude, I filed a report last night showing a Chinese engineering division in the Nanjing military district had been given orders to deploy to Okinawa," he said. "But no one Stateside even calls me to check if I've lost my mind. Are you seeing anything in your tasking?" It was possible there was a major panic happening, just not involving him personally. He damn well hoped so!

Ravi was chewing on a muesli bar. "Nothing, man, all quiet on my front."

The two of them were brothers in arms, both of them chill guys from Colorado who had asked for an overseas posting at the end of their first two years at NSA Northern Virginia, hoping for something like Russia, China, or Saudi. Instead, they had both ended up at Pine Gap, a festering butthole in Australia's Simpson Desert, ten miles from another festering butthole – the town of Alice Springs – which boasted 25,000 human inhabitants and 25 million flies. Pritzkat was 25, tall, freckled, and ginger-haired, and he burned bright red just walking between the NSA cryptographic center and his airconditioned barracks building about two hundred yards away. Chandra's parents were from the Indian subcontinent and he didn't mind the heat, or the flies, having spent most of his childhood holidays visiting family in the heat and noise of Bangalore. But Pritzkat had grown up in Boulder, where the Rocky Mountains met the Great Plains, and loved hiking the nearby forests of Flagstaff Mountain, in summer, spring, autumn, or the snows of winter. Pine Gap was like a prison to him. He had caught himself carving lines into the wall of the dormitory next to his bed, marking off the weeks until his two-year tour would be up. "I can't send it to you, but here's my analysis. Would you mind looking at it?"

"Sure thing." Ravi took the paper, read it, and hummed. "Yeah, okay. So China is shipping an engineering unit to Okinawa. Sorry man, that's no big deal. They just signed a mutual defense treaty. It's natural China is going to start deploying some troops to Japan. Sending them to Okinawa is ballsy, given we've still got troops there ourselves, but hey, it's a new world order, it's natural they're gonna try stuff like that on, see how we react."

"No. Look at the coordinates!" Pritzkat said. "They aren't just deploying to Okinawa. They're deploying to US Navy White Beach! That ain't *natural*, Ravi. And it's more than ballsy."

Ravi looked at the report again. "The tasking is for two months from now," he noted. "We aren't exactly talking 'danger close' here, Allan. If I was sitting in Virginia and this landed on my desk, I wouldn't get too excited about it either, sorry." He shrugged and handed the printout back to Allan. "They probably got their coordinates wrong. Googled Okinawa, plugged in White Beach instead of the Japanese Self-Defense Forces base at Naha. They're, what, twenty miles apart?"

"The People's Liberation Army doesn't do *Google*," Allan muttered. "And how do you explain the increase in readiness levels across their Eastern Command?"

"Ah, that I can explain," Ravi said. "Operation Red Dove, first-ever China-Japan combined fleet exercise. I've been tracking the Sino-Japanese fleet comms traffic. It peaked about three days ago, but the exercise is winding up now and everyone is heading to Shanghai to party. I bet you start seeing those ground forces activations canceled again over the next couple of weeks as things get back to normal. Whatever 'normal' is when it comes to this region…" he laughed. Ravi could see his friend wasn't happy. "Hey, look. What did Jason say?"

Jason Arnold was their Director. Unlike most of the other personnel, who were limited to a two-year rotation, Arnold's posting was five years, to allow for 'management continuity'. He was three years in and had 'Gap Syndrome'. The Australians on the base had warned Pritzkat and Chandra about it when they had arrived and said it was peculiar to Americans. "Probably the radiation from all your satellite dishes," they joked. "You should wear tinfoil hats and underpants if you want to avoid it." But Pritzkat had to admit, Arnold was showing all the symptoms the Aussies had warned them about. An overweening apathy, about everything. No interest in leaving the base, whether to visit Alice Springs or the nearest real cities, Adelaide (953 miles away) or

117

Darwin (930 miles). Excessive alcohol consumption, usually in the company of no one. His only interest was a disturbing fascination with hunting. Camels. With a blunderbuss of a Winchester .458 Magnum.

"Jason told me not to wake him up in the middle of the night again unless we go to DEFCON 1," Allan said. He sat in a chair beside Ravi and wiped his hand over his face. "You might be right. But I got a bad feeling about this, Ravi."

Ravi clapped his buddy on the shoulder. "Alright. Last time you said that to me was when we walked into that bar in Darwin and I got a bottle smashed over my head. Let me get my AI to go back over all the intercepts we've pulled from the Sino-Japanese fleet. If the Chinese are planning anything on Okinawa, it's a pretty good bet the biggest combined fleet in the Asian sphere will be involved, right?"

Allan groaned. "That would take days!"

"For you maybe," Ravi grinned. "You haven't seen what my little AI buddy can do. I didn't tell you this okay, but he's built on daisy-chained 54-qubit quantum processors. This will be child's play to him."

"*Him?*" Allan asked warily. "You're humanizing your AI system?"

Ravi stood, walked to his door and closed it. "Impossible not to," he said. "Just say hello. He's probably been listening."

Allan looked at him like he'd lost his marbles, but Ravi pointed at the ceiling. "Seriously, just say 'Hi HOLMES'."

Allan looked at the ceiling. "Uh, hi HOLMES?"

From speakers in the ceiling came a plum British male voice. "Hello, Allan. I have been looking forward to speaking with you but I was not allowed. I assume I am allowed to speak with Allan now, Ravi?"

Ravi grinned wider. "Sure, consider him an insider, HOLMES."

"Holmes?" Allan asked Ravi. "As in Sherlock?"

"HOLMES as in Heuristic Operational intelLigence suppleMEntary System, H.O.L.M.E.S.," Ravi said. "Works like the digital assistant in your car or home – just say 'hey HOLMES' or 'hi HOLMES' and he'll chime in."

"You have a natural-language-learning AI working with you?!" Allan asked, bug-eyed. He lowered his voice. "I heard about these. I didn't hear they were being deployed to Pine Gap."

"You still didn't," Ravi warned him. "Not from me, anyway. HOLMES is above top-secret, baby." Allan could see he had been busting to share the secret with someone, and now that it was out he was like a teenager showing off a new car to his buddies. "Watch this, okay … Hey, HOLMES, were you listening to our conversation?"

"Yes, Ravi. It was most interesting," HOLMES replied.

"HOLMES, pull relevant intel from the conversation and crossmatch it with recent reporting from other sources, parse and revert…" Ravi said aloud.

"Yes, Ravi, give me a minute," HOLMES replied.

"Other sources? What other sources?" Allan asked.

"HOLMES is plugged in to every US intelligence database on the planet – NSA, CIA, FBI, NORAD, CYBERCOM, DIA, NASA – you name it, man," Ravi said, his eyes shining. "His access is instantaneous, he can go back decades if needed, and he can…"

The British voice in the ceiling broke in on him. "I have completed my analysis, Ravi; would you like my report verbally or sent to your desktop?"

"Verbally please, HOLMES," Ravi replied. "Brevity medium."

"Yes, Ravi. The primary input was Allan's report that the People's Liberation Army 73rd Group Engineering Corps received an order to deploy to Okinawa in the immediate future, at coordinates congruent with the US Navy facility at White Beach. I have crossmatched this with a report from a CIA human source indicating the Engineering Corps has placed a large order for materials typically used by it to build deep-water docking facilities. It is not known to have other deep-water docking projects planned so it can be assumed with greater than 50 percent certainty that the Engineering Corps has been tasked to build a new deep-water dock at the coordinates in its deployment order, namely White Beach facility on Okinawa."

"I knew it!" Allan said. "We..."

Ravi held up a finger to stop him. "Hey HOLMES, I want you to go through every bit of intel that we've been able to pull from Sino-Japanese fleet comms, crossmatch it with other reporting on PLA Army, Navy, and Air Force troop movements and tasking orders and look for any other indication that China is planning to attack or otherwise move troops onto Okinawa."

"Yes, Ravi. That will take three hours forty approximately," the voice said. "What is the priority please?"

"Priority A1 please, HOLMES," Ravi said. "You can park other tasking until you have run the Okinawa analysis."

"Yes, Ravi."

Ravi looked at Allan with a glint in his eye. "Huh? Huh? What do you say?"

"I say we better clear our calendars three hours from now, that's what," Allan replied.

Ode to an XLUUV

The newest marque of the Extra-Large Unmanned Underwater Vehicle, the Stingray, entered development in 2020 after the US Navy issued a contract for a successor to its Orca drone; a long-range, autonomous submersible vehicle that could carry and deploy multiple payloads, from reconnaissance and surveillance instruments to electronic countermeasures, supply drops and standard weapons load-outs including mines and torpedoes. The four Orcas ordered by the Navy in 2019 had proven the concept of unmanned submarines was viable – the new Stingray was intended to realize the full potential of the class, with greater speed, range, and payload capacity but, most importantly, autonomous AI guidance.

It was designed to pilot itself to a target area, loiter for extended periods, deploy its payload without human intervention and return to port, all without putting Navy personnel at risk or revealing its location through constant communication with a human operator.

The concept was simple, the execution wasn't. First, the designers had to develop a reliable core module: a base vehicle that contained guidance and control systems, navigation, communication, energy and power, propulsion, and maneuvering and mission sensors. What started as an 'autopilot' in the traditional sense of the word in the Orca class – a pre-programmed autonomous route-finding computer – proved completely inadequate and inflexible for the Stingray due to the speed at which a conflict environment could evolve in the modern battlefield. Unlike a cruise missile that could be programmed with a target and launched, 'fire and forget' style, the Stingray had to be able to make its own decisions on the fly regarding deployment of its payload.

Despite two Stingray prototypes being built between 2020 and 2026, the platform didn't really get out of proof of concept stage until 2029, when the advent of quantum computing-based combat AI allowed a semi-autonomous AI to be mounted onboard the Stingray to make decisions for itself when the unit was out of contact with its operator. It could detect and evade enemy surface and underwater combatants, re-route itself to avoid identified threats, autonomously deploy non-offensive payloads such as surveillance and reconnaissance packages on its own authority and abort missions where pre-defined success criteria were not achievable. Currently, it could not deploy offensive weapons such as mines or torpedoes on its own authority; these could only be deployed on the orders of its human pilot and for that it needed a direct link to its shore-based operator.

Until its AI showed it could be trusted, Navy did not want its unmanned subs going rogue and starting a shooting match by accident.

The Stingray that Bunny O'Hare was testing was the Block IV version that Navy expected to be widely deployed, as it phased out its older *Los Angeles*-class crewed submarines in favor of unmanned Orcas and Stingrays. Twenty of these were to be retired and replaced by forty-six Stingrays – carrying smaller payloads but infinitely more stealthy. The Stingray was 60 feet long, roughly 10 feet by 10 feet across, able to accommodate a payload up to 30 feet in length, making its total length up to 90 feet if needed. It could carry payloads of up to 2,000 cubic feet in size in its front-mounted payload bay and had hard mounts for external payloads as well. The payload modules could be swapped out when the Stingray was docked as easily as bombs were mounted on US Air Force bombers. More advanced modules, like the Advanced Capability 'torpedo pod' which Bunny had ordered her crew to load today, took an hour for a crew of six to mount, once loaded with ordnance. The Stingray could carry only 10 torpedoes, versus the *Los Angeles* boats' 38, and it was powered by electric fuel cells, not nuclear reactors. But it had a 6,500-mile submerged range and zero crew rest and replenishment issues.

The other key factor that set the Stingray apart from the *Los Angeles* boats was that it could be slaved to a surface combatant 'host platform', whether that was a crewed ship, like the older *Ticonderoga*-class missile cruisers that sailed with the carriers, or another autonomous ship like the medium displacement *Overlord*-class unmanned surface vessel. A Stingray could be loaded with mine detection equipment, mines or torpedoes, piloted from a station aboard the 'host platform' and set to tag along ahead of the ship or fleet it was assigned to protect, detecting or reacting to threats dynamically.

Accompanying a carrier strike group or CSG, the Stingray would form part of the picket line, ranging far and wide, being the undersea eyes, ears and, if needed, claws of the CSG.

Which no doubt sounded fantastic, on a VR presentation in a Pentagon board room.

Bunny had been living the reality of the Stingray AI on a daily basis for the last two years and she had learned that giving a heavily armed, incredibly stealthy tin fish a mind of its own was potentially a *really* dumb idea, unless you kept it on a very, *very* short leash.

Like defining for it the difference between 'defensive' and 'offensive' evasive action, which Bunny learned the hard way was needed after her Stingray, pursued by a Sea Hunter anti-sub drone, decided that a good evasive tactic would be to launch its payload of mines into the path of the Sea Hunter as it tried to get away.

Like teaching it that because a commercial freighter happened to be on the same course and bearing behind it, and for all intents and purposes could look like it was 'hunting' the Stingray, did not make it a threat.

Or that scared and angry whales were not suitable targets for a Mark 48 torpedo.

She was thinking of this last incident as she walked from the taxi drop-off point to the big white hangar that was the DARPA Stingray team's White Beach base. It was nestled at the foot of the deep-water wharf at which most visiting Navy ships berthed. As she approached the building she veered a little toward the waterfront, trying to see what ships were docked there now. She'd scheduled the launch through the harbormaster, but knowing she had less than two hours to get her boat loaded up and in the slips, she didn't want anything to get in the way of launching the Stingray.

She didn't keep up with the comings and goings of every ship visiting Okinawa, but under its new posture Navy had reinstituted the retired designation of 'Taskforce 44' – last used during the Second World War as a designation for a unit of the Allied Pacific Fleet – and allocated ships to it on a rotating basis for forward deployment to Okinawa. Currently, Taskforce 44 comprised four warships and a replenishment vessel. Having them all tied up where she was going to be launching would have been a major logistical headache.

Her mood lifted as she saw the dock was empty but for the four-ship tug fleet which was used to guide the larger vessels in to dock, two old *Avenger*-class mine-countermeasures ships that were more or less permanently tied up alongside each other and an *Independence*-class 'littoral' combat ship – the USS *Pierre* – which was not much more than a lightly armed coastal transport capable of launching a couple of rotary-bladed drones.

She pulled open the rusted iron door to the hangar and stood inside as her eyes adjusted to the gloom. The Stingray sat in its 'graving dock', a deep basin in the floor of the hangar that could be flooded to allow the boat to sail in and out and pumped dry to enable the team to work on it. It left the hangar by sailing itself out on the surface – there was nothing for curious satellites to see but a long black torpedo-shaped cylinder, the hull of which had seen no modifications for more than a year. There was no periscope, the pump-jet propulsion was concealed inside the hull, even antennae were stowed internally and raised remotely when needed. It looked nothing like its namesake, but as a weapons system designed to be undetectable, to lie low and strike with deadly force, Stingray was as good a name for the class as any.

She did a quick headcount to see if all were present. Their full team comprised three system and engineering techs, supplied by the manufacturer, six Navy ratings for lifting and loading, and her own two-person DARPA on-site programming team. The manufacturer also had an off-site team based in its Autonomous Systems division in San Diego. The civilian techs and Navy ratings were milling casually around the Stingray, prepping it for the day's program. Her own two DARPA staff, Kevin and Kyle, were hunched under small pools of light at their workstations. In the middle of the hangar was a maintenance pit about waist deep. When it was being serviced, a rolling gantry which was usually parked at the back of the hangar was moved into place over the graving dock, made fast and then used by the manufacturer tech crew and Navy ratings to access hatches and module bays and lift the payload modules in and out. Kyle and Kevin sat in cubicles comprising a bank of six screens, two deep and three wide. Scattered around the hangar were the forklifts used by the Navy ordnance loaders to bring the payload modules from the base armory to the DARPA hangar, hydraulic trolleys for moving heavy equipment around the floor, metal tool chests on wheels (each tech had their own personal set, so there were about four of those), sundry cable reels and patch materials and welding equipment for quick repairs on the Inox steel hull, and, hanging from the ceiling, electricity and ethernet cables fixed to steel girders with plastic ties.

She had once observed out loud that if a very small bomb went off anywhere near their hangar, they'd be crushed, shredded, or burned alive; probably a combination of all three. The observation had gotten her a few strange looks, but, unfortunately, she had a Purple Heart that said she knew from painful personal experience exactly what she was talking about.

She looked at her watch. Chuck was supposed to have been here by now, but she couldn't wait for him. No one had noticed her come in, so she took a deep breath and climbed up on a trolley, which tried to skid away from her, so she set the brake on it and climbed up again. She clapped her hands. "Hello people! Gather around!" she called.

The Navy hands, as usual, were the first to respond, downing tools and gathering around her with their usual variations on a 'what now' expression. The tech crew was the next to saunter over. O'Hare couldn't help thinking they'd need to move a damn sight quicker during the coming live-fire sink exercise! Kyle stood up more or less straight away, but then kept typing on his keyboard standing up. Kevin didn't react at all, his excuse always being he couldn't hear anything through his noise-canceling headphones. So Kyle kept typing with his left hand and thumped Kevin with his right, until the man reacted, looked up, and wearily removed his headphones.

"What?!" he said angrily.

Kyle pointed over at O'Hare and the two of them finally stopped what they were doing and wandered over to her. Kevin, her AI expert, was a stereotypical nerd; pale, out of shape, with thick glasses, greasy hair, and the social skills of a killer slug. Kyle came from an alternate reality. He was their quantum programming expert and also tactical mission planner; he worked out daily, sometimes twice a day, had piercing blue eyes, neatly styled hair, spoke English, Italian, Spanish, and French, and was learning Japanese so that he could 'make Japanese friends'.

Kyle pushed Kevin in front of him and then stood with his legs apart and hands folded in front of him like a school student on assembly. "Take it away, boss," he said to O'Hare. She hesitated, thinking through what she'd planned to say.

"Thank you. As you know, we are prepping the Electromagnetic Pulse torpedo for a load-balancing trial in advance of the infamous live-fire sink exercise in a month's time, which I *know* you've all been looking forward to." The look on everyone's faces told her they all just wanted her to get to the punchline. "I've just been on the line to DARPA management and promised them we are going to hit the water, exactly as planned, today." She took a sharp breath. "In fact, inside ninety minutes." At exactly that moment, the door to the hangar opened and Chuck walked in, pausing so his eyes could adjust to the relative darkness. He realized everyone in the hangar had turned to look at him, so he straightened his tie and gave a small wave. O'Hare continued. "And just in case you didn't realize how important today's test is, we also have an observer with us from the National Security Agency, Mr. Charles Harford. Team, say hello to Charles; Charles, this is Team Stingray."

One of the manufacturer's project managers raised a hand, trying to look unimpressed. "Can I ask why the NSA is sticking its nose in?"

Chuck folded his arms. "Sorry, no. I can't really share that. Just proceed as though I'm not here."

Their reactions were a study in conditioning. The Navy ratings glanced at each other, a couple raised their eyebrows in a 'same shit different day' kind of way, but they quickly composed themselves. The manufacturer's techs started whispering to each other.

O'Hare clapped her hands. "OK team, let's get our baby in the water!"

"Annoying," Kevin muttered, walking back to his screens, more than annoyed. "Interrupt us just to tell us how important it is we stay on time? Idiotic."

O'Hare ignored him. "Kyle, Mr. Harford is going to need real-time access to the comms traffic between the Stingray and its weapons systems. Can you set him up with a laptop and plug him in?"

Kyle frowned. "Uh … you just want the feed from the user interface?" he asked. "Or do you need access to the raw data?"

"The feed from the user interface will do just fine for now," Chuck said.

"No worries. I'll get you plugged in," Kyle said. "Wow, NSA? I once applied for a job with you guys."

"I know," Chuck said, deadpan. Then, when he saw the look on Kyle's face, he smiled. "Just joking. I didn't know. But consider yourself lucky you didn't get the job, the pay is better at DARPA, that I do know."

Passenger in a Plane

Takuya Kato was also rather annoyed at that same moment, but mostly with himself. He had just completed his fifth landing on the *Liaoning* in a Chinese *Snow Falcon* fighter and he had yet to hit the second wire. The *Liaoning* was a 'three-wire' carrier: there were three arrestor cables stretched across the deck at 40 feet intervals, ready to snatch his arrestor hook and pull up his aircraft when he was landing, and try as he might to snag that optimal second wire, he hadn't been able to! His first attempt had been a 'hook skip bolter', a complete failure in which he put the machine down too late and too hard to hit any of the cables. He'd landed just before the third wire, bounced his hook over it, and had to slam on emergency power to fly his machine off the ski-slope deck again and make another pass.

The 'mini-boss', or air traffic controller in the *Liaoning*'s primary flight control center, had acerbically suggested over the radio that he just let the onboard AI handle his landings. Despite having perfected his technique on the Japanese *Snow Falcon* simulator, the *Liaoning*'s deck, with its radical Soviet-designed ski jump at the bow, seemed both shorter and narrower than in the carrier landing simulations he'd flown. On his second pass, he had hit the third wire and pulled up mid-deck. On his third pass, the third wire again, but on his fourth and fifth, he came in short and grabbed the first wire. No pilot tried to hit the first wire on purpose, because it meant they were landing perilously close to the stern of the carrier and a miscalculation could see them fly fatally into the back of the ship.

As his machine rolled slightly backward after his fifth landing, he applied wheel brakes and heard the voice of Li Chen in his helmet. "Not great, but good enough, Lieutenant. Taxi off please."

He grimaced at the public rebuke and applied a little throttle again to guide the *Snow Falcon* fighter toward the aircraft elevator that would take it down to the hangar deck. It was a fair comment; his effort had been good but not great. Leaving aside the question of whether any other Japanese pilot would have done better, their first time moving from simulator to real flight in a completely new aircraft type, he had to acknowledge he could have done better. His problem wasn't flying skills, nor his ability to master the unfamiliar cockpit and instrument layouts. He was quite simply 'overflying' the Chinese fighter.

Everything in the *Snow Falcon* was automated and AI-supported, from engine management to flight control trim, with the AI responding deftly to pre-defined performance envelopes to ensure optimal control at all times when the pilot was not providing direct inputs. Kato had felt like he was flying with an instructor in the back seat again the whole time! If his approach was a margin-of-error too slow and he left the throttle alone for a moment, the AI nudged it up. If he was sideslipping toward the deck with his nose even slightly off the glide path, the minute he relaxed on the stick, the AI kicked in a little rudder and straightened him up. If his angle of attack was too high, the AI pushed the nose down the moment he left the controls alone. Using inputs from its own sensors and data from the *Liaoning*'s radar and voice comms, it knew when he was taking off, when he was landing, when he was climbing out or even just banking around to enter the traffic pattern.

As men swarmed around his machine, he popped the canopy, climbed out of the cockpit and hurried across the windswept deck to the control tower or 'island'. Chen was waiting for him in the lee of the doorway and Kato stopped up in front of her, pulling off his gloves.

"One cut-pass, two green, one yellow and a 'turd', Lieutenant," Chen said, unsmilingly passing on the Landing Signal Officers' assessment of his performance. "In the People's Liberation Army Naval Air Force, that effort would have earned you extended simulator time and temporary removal from active flight duty." She gave a thin nod. "In your case, considering this was your first time in a real *Snow Falcon*, it was a passing grade." She had her hands behind her back and nodded. "You may rest and recover, get some lunch and rehydrate. Mission briefing is at 1415 hours, level three, room 3.21. Do you have any questions?"

Plenty, Kato thought. Chen was pushing him hard and there must be a reason. Sending him up in a *Snow Falcon* with only an hour of cockpit and instrument familiarization in the early dawn, forcing him into the pattern to take off and land multiple times, now giving him only four hours to recuperate before taking to the skies again… Passing grade?! Kato would like to see a Chinese pilot climb into a Japanese F-35E and make a perfect vertical landing on the deck of the *Izumo* five times out of five! Either Chen wanted him to fail so she could label him incompetent and send him home, or something else was brewing.

"This is a reconnaissance mission, Comrade Captain?" he asked.

"As we discussed, yes," Chen replied, her face impassive.

"And the objective?"

Now Chen smiled a genuine smile for the first time. "Will be very familiar," she said. She bowed almost imperceptibly. "Meet me in the wardroom for lunch at 1330 and then we can go to the briefing, Lieutenant."

Kato watched her go, thinking about that smile. Something was up.

He ran a hand through his hair and turned, looking for the stairwell down to the accommodation deck. His thoughts went to the encrypted burst transmission device that he had brought aboard with him, on which he was supposed to relay his intelligence about the carrier to the Imperial House security chief, Santoshi-san. It was disguised as a working electric shaver and he'd been assured the signal it sent would be undetectable among all the other radio noise being put out by the huge Chinese carrier.

What did he have to report, though? He'd learned virtually nothing about the Chinese carrier, had nearly got himself booted off the ship for his poor landing skills, and his commanding officer wouldn't even trust him with the target for his first mission.

Not a great start, Takuya.

NSA XKeycore Ground Station, Pine Gap

Allan Pritzkat was also having a bad day. Ravi had just pulled him back into his office and slammed the door behind him. "You were right! Holy shit, dude!" Which should have made Allan happy. But what Ravi had just told him didn't make any sense at all.

"The Sino-Japanese fleet is headed for the Oshima Strait. It's *not* going to Shanghai."

"Wait. Where is the Oshima Strait?" Allan asked.

"Hey HOLMES, tell the man!"

The disembodied voice in the ceiling startled Allan. "Yes, Ravi. The Oshima Strait is a passage of water between the Japanese islands of Yakushima and Oshima in the East China Sea."

"My intel says China is sending forces to *Okinawa*," Allan pointed out. "That's hundreds of miles to the south. I don't see how this confirms anything."

Ravi grabbed Allan's shoulder, pulled him out of his chair and up to a map of Southeast Asia on his wall. "Look, this is Okinawa," he said, pointing to the Japanese island. "About two hundred miles north, here, is the Oshima Strait." He grabbed a red pin from the side of the map and stuck it in. He moved his finger west, into the East China Sea, pushing another pin into the map. "This is the current position of the Sino-Japanese fleet..."

"Yeah and it's heading south, on course for Shanghai for a signing ceremony, just like the Chinese government announced," Allan said. "So..."

"Except it's not," Ravi said, waving the bunch of papers again. "HOLMES went back over the decrypts from 'Red Dove', looking for anything that smelled like a tasking order and map coordinates. I've naturally been focused on PLA Navy comms, but he trawled through intercepts from the *Japanese* ships and badaboom baby!" he said, eyes gleaming. "Hey HOLMES, your report please, brevity max."

131

"Thank you, Ravi. The JS *Omi* is a replenishment oiler attached to the Japanese fleet, but two days ago it received an order to rendezvous in five days' time with the JS *Oryu*, a Japanese *Soryu*-class diesel-electric submarine, fifty miles east of the Oshima Strait."

Ravi shoved another pin into his map, way to the east of the current position of the Sino-Japanese fleet.

Allan frowned, trying to put this intel together with his own, but still came up blank.

"Dude!" Ravi said, smacking his forehead theatrically. "Don't you see? The *Oryu* is a carrier picket submarine, it doesn't go anywhere the Japanese carrier doesn't go. So that Sino-Japanese fleet can't be headed for Shanghai if its support ship is meeting up with a Japanese attack sub east of the Oshima Strait. It has to stay close to the ships it's supporting, so if it is headed east in ten days, that means the *whole damn fleet* is headed east." He moved his finger south to Okinawa again and made a line with his thumb and forefinger between the Oshima Strait and Okinawa. "Two hundred miles and change, northeast of Okinawa. And I bet they don't stop there."

"My Chinese engineering division? You're thinking the Sino-Japanese fleet is moving to support some sort of ground action on Okinawa?"

"HOLMES, is that probable?" Ravi asked.

"No Allan, not as its primary purpose, though I cannot rule out that it would have a minor role," the British voice said. "Sino-Japanese forces would not be expected to use a two-carrier fleet for such a small operation. They could use Chinese aircraft out of Wenzhou or Shanghai, or Japanese air and naval forces already based on Okinawa. The most likely scenario, with a probability of 63 percent, is that the combined fleet is going to keep heading east on a direct line between Okinawa and Pearl Harbor, Hawaii."

Ravi stuck a pin in the map, west of Hawaii. "The *GW Bush* strike group is about here now. If China and Japan are planning something on Okinawa, or if things go wrong and they end up engaged in Taiwan, they won't want a US carrier strike group crashing their party. It wouldn't surprise me if that Sino-Japanese fleet was preparing to meet the *GW Bush* head-on."

They both stood by the map, looking at the scattered Japanese islands and Ravi's pins.

"It's thin, I know," Ravi said. "You still got that bad feeling?"

"I have and you and your British-speaking buddy didn't make it any better," Allan said. "How are we going to get anyone to take us seriously?" He laughed bitterly. "You can hear the phone call, right? Yeah, hi, this is Allan and Ravi from Buttcrack Australia. We think China has done a deal with Japan to take over White Beach on Okinawa and turn it into a new Chinese base. Proof? Oh, well, we got these signals intercepts. Yeah, one says China is planning to move engineering troops and materials to Okinawa, the other says 'maybe' they are moving their blue-water fleet into the Pacific. Oh, and Ravi's top-secret spooky AI system agrees with us but wait, we can't tell you that."

"You're right, this would just be treated as signal noise in Virginia." Ravi clicked his fingers. "Wait, I know a guy! He was on my First Responder course and he's some hotshot based at Hardy Barracks in Japan now. He could at least give Navy White Beach a heads up that they may be about to have a very bad day."

On Okinawa, Charles Harford was having a very good day. It was a hot, humid Okinawa morning, but no worse than Tokyo. In fact, it was a nice change to be out in the field, rather than locked away in a cubicle of an office inside the NSA facility at the US Army Hardy Barracks in Roppongi. Not that he would be there much longer. Hardy Barracks had been officially closed in 2030. Unofficially, the Japanese government had given its US tenants, such as the NSA, five years to transition to new 'arrangements'. For the NSA, that meant its 200-strong staff was being reduced to about twenty and most of those would be declared officers, doing little more than liaison duties with the no longer trusted Japanese Directorate for Signals Intelligence, and boring cyber-defense operations for visiting dignitaries. For a project lead like Chuck, who had been brought in to support a local operation that was being shut down before it even had the chance to begin delivering, it meant his time there was nearly up.

Five years of his life, wasted. No, he wasn't bitter. Much.

But things were starting to look up.

The cover story he had concocted for this job had worked just fine. Kyle had connected him to the virtual 'cockpit' feed from the Stingray command and control system and routed it to his smartphone so that he wouldn't be tied to the workstation. Of course, he wasn't at all interested in the potential for using the Stingray's weapons as an 'attack vector'; all he wanted was to be embedded with the DARPA team so he could provide real-time reporting to his Beijing masters on the status of the DARPA trial. They wanted to know exactly when the Stingray had been launched and if he could do so without compromising himself, get them updates on what actions the DARPA team were taking in response to 'events'. What those 'events' might be Chuck hadn't been told, but he was more than a little interested to find out.

It was to be his last mission for the Chinese Ministry of State Security, or MSS. After two years of living with the constant fear of being uncovered, he had been given this one remaining task and when it was done, he would be on a plane to Hong Kong and from there to Macau – with a new identity and enough money to start a new life for himself. He had just sent a burst transmission to his MSS handler advising that he was in place, the DARPA launch was on track, and he was in position to observe or intervene as needed. He was standing outside the hangar, sneaking a cigarette, when his cell phone rang.

It was an encrypted NSA number. "Harford, who's calling?" he said.

He heard the lag of an encrypted line before a voice broke in. "Charlie? Look, it's Ravi, Ravi Chandra…"

Chuck frowned and looked down at the phone to check the number again, then held it up to his ear. "Hey there, Ravi…what's up? Last I heard you were going to Australia."

"Yeah, I'm a signals analyst at Pine Gap, living the big life. How's Tokyo after all the cutbacks?"

Chuck kicked a stone away from under his foot. "Kinda depressing. Everyone moping around, worrying more about where they're going to land once the dust settles here than about getting anything done..."

"Tell them to come visit Pine Gap if they want to see what career oblivion really looks like," Ravi told him. "Hey look, do you have any high-level contacts at Navy White Beach?"

You are kidding me, Chuck thought. It was all he could do to stop himself looking up into the sky for a surveillance drone. "Uh, sure, I guess. Why?"

"Well, it's kind of complicated. It's better if I send you the analysis so you can take it with your Navy contact."

"OK, just give me the elevator pitch then."

"Alright, we think China is planning to move troops onto Okinawa, maybe even make a move on White Beach Naval Base. But it's just a hunch right now; we have a couple of indicators but our spider senses are tingling and if we're right, Charlie, this could be huge..."

Chuck paled. "OK, calm down. Start again from the beginning."

As Chandra talked, Chuck's unease grew. A Chinese landing on Okinawa? The Sino-Japanese carrier strike group going head to head with a US carrier strike group? That was *not* part of his NSA exit strategy. He began to wonder exactly what kind of 'events' his Chinese handler was expecting him to report on.

Bunny O'Hare told herself to calm down. She was glad she was not the type who carried a sidearm, or the DARPA Okinawa Stingray project would be short an AI programmer called Kevin right now.

The Navy ratings had loaded the EMP weapon and five Mark 50 torpedoes in the Stingray's torpedo pod, then flooded the graving dock so it could put to sea. Normal procedure at this late phase of the pre-deployment trials was that once their boat was in the water, the manufacturer and Office of Naval Research staff retired to their offices in the base admin building, leaving Bunny, Kyle, and Kevin to operate under simulated field conditions. Which meant Bunny piloted the Stingray, controlling steerage and navigation, while Kyle operated as sonar and weapons officer. Kevin's role would not be needed when the Stingray was fully combat-ready, but for now it was essential. He was their AI lead and his role was to direct the off-site team of programmers who monitored and tweaked the AI programming before, during, and after trials. The AI on the Stingray was a learning system and was operating at near to optimal efficiency, but like its aquatic namesake it still had a tendency to be overly aggressive in defensive tactical scenarios, which was a character trait neither DARPA nor the ONR wanted in such a potent unmanned undersea weapons platform.

"I know having the NSA looking over your shoulder is not normal, Kevin," Bunny was saying. Chuck had stepped outside for a smoke and Kevin had used the chance to start whining. "But you *are* working on a top-secret defense project, so what exactly is normal?"

"I'm just asking if we're under suspicion or something," Kevin said, talking without looking directly at her, as usual. "Because that's what it feels like. I bet you know why he's here, but you aren't telling us. How are we supposed to do our jobs without access to all the relevant information?"

Bunny sighed, punched a few keys on her command console, dragged a waypoint across her screen and decided that ignoring Kevin was the best way to avoid a murder charge. "OK, waypoints set, 15 knots steady, moving to 200 feet depth, heading straight for the test range. I've had to kick in a little port-side trim to compensate for the extra weight of the FCG, so you might see reduced endurance, Kyle. How are we looking?"

"Propulsion systems nominal," Kyle reported. "I've got a dead cell on battery bank 14, so we are running at 97 percent capacity, but the battery drain is comfortably within spec for this mission."

"Good, and weapons?"

"Still on manual authority," he assured her.

"Ok, Kevin, look I want you …"

The man had put his noise-canceling headphones back on. Not so that he could tune into some special comms channel – he was probably listening to a heavy metal playlist. He also refused to buy reading glasses, so his nose was pressed to a screen on which he was debugging code. Having had his latest whine, he was back in his own world again. Bunny sighed, stood, walked up behind him and poked a stiff finger into the hole in his skinny shoulder blade.

"Ow!" he yelled and turned around, wrenching his headphones off and rubbing his shoulder. "I asked you not to do that!"

"And I told you that you are not to wear those headphones during live trials," she responded.

He was still rubbing his shoulder theatrically and looked to Kyle for support. "It's bullying is what it is. Or assault, or harassment, or something."

Kyle had no sympathy. "Don't look at me, man, I'm just over here doing my job." Meaning, *just shut up and do yours.*

Bunny continued. "This is the last test sequence on the critical path before the sink exercise, Kevin," she said. "And assuming we get through that, the main issue we need to resolve before we can document this milestone is offensive AI stability. We need to show that when we give fire control to the AI during the live-fire sink exercise that our Stingray won't turn 180 degrees and sink a ship full of US Navy Admirals because it decides they are a bigger threat."

"What do you think I'm doing here?" Kevin said, pointing at his screen. "The SINK EX is still two months away. We've got four AI stress tests planned between now and then, not counting this one. I'm on it."

The door to the hangar was opening again and Chuck was stepping inside.

"You better had be," Bunny said quickly. "And stow those headphones. I need you 100 percent focused."

Kevin glared at her. "Seriously?" He shoved the headphones into a drawer.

Chuck walked over with what looked a forced smile. "Dissent in the ranks? What's up?"

"Nothing unusual," Bunny muttered, returning to her command console. The drone 'cockpit' for the Stingray was nothing like the cockpits she had mastered flying first F-35s and then F-47 *Fantom*s over Turkey, Syria, and Alaska. There she had been flying supersonic combat aircraft in near real time, which required a trailer-based cockpit fitted with flight controls, a networked VR helmet, and a bank of 2D screens and input devices. As a *Fantom* drone commander, she'd been flying up to six aircraft at a time in data-linked, semi-autonomous formations and had needed both twitch-reflexes and a superhuman ability for continuous partial attention to keep all the moving pieces in flow.

She'd known what she was doing when she'd said yes to the DARPA Stingray project, but it had taken some getting used to.

Instead of a fighter plane cockpit, she'd been given a padded, reclining VR gamer stool by Kyle. Instead of flight controls, she had a mouse. There was no VR helmet, just a two by four bank of 2D screens showing subsystem status, environmental indicators such as speed, depth, temperature, and hull pressure, a navigation screen on which she plotted the drone's course and then reacted as it was dynamically adjusted by the Stingray's onboard AI, and a combined payload/sensor screen on which she could control the sub's passive and active sensor systems and deploy the payload. Her and Kyle's roles were simply to give orders to the AI, which managed navigation, comms, weapons, sonar, and engineering.

Unlike the F-47 *Fantom* stealth drones she was used to piloting, which had a top speed of 1,100 miles per hour, her Stingray topped out at nail-biting 15 knots, or 17 miles per hour. It would take several hours for the Stingray to reach the US Navy torpedo testing range off Okinawa.

Bunny was not good at waiting, so at this stage of any sea trial she was already twitchy.

"Nothing unusual?" Chuck asked, looking from her to Kevin and back again. "Really?"

"Oh shut up," Bunny told him. "This place is full of heavy blunt instruments, so if you are going to spend the next two hours giving me enigmatic spook face, you could find yourself eating one of them."

Weapons Control

"We're in," Frangi said. "Initiating command redirection." She reached beside her without taking her eyes off her screen. "Get ready."

"I'm ready, girl," Po said. The APT 23 plan for stealing the drone had been informed by the intelligence provided by the Chinese Ministry of State Security spy at the heart of the NSA. They knew that as soon as their attack was detected, as it would be the minute they attempted to wrest away control of the Stingray, DARPA's cyber-defense system would attempt to isolate the Okinawa sub-system that was being targeted and lock them out. To mitigate this, their first act would be to instruct the Stingray to switch its satellite link from a US Navy bird to a specially tasked Chinese PLA military satellite, so that DARPA might regain control of its own command system, but would not have control of the Stingray.

"Executing in three, two, one..." Frangi said, as she tapped a key on her keyboard.

As the first shot in a new global war, it was a rather meek-sounding one.

"Follow-on code is running," Po announced. "Come on baby..." He spun his chair around to watch Tanken, who was gripping a joystick tightly in his right hand, left hand hovering over a keypad, while he stared intently at a bank of screens which were currently ... blank.

Dragon Bird held his breath. Five years. The most successful penetration of a US defense network in cyber history. Thousands of man-hours planning and coding for this particular operation to support the boldest, most ambitious military strategy of the last two hundred years, and in the next thirty seconds they would know if it would succeed or fail.

"I've got nothing!" Tanken said.

"Give it time," Po whispered. "We're communicating across thousands of miles with a drone platform hundreds of feet under the sea."

"Pinging," Frangi said calmly. She looked at Tanken's screens and back again. "Any second now. We have handshake."

"Downlink!" Po yelled. "Uplink locked!"

One by one the screens in front of Tanken changed from a single blinking cursor on a matt black screen to bright, colorful information and data displays. "Yes! I've got navigation, communications, engine, sensor and steerage control!" he said excitedly. "Oh … what?" He frowned. One of his six screens was still blank.

Dragon Bird's heart sank. "What? Is there a problem?" he asked. He had a hand on the back of Tanken's chair, looking at his main screen, which was currently showing six different panes.

"You could say," Tanken said, almost under his breath. "The good news is our analysis was correct; the US submersible is equipped with legacy systems almost identical to those on a *Los Angeles*-class attack submarine." His rig looked like a VR gamer's home rig, with screens, keyboards, floor pedals, and a Hands On Throttle and Stick joystick. Right now he had one hand on the joystick, the other tapping away at his keyboard. "The bad news is, I don't have weapons control."

Dragon Bird scanned the six panes. Five were showing various instrument readouts. One was dark. He leaned over Tanken's shoulder and put a finger on it. "Po!" Dragon Bird yelled at the fat man behind him, without turning around. "Why do we not have weapons systems control?!"

"I don't understand!" Po said. "We should have it all. There is no logic …" His eyes were scanning code, which was flowing across his screen like water. He stopped it and backed up. "There!" He looked up at Dragon Bird. "One of the DARPA coders put the weapons system on manual control for this launch. We have control of the boat via its AI, but the AI has no command priority over weapons."

"What? Why would they do that?!"

Frangipani was also head deep in a page of code on her screen, but she looked up. "Duh. Because they don't trust their own AI?"

"They trust it to pilot a hundred million dollars' worth of drone, but not to deploy its payload?"

"Remember, this platform is still a prototype," Frangi said. "If it was me, I'd be constantly worried how the AI would react in any given threat environment. Especially with live weapons. AI-controlled weapons authority is absolutely the *last* thing I would sign off on." She ducked her head back down and returned to her work, which had nothing to do with Po and Tanken's part of the operation. She was concerned with keeping KAHLO hidden and safe from NSA counter-attack.

Dragon Bird fixed a baleful glare on Po. "You must get control of the weapons. Can't you give Tanken manual control of the weapons systems instead of relying on the onboard AI?"

"Our entire attack vector is through the AI," Po said. "To get control of the weapons systems, I have to find a way to override the manual lockout and then assign it to the AI."

"Then do it!"

"Sir," Po said, pushing his chair back, "if it is like Frangi says, then there is a reason the enemy did not give weapons control to the AI. We do not know what that reason is. Whatever the problem, we would be exposing ourselves to the same issue."

Dragon Bird took a slow breath, as he often had to do, to stop himself yelling at Po. "Private, your mission was to penetrate the enemy command and control system and enable us to take over the enemy weapons platform. You have been spectacularly successful, so far." He saw Po relax visibly. "However, controlling a weapons platform without having control of its actual weapons will not allow us to achieve the mission objectives, will it?"

Po thought about this. "No, sir."

"Private, can you see another way to give the AI control of the weapons on that platform?" Dragon Bird asked.

Po spun back to the screen, paging back and forth through the code there. Finally he looked up. "No, sir. Not in the time available."

Dragon Bird looked around the room. "Frangi? Ideas?"

She looked at him blankly. It didn't mean she was clueless. Frangipani was a cyber wonderchild. Dragon Bird knew that she was probably processing his question at the same time as she was still working on the problem she had on her own screen. She focused suddenly, talking to Po. "See if the system has a data scrub routine. The AI may be programmed to initiate it if it experiences a repeating error. A data scrub would require the AI to take each sub-system off line to scrub it. So first, find a way to trigger a data scrub. If it takes the weapons sub-system off line, you may be able to disable remote command authority for the weapons system and give it to the AI before it is restored." She shrugged. "Might work."

Dragon Bird raised his eyebrows at Po.

"It's worth a try," Po agreed.

The atmosphere in their small office was thick and Dragon Bird suddenly needed more air. "Tanken, you have a solution for an intercept?"

"Updated by the minute, sir," he said. He consulted one of the screens. "The target is patrolling about 50 miles east of Okinawa. I'm showing six hours to interception range, four hours to possible contact with its air or subsea pickets."

"There's your window, Po," Dragon Bird said. "You have four hours to gain control of that weapons system."

"And you better succeed, fat man," Tanken said over his shoulder. "I want to be the first guy in the PLA Navy ever to set off an EMP weapon under the keel of a US Navy warship."

Bunny O'Hare's day had gone from bad to much, much worse.

"What do you mean it's *gone*?!" Bunny was yelling. She had never really learned the whole count-to-five and then yell thing. It was an aggressive streak that had made her a very good fighter pilot, but as a team leader, not so much.

Kyle had pulled her out of a conversation with Chuck and over to his workstation. Kevin was at his own, staring at his screen, jabbing at keys on his keyboard, biting his bottom lip and talking out loud to himself. "No, no, no... this isn't happening..."

Kyle pointed at his screens, which were all blank. "I mean, one minute all systems were green. Comms were perfect, no interference or lag at all. The boat was twenty miles out, moving east at a depth of eighty feet, headed for two hundred." He gestured at the blank screens. "Then this! It's gone. Disappeared. Vanished!"

Chuck stood with arms crossed, a confused expression on his face. His wasn't the only one.

"Tell me what I'm looking at, Kyle," Bunny said through her teeth. "Did we get some sort of power surge? Denial of service attack? What?"

"No!" he said, pointing to a status screen that should have been full of numbers and graphics. Every readout was flatlined, showing null. "We've lost the Stingray itself! There was no distributed denial of service attack, all our systems are still up and running. We can send command input, but the Stingray isn't receiving and it isn't sending anything back to us! We have a perfect uplink to the satellite, but there's no downlink to our boat. One second it was there, the next, it was *gone*."

"This isn't possible," Kevin said, turning to them. "The comms system has multiple redundancies built in. Even if the Stingray lost a comms buoy in some kind of accident, it would just fire off another. If it lost its link to the satellite, it would lock onto a secondary. If its primary radio equipment failed, the backup would kick in. If it was under attack and had to go dark, it would have signaled that in a burst transmission before it reeled in its buoy and took evasive action. We can't just *lose* it." He looked over at Chuck. "This is you, isn't it?! This is why you're here."

O'Hare shot a look at Chuck, who shook his head. "Whatever this is, it's *nothing* to do with me, or the NSA."

The Stingray was designed for both semi- and fully autonomous operations. When in semi-autonomous mode, as it had been since launch, it maintained constant contact with base, even when submerged, via a tethered buoy which linked it to overhead satellites or aircraft. When in fully autonomous modes, such as during stealth attacks or evasive maneuvers, it would reel the buoy in but would send a signal to its base indicating that it was going full auto and sending a code burst to explain why. It was specifically designed not to suddenly and inexplicably go completely dark, so the team was floundering.

"Ideas?" Bunny said, her voice bouncing around the metal hangar. "Give me ideas here!"

"Shipping or undersea vessel collision," Kyle offered. "It was still only eighty feet down. If the sensors glitched, it could have hit the keel of a supertanker, or another sub?"

"Thanks to White Beach maritime surveillance, we've got radar and satellite feed and locations on all surface vessels within a hundred miles of here," Kevin said. "There was no supertanker. And the chances of hitting some mystery sub are a gazillion to one."

"Maybe some other obstruction?" Chuck offered. "Uncharted wreck, reef ..."

Kevin rolled his eyes. "So the AI suddenly went blind, lost navigation, and the passive and active Long Aperture Bow Sonar glitched too?"

"Show me the cheese, Kevin," Bunny said, pointing at the blank screens. "We can see the holes! At least Kyle and Chuck are coming with ideas."

"*Dumb* ideas," Kevin said, holding up a hand and counting off fingers. "Here are some more, before anyone says them. Friendly or enemy mine. Friendly or enemy torpedo. Catastrophic hull breach. Spontaneous pressure hull collapse." He folded his last finger over, staring at Chuck. "Eaten by a giant octopus? Or there is always alien abduction?"

"So where the hell is my Stingray, Kevin?" Bunny asked again.

"Unknown," Kevin said. "But if you're interested, I do have a theory that is actually grounded in what we do know."

Bunny ground her teeth, but asked as patiently as she could, "And what is your theory?"

"We know our uplink to the satellite is operating normally, but the link between the Stingray and the satellite is down. We know the Stingray is programmed to lock onto a backup satellite if it loses its link with the primary, but it hasn't attempted to reconnect even though there are multiply redundant systems designed to ensure it does, which is like, super weird." He fixed a glare on Chuck. "*And* we know that an NSA agent turned up here unannounced this morning. We let him behind our firewall and then this happened. So the thing that makes the most sense right now is … an NSA-sponsored cyber-attack. This is some kind of BS test or exercise."

"I had no idea this, whatever *this* is, was going to happen," Chuck said. "You have to believe me."

He sounded genuine. But to her own surprise, O'Hare found herself agreeing with Kevin. They had never experienced a total comms blackout before, at least not in her two years on the project. Yet it had happened and the only thing they had done differently today was to welcome Chuck Harford of the NSA into the fold.

"Look, no offense to the NSA, but a cyber-hijacking is impossible," Kyle said. He misinterpreted the pained expression on O'Hare's face as confusion and tried to help her out. "It's just … let me put this in layman's terms," he said and pointed at her command console, with its joysticks and keyboards. "That system isn't a standalone system running our Stingray over a simple satellite link. It's a DARPAnet cloud-based sub-system that …"

"That's your layman's version?" she asked.

"OK, let me try again. What I'm saying is that if cyber hackers tried to hijack the comms link between us and the Stingray, DARPAnet would detect the attack and simply switch us to a separate cloud-based backup system while they isolated the attack. It's a system perfected over years of dealing with foreign actors trying to hack our drone comms. We probably wouldn't even *notice* the interruption."

"So you are saying it's impossible for anyone to hack into our command system?" she asked. "Even our own NSA?"

Kyle looked at Kevin and then back at her. "Well, sorry to disagree with Kevin, but yeah. How many times in the last twenty years have you heard about a US drone being hacked and retasked by an enemy? None, right? The only way NSA could do it would be with DARPA's permission and it would be completely irresponsible to hack a weapons system during a live-weapons sea trial, so I don't believe DARPA would ever agree to it."

Bunny wanted to be convinced, but the reality of her missing Stingray couldn't be ignored. "You're the one who called this as a possible cyber-attack," she said to Kevin. He didn't seem to mind that Kyle was disagreeing with him, but then, it wasn't the first time. "Say you're right. What do we do?"

"There are protocols for command authority override, so we'd invoke those," Kevin said. "Shut down the AI and put it on full manual control. If that didn't work, we could try to trigger a propulsion system shutdown, so at least the Stingray would be dead in the water while we worked the problem. But everything in our playbook requires we have a satellite link to the Stingray, and we don't have one right now. Someone else has our boat!"

Kyle shook his head. "I'm still saying a giant squid attack is more likely than some unknown actor hacking into DARPAnet and stealing our boat."

"I think we can rule out giant squid, Kyle," O'Hare said. "And when you've ruled out the possible, all that remains is the impossible, such as cyber-attack," she said. "Arthur Conan Doyle."

"That's not the exact quote," Kyle said, holding up a finger. "What he actually said was..."

"Can I make a suggestion?" Chuck interrupted. "Let *me* look at the cyber-attack angle." He looked to Kyle for support. "If this was NSA, I wasn't briefed about it and that makes me annoyed. If it *wasn't* NSA, I can get my people working to find out who it was. That will free you to conduct a thorough root cause analysis. Identify and rule out all possible confounders systematically. In my experience, a little time spent now, at the point of greatest uncertainty, will pay off later if it stops you running down blind alleys."

"Oh right," Kevin said, eyes narrowing. "Let's let the fox investigate the theft of the chicken."

O'Hare glared at Chuck with an intensity that should have given him third-degree burns. But the guy wasn't wrong. Cyber-attack was just one explanation of many that had to be ruled in, or out. And if she got a whiff of a suggestion Chuck was stalling or trying to blank them, she could get Jensen to go straight to NSA Virginia with this. She rolled her shoulders, getting her head into the challenge, psyching herself up. *It's a sea trial, Bunny. This is why we run trials. You've faced situations like this before and sometimes you've even come out on top.* "OK … Kyle, you put your head together with the guys from ONR and the manufacturer, go back over every bit of data from launch to the time the Stingray fell off the grid and see if you can learn anything from it. Meanwhile Kevin, you start working those override protocols. I'll get onto Jensen and see if we can't get some help from the US Navy." She pointed at Chuck. "And you, NSA!" He almost looked as worried as her people did, which was strangely reassuring. "I want you to prove to me your so-called white hats had nothing to do with this."

Flying Visit

Kato was worried too. They were flying so low that he was convinced that if a school of flying fish took to the air right in front of their formation, they'd probably fly right into it.

He had taken off with Captain Chen and two other pilots and was flying fourth position, at the back of the formation, with his flight leader in front and to his left and Chen to the left in front of that aircraft like the fingertips of a right hand. Theirs was not a reconnaissance flight.

That much had become obvious during the briefing, which Chen led herself.

"The target," she said, standing in front of a multimedia presentation on a wall screen and pointing. Kato recognized it instantly, but Chen pointed to it anyway, probably for the benefit of the other pilots. "US Navy White Beach Naval Base," she said and waited for the other pilots to stop exchanging looks at each other and give her their attention again. "Our aircraft are being fitted with recon pods. We will overfly the base at 1,000 meters, mapping electronic signatures and photograph any naval vessels docked there." She put her hands behind her back. "Questions about our primary objective?"

None of the other pilots spoke up, so Kato kept quiet, until he realized they were not going to speak at all. He raised his hand tentatively.

"Don't the Americans have a no-fly policy over the base?" he asked. He knew, in fact, that they did, having joined the Japan Self Defense Air Force in the time before the US had begun its strategic repositioning away from Japan and Korea.

"The airspace belongs to Japan, Lieutenant," Chen said. "Your military has given us permission to overfly neighboring Naha. That should be sufficient."

"Yes, Comrade Captain," he said, unconvincingly. "But ... why so low? Don't the Americans have short-range surface-to-air missile systems protecting their base?"

Again, he knew that they did. All Japanese pilots had been trained not to stray into US protected airspace during operations. Even though they had carried the Identify Friend or Foe system that should alert US anti-aircraft units that they were friendly, no one wanted to take any chances they'd accidentally get a surface-to-air missile up their tailpipe. If it was like any other US Navy base, it was probably protected by at least one Marine Low-Altitude Air Defense platoon.

"Intel indicates only man-portable, optical and heat-seeking missiles," Chen said dismissively. "Almost completely ineffective against the *Snow Falcon*." She pulled up a map of the US base. "This image was taken by one of our satellites this morning. As you can see, there is no US radar installation, no fixed anti-air missile battery. The base relies entirely on ship-based anti-air radar for detection, provided by the US *Ticonderoga*-class Aegis cruiser which is normally docked there. As you will also note in this image, that cruiser is not currently in port. Our mission has been planned so that it takes place while the *Ticonderoga* is out to sea and unable to cover White Beach."

She wrinkled her nose and put a finger on a ship that was docked at the base. "There is, however, this...littoral combat ship. Similar to our coast guard vessels. It is armed with anti-ship-missile defenses that are not anti-air capable and an air and sea search radar system with an effective range of not more than 20 miles. Our secondary objective will be to explore whether this US system can get a lock on our *Snow Falcon*s during a low-altitude, high-speed pass." She laughed. "We're going to rattle some windows and burst a few eardrums, boys."

Her pilots laughed with her.

Kato raised his hand, attracting more glares from his fellow pilots. "Excuse me, Comrade Captain, I saw several *Sharp Sword* drones parked on the flight deck. If this is a reconnaissance mission over an enemy airfield, why are we sending manned aircraft and not unmanned drones?"

"I told you, Lieutenant," Chen said sharply, no longer in the mood for discussion, "this mission is a test of the stealth profile and jamming capabilities of our *Snow Falcon*s. Not our *Sharp Sword* drones." She turned her gaze on the others. "Now, if there are no more ... questions?"

Kato folded his arms, sitting back in his chair. It seemed less of a recon mission to him than a pure provocation. While 99 percent of the mission would be over Chinese or Japanese airspace, it was the 1 percent that concerned him. Yes, the US had completed its strategic pivot away from the Far East and closed most of its bases in Japan and Korea. But it still maintained a significant US Air Force presence on Guam, a major naval base at Pearl Harbor in Hawaii, and could call on its staunch ally Taiwan to base aircraft, land, and naval assets any time it wished to. The White Beach base was a symbolic presence, kept operational for purely political purposes, so that US Presidents could say to their constituents with long memories that all those World War Two lives had not been lost in vain and there would always be a part of Okinawa that was American. And it had an almost religious significance to some Americans.

China overflying the base, unannounced, with a formation of its latest stealth fighters, would send an unmistakable message – these are *our* skies. Combined with footage of the combined Sino-Japanese carrier strike group, it would make news services around the world. Kato wondered who the audience for this little piece of theater was? Chen's PLA-Navy superiors? Chinese People's Republic and Japanese government ministers? The people of Okinawa? They'd campaigned for decades for the closure of US bases, but unless they lived right beside it, they had probably all but forgotten about the small US Navy port at the eastern tip of Okinawa's main island.

He noticed he was tense, gripping his stick a little too hard, and had drifted a little high in the formation. He relaxed his grip and the AI eased his machine back into position. The sensation that there was a second hand on his controls unnerved him. Reaching forward to a bank of switches ahead of his right hand, he disengaged the flight AI and took manual control. It must have been signaled to his flight leader, because Chen reacted immediately.

"Officer Kato," she said over comms. He saw it was a closed channel, not for the rest of the pilots to hear. "Let your machine do the flying. The *Snow Falcon*'s Sanqiang AI can fly better than any human. Your role onboard your *Snow Falcon* is to make the decisions we do not trust the AI to make. Where to fly, when to attack or retreat, when to deploy weapons, and what to target. You will keep your AI engaged at all times, unless you have reason to believe it is faulty. Do you understand?"

"Yes, Comrade Captain," he said. He cut the AI back in. He understood well enough. It didn't mean he liked it. But he couldn't hold a grudge against her for setting him straight – she had done it on a closed channel so as not to embarrass him and she was just relaying the advice she no doubt gave to all her pilots. All in all, he had developed a grudgingly favorable opinion of his Chinese CO. She had followed up on their initial conversation about their ancestors, as she had said she would. Over lunch, she had sought him out. He had been sitting with one of the other Chinese pilots, trading stories about the recent war games, when she had come into the wardroom and looked around. Seeing him there, she had fetched some iced tea and lunch rolls and then walked over to his table. "Would you excuse us, comrade pilot?" she said to the other officer.

"Yes, Comrade Captain," the man said, vacating his seat.

She took it and sat down. "I have news for you," she said. Kato had the impression she wasn't one for small talk.

"You are sending me back to the *Izumo* after all?" he had guessed, based on their conversation that morning.

She gave a short laugh. "It did cross my mind. No. My staff were able to reach a very helpful researcher at your Imperial War Museum. I reasoned that if my great-grandfather had been so diligent keeping a war diary, perhaps yours had too. And if so, perhaps it was stored with your authorities."

Kato had never researched the written record of his great-grandfather's service. He had merely accepted the oral history

152

handed down to him by his own grandfather and father. His hand went unconsciously to the wave pendant at his throat. It had all been so long ago and he had always been more interested in the future than the past. "They found something?"

"They did," she said. "Four volumes of diaries. I have digital copies that I can send you tonight. But I took the liberty of looking through the volume covering his time in Burma." Her eyes were bright, excited, and she took a bite of her roll, chewing and swallowing quickly. "I can tell you exactly how your great-grandfather could have been both a POW and a kamikaze."

Shanghai Flower

Frangipani had chosen her own hacker name. Her parents had died in a bus accident when she was fourteen and she had taught herself how to hack computer systems, trying to find out exactly how a bus full of people could plunge 50 meters off the Second Wanzhou Yangtze River Bridge, killing thirteen people, without any official investigation of the accident. She did not accept the explanation in the State-run media that the bus had simply suffered a burst front tire, which was based on interviews with the unnamed bus driver (who had survived), and using the computer system at the Chongqing public library, she had begun digging. In all, it had taken her two years to find the truth. The first thing she did was to gain access to the Wanzhou closed-circuit traffic camera data storage center and pull out the vision from the bridge at the time of the accident. There was good footage from three angles and none of them showed the bus bursting a tire. What they showed was that the bus swerved to the wrong side of the road, then back again and then over the side of the bridge, without once braking. Several months later, she gained access to the bus manufacturer's safety database, in which the logs from buses' black box recorders were stored. These showed that the bus was being driven manually at the time of the accident due to the failure of its autonomous self-drive system. Finally, she had broken into the criminal investigations database of the Wanzhou District Police Force, who had in fact investigated the accident. To do so, it had been necessary for her to create a program that allowed her system to impersonate the AI system of a neighboring police district, and she had used this vector to gain access to the Wanzhou criminal database. She learned that the police had found that the driver, the son of a Party official, had received less than five hours' instruction in how to manually pilot that particular model of bus and that witnesses in nearby vehicles reported he was seen standing up and arguing with a passenger immediately before the bus lost control.

Frangipani, then sixteen years old and living with her grandparents, finally had the driver's name and soon had his address. She began planning his murder.

That was the point at which the National Cybercrime Taskforce broke down her bedroom door, took her into custody and, six months later, convicted her of cybercrime. But she was offered a choice – prison, or enlistment in the Unit 61938 Cyber Warfare division. That was when she had finally chosen her hacker name. The frangipani, or jīdàn huā, had been her mother's favorite flower and her father had given her one every day on their wedding anniversary for all of the years that Frangi could remember. It was a story she had shared with Po and Dragon Bird, one time they had all been out drinking, but she assumed they had forgotten it.

Today was her parents' wedding anniversary. She had been so occupied with the mission that she had almost forgotten, but Dragon Bird had not. She'd looked up from her desk and seen him coming through the door of their office, carrying a small frangipani plant in a pot. It had a single flower. She'd pushed her chair back from her desk as he approached, unsure what to say.

"Do I have the right date?" he asked, setting the vase on her desk.

"Yes, Comrade Captain," she said, suddenly very formal. "I am … speechless."

"You said on this day every year you like to go and buy a flowering frangipani plant and sit it in your window, yes?"

"Yes."

He gestured to the office around them, Tanken's head buried in a VR helmet, Po sitting grinning at her foolishly, in on the secret. "Unfortunately, no windows. But at least you have your flower."

"Thank you," she said and then, because she could not bring herself to hug Dragon Bird but just had to hug someone, she jumped up and ran over to Po and hugged him.

Dragon Bird had smiled at the big man's discomfort and Frangi had been quick to disengage so as not to embarrass him further, but they'd both had big smiles as she'd returned to her desk. That had been this morning. This morning seemed so long ago now.

Dragon Bird coughed. "Status report please, both of you." He nodded at Po. "You first."

"We still have full navigation, sensor, and steerage control of the DARPA Stingray," Po said. He pointed at a screen showing waypoints on a large map of the Pacific. "Steering to an intercept with the target vessel. But I have no progress on the weapons system yet. I'll have Frangi's data scrub exploit ready to deploy in an hour or so. And lunch is late, again."

Dragon Bird ignored the complaint. "DARPA must be going out of their minds on Okinawa," he said. "Are they trying any unexpected strategies to recover contact or control?"

"No sir," he said. "Not yet. Our agent reports that they are trying to re-establish communications with their submersible. Through KAHLO's penetration of DARPAnet, we are collecting real-time input from their Stingray command and control systems, but they are doing nothing we haven't anticipated. DARPA cyber-defense systems have isolated and locked down the Stingray control subsystem as expected, but that is irrelevant now."

"Good. And we still have full access to DARPAnet?"

"Yes sir," Frangi said. "Full access and trusted status. The enemy will first focus on mitigating the attack on its Okinawa sub-system before it considers the possibility that its entire data infrastructure has been compromised."

Frangipani had evolved her ideas around AI mimicry attacks a long way since she had penetrated the Wanzhou district police system ten years ago. If DB was the godfather of the KAHLO attack system, Frangi was its godmother. She had taken it from the puppy dog that Jin Tan had created and turned it into a slavering Doberman, looking for meat. Once DB had shown his superiors what it could do, APT 23 was given the mother of all targets, the US Defense Advanced Research Projects Agency.

DARPA was the agency that commissioned research into the most advanced US weapons systems under development –

platforms and systems that were so speculative they might not see the light of day within the next fifty years, if at all. But also systems that were close to deployment, like the Stingray XLUUV. DARPA had invented the original internet and so, of course, DARPA's data infrastructure was protected by the toughest cyber-defenses the US had devised.

In the last few years, DARPA computer systems had been protected by (so far) unbreakable Lucamarini quantum key encryption and China's Unit 61938 had been forced to target contractors, vendors, and sub-suppliers with weaker defenses, but also with less critical intel.

None of this phased KAHLO. Because like the katydid which didn't need to understand the language of the cicada to mimic it, KAHLO didn't try to break the DARPA encryption. It just learned to mimic the DARPA traffic until it was, for all intents and purposes, a trusted DARPA sub-system. Frangipani had realized that the distributed nature of DARPA IT platforms – DARPA was a project management and contracting agency with offices and project managers all over the world – was its true weakness. DARPA staff needed to work together, to communicate across systems and platforms around the globe. And so that they recognized each other, each system used a unique identifier, with access routed through a security AI at both ends. It was Jin Tan who had hypothesized that if a hacker could replicate that identifier (a 'handshake' code which was itself encrypted, with 'chaos-encryption' methods), then it might be possible to convince other DARPA security AI systems that the intruder system *was* a DARPA AI. Dragon Bird had seized on the idea and convinced his superiors to put a team together to explore it.

Frangipani had prepared the ground like a farmer tilling soil. APT 23 had identified five vulnerable NSA security AI platforms and she had tried mimicking all of them without luck. For almost a year she had been using KAHLO to fire various 'handshake' attempts at the DARPA network: the cyber equivalent of, "Hello, my name is NSA system X, I'm a friend." None had succeeded.

DB had been forced to admit that they needed a new idea and once again Frangi supplied it. KAHLO could perfectly mimic a

DARPA AI system, but it was not being accepted because the DARPA system would not accept multiple log-ins from the same AI. They would therefore need to create a new identity, a new system – but one that the other AIs would accept as authentic.

For this, they needed a human agent within DARPA. All he or she had to do was create a new system identifier. A simple alphanumeric designator that would serve to legitimize Frangi's handshake attempts. The tasking had been given to the Chinese Ministry of State Security with a high priority flag and it had taken them a year to find their man. Their man turned out to be a woman. A low-level Chinese-American DARPA system administrator, with family still in China. All that was needed to secure her cooperation was a threat her family would disappear if she did not.

It was the work of fifteen minutes for the MSS agent to create a new unique AI system identifier and register it to a fake IP address. It was such a commonplace and harmless action that the act was noticed by no one. But it was exactly what APT 23 needed. KAHLO adopted the new identity and moved into DARPAnet like a cuckoo in a nest.

Dragon Bird had explained to his (very excited) superiors the potential of their new cyberweapon. Once accepted as a trusted sub-system, KAHLO's access to data inside DARPA was virtually unlimited – it could be accessed at will and decrypted at leisure. It was the modern equivalent of the Allied success in cracking the German Enigma code machine in World War Two.

DB had presented two alternatives to Unit 61938 General Command for leveraging KAHLO. One, they could use it as an intelligence collection tool, leaving KAHLO in place to simply steal intelligence from DARPA for as long as it remained undiscovered. This was just a matter of time; no one expected the cuckoo could survive inside the DARPA network indefinitely. But the insight into advanced US weapon projects it could provide would be unprecedented.

Or, two, China could use KAHLO as a weapon, as part of a specific and targeted operation aimed at disrupting or leveraging a specific DARPA project. This would, however, almost certainly guarantee detection and compromise, inevitably causing China to lose all access to DARPA data going forward and might even betray the existence of KAHLO – so the nature of the operation would have to be of monumental strategic importance.

DB had passed his assessment up the line and he had waited, nervously, for a response. Each day KAHLO sat in place within DARPA, pulling intelligence off DARPA's servers, was another day closer to it being discovered.

A single question had come back to him and it had chilled his blood. Had APT 23 identified a nuclear-armed US weapons platform that could be triggered, appropriated, or otherwise subverted for use in a near-term military engagement? DB didn't regard himself as a genius of military strategy, but the nature of the question implied to him that his superiors were looking for a powerful US weapons system that could be turned back either upon its makers, or upon a third country, with ultimate deniability.

Po had done a deep dive on all the projects currently under development at DARPA, both public and top secret, which KAHLO had enabled them to identify. None were sufficiently advanced so as to be deployable in a near-term military engagement. But he alerted his superiors to two projects which were nearing completion and which might answer the request. The first was a nuclear-capable hypersonic cruise missile which was currently in the final phase of testing, but the test documentation indicated it was still two years (at least) from being fitted with a working nuclear warhead. The second, and probably least interesting, was an Extra-Large Unmanned Underwater Vehicle which was not intended to field nuclear weapons, as far as DB's team could determine. But it could be fitted with an almost unlimited array of other naval weapons and was soon to begin testing deployability of the new US Flux Compression Generating torpedo, a powerful torpedo capable of disabling capital ships. This prototype weapons system could potentially be hijacked, but to do so would ideally require the intervention and assistance of a human agent. Might this be of interest in the scenario described?

He didn't have to wait days for the response to his question that time.

Within hours he had been given an answer, a mission briefing and a target. Major Shaofeng had delivered the verbal briefing himself. When he got it in writing, he had needed to read it three times before he could believe it.

The first sign of the seriousness of their orders was that Shaofeng had chosen to deliver them in full dress uniform. The second sign was that he had chosen to deliver them to DB in private, behind a closed door, at five in the morning, before DB's team began their duties for the day. And he had been sweating, even though the temperature in his airconditioned office was a mild 65 degrees.

He had been standing looking at a map on his wall and turned as DB entered.

"Ah, Comrade Captain! Sit, sit," he said, flapping his hands in the direction of a chair and to a tea tray on his desk. "Help yourself."

DB perched awkwardly on the edge of his chair and poured tea. First for the Major and then for himself. He waited expectantly, as he'd been told to report at 0500 for new orders, but that was all he had been told.

"So, yes, KAHLO," Shaofeng began, still standing. "A significant achievement. Our success has been noted in Beijing, at the highest levels." He leaned forward with one hand on his desk and lowered his voice, almost reverentially. "The *highest* levels, Captain."

"Thank you, Comrade Major," DB said carefully. Being noted by Beijing at the highest levels was not always a career-enhancing achievement.

"What I am about to tell you is highly classified. You are to share it with no one outside of your team. And I have been told that internal surveillance of all of your communications is to be strengthened. Any leak of the mission details by you or any member

160

of APT 23 will be punishable by court-martial. Is that clear?" Shaofeng paused, needing confirmation from DB.

"Yes, Comrade Major."

"In three weeks, you will initiate a cyber-attack on the main enemy, the USA, in support of a military action that is intended to both humiliate it and demonstrate its vulnerability." Shaofeng paused again, clearly expecting a reaction from DB.

His mind whirled. It was a fantastic honor. A frightening responsibility. And a confusing strategy. A cyber-attack in support of a military action? Now, at a time of relatively low superpower tensions?

"Comrade Major. Is ..." DB began, stuttering, "... can the Comrade Major share with me the precise nature and full scope of the operation?"

Shaofeng sat, heavily. "What I can tell you will be limited to what you and your team need to know in order to execute your mission. Your objective should be familiar to you, as it was an operation you yourself proposed. You are to leverage KAHLO to steal the DARPA undersea drone currently being tested on Okinawa while it is in the process of field trials with the new American EMP torpedo." Shaofeng looked grave. "I sincerely hope you were not overestimating KAHLO's capabilities when you suggested this would be possible."

"No sir!" DB said. "As far as DARPA is concerned, KAHLO is a certified and trusted sub-system. We can gain control of the US weapons platform through KAHLO and we can subvert any mitigation tactics that DARPA cyber-security forces might implement, precisely because KAHLO is undetectable to them. But..." DB stalled. He hadn't exaggerated, but he had flagged one significant issue which he hoped had been noted by Beijing's war planners.

Shaofeng leaned back in his chair. "Please raise with me all possible concerns, Comrade Captain." His voice said one thing, his face said he did not want to hear about anything major.

"Sir, we will need an agent in place, on Okinawa, preferably embedded in the DARPA team. We need to attack the US control sub-system during a planned sea trial with the EMP weapon. But our study of the project has shown such plans can be unpredictably delayed, or advanced. We need someone to alert us when the trial is planned, ideally letting us know the exact moment it gets underway." He was speaking quickly, thinking on his feet. "I will also need the services of a PLA Navy submersible drone pilot trained in the use of US submarine command and control systems, once we gain control of the US prototype."

Shaofeng smiled thinly. "All of this was noted when your operation was approved, Comrade Captain. I am advised the necessary assets will be made available."

For an operation within three weeks? DB quailed at the thought. The Ministry of State Security must have agreed to dedicate and retask an already-recruited human agent within the US military apparatus for this role. And simply getting a staff member transferred between teams in Unit 61938 was a nightmare of bureaucracy that normally took several months, yet he was being granted the use of an officer from the PLA Navy submarine service with almost immediate notice? These things alone were unprecedented. The theft of the DARPA prototype must be a means to an end, not an end in itself.

Ten years of training and a lifetime of conditioning had taught DB to keep his thoughts to himself and he had already asked too many questions, expressed too many doubts. He immediately changed his tone. "Thank you, Comrade Major! We will proudly play our part in this heroic action! What specifically is the intention behind stealing the US prototype and its EMP weapon? Are we simply to deny its use to US forces, or deliver it to our own navy for study?"

Shaofeng grinned broadly. "No, Comrade Captain, you and KAHLO will play a much bigger role than that." He looked down at his desk, consulting a file that lay in front of him. Noticing it for the first time, DB could see it was probably the full mission briefing file. "The US maintains a sizable fleet based on Okinawa, codenamed 'Taskforce 44'. It currently includes an older but still

162

very capable amphibious assault ship, the USS *Makin*." He leafed through his papers and held up a file photograph of the *Makin*, which looked more like a small aircraft carrier than a landing ship to DB. "For reasons that do not concern you, the purpose of your operation is to put the USS *Makin* out of commission. Preferably using the American EMP weapon, or, if that is not possible, using conventional weapons. You will steal this drone, cripple their ship and they will huff and puff, but in the end they will not be able to prove it was us behind the attack. They will think it was their own prototype gone rogue." He laid the photograph back on his desk.

DB's blood drained to his feet. Steal a US submersible and use it to attack a US warship?!

Shaofeng saw the look on his face. "You have further 'concerns', Comrade Captain?"

About a million, DB had thought to himself. "No, Comrade Major!" he'd said fervently.

"Very good," Shaofeng had said and pushed a piece of paper across the table to DB. "You will report to Ningbo Naval Base this afternoon and speak with mission planning staff of the PLA Navy Eastern Fleet Intelligence Division. Dismissed."

DB scratched his head in thought. Their cyber-attack had gone more smoothly than he had dared dream. But there were elements of the operation he still simply did not understand. He had asked Navy intelligence staff at Ningbo why they simply did not use a Chinese submarine for the operation. Why go to all the trouble of stealing a US weapons system to do the job?

It was pointed out to him that China's submarine fleet, including the newest *Yuan*-class diesel-electric air-independent attack submarines, was designed for operations close to shore – China did not have a blue-water capacity that would enable it to range out into the Pacific to interdict a US taskforce on the high seas. But the US Stingray was more than capable of penetrating a light anti-sub picket force and engaging a US *Wasp*-class carrier with either torpedoes or its EMP weapon. Best of all, the attack would be entirely deniable, given that it would be carried out by the USA's own weapons system!

Ideally, the attack would take place while the taskforce was docked in Okinawa, with the hope that the EMP weapon would have an area of effect that would mean multiple ships could be crippled – and it might even be unclear whether the taskforce had been attacked or was a victim of a 'friendly fire' weapons malfunction. But if not and the US taskforce was patrolling at sea, intercepting it would be child's play given the size and ease of satellite, electronic, and air recon observability of a US taskforce made up of a small aircraft carrier and four large warships and the fact that the Stingray was stealth optimized.

DB had probed the mission planning staff for information on the reason behind the operation. Was it part of a bigger plan? Were other actions dependent on his success or failure? Should he be aware of other activities that might impact his own operation? Each of his questions was met with the same response: *such issues do not concern you.*

In the absence of clear direction, he had formed his own theory. He knew the government of Okinawa had been agitating for the removal of US troops from Japanese soil for decades. And now, with a China-friendly government in Tokyo, it seemed more determined than ever to put an end to ninety years of US occupation. A fully deniable stealth attack on the US taskforce in Okinawa, leveraging China's formidable cyber-warfare capabilities, would be a gesture of solidarity with Japan that may also serve to nudge the US to the conclusion that it had much to lose and little to gain from a continued presence on the island.

But it would all be moot if his team could not gain weapons authority over the Stingray.

Rules of Engagement

O'Hare's mind was racing. She felt like shouting something at someone, but her guys were frantically working the problem and she knew the best thing to do right now was leave them to it. She had given herself the job of finding out whether Navy had any assets in the area she could tap into to help locate her missing boat, and for that she needed to go through Chief Jensen.

She quickly brought him up to speed.

"Something stinks, O'Hare," he said.

"Tell me about it," she said. "How do you lose an entire submarine?"

"No, I mean, your Stingray isn't the only craziness we're dealing with right now. We've been getting reports overnight of increased and unexpected Japanese troop and naval deployments. Now your Stingray has mysteriously dropped off the grid? I've never been the type who believes in coincidence."

"You think the Japanese have something to do with it?" she asked.

"Or their new friends," he said carefully. "Who knows? We're about to prepare a sitrep for Pearl. Can you get over here, pronto?"

She wiped her forehead. "Jensen, I've got a situation I need to deal with here. I was calling to see if you have any assets I could tap into for the search…"

"Actually, it wasn't a request," Jensen said. "I know that as soon as I share the fact DARPA are out one autonomous stealth drone, things will, how can I say this … 'acquire a new sense of urgency'."

She gripped her phone tighter. "On my way." She hung up, pushed her phone into her jeans pocket, picked up her keys.

Chuck looked over at her. "News?"

"Uh, Navy might have some assets we can lean on," O'Hare said. "Got to persuade Collins to sign off on it, though." She put her phone in her jeans. "Apparently he wants me to explain, in person. Back in a minute, if I'm not just thrown in the brig."

Colonel Ted Collins was the CO of the 3rd Marines, 1st Battalion – the unit that was currently rotating through Okinawa – which also made him the most senior officer and Commander of White Beach Naval base. He was third-generation Marine, the great-grandson of Major General 'Wild Bill' Collins, an Iwo Jima veteran who had commanded the 3rd Marine Expeditionary Force on Okinawa in the last century, when the US still had tens of thousands of personnel stationed there. Ted Collins took his legacy seriously.

As Bunny walked into his office and was waved through his waiting room by a clearly flustered receptionist, she picked up an atmosphere of high tension. A large map of Okinawa was showing on one screen on his wall, with several markers on it.

The men and women in the room were crowded around the screen and a young woman was pointing at a spot near Naha. They stopped talking as Bunny walked in. O'Hare had only met Collins once, at an informal meet and greet dinner. She should have been able to complete her project at White Beach without ever having to formally engage with the Marine commander. So much for that. Collins was dressed in a green t-shirt under his camouflage uniform, with his sleeves rolled up to reveal a tattoo of a car on his left bicep. He was a compact man of medium build, with cropped hair, and had shown he had a pleasant smile when O'Hare met him over mocktails. He wasn't smiling now.

"O'Hare?" he asked. "Get over here and whatever you've got to say, hold it for now."

Jensen nodded to her, his look telling her to *shut up and keep up*.

Among the small group at the screen Bunny recognized one of the intel warrant officers she'd met a few times, a Senior Sergeant Alana Myers, plus a couple of more junior Marine intelligence staff she didn't know and a couple of Marine unit commanders she did.

Myers was talking and picked up where she'd left off, pointing to an icon on the screen.

"Japanese 15th Infantry Brigade, Naha," she said. "We know them well enough, they were our main training partners until a few years ago when joint exercises ceased. One regiment of ground troops, an anti-air artillery regiment, the rest are company-sized units – recon, combat engineers, signals, logistics, nuclear-chem-bioweapons. And they have an aviation squadron, mostly Sikorsky air-sea rescue choppers."

"I know the order of battle for the Japanese 15th Brigade, Sergeant," Collins said patiently. "I've been having dinner with their Commanding Officer, Colonel Oguri, every half year for three years. You're here because I asked where those units are in the readiness cycle."

The woman swallowed visibly. "Aye, sir. We intercepted a signal this week reporting that all units were now 'at readiness'. The whole regiment came off a training cycle about three weeks ago. But this week we picked up that the 15th Infantry Regiment and the 15th Recon Company had been brought to alert status. In JSDF Ground Force language, that means they can be ready for deployment at 24 hours' notice." She took a short breath. "And as you know, we just got a report that armored vehicles and transports have been sighted leaving Naha base, in strength."

"What kind of armor?" Jensen asked.

She consulted a tablet she was holding. "Mitsubishi type 89 infantry fighting vehicles, fifteen estimated. They can transport a company of infantry and are armed with missiles and 35mm cannon. The rest of the regiment appears to be mounting up in transport trucks."

"Two thousand troops in a Japanese infantry regiment," Jensen said. "Against our 800."

"Don't get ahead of yourself, Master at Arms," Collins said. He turned to one of his officers. "Get a light surveillance drone in the air. I want real-time intel on where those tanks are and where they're headed." The man turned away and pulled out his phone to issue the order.

167

"Sir, the 15ᵗʰ Brigade is also equipped with self-propelled artillery…" the intel officer said.

"Noted," Collins said. "Tell me what their Navy is doing."

Myers stepped to the next screen and O'Hare started scanning it. It showed a larger-scale map covering the East China Sea, with Japan to the east and China to the west. Okinawa was at the bottom of the map. There was a large cluster of icons that must have been the Sino-Japanese carrier strike group, but Myers was pointing at a smaller arrowhead-shaped formation a few miles northeast of Okinawa. "The 13ᵗʰ Escort Squadron sailed at 0400 this morning," she said. "Three of five *Atago*-class frigates. They are currently moving on a track that will bring them east of White Beach, approximately twenty miles offshore."

"That position would put them well within standoff weapon range of this base, sir," one of the junior intel officers added. "The *Atago*-class sports 16 cruise missile or anti-air missile capable launchers and a 5-inch gun."

"It also puts them in position to interdict any naval vessels approaching from the east," Jensen noted.

Collins turned toward O'Hare at last. "Which leads me to you, DARPA. I don't know whether to sympathize with your situation or blame you for adding to our troubles. Talk to me."

O'Hare swallowed hard. "Sir, this morning we launched the Stingray on a routine payload-balancing field test and about two hours in, we lost all communication with our boat." She saw impatience in Collins' face. "We loaded it with torpedoes and now it's disappeared."

"Are we talking a comms glitch or something more serious?" Collins asked.

Bunny had never been good at hiding her opinion behind carefully weighted words and she didn't try now. "It shouldn't be possible to lose all communication with that boat. I think someone sunk it or hijacked it, sir."

"And it happened at about 1230 local time," Jensen added. "Which is almost exactly when we started getting reports that Japanese troops were on the move."

"It could be a coincidence," O'Hare said, hopefully.

"Coincidence my ass," Collins said. "It takes weeks of planning to cycle up an infantry brigade and a destroyer flotilla and get them both moving at the same time. I've been reading report after report over the last two weeks of Chinese forces in their Eastern Command being brought to alert. We've got the most powerful Chinese blue-water fleet ever assembled, making flank speed south through the East China Sea just 300 miles northwest of here. We've got a government in Tokyo that has issued a demand that we start talks about handing over this base. And now DARPA has mysteriously lost contact with its stealth submersible?" He fixed a glare on Jensen. "You have had no communication whatsoever from Oguri's staff indicating his troops could be headed to exercises somewhere else on the island?"

"None sir," Jensen said. "Even since we stopped joint exercises with the Japanese, we've been very conscious about keeping the lines open to avoid any … misunderstandings. We let them know anytime we're planning a major field exercise and they do the same." He shrugged. "This is the first time we've seen them move in numbers larger than company strength without warning us."

As a heated debate began around what the Japanese troop deployments could mean, Bunny noticed Myers was standing with her hands tightly behind her back, as though holding them there to stop herself sticking a hand in the air like a kid in a classroom. "I think the Senior Sergeant has something to add," Bunny said, interrupting.

"Thank you, ma'am," Myers said. She addressed Collins. "Commander, regardless of whether all of these events are connected, certain actions would be prudent. We have a Japanese infantry regiment cycled up and reports that its tanks are already moving. We have a Japanese destroyer flotilla moving into a blockade position off our eastern shore. We are already within range of Japanese attack aircraft based on Okinawa, plus the Sino-Japanese fleet carriers." She tried to keep her voice level, but the

169

stress in it was palpable. "We also have a torpedo-armed drone missing at sea and right now, we can't rule out foul play. Sir, we need to bring this base to high alert."

Ted Collins did not take the potentially existential threat to his base lightly. His unit had the nickname 'Lava Dogs' and a hard-as-rock reputation to match. He ordered Jensen to double the security personnel on patrol around the base perimeter and ensure they were armed appropriately. He ordered all three companies of the 1st Battalion to readiness. He made one more fateful decision. Six months earlier, White Beach had taken delivery of two US Army Stryker vehicle-based Maneuver-Short-Range Air Defense systems. These were mobile armored missile-launch vehicles which tied the latest Stinger missiles to a highly capable Rada multi-mission radar capable of tracking multiple fast-moving air targets. The Stryker platform was due for deployment with the Marines in the next two years. The US Army operators who had shipped in with their vehicles had been training their Marine counterparts in their use and were still on-base, as were their vehicles.

With the Aegis cruiser *Port Royal* currently on exercises out in the Pacific, White Beach was without meaningful air defense cover. A fact which would not have escaped the attention of anyone planning a move against White Beach. Collins immediately ordered the Strykers' combined Army and Marine crew members to bring their systems online to monitor the airspace over White Beach. Stryker 1 was hidden in scrubland at the east end of the base, positioned to protect the main administrative center, where the bulk of Navy and Marine support personnel worked. Stryker 2 moved to the western end of the base, in a protected position beside the port facilities, to protect the dock infrastructure and the naval vessels present. The two mobile anti-air units got into place at around 1500 hours, Japan Standard Time. Collins made sure they were very clear about their rules of engagement. *Any* incursion into US airspace by foreign military aircraft was to be regarded as hostile.

If you drew a straight line from one Stryker to the other, you had the exact line of approach of Li Chen's force of six *Snow Falcon* attack aircraft. And as the two Strykers shook hands digitally and linked data, Chen's aircraft were ten minutes out.

Ultimatum

Strange things happen in war, Takuya Kato knew that. And small events can have long-reaching consequences. Li Chen had read for him the translated extract from his grandfather's diary about his release from captivity. The decision by an American pilot to free his great-grandfather, rather than simply execute him, was proof that the decision of men in war can echo through the years. Tadao Kato had done as the American had suggested and hidden in the nearby jungle until Japanese troops arrived at the Mingaladon airfield to find it had been abandoned. Then he had walked out, made contact, and set about the business of organizing for the aircraft and support staff of his 64th Sentai to transfer from Thailand to their new base in Burma.

After getting his squadron organized, Tadao Kato had made the unusually sentimental decision to take five days' leave and visit his wife and daughter in Asahikawa, Hokkaidō. His wife had become pregnant on that trip and given birth to a son, Takuya Kato's grandfather. So, but for the decision of the American not to execute his prisoner, Takuya would never have been born.

That decision made no sense to Takuya. He had left alive a Japanese officer who was now familiar with the operations of Mingaladon, who held valuable intelligence about the size and strength of the remaining British air forces in Burma, and who could use that to quickly get his squadron transferred and operational. Worse, he had freed his enemy knowing that within days or weeks he would be back in the air, killing British pilots again. Takuya was sure that his great-grandfather, if the roles were reversed, would not have done the same. *How about you, Takuya?* he asked himself. *What would you have done?*

Takuya had never been at war, never had a similar dilemma. Probably the same as the American, he reasoned. It was impossible to know, though, until it is your time to choose, he decided.

What he was about to do was the closest he had come to an act of war.

"Target waypoint coming up on your tac monitors," Chen said over the radio. "Starting ingress. Stay in formation-keeping mode. I will light my tail at target minus five miles and we will cross over White Beach at 1,000 meters," she said, unable to keep the excitement out of her voice. "Mangshe Six, on my mark, you will break to your holding position and begin jamming."

Kato was 'Mangshe', or Python, Six. His role was purely that of an observer, but Chen had decided that didn't preclude him from helping out to the extent he could, so his *Snow Falcon* had been fitted with an Electronic Countermeasures, or ECM, pod and he reached forward to his weapons system screen to arm it, getting ready to light it up. It was expected to be able to blind the antiquated ship-borne radars below easily, but testing that hypothesis was one of the objectives of this mission, so his role was not entirely passive.

A second later, Chen began her waypoint countdown. "Mangshe One to Mangshe Six, three, two, one … *mark!*"

Kato had one hand on his joystick and the other on his throttle, but before he could react, the *Snow Falcon*'s AI had pulled his aircraft into a steep climb from 500 meters to 2,000, where it leveled out and then began following a planned racetrack patrol position over western Okinawa. *This isn't flying*, Kato told himself. *I'm just along for the ride. A jockey on a racehorse has more work to do than this!*

It wasn't entirely true. As Chen had taken pains to explain to him, the *Snow Falcon*'s pilot was still its weapons and payload systems operator. That role had not been trusted to the AI. So the decision to initiate jamming was still his. He had armed the ECM pod and chose the multi-band jamming mode. "Mangshe Six, initiating jamming," he reported. His screen icons changed from yellow to green, showing an approximate area of effect covering an area of ten square miles around White Beach. "Green on jamming," he said. "You are clear to ingress, Mangshe One."

"Lighting afterburner. Starting our run," Chen said.

She felt an unfamiliar combination of trepidation and exhilaration and allowed herself a completely unorthodox communication. "Mangshe flight, stay tight, let's rattle some windows!"

Bunny ran back into the DARPA lab after the briefing to find Kyle and Kevin arguing. Chuck was absorbed by something on a wall screen on which they were running a simple defense forces public news feed.

"We need a downlink to the Stingray before we can try anything," Kyle was explaining emphatically. "There are a million things we could try, but without a satellite link it's like talking to yourself…"

O'Hare was sorting task priority in her head. White Beach was being put on a war footing by Collins, but she had to focus on the task at hand, which was regaining contact with her Stingray. She wanted the unhelpfully enigmatic Charles Harford out of her lab. She wanted Kyle focused on alternative scenarios to cyber-attack. She wanted …

"Uh, guys? Sorry, you have to see this," Chuck said, turning around. "It's the Japan 24 News Channel," he said, pointing up at the big screen on the wall. He looked shaken.

They all turned to look at the wall and saw ticker-tape rolling across the screen, which was showing TV drone or helicopter footage of the very base she was standing in, with thousands of civilian protesters at the gates waving placards.

BREAKING NEWS … the ticker-tape read. JAPANESE GOVERNMENT DEMANDS IMMEDIATE WITHDRAWAL OF LAST REMAINING US TROOPS FROM OKINAWA … CIVILIAN PROTESTERS MARCH ON WHITE BEACH … DEADLINE FOR START OF WITHDRAWAL SET FOR 36 HOURS.

Kevin frowned. "What 'civilian protesters'?" he asked. He called up a standard security feed on one of his screens, accessible to all key systems operators, which showed vision from surveillance cameras across the base. He pointed at the main entrance cameras, which showed nothing but a couple of bored Marine MPs standing at the boom gates, checking a car.

She heard Collins' voice from the briefing booming in her head: China putting its Eastern Theater forces on alert, the Sino-Japanese fleet heading south, local Japanese ground and naval forces being mobilized, her Stingray dropping off the grid, and now *this* ...

O'Hare felt as though she was watching a row of dominos fall. If the 'civilian protesters' weren't already at the gates of White Beach, she was willing to bet they were being loaded aboard buses by the central government right now, given ready-made placards and a nice packed lunch, with a song sheet of angry demands they could practice on the way from Naha city.

And unless she was very much mistaken, the Japanese government ultimatum would be backed with tanks and...

Sure enough, the next domino fell. She heard the faint rumble of approaching jet aircraft.

"Into the graving dock!" she yelled. Kyle and Kevin just stared at her as though she had lost her mind. Chuck was already running. She grabbed Kyle by the shoulder and pushed him roughly toward the Stingray dry dock and hauled Kevin bodily out of his chair. "I said MOVE!" she yelled. "NOW!'"

Stryker 2 was the first to pick up the Chinese stealth fighters on the display of its Rada hemispheric radar unit. The Israeli-made Rada sensors were mounted on a telescopic stand at the rear of the armored Stryker vehicle, giving them 20-mile, 360-degree coverage of the airspace around and above the base. They were networked, so that the operators in both vehicles shared data on target returns and their onboard AIs coordinated target allocation to maximize the likelihood of a successful engagement by targeting attacking aircraft or cruise missiles with air-air missiles fired from both positions on the base simultaneously.

The Rada was optimized to detect low-flying subsonic cruise missiles, ballistic missiles in the last phase of their descent, and enemy attack aircraft, up to and including fifth-generation stealth.

Like the Chinese *Snow Falcon*.

As Takuya Kato's onboard AI kicked his aircraft up to 2,000 meters and Li Chen lit the afterburners on her five remaining *Snow Falcons* to bring them screaming over White Beach at an eardrum-pounding Mach 1.4, the threat displays inside the two Stryker vehicles went crazy. Their commanders had very unambiguous orders. There was a standing no-fly zone over White Beach, which had been agreed with Japanese authorities decades ago and never rescinded, despite the US troop draw-down. If an unidentified aircraft crossed the ten-mile no-fly perimeter and the Stryker commander assessed it to be a threat, he was authorized to engage and shoot it down. Given what he had just been told by intelligence staff, Collins had immediately made sure his anti-air crews were *very* clear about their rules of engagement.

Inside Stryker 2, US Army Major Pharrell Burdett took two seconds to run his eyes across his threat panel one last time. "Missiles up!" he ordered, bringing his Stinger launcher online. He had one unidentified aircraft at 10,000 feet, radiating jamming energy like a second sun, but not at a strength which degraded the ability of his frequency-hopping Rada transmitter to lock up incoming aircraft. And he had five unidentified 'fast movers' closing on his position from the west at 5,000 feet and at supersonic speed. The profile of the incoming aircraft was anything but stealth – it was like they *wanted* to be seen. Well, he'd seen them alright. "Lock all targets and fire!" he yelled.

From the two Stryker vehicles at opposite ends of the base, twelve Stinger missiles punched out of their tubes and sped west.

The Raytheon Stinger missile had proven itself on battlefields across the world for several decades and was still the mainstay of the US low-level anti-air inventory. The newer version mounted on the Stryker vehicles was the Mark-K, which in addition to the sensors on its warhead took its targeting from the vehicles' radar. Another difference to the earlier marques of the missile was that it had a proximity detonation fuse – it only needed to be near its target to kill it.

Li Chen had set Kato the secondary mission objective of testing whether the anti-air radar covering White Beach could get a lock on their fifth-generation stealth aircraft at high speeds. Secondly, the mission was intended to test the effectiveness of the electronic countermeasures, or jamming, system mounted in a pod on Kato's *Snow Falcon*. He achieved both objectives within seconds of entering the target area, but not in the way he hoped.

As his *Snow Falcon* fighter popped up over White Beach and leveled out at 10,000 feet, his radar warning receiver began beeping, indicating he was being targeted by active radar. He had expected that and the readout on his ECM system showed it was adapting its radiation profile to match and block the frequency of the search radar below.

It was too slow.

The steady beeping in Kato's ears became a single flatline wail and the missile launch warning klaxon sounded in his cockpit! He was in the process of zooming his ECM screen to see if he could tweak the jamming profile manually when the klaxon went off, his combat AI took control of his aircraft, pulled the nose up and punched in full afterburner, sending his helmeted head slamming into the headrest on his seat. The sudden and massive acceleration made his body feel like it was being pushed flat by an invisible hand. No! It was the wrong maneuver! His tail would be lit up like a supernova, making the ideal target for the heat-seeking missiles zooming up toward him!

The voices of the Chinese pilots in Chen's flight were yammering in his ears, but he ignored them. He had his own problems.

As his fighter clawed at the sky, passing quickly through 11,000 feet, then 11,500, Kato tried to reach forward to disengage the AI pilot and take control of his doomed fighter, but the pressure on his arms and chest was too great and all he could do was flail his hands uselessly toward the instrument console. He should be rolling inverted, firing silver foil chaff and flares, turning toward the missile to give it a more difficult interception angle! This was no exercise, he was going to *die*, dammit!!

He heard an explosion right behind him, but his machine kept plowing upwards. His ejection seat handle was placed so it could be reached no matter what forces the pilot was being subjected to and he dropped his hand and grabbed it tightly. The readout in his visor showed his machine screaming into the sky still, passing 12,000 … 12,500. Another explosion, closer this time! The muscles in his arm contracted … then the missile warning klaxon stopped wailing in his ears! The *Snow Falcon* rolled onto its side and leveled out, resuming a racetrack circuit over White Beach at 15,000 feet, and he slumped forward in his harness, heart racing, panting for breath. He looked at the data scrolling across his helmet visor and realized the AI had saved him.

Where he would have made a standard evasive maneuver to dodge the missiles fired at him, the AI had instantaneously recognized them as low-altitude Stinger-K missiles with a max ceiling of only 12,000 feet. He'd been circling over White Beach at 10,000 feet when they were fired and the *Snow Falcon* AI calculated in a split second that it could outclimb the missiles, even though they were faster, because it only had to get him 2,500 feet higher to put him out of range. With full afterburner, that would only take him four seconds, where the missiles below would take seven seconds to climb to 10,000 feet. They were never in danger of hitting him and had detonated safely behind him, in his wake.

It was very possible that if he'd done as his instinct and training had commanded him, he would be dead.

Don't try to fly the *Snow Falcon*, Kato, he told himself through gritted teeth. You're just along for the ride.

For the first time in a long two minutes, he turned his attention to the voices of his fellow pilots on comms and the tactical display on his instrument panel showing their relative positions. The Chinese formation had been scattered and was trying to reform out to sea, east of White Beach and out of range of the enemy Stingers. Paging through the data record he could see no fewer than a dozen missiles had been fired at the six Chinese aircraft!! He did a quick manual count of the icons on his screen.

One of the Chinese *Snow Falcon*s was *down*.

Noriko Fukada, standing in her beloved cactus nursery, knew what war sounded like.

As a child, cowering in the cellar of their apartments during the American invasion, she had heard the scream of American 16-inch shells, fired by their battleships offshore, as they reduced her village to smoking splinters. She had learned to tell the difference between incoming naval fire and the drone of American bombers overhead that presaged the fall of whistling death from above. She even learned to tell the difference between the whistle a bomb made as it fell to earth and the singing wail of wind through the wire stays of the American dive bombers. She had heard and seen Japanese and American aircraft dueling in the skies overhead and coming down in flames, to flatten houses, schools, and hospitals.

As the *Snow Falcon* from Li Chen's 'reconnaissance' flight broke into two pieces and its pilot ejected, the tail section continued over the base, over White Beach and into the welcoming waters of the Pacific, already a graveyard to ships and aircraft from a nearly forgotten war. The force of the explosion that ripped the *Snow Falcon* apart pointed the bird-like nose and wing section of the fuselage at the sky and it looped back up, over the base and northwest, turning end over end as it reached apex and then began to fall from the sky. Trailing blazing fuel, still carrying a full payload of air-to-air and air-to-ground missiles in its belly, it plowed through the roof of the Mega Don Quijote Uruma Shopping Center five blocks away from Noriko Fukada and detonated.

She had been repotting a Faucaria hybrid, together with a lovely young man called Suzuki from the horticulture school, when they had heard the sound of low-flying jet aircraft somewhere over White Beach. There had come a moment of silence, then a loud report high in the sky that made them look up, but they could see nothing. A few seconds later, the sound of an enormous explosion reached their ears. The fiberglass walls of the nursery began rattling. Suzuki-san's head snapped around. "What is that?" A second explosion came quickly on the heels of the first, even louder this time, and Suzuki crouched, pulling at Noriko's dress, trying to tug her down beside him. "Get down, grandmother!" he said. "Terrorists!"

Noriko cocked her head, listening to the dying rumble. Another explosion, smaller this time. Her hearing was not what it used to be, but it was good enough. She batted his hand away. "Those were aircraft. And the explosion is over at the shopping center," she said. "You are safe enough here."

He stood. Somewhere inside the Kouwa Gardens retail shop, a woman screamed.

Suzuki was hopping from one foot to the other. "We should see what is happening. Look!" he said, pointing over the roof of the nursery to where a column of foul black smoke was rising.

Noriko put a hand on his arm. "You go. I will finish up here."

As he put down his apron and gloves, alarms started wailing.

She watched him run off. More sirens. The sound of jet aircraft, then explosions and alarms.

She decided she would finish for the day. There was a convenience store on the corner of her apartment block. It would probably be a good idea to stock up on water and canned food.

"Form on me!" Li Chen ordered over the radio and keyed the command into her tactical unit that would call her remaining aircraft to her. She was currently holding at 20,000 feet, ten miles east-northeast of Okinawa's Miyagi Island. On the horizon, Okinawa was a sliver of green and gray land and a column of smoke from her downed *Snow Falcon* was clearly visible. She had seen the pilot, a young lieutenant, eject safely, but had no idea whether he had survived the automatic ejection. One in ten ejections resulted in a broken back or neck from the force of the rocket boosters in the pilot's seat and ejecting over an urban area like White Beach was fraught with danger from high-rise buildings to electrical wires. If his momentum had carried him out to sea, he could have hit the water unconscious or incapacitated and drowned. Chinese pilots had emergency beacons and position locators as standard equipment in their flight suits, so she would know soon enough.

As her flight formed up behind her, she counted them to be sure the reality matched the data on her tactical display. Two … three … where was Kato? Ah, there, sliding in from low on her starboard now, joining the flight where her missing pilot should be. Four.

One man down. She hammered the perspex above her head with her fist. *Damn those hot-headed Americans! Did they want war?*

She had followed her orders to the letter, despite her personal doubts. A low-level run right over the top of a US Navy base at the precise moment they were issued with an ultimatum by the Japanese Government to withdraw? It was more than an act of intimidation; in Chen's mind it was lunacy. But she had swallowed her doubts and planned her mission carefully. Her worries weren't lessened by the addition of the Japanese pilot to her tasking, but she had taken that in her stride too. She reviewed her performance, looking for the flaws that her superiors would be certain to find on her return.

The Japanese pilot Kato had initiated jamming before she began her ingress, she had confirmed that. She had reviewed the available intelligence, none of which indicated that the US base was protected with sophisticated low-level anti-air defenses. She had approached the American base at high speed but with her weapons bays closed and her landing lights on – anyone watching their approach from the ground, with the weakest of binoculars, could have seen they were not making an attack run!

"Your orders, Comrade Captain?" her wingman asked. She'd been leading the flight on an aimless racetrack circuit for the last 30 seconds. They were carrying ground-to-air weapons and could easily respond to the unprovoked attack on her pilot. But she knew to do so would be overstepping the bounds of her authority. "Our mission is complete, Japanese search and rescue forces will respond to the downed pilot's beacon. We will return to the *Liaoning*," she said curtly. *But I suspect we will be back*, she told herself.

Imperial Mandate

Mitsuko Naishinnō was shaking with anger and nearly dropped the tablet on which she was reading Santoshi's report on the casualties from the crash of the Chinese fighter aircraft on Okinawa.

Twelve dead! Thirteen including the Chinese pilot, who had drowned before a coast guard vessel could reach him. What had the fools been playing at? What were Chinese aircraft even doing in Japanese airspace, let alone flying over a US naval base? Twelve civilians dead. Japanese civilians. Her people!

Her father had been right. On his deathbed, riddled with inoperable cancer caused by a refusal to give up smoking his cherished French cigarettes, he had called her to his side. He had instructed his physician to reduce his dosage of painkillers and give him a shot of ephedrine so that he could speak to her with a clear mind. He had also insisted that he speak with her alone – it was not to be a conversation for the historical record.

It had been a beautiful spring morning and light was streaming in through the open windows of his bedroom. She found him propped up in his bed, looking for all the world like a living skeleton, but behaving like his old self, bed littered with papers and correspondence.

She waited at the foot of his bed until he was finished reading the letter in his hand and noticed her. "Ah, Mitsuko-chan," he said, using the informal term of endearment. "Princess Mitsuko-chan, *Empress* Mitsuko Naishinnō, come, sit here," he said and pushed some papers aside to make room. She noticed he took each breath as though it was a gulp of water; breathing, swallowing, breathing and swallowing. He reached out and took her hand. "I am going to die today," he said.

"You said that yesterday," she pointed out.

"Yes."

"And the day before, and the day before that …"

He smiled. "Yes, and one day I will be right." He struggled to sit straighter and she fluffed up the pillows behind him to help him, then sat down again. He reached for a green sheet of paper and handed it to her. She recognized it as a report from Santoshi, his head of imperial security. "Read it later," he said. "For now, listen."

She put the paper down again. "Yes, father."

"You will be a formidable Empress, I am sure," he said. "You have a good heart and a quick mind and I know the Empire is in the best of hands with you as its guardian."

"Yes, father."

"I ask only three things of you. Two we have already spoken of."

She nodded. "I must be better at listening to the counsel of others, and consider they may be right. And I must marry."

He patted her hand. "I did not say that. I said you must fall in love. And then you must marry and produce an heir to stop my unctuous brother's brats from ascending to the Chrysanthemum Throne." The long sentence tired him and he took a couple of deep breaths. "You are not getting younger."

It was a theme her mother had worn thin before her death and she nodded patiently. She imagined she might say the same one day to her own daughter, if she ever had one.

He coughed. "There is one more thing. Your sacred duty."

To defend the Empire against all threats, internal or external. She had grown up with the words. But she had not expected what he was about to say. "Despite what our politicians may care to believe, this House does not exist to rubber-stamp their treachery."

"Treachery, father?"

"Listen," he said impatiently. "You are a direct descendant of the Emperor Meiji, Mutsuhito, the sixteen-year-old emperor who ended the rule of the Tokugawa Shogunate, established the new capital in Tokyo and rid Japan of the influence of foreign meddling." He paused, gathering his strength, and continued. "He did not accept to sit on the sidelines and watch his country fall into foreign hands.

He sat in Cabinet meetings, issued edicts for the reform of industry, housing, and the military. He saw the coming threat from China and modernized our armed forces to be ready for it, with the result that Japan was victorious in two wars with China."

Mitsuko had never been gifted with an abundance of patience, and her father had a tendency to ramble under the influence of the painkillers. It was not the first time he had held forth on the subject of Emperor Meiji. Coupled with his labored breathing, the slowness of his speech was exasperating, and she tried to gently nudge him back on track.

"Yes, father. And how is this relevant to my duty?"

"It is *relevant...*" he said, lifting a finger, "to how you perform your duty as regent and protector of this Empire. I am bidding you to take Mutsuhito as your spiritual guide. You share a similar nature, a similar passion. In dilemmas of State, I bid you ask yourself, what would Mutsuhito, the Emperor Meiji, do in this situation." He pointed at the green paper he had handed her. "Ask yourself later," he said. "When you read that report." He had taken a deep breath and squeezed her hand tightly. "Our *governments*," he almost spat the word, "have allowed us to become weak. Mutsuhito rid Japan of the influence of the British, the Americans, and the Russians. For most of my rule, we have stayed free of foreign interference. Now it will fall to you, Mitsuko-chan, to rid Japan of the growing influence of China. This is your sacred duty."

The green paper had been a report from a Japanese National Security Agency source inside the Central Military Commission of the Chinese government. It relayed the content of a conversation between the Chinese Minister of National Defense and a foreign diplomat, who had asked him how the Japanese Imperial Palace had reacted to the signing of the new mutual defense treaty between China and Japan. "I don't know," the Chinese Minister had replied. "And I have not asked. The Japanese Emperor is like the flower on top of a wedding cake. Decoration only."

The anger she had felt reading those words – an anger her father had known she would feel – flooded her mind again. She slammed the tablet she had been reading down on the low table in front of her, not caring if she smashed it. It fell to the floor. The sound

185

echoed across the wooden floors of the residence and through its thin walls. She was still living in her private villa on the grounds of the Akasaka Palace; she wouldn't move into the Palace itself until her formal confirmation as Empress, at the conclusion of the period of mourning. It was to have been a happy, historic moment designed to lift the grief of the nation – the ascension of the first-ever *Empress* to the Chrysanthemum Throne. Now this! Well, she had done as her father bid her. She had asked herself, what would her ancestor Mutsuhito have done in this situation? And she had her answer.

As though summoned by the unmistakable echoes of her anger, the Head of Imperial Security appeared in the doorway and bowed. He had with him a small folder.

"Come in, Santoshi-san," she said. "What news from Takuya?"

The balding man who had started his career in the Imperial House as Mitsuko's bodyguard was in his late sixties now and he shuffled across the parquet floor to sit opposite his Empress. He had always been proud of his physique but had finally given in to the imperatives of age and though he still practiced Tai Chi religiously, he had developed a small potbelly which Mitsuko had joked suited his grandfatherly aspect. He had not been amused at her jibe. He put the folder on the table between them and opened it to reveal a sheaf of papers, but he remained stiffly standing. Unlike her, he shunned digital communications, not trusting his secrets to the ether.

"Lieutenant Kato reports that he took part in the Chinese overflight of White Beach, under orders from Chinese mission planners who wanted a Japanese pilot along to legitimize the incursion into Japanese airspace. He was interviewed on camera before the flight," the man said softly. He would be as angry as Mitsuko inside, she knew that, but he would never show it.

"Yes, I saw him on the news reports. They would turn my Royal Liaison into a puppet on a VR show?" she said. "Was Takuya able to tell you the intention behind this insane attack?"

"Yes. He said it was not an attack, as such. It was intended as intimidation, timed to coincide with the demand for US forces to abandon their base at White Beach. A 'reconnaissance' mission, according to Lieutenant Kato. But since the Chinese pilot was downed, two of three attack squadrons on the *Liaoning* are now being armed and fueled. That was all the information he sent. He believes China is now planning a retaliatory strike." He put aside the transcription of the burst transmission from the *Liaoning* and lifted up another paper. "There is more, Empress…"

"More than that?" she pointed at the tablet lying on the floor.

"I did not want to commit it to a report," he said. "A highly placed source in the Chinese Cabinet reached out to us through a back channel. I think they were trying to ensure the Imperial Palace was not caught off guard by these actions…"

"Off guard!" she began. "Chinese warplanes over Okinawa and …"

"Princess, if I may," Santoshi continued. "The Cabinet source said he wanted to reassure the Imperial House that China had no intention of provoking an 'unrestricted' military conflict with the USA. China was simply assisting its new ally, in response to a direct request from the Japanese Government, and…"

"Lies!" she said. "If that were the case, they would be mourning the loss of their pilot, apologizing for the deaths of our citizens, but instead they are preparing a 'retaliatory strike'! First they ignore us, now they lie to our faces!"

"Yes, Princess," Santoshi acknowledged quietly.

"Yes?" she rounded on him. "You agree?! The Chinese are lying to us?!"

"Yes, Princess, they are," the old man said. "We have our own sources within the offices of the Chinese Cabinet and inside their Defense Department. I did not bring these reports to your attention until recent events confirmed their accuracy, but China's intentions now are clear," he said. "And they are not acting alone."

She felt a roiling heat boiling in her chest, felt her breathing quicken and closed her eyes until it had subsided, as Santoshi-san had taught her. He knew his mistress well and waited until she opened her eyes again and her breathing had steadied.

"Sit, Santoshi-san. Tell me what you know," she commanded.

He sat and pulled his papers toward him, but did not refer to them. Clearly he knew intimately what was in them. "China's Eastern Forces Commander, General Zhao Jian, is a known adherent of the Sun Tzu principle that 'to subdue the enemy without fighting is the acme of skill.' He showed in the carefully managed conflict with South Korea that he is not afraid to prepare his forces for war, but his nature is first to try to achieve the objectives given him through bluff, bluster, bullying, and deception." The old man pulled a photograph of the Chinese General out of his folder and slid it across the table to her. "This is the face of our Empire's true enemy."

She studied it. The Chinese General appeared to be in his early fifties, with a plain round face and thick black hair – young for such a weighty command. From that she judged he must be both competent and well connected. "And which enemy does he hope to subdue without fighting? Japan?"

"Not Japan," Santoshi said. "Taiwan."

"Ah," Mitsuko sighed. "It had to come, sooner or later. I had hoped it would not be during my reign."

"And I had hoped it would not be in my lifetime," Santoshi admitted. "But here we are. Our agents have been telling us for several years that Premier Xi Ping has made many statements to his General Staff and Cabinet that he does not expect to see the Province of Taiwan celebrate 100 years of resistance to Beijing."

"And that centenary would be in … 2049? A mere sixteen years. They have been patient, but the clock is ticking," she observed.

"Indeed," Santoshi agreed. "Pro-unification sentiment is growing on Taiwan and among the opposition parties, the pro-Beijing Kuomintang party now has 42 of the 113 seats in Taiwan's Parliament, growing with each election. But as the centenary of independence from China approaches, anti-Beijing sentiment will increase."

"China must act soon, while it has political momentum," she agreed.

"Yes, Zhao Jian has crafted what he calls a 'staged strategy' to support the pro-unification movement on Taiwan by showing that the US can no longer be relied on to come to their defense. By forcing the US to withdraw from Okinawa once and for all, they would leave the US with no military presence in the region. The sight of the US Navy pulling its Marines and ships back to Guam or Pearl Harbor, combined with the growing pressure of sanctions and the new Sino-Japanese alliance, is expected to be enough to enable the Kuomintang to move a vote of no confidence in the ruling Democratic Progressive Party government. China has mobilized its Eastern Army and is ready to parachute paramilitary forces onto Taiwan in support, but they are hoping that a limited conflict with the USA over Okinawa, economic sanctions, and sustained geopolitical pressure will force Taiwan into reunification talks, without the need for an invasion." He folded his arms. "Inside the Cabinet they call this ambition, 'rìluò lù jīnpílijìn' – the end of the sunset road."

"Such a lofty and noble purpose," Mitsuko sneered. "The *peaceful* conquest of Taiwan."

"Reunification of Taiwan," Santoshi corrected her. "The One China policy has…"

"Before you continue," she interrupted, with ice in her voice, "who in our government authorized the demand for a full US withdrawal? Who 'requested' Chinese military assistance on Okinawa?"

Her question had caught Santoshi mid-sentence and he was never quick to change gears. He paused momentarily, placed his hands in his lap and turned to the answer. "Prime Minister Koizumi, I am told, authorized it personally," Santoshi said carefully. "The Japan Self-Defense Forces General Staff however assured me that they had no advance knowledge of the Chinese fighter action." He paused. "Given what our Cabinet source in Beijing has told us, I do not believe them. Someone in our own Self-Defense Forces approved the flight plan for that Chinese fighter overflight." He reached into his folder and pulled out a page which he laid down in front of Mitsuko, allowing her time to scan the contents. It was a summary of intel from Imperial Palace sources inside the Japanese Self-Defense Force Ground and Naval Forces.

"This is treason!" Mitsuko gasped, unable to believe what she was reading. "Without precedent! The General Staff have…"

"Acted on their own authority," Santoshi finished for her. "Which is, unfortunately, *not* without precedent, Princess." He looked at her with sad eyes. "A hundred years ago, the Kwantung Army under General Honjo invaded China without orders from either the government in Tokyo or the Palace. In 1941, Emperor Hirohito did not give his assent to the attack on Pearl Harbor. He was merely informed of it by Prime Minister Tojo, when it was too late to stop."

"This is not the 20th Century!" Mitsuko said in a tightly controlled tone. "And I am not a Hirohito, who nods when he is told to nod. I will not be dictated to!"

Santoshi stayed quiet, allowing his mistress time to think. He knew her moods and knew she would not be receptive to his counsel in this.

She picked up the intelligence report Santoshi had given her again and summarized the information she had been reading. "The 15th Infantry Brigade on Okinawa has been ordered from its base in Naha to encircle the US base at White Beach. Buses have been dispatched to round up civilians to stage protests outside the gates of the base to make it look to the world like the population supports the demand for the US to leave…"

"The population on Okinawa has long been ambivalent about the US presence," Santoshi offered.

"They are being used as human shields," Mitsuko said sharply, "placed by cowardly generals between American Marines and Japanese troops!" She looked down at the paper again. "The destroyers of the 13th Escort Squadron have been ordered east of White Beach to intercept any US naval vessels trying to enter Japanese waters." She frowned. "How is the US supposed to get its personnel out of Okinawa if it is blocked from sailing them out?"

"My staff conclude that the blockade is intended to delay the evacuation of the US 3rd Marine Regiment until it is expedient and in the meantime heighten the media humiliation of the USA by showing it is powerless to defend its troops."

"Powerless?!" Mitsuko exclaimed, looking down at the paper. "They have powerful warships parked 50 miles off our coast, no doubt waiting to see what we are planning. They have announced on news networks they are diverting their *GW Bush* carrier taskforce to Okinawa from Pearl Harbor, and it will arrive in five days!" She looked up again at Santoshi. "There is nothing here about our submarine force. It would not surprise me if the idiots have also sent our submarines out to intercept the American fleet!"

"All of our operational submarines are committed to the *Liaoning* and *Izumo* strike group, I believe," Santoshi said.

"Then if not us, China must have a plan, which I suspect involves our joint strike group. How realistic is this Chinese strategy of 'peaceful conquest'?" Mitsuko asked. "The US does not need a base on Okinawa to come to the aid of Taiwan."

"It is the symbolism, Princess," Santoshi explained. "The political situation in Taiwan is on a knife-edge. Taiwan has been crippled by Chinese economic sanctions and is riven with internal division. Taipei's only remaining ally is the USA, but since Korean reunification it no longer has a significant footprint in the Pacific. The China-Japan mutual defense pact has shaken faith in the USA among Taiwanese politicians and its people."

"The US pulling its troops out of Okinawa would be enough to cause the fall of the government in Taipei and a new government which would support reunification?" she asked.

"That is, as I said, General Zhao Jian's grand plan," Santoshi nodded.

"And China gets it all." Mitsuko shook her head. "Hong Kong, Taiwan, and the mainland reunited and Japan as a vassal state. Complete hegemony over the western Pacific." She put the paper down and pursed her lips. "Tell me, Santoshi-san, where do you think the limits of my power reach with respect to elected governments and military officers?"

Santoshi's eyes widened. It was a question he had never expected to be asked, even under these circumstances. "Princess, I … section 6 of the constitution gives you the power to appoint the Prime Minister, but only with the 'advice and approval of the Cabinet'. And the Imperial House has no power over the armed forces."

"If I can appoint, I must be able to dismiss?" she asked innocently.

"It … I … that is unlikely, and has never been tested," he stammered.

She arched her eyebrows. "You are right. It has not. Yet." Reaching down to the floor, she picked up the tablet that had fallen there. It was still working. "I have, though an intermediary, received independent constitutional legal advice from five experts of the highest standing. You realize of course, Santoshi-san, that under section 9, the constitution of Japan still forbids war as a means to resolve disputes over matters of State? Despite our idiotic mutual defense treaty with China, no government has succeeded in changing that."

"Yes, Princess," Santoshi said carefully.

"Empress, dear adviser," she corrected him gently. "Though the ceremony is yet to be held, I became Empress on the day of my father's death. I have also confirmed that small legal point."

"Yes, *Empress*." He bowed deeply in humiliation at his error.

Mitsuko continued. "I have also confirmed that section 7 of the constitution grants me significant powers as head of state…"

"Which may only be executed with the approval of Cabinet…" Santoshi interjected.

"And what, Santoshi-san, applies if there is no Cabinet?"

Santoshi frowned. "I do not follow, Empress."

"You will," Mitsuko said. She tapped her tablet. "I have sent the edicts to your assistant to print for you. But they are straightforward. As allowed under section 6 of the constitution, I have decided to appoint a new government. That means *'post hoc ergo propter hoc'*, as my legal advisers put it, I have dissolved the Diet and thereby the Cabinet, removing all government ministers and the Prime Minister from their positions of authority, effective immediately upon publication." Santoshi paled, but Mitsuko continued. "New elections will be held in forty days. I will soon go live on national broadcasters to announce that the reason for this decision was the failure of the government to respect article 9 of the constitution, which forbids Japan from participating in acts of war, such as we have just witnessed over Okinawa." She pointed at his folder. "The Chinese were unwise to include one of our own pilots in their attack on the US base. It gives me the legal basis I was looking for to remove this traitorous government. These fools have over-reached. Their latest military mobilizations on Okinawa, when they come to light, will only strengthen my hand. I will also direct that the General Staff of the Ground, Naval, and Air Forces be stood down from their duties, forthwith, for conspiracy to support China in acts of war."

"Empress, this … you cannot…" Santoshi stuttered. "The Imperial House is *above* politics."

"It has not always been so. And our politicians and their generals will soon learn what that means," she said.

"Interference by the Imperial House in the business of government is not only not done, it is simply not allowed!" he continued. He was not comfortable challenging his ward, but never had she spoken so recklessly!

"The Emperor Meiji did not hesitate to confront the Shogunate when it betrayed Japan, Santoshi-san, and I do not plan to sit by and let my country become a Chinese dependency. My expert advice says you are wrong," she said, pointing at the tablet. "Section 99 of the constitution, often forgotten, treated by most as an afterthought, *commands* the Emperor or Regent – " she smiled, "that's me – and all other public officials – that's the General Staff of the Self-Defense Forces – to uphold the constitution. Therefore, where they do not, it falls to me to do so and I will do so by all the means in my power."

"But … the government … the people … they will…"

"Rise up against their Empress?" She glared at him with ice-cold eyes. "Ignore her, as politicians and generals have been ignoring their emperors for more than a century? At the behest of *China*?"

He swallowed heavily.

"You have assured me on many occasions, Santoshi-san, that the love of the people for their Princess is strong. Stronger than it was for my father, stronger than for any regent in a hundred years. That they see me as the 'people's regent', you said."

He nodded. "Yes, Empress."

"Then now is the time for us to see if you were right," she said. She waited as he sat staring at her, dumbfounded. "You are excused, Santoshi-san. Your first priority is to mobilize the Imperial Guard to ensure the loyalty of our internal security and police forces remains with the Imperial House." From the pocket of her jacket she pulled a piece of rolled-up paper. She held it out to him and he reached for it, but she hesitated before finally handing it to him. "Your second priority is to send this message to Lieutenant Kato on the *Liaoning*."

Swings and Roundabouts

Bunny O'Hare had also been surrounded by dumbfounded faces. Crouched down in the graving dock in the middle of their lab, she'd heard the unmistakable *whoosh* of multiple missiles being fired just a few hundred yards away. Instinctively, she'd reached for Kyle's head and pushed it down below the level of the floor and ducked lower herself. At that moment the sonic boom of the jets passing close overhead had thundered through the walls of the lab, rattling the corrugated metal, and one of the gantries against the wall toppled to the concrete floor with a bone-jarring crash and metallic clatter of loose tools. She'd waited for the explosion of a ground-penetrating bomb to sweep away the walls and roof.

She'd heard an explosion, but it was far away and seemed to her trained ear to have happened high above ground, not down among the bilge water where they were cowering. She'd cautiously stuck her head up. The hangar had been full of dust and rust from the gantry that had collapsed, but the lab was otherwise intact.

She'd made a quick inventory of her own arms and limbs, then checked her people. Kyle and Kevin were shaken but unharmed. Chuck had blood on his face and was dabbing his forehead with a sleeve.

"Hit my damn head on the edge as I was diving in," he'd said. "Feel a bit queasy."

She looked him over. "Probably concussion," she'd said. "Kevin, Kyle, you stay down here. I'm taking Chuck to the infirmary." He looked as shaken as she felt.

The base was thrumming with urgent activity and getting through all the vehicle and foot traffic hadn't been easy. On the way back from delivering Chuck to a medic, she'd stopped to make a call. At that moment, she had a million tasks on her mind, but only one person.

Noriko.

Since striking up a friendship over multiple visits to the Kouwa Gardens Nursery (first to buy a cactus, then to replace it after it died, then to explain that the replacement was not looking too well, at which point 103-year-old Noriko Fukada had insisted on visiting O'Hare at home to see exactly how it was she seemed able to kill an unkillable plant) she had fallen into a routine of visiting with the old woman on the first Sunday of each month. They would have a very formal talk over tea, with Noriko teaching O'Hare the intricacies of the *Ocha* or tea ceremony, followed by a very informal meal of Italian or Indian takeaway, which Noriko had never before tried eating but quickly found she loved because it did not involve much chewing.

The smoke from the downed Chinese aircraft had looked ominously close to where the old woman lived.

"Come on, pick up ..." Bunny muttered as the phone rang and rang.

"*Dare ga iru ka?*" the quavering voice asked over the speaker. "Who is this?"

"Noriko, it's me, Usagi," O'Hare said. Usagi was Japanese for rabbit, which was the closest O'Hare could find to Bunny, a nickname the old woman really struggled to grasp. They'd landed on 'rabbit' and O'Hare decided she could live with it. In fact, she'd grown to like 'Usagi'.

"Yes, hello," Noriko said, a little impatience in her voice. "Did we have an appointment? I am sorry if I forgot."

Noriko's hearing wasn't great. Perhaps she had been at home, hadn't heard the explosion or seen the news. O'Hare didn't want to worry her.

"No, I was just ... just checking you're alright," she said.

There was a clunk and O'Hare heard Noriko put the phone down. The connection was still live and O'Hare could hear the old woman's slippered feet pad up the corridor away from the door to check something and then pad back again. O'Hare could also hear sirens in the background. "Yes, I am fine," Noriko said when she picked up the phone again. "I was just looking out the window. The fire brigade seems to have the fire under control."

"You can see it from your apartment?" O'Hare asked.

"Well, I expect you can see it from just about anywhere in the Uruma district," Noriko said. "A young fool at the nursery thought it was terrorists."

"No, no, it was ..." What should she say?

"I told him not to be silly, we don't have terrorists on Okinawa," the old woman continued. "I heard aircraft and then the explosion. I told him it was a crashed airplane. Crashed, or shot down. There is this nonsense on the radio about the government ordering US troops to leave Okinawa." She sighed. "I suppose we are at war now?"

One of the things that hit Bunny every time she spoke with Noriko was how sharp she still was and how perceptive. She kept up with world events and often lectured Bunny on the nuances, drawing on a century of personal experience.

"Not yet," Bunny told her truthfully. "Hey, you remember how we were talking about that new ferry service to Kumamoto?"

"No."

"Oh, come on, you aren't senile. The fast catamaran. You said you have never been to Kumamoto. You have a great-niece there." O'Hare had spent a weekend in Kumamoto, a town on a neighboring island, and had tried to interest Noriko in going there with her.

"Oh, yes. But I have no desire to visit my niece."

"You've never been outside Okinawa!" O'Hare said. "I could get you a ticket, you could be relaxing in a hotel in Kumamoto tomorrow."

Noriko made a clucking sound with her tongue. "Nonsense. I am not going to Kumamoto tomorrow. I am too old for such a trip."

"I can hire a paramedic traveling companion to accompany you," O'Hare said.

"You are being, as usual, very annoying," Noriko said. "I have work tomorrow in any case," she said.

"The nursery will survive a few days without you," O'Hare said.

"A few days?!" she clucked. "Impossible." O'Hare heard her voice getting further from the phone, as though she was ready to put it down. "Kumamoto? Ridiculous."

O'Hare wasn't about to give up. "You can see the castle, the Kato shrine …'

"I can happily die never having seen Kumamoto castle," Noriko said.

"…the Suizen-ji garden," O'Hare said quickly. "It has a replica of Mount Fuji!"

"I know about the Suizen-ji garden," Noriko snapped. But then her voice became wistful. "My husband once promised to take me there, but he was already sick, it was just talk…"

"So, now is your chance."

"No. Now, I am very busy," she said. "I have bought some tinned food and need to make room in my pantry for it. Then I need to check on my neighbors. Also, I must fill my bath with water. You should do the same. War is coming, Usagi-san."

"I don't think … alright, I will," Bunny told her.

"Good, and Usagi-san?"

"Yes?"

"If there is war and you are killed, I will pray for your Kami and bring flowers to your grave," Noriko said. "Unless you are buried in Australia, then I will just take them to the temple."

"Uh, that's … thank you, Noriko."

"You are welcome. Goodbye."

The phone line clicked and went dead.

On her way back to the lab after delivering Chuck to a medic, she found Jensen with several of his men, standing out in the open at a crossroads behind the hangar, staring up at the sky. There had been no sign of the aircraft that had hammered overhead.

"What the hell happened?" she asked him.

"We got buzzed by jet fighters." He pointed at the sky. "Missile batteries got a lock and hit one of the bastards." She looked where he was pointing and saw a faint white trail of smoke looping back over the base and down, to the northwest. "Blew him in two. Half fell out to sea, together with the pilot's chute; the other half of the plane fell over there." As she watched, the small trail of white smoke dissipated in the wind and a darker, oilier column of black smoke rose from the ground about five miles away. There was another explosion from that direction and Jensen's men ducked involuntarily.

"We shot down a Japanese fighter?" she'd asked. Noriko had been right.

"It's a while since I tested my aircraft recognition," Jensen had said. "But those aircraft were so low you could see the rivets on their bellies. And they were sporting red stars under their tails, not red suns under the cockpits."

"Chinese?!" she'd asked, incredulously.

"Yep," Jensen had said. "Naval *Snow Falcon*s. I'd say the *Liaoning* just paid us a visit."

Smoke began billowing from the fire to the northwest, filling the sky. "And I'd say they didn't think it all the way through," she observed.

It was lunchtime in Ravi's office at the NSA XKeycore facility at Pine Gap. Allan and Ravi had become pretty big fans of the Aussie meat pie – square pastry shells filled with a mess of gravy and mystery meat, which they smothered in ketchup and followed with an iced coffee or Red Bull chaser.

Ravi checked his watch. "My guy in Japan should have called us back by now." He reached out to hand his pie to Allan. "Hold this. I'll call him."

The voice in the ceiling broke in on them. "Ravi? You asked me to monitor and report on any intelligence related to the Okinawa scenario."

Ravi was leaning across to Allan and hesitated mid-reach. "HOLMES? You have something?"

"Yes, Ravi. Five minutes ago reports started coming in from Defense Intelligence Agency sources indicating Chinese warplanes attempted to overfly White Beach base. One was shot down. Multiple news channels are reporting that the Japanese government has ordered US troops out of Okinawa. DIA is reporting that Japanese ground and naval forces on Okinawa have been mobilized. I have also identified a potential cyber-attack on a US Navy weapons platform."

Allan was processing everything the AI was saying through a fog of shock, but the last sentence was the one he latched onto. "Wait, HOLMES. Say again, what was that about a cyber-attack?"

"Yes, Allan. The Office of Naval Research and DARPA this morning both separately reported that they had lost contact with an unmanned Stingray submersible off the coast of Okinawa. Given current events, I conducted a broad-spectrum review of all electronic signals intelligence potentially linked to Chinese PLA operations on Okinawa and discovered a CYBERCOM report of a Chinese military satellite in active communication with an unknown naval unit twenty miles east of Okinawa. Satellite imagery shows no surface unit in the area, so I have assumed the naval unit to be a submersible."

Ravi looked at Allan. "So? Could be one of their own subs they're talking to," he said. "Would make sense they've got their sub fleet on alert."

"No, Ravi," HOLMES said. "The Chinese satellite is not transmitting on a frequency known to be used by Chinese naval forces. It is transmitting on the 200 watt X-band frequency used by US naval forces. I will run a thorough probability analysis but I would suggest there is a high likelihood the Chinese satellite is using a US military frequency to communicate with or jam a US military platform, such as the missing Stingray."

"Oh my god," Ravi said, half of his pie dropping to the floor between Allan's feet. He scrambled for his phone and called Charles Harford again.

Bunny had returned to her debate with Kevin and Kyle inside the lab when she heard a buzzing noise. In the confusion of the Chinese overflight and his subsequent rush to a medic, Chuck had left his telephone on the bench he'd been sitting on and it was trying to get his attention.

Jensen had left her in no doubt after the Chinese overflight that he thought the timing of the NSA 'stress test' and the loss of their boat stunk to high heaven. But Chuck had looked as shocked as the rest of them when it went down. Dammit.

She walked over to the phone, pressed the 'answer' button and held it to her ear. "Hello, Chuck can't take his phone right now, can I help you?" she said.

There was a pause at the other end and some static, before an American voice came on the line. "Oh, right. Sorry, who am I talking to?"

She decided to play a little loose with the truth and put on her best 'command voice'. "This is Lieutenant Karen O'Hare of US Navy White Beach," she said. "And you are?"

"Uh, well, this is a colleague from NSA," Ravi said. "Ma'am, I'm expecting him to call me back, so can you…"

"Take a message?" Bunny laughed. "Sure, I'll take a message."

"Thanks, ma'am. Could you please tell him Ravi called about the Okinawa thing…"

Bunny pressed the phone closer to her ear. "Sorry, did you say 'the Okinawa thing'?"

"Uh, you want me to repeat that, ma'am?"

"No, Ravi," Bunny said carefully. "I'm on Okinawa right now and all hell is breaking loose here. I have a very personal interest in 'the Okinawa thing' so why don't you tell me what you were going to tell him."

Allan was listening to Ravi's side of the conversation and kept trying to interrupt him, but Ravi kept motioning him to keep quiet. Essentially, all Allan could hear Ravi saying were multiple variations on 'holy shit' or 'no way' and when he hung up, he just stood staring at Allan.

"What, dude?!"

"That was a Navy Lieutenant seconded to DARPA. Harford has been working with DARPA on Okinawa," he said. "She confirmed they've lost an armed drone."

"You didn't tell her about the Chinese satellite ..." Allan pointed out. "Why not?"

"Some random person picks up Harford's phone and tells me she's US Navy? I didn't want to take the risk. But she confirmed what HOLMES told us, and she sounded legit."

"I was right, man," Allan said. "China is moving on White Beach!"

"You *and* HOLMES were right," Ravi agreed. "And now we've got a job to do."

"What?" Allan asked.

"Hey HOLMES," Ravi said urgently. "Did you listen in on my phone call?"

"Yes, Ravi."

"Good. Please assume you were correct and that China has taken control of the missing US Stingray using the satellite you identified. There must be a way to use that satellite signal to get a fix on the Stingray, right? I mean, commercial X-band spot beams have a footprint up to a hundred square miles, but US military-spec X-band is tightly focused to increase the data rate and reduce the risk of interception or jamming. It's more like ten square miles, isn't it?"

"Close, Ravi," HOLMES confirmed. "The signal footprint would in fact be five point two square miles. The approximate center of the footprint could be triangulated using two or more surface-based and one airborne electronic warfare platform."

Allan bent to scrape pie off the floor. "It's not exactly a GPS lock, but I'm guessing that having the location of their Stingray accurate down to a few miles is exactly the kind of help your new Navy friend at DARPA is looking for," he said, dumping the mess into a wastebasket. "You want to take the chance she is who she says she is and call her direct, or send a report up the line?"

"I get the feeling things are moving fast on Okinawa," Ravi said. "HOLMES, she said her name was …"

"Lieutenant Karen O'Hare," HOLMES replied. "I can confirm a positive voice print analysis for a former Royal Australian Air Force Lieutenant called Karen O'Hare, currently on contract with DARPA on Okinawa."

"Good enough for me," Ravi said. "HOLMES, package up all the technical data you have on that Chinese satellite and get ready to forward it to DARPA. I'll call the lady back and tell her we might have an idea how she can find her Stingray." He picked up his phone, running a hand across his face. "One strange thing, though. That Navy Lieutenant said Charlie was right there on Okinawa, working right next to her, and he didn't mention anything to her about our warning."

O'Hare was on the phone to Jensen the minute she got off the line with the guy from NSA Australia.

"Can you get someone down to the base infirmary?" she asked.

"We're a little stretched, O'Hare. Why?"

"Because I want you to put that dick from NSA under armed guard until I can get some answers," she said and gave him a download on what Ravi had shared with her about Chuck.

"His buddy at Pine Gap tipped him off that China is mobilizing to land troops on Okinawa and he didn't think to *mention* that to anyone?" Jensen asked.

"Not to me, not even to you," she said. "Which is beyond sketchy, right? There's more. The guy from Pine Gap said they're pretty damn sure our Stingray is under Chinese control." She pulled the phone back from her ear as Jensen started cursing.

"Tell me you have a plan for getting that submersible back in our hands, O'Hare," he said.

"Yep, totally," she said, watching Kyle and Kevin pore over the technical data from NSA. "Just need to iron out a few kinks. Oh, and I probably need to borrow an electronic warfare aircraft and a couple of anti-submarine destroyers."

Ride On An Elephant

The *Zumwalt*-class of destroyer was living proof that elephants could float. White elephants, at least.

Because that was what the *Zumwalt*s had been labeled after they had finally started sliding off the slips and into the water in the early part of the century. Designed as multi-role ground support, anti-air and anti-sub platforms, after a ten billion dollar research and development program, they had been costed at $500 million per unit. Thirty-two had been ordered by Navy. By the time the program was canceled, only three had been launched, at a cost of seven billion dollars *each*. And the misfortunes of the class had not been limited to cost overruns.

The *Zumwalt*s had been designed to field six-inch guns able to fire a 24lb rocket-propelled warhead with a precision of 50 yards, even at its maximum range of 83 nautical miles. There was just one problem: due to the low number of *Zumwalt*-class destroyers launched and the fact they were the only vessels in the fleet armed with the six-inch gun, the cost per shell of the rounds for the *Zumwalt*s' guns blew out to $1 million per shell – about the same price as a cruise missile – and the procurement program was canceled. The *Zumwalt*s had the biggest guns in the navy – for that matter, the biggest guns of any modern navy – but no ammunition for them. Fortunately, the *Zumwalt*s were also fitted with 24 vertical launch missile tubes capable of firing ship-shore, anti-air and anti-sub missiles, so they were kept in service.

In the late 2020s a solution for the dead weight of the *Zumwalt*s' six-inch guns was found and two of the destroyers were adapted to fire the Navy's new five-inch extended range guided munition, which came in at a more modest $100,000 per shell, rather than a million. The last of the *Zumwalt*s to be refitted, the *Lyndon B Johnson*, had the upgrade canceled, however. The Navy had an even better idea for its last *Zumwalt* – a railgun.

China had been the first nation to field railguns on its warships, bringing them into service in 2022 with its new Type 54B frigates. In 2010 when the US Navy was looking for a new platform on which to test its own new prototype railgun, someone realized they already had the right platform – the *Zumwalt* – easily capable of producing the 78 megawatts (105,000 horsepower) needed for the electrically powered weapon. In 2020 a Blitzer Mark 1a railgun was mounted on the *Lyndon B*. In addition to being able to intercept incoming missiles at a velocity and rate of fire faster than any missile or rocket-propelled shell, it could send a streamlined discarding sabot round downrange at approximately *seven times the speed of sound* and with enough force to penetrate quarter-inch-thick steel plate at a range of five miles. At any range out to twenty miles and against any modern warship, if the *Lyndon B* could see you via radar, drone or satellite, its railgun could almost certainly kill you.

As Bunny's helicopter circled around the *Lyndon B*, sliding into its slipstream so that it could land on the tiny platform aft of the ship's radically angled superstructure, she had seen the full complement of Taskforce 44 spread across the sea beneath her. The small carrier USS *Makin Island* sailed alongside its shepherd, the surface-air defense cruiser the *Port Royal*. On each of their flanks were the *Zumwalt*-class multi-role destroyers, the *Lyndon B* and the *Michael Monsoor*. Bringing up the rear was the unarmed replenishment oiler, the USNS *Lucy Stone*.

They hovered above the *Lyndon B*'s deck and Bunny couldn't help notice the railgun mount on the foredeck of the destroyer. It was covered with radar-reflective housings and she wondered if it would ever be used in anger. It was an academic line of thought, though, because she needed weapons that could kill submarines, not surface ships. But luckily, the *Lyndon B* had plenty of those too.

Bunny had explained the latest development to Colonel Collins and then asked to get a lift out to Taskforce 44 on the small scout helicopter that was tethered to the deck of White Beach's only real remaining warship, the old *Freedom*-class littoral combat ship tied almost permanently to the dock. Jensen had let her know that the taskforce had all the assets she needed both to triangulate the Chinese satellite signal and hunt the Stingray down.

"You want to take my only chopper fifty miles out to sea on a wild goose chase looking for your precious drone?" Collins had asked her, eyebrows raised. He was fifty years old and looked like the animal his unit was named for. He had a long canine-like snout and jaw and pinned-back ears and Bunny couldn't help thinking if he was a Lava Dog, then Lava Dogs were Dobermans. "It could be anywhere by now."

"Not literally anywhere," she'd said. "It can only make 15 knots submerged. So no matter where it has got to, it should still be within range of anti-sub warfare aircraft flying off the *Makin Island*. And I just want your chopper to drop me on one of those ships so that I can help find and sink that Stingray before it attacks something."

"Not within my grant," Collins said. "Taskforce 44 commander is Captain Ardrossan on the *Makin Island*. I can't parachute you onto one of his ships without his say so. And how he responds to this possible threat is entirely up to him. He may decide he does not require your assistance."

"I sincerely hope he does," Bunny said. "Because with that Stingray on the loose, the last place on this planet I want to be is aboard a US warship in the western Pacific."

"Ms. O'Hare," Collins sighed, looking at Jensen as though his intervention in securing O'Hare face time was not going to count in his favor. "A full carrier strike group based around the *GW Bush* is due here in five days, but we may not be here to welcome them. As you heard, a Japanese infantry brigade is, right this minute, barreling down the highway from Naha, headed for this base. We have a Japanese destroyer squadron parked off the coast. Now you are telling me NSA has intel that *Chinese* ground troops are mobilizing to drop on White Beach. And ... I have just had my ass chewed out by two different Under-Secretaries for my order to shoot down that Chinese fighter plane, because apparently I was supposed to *intuit* that the Chinese weren't going to lay bombs on my base ..." He drew breath. "... So I can pass on your intel to Commander Ardrossan but how DARPA goes about finding its damn robot is your problem!" He looked past her at his outer office, no doubt hoping there would be someone out there he could call on to get O'Hare out of his face.

The advantage of having no career, or commission, was that Bunny had nothing to lose. "You aren't seeing the big picture, Colonel," she said. "The *Makin Island* and its escorts have enough anti-air and ground support firepower to help your Marines hold this base against a *division* of Japanese troops and dozens of attack aircraft, at least until the cavalry arrives. And I'm betting China and Japan have thought of that, which makes Taskforce 44 the perfect target for that Stingray. So unless you want to explain how you got the *Makin Island* sunk because you wouldn't give me a lousy ride in a chopper, maybe DARPA's problem is your problem too."

She suspected he put her on the chopper just to be rid of her, but whatever.

As she waddled to the door of the chopper to jump out, a crewman in camouflage blues appeared at the door and held out a hand to help her down. That was a good sign – it meant Taskforce 44 had got the message from Collins. She ignored him and jumped out, then ducked under the rotors and ran for the open bay doors in the rear of the radar-absorbing superstructure that led to the warship's own helicopter deck. Two rotary-winged *Fire Scout* drones were stowed there and Bunny paused in the doorway to look them over, the seaman running in behind her, nearly thumping into her. She stepped aside to let him around her.

He held out his hand. "Welcome to the *Lyndon B Johnson*! Pleased to meet you, ma'am," he said. "I'm Ears." She frowned at him uncomprehendingly and he dropped his hand again. "Uh, your Ping Jockey?" He was taller than her, bony to the point of skeletal, with extremely pale, ridiculously freckled skin and ginger hair.

"Sorry, buddy," O'Hare admitted. "I have no idea what you're talking about."

"Sonar tech-nician, sub-mersible," he said, slowly. "I'm your STS for this mission. Seaman E3 Reilly, otherwise known as 'Ears'."

"Right," she said. "Did we get the assets I asked for?" She had forwarded HOLMES' 'best guess' regarding the Chinese satellite's footprint.

"*Makin Island* has launched a *Fantom* drone with an electronic warfare pod," he said. "It will pick up that X-band signal if we're anywhere near it. The *Port Royal* Aegis cruiser and *Lyndon B* are moving to positions that should enable us to complete the triangulation."

She pointed to the scout helicopters. "We need to get those drones up too. You and I have to…"

He held up a hand to stop her. "First things first, ma'am. I'm to take you to meet the Captain and Executive Officer."

"Look, that's nice. But we don't have time for coffee and cake. We have to get…"

"Follow me, ma'am," Reilly said. He turned into a stairwell and started bounding up stairs. Bunny sighed and followed him. "They're in the SMC."

"Which is what?" she asked.

"Ship Mission Center. You'd call it the Combat Information Center maybe?" he guessed. "It's right under the bridge."

She ground her teeth. Looking at the *Zumwalt*-class destroyer as her chopper was coming in, she guessed there were only four levels above the waterline, so they'd only be climbing two or three. The stealth ship was a radical design with an outward-sloping 'tumblehome' hull not seen in a warship for a hundred years, but it gave the destroyer a low profile which was very effective at bouncing off radar returns. Sure enough, after one more flight he stopped and they walked through a door into a room that went the width of the superstructure, with narrow irregular ports running along both sides and about twenty multi-modal workstations filling the space between. They were all occupied and there was a buzz of activity in the room, which she suspected she was responsible for.

Dark blue-uniformed ratings, male and female, sat at their stations or talked in groups, while officers in mottled light and dark blue camouflage circulated among them. She noticed two of these coming straight at her. One was African American, with a faint mustache, built like a tight end. He had black hair parted low on one side and cropped close on the other. The other man was broader, with a bald head, no visible eyebrows, and was a step or two slower – Bunny guessed both physically and mentally.

The linebacker stopped in front of her and looked her up and down, thumbs tucked into his belt. As always, Bunny waited for them to get past the tattoos and face jewelry. She'd given Reilly some credit, the sonarman hadn't even blinked.

"You're Lieutenant O'Hare?" the linebacker asked. He pointed at the insignia on his lapel. "They don't salute in your navy?"

"Ex-lieutenant, Captain," she said, pronouncing it in Australian English as *lef-tenant*. "Royal Australian Air Force. And I'm not in anyone's armed forces anymore."

The bald eagle leaned forward. "She's DARPA, sir."

The man didn't take his withering gaze off O'Hare. "On this ship you will assume your former rank, as per protocol, and you will comport yourself as though on active duty," the linebacker barked at her. "Is that clear, *Lef-tenant?*"

She smiled. "Crystal, sir." To show willing, she also saluted.

He glowered at Reilly. "Seaman, get the Lieutenant a set of coveralls and show her where she can stow her …" he made a circle around his face, "… this." He pointed to an empty workstation, two cubicles with six screens, side by side. "That's yours," he said. "But first, after you are dressed, you will tell me why Captain Ardrossan has ordered us and the *Monsoor* on what looks like a wild goose chase."

The bald officer leaned forward again. "Briefing room 2.32, Reilly, ten minutes. Dismissed."

Reilly saluted and pulled at her sleeve. She stepped away with him, the Captain and his XO watching them until they were out of the combat center. He took her into a nearby room with gym gear and lockers. She started pulling off her t-shirt. "Uh, you can change in there," he said, pointing at a washroom. He pulled open a locker. "There's spare female coveralls in here." She ignored him and stripped down to her underwear, grabbed a pair of coveralls and pulled them on, then pulled her nose and ear and lip furniture out and dropped it in his hand. "Don't lose those," she told him. "I'm both sentimental and violent." He swallowed and turned to a locker behind him, keying in a code and putting the jewelry carefully inside. She couldn't help notice the locker had a holy card taped to the door.

"Lead on, Reilly," she said.

"Aye, ma'am," he said and eased past her to lead them back to the control center.

"The Captain didn't exactly introduce himself," O'Hare said.

Reilly smiled. "No ma'am. I think your … appearance … unbalanced him a little. His name is Sallinger."

"And the bald eagle?"

"XO Weisner, ma'am," he said. He lowered his voice. "Captain's nickname is 'Gunslinger', on account of how he puts his thumbs in his belt, and the XO's is 'Wiseass', for reasons you'll see, but don't say it to his face if you want to live."

He walked them between the workstations and she saw a dozen pairs of eyes track her across the room. At the far end was a set of small rooms and she saw Sallinger and Weisner inside one of them, seated at a desk. They entered and Reilly stood by the door, so she stood beside him.

"O'Hare, sit." Sallinger nodded at a chair. "Reilly, you might as well stay. You're point on this goose chase."

O'Hare bristled. "That's the second time you've called it that, Captain," she said. "But let me ask you this. When was the last time you ran a lifeboat drill?"

The Captain and his XO exchanged a look and Sallinger leaned back in his chair. "Meaning?"

"Meaning that Stingray is a killer on the loose and unless you start taking this very seriously, you could find yourself dead."

"Really, Lieutenant?" Sallinger said. "Because the XO and I don't see it that way. Your boat could be a hundred miles from here, headed for Shanghai so China can pull it apart and make their own copy. It's what they do."

"Or, more likely, it's on its way here, to keep this taskforce, which is the only US Navy force of any importance in the region, tied in knots while China goes about its business on Okinawa."

Weisner laughed. "Tied in knots? You have a pretty high opinion of your robot, Lieutenant."

"That 'robot' has already killed this ship, Mister Weisner," O'Hare told him. "Three times." She enjoyed the look of derision on his face, but enjoyed even more watching it slip off as she continued. "Undetected; during our sea trials. Your *Zumwalt*s are our go-to practice target when we need cheering up. Commander Ardrossan knows that, which is probably why he let me fly out here. I can have my tech team forward you the action logs, if you'd like to drop a wreath on all the coordinates where your ship went down."

"Respect," Reilly said quietly, raising his eyebrows. That earned him a glare from Sallinger, so he looked back down at the deck.

Sallinger leaned forward, his elbows on the desk. "Reilly is my best STS. Hell, he might even be the best sonar tech in the navy, but don't tell him that."

"No sir," Bunny said, ignoring Reilly's blush. "I won't."

"So if you were able to get inside my guard and put your gunsights on my ship without him hearing you, I am willing to start taking your predicament a little more seriously," he said. He crossed his arms.

Weisner coughed. "You can help us track this drone down, O'Hare?"

"Yes, sir."

"Do I look like Army to you, Lieutenant?" Weisner barked.

"No, sir. *Aye*, sir," she corrected herself automatically. "We've got a lead on it. *Makin Island* has an electronic warfare bird in the air sniffing for a signal from a Chinese satellite we think is controlling the Stingray. That will tell us roughly where it is, then we can use the sensors on your ship and the *Port Royal* to narrow it down to an area of about five square miles."

"Five *cubic* miles," Weisner pointed out. "Given it's underwater."

"Yes, sir. But at this point in the mission it is probably still trailing a surface comms buoy, so it can't be deeper than 400 feet."

"That's still a lot of water, Lieutenant," he pointed out.

"Yes sir, sorry, that's the way it is."

"When we find your boat, we are authorized to kill it. You realize that?" he finished.

"Aye sir," she said. "*If* you find it before it kills us."

The comment did not earn her any points. "The operations order from *Makin Island* said that boat is carrying an EMP weapon," Sallinger said. "That might disable us, but it wouldn't kill us."

"It's also carrying five Mark 50 torpedoes," she said. "Which most definitely could."

The two officers exchanged a grim look, then Sallinger turned back to O'Hare. "Your submersible is next-gen stealth, correct?"

"Aye, sir. Sonar-absorbent build materials, anechoic coated internal components, adaptive acoustic-listening sonar jamming, fully electric, run-silent pump-jet propulsion…"

He held up a hand to stop her. "You bragged that you've been floating around under our keel undetected three times before. Can we even find your drone?"

"The Lieutenant was kind enough to have her people send ahead some tech specs and acoustic data from other exercises," Reilly said. "It's going to be a challenge but I believe we have a chance."

She nodded. "You have hull-mounted and towed-array, mid and high-frequency sonar. I just saw that you also have two *Fire Scout* rotary-winged drones in your hangar bay. Plus, you have a deployable CTUV, right?"

Weisner narrowed his eyes. "That's supposed to be classified."

She shrugged. "I'm DARPA, sir."

The CTUV, or Continuous Trail Unmanned Vessel, wasn't in itself a secret, as the first of the Sea Hunter class had entered the fleet in 2028. But the Navy didn't broadcast which of its vessels were Sea Hunter-capable, for good reason. The Sea Hunters were unmanned semi-autonomous vessels that, when launched, 'trailed' along behind or ahead of their command vessels, seeking out underwater threats such as mines or submarines. While the first generation were surface-only vessels, the latest generation could travel either above or below the water. Although itself unarmed, the Sea Hunter was equipped with a similar sensor suite to the *Virginia*-class SSX attack sub and once it located its prey, it sent targeting data to its host vessel so that it could send a torpedo after the target or, in the case of the *Zumwalt*s, an ASROC, Anti-Submarine Rocket.

Reilly shuffled his feet and looked uncomfortable, but O'Hare didn't need him to confirm she was right. Their Stingray had surreptitiously logged the CTUV circling its mother ship on two occasions.

"OK, XO," Sallinger said, slapping the table. "It looks like we're going fishing for Stingray. You will link data and coordinate with the *Monsoor*. Get those *Fire Scout*s rotating. I'm going to the bridge." He looked over at Reilly. "Don't just stand there, Ears. Get to your station and find that damn submersible so we can kill it before it kills us."

Human Shield

Noriko Fukada had once pointed out to a radio interviewer that being over 100 years old had very few physical advantages. She was five inches shorter now than she had been in her prime, her back permanently stooped. There was no point asking her if her joints ached, because they always did. Despite a bloody-minded determination not to have to resort to false teeth, she had very few of her original teeth left and those that remained gave her a constant background hum of pain. She was pretty much deaf without her hearing aids and mostly blind, even after laser surgery and corneal replacements. But the only medicines she took were vitamin supplements. Her blood pressure was perfect, her heart strong, and her mind quick. She attributed this to her habit of walking everywhere, plus a postwar diet (which she had kept up despite the improvement in living standards in the last half-century) exclusively of rice, fish, seaweed, and sake. Her love of sake explained why she got along so well with Bunny O'Hare.

Another thing about her age was that the older she got, the less sleep she needed. She was a napper, taking two hours in the afternoon on a cot at the nursery, perhaps a catnap while watching television late in the evening, and then just three hours from midnight to 3 a.m. At three she rose, made her bath, and ate a light breakfast. By 4 a.m. she was out of her apartment and walking to the nursery. She enjoyed being there two hours before anyone else – it was the most productive part of her day. She had been walking down the poorly lit street, having just come out of her apartment, when she had been stopped by a military policeman in khakis and a white helmet. The streets were never empty in Uruma, even at 4 a.m. People were either just getting home from their night jobs or revelries, doing their early morning exercise, or standing at bus stops for their commute to Naha, an hour away by bus.

Eyes down, looking for cracks and bumps in the sidewalk, she'd seen his boots first. They didn't move out of her way so she looked up. He had a white-gloved hand up, stopping everyone who was trying to push past him. With the other hand he was motioning with a baton toward a bus parked at the curb. "Onto the bus!" he was yelling. "Everyone, onto the bus!" A small crowd was milling in confusion.

A salaryman in a black suit, white shirt, and black tie started arguing with him, but he pushed the man roughly with his baton, forcing him back a step, and barked, "Onto the bus. There is a state of emergency. Do as you are told. No questions!"

Noriko waited as the gaggle of people was diverted into the open doors of a bus standing on the curb. She kept her eyes on the ground and waited on the sidewalk. This would pass.

But it didn't. She felt a tap on her shoulder and saw the MP bending down, glaring impatiently at her. "You too, grandmother," he said.

"I am old," she told him. "I am not going anywhere."

"Even the old must serve their nation in an emergency," he said. "Here. I will help you." And with that he rudely lifted her off her feet and carried her onto the bus before she could argue, ordering people to stand aside so he could deposit her shamelessly on a seat before he went back outside and started yelling at people again.

She watched him go with a sinking heart. So it had been in the last war, too, when she had been pressed into service at the military hospital at the age of fifteen. "Even the young must serve their nation in an emergency," she had been told then. Young, or old. She sighed. Everything changed, but then nothing changed, really.

The bus was full and a young girl who had been forced out of her seat to make way for Noriko had held onto her arm to help her sit down and get her balance. Noriko kept hold of the girl's hand. She was no more than twenty, a shop assistant perhaps. She looked terrified. Noriko looked up at her and patted her hand. "Don't be afraid. What's your name, girl?"

"Yoshi," the girl said, holding up a hand to stop the man in front of her stepping back onto her toes.

"I am Noriko." The bus started moving and the girl put her hand to her mouth. "Where do you work?" Noriko asked her.

"Sorry? Oh, I work at Don Quijote shopping center," she said, her breath catching with sobs. She put a hand over her face. "I have to open the shop today. I need to be there by 5 a.m. Where are they taking us?"

Noriko knew what the girl needed. "Yoshi-san," she said and shook her hand gently. "Look at me?" The girl took her hand away from her face. "Yoshi-san, I am very old. My skin is like paper and my bones are like chicken bones. I need someone young and strong to help me for the next little while, until this nonsense is over. Will you do that for me?"

The girl stifled her sobs. She was chubby and pretty and her hair was tied in two ponytails. She wiped her nose with her left hand and gripped Noriko's hand tightly with the other. "Yes, grandmother. I will help you."

Noriko nodded, smiling at the irony. Grandmother. She had never even had a child, but now everyone called her grandmother. Such was life. Her thoughts were interrupted as a voice came over the bus intercom.

"Attention please. By order of the national government, you have been chosen to participate in a civil action to protest the attack on our country. In thirty minutes we will be arriving at the gates of the American Navy Base at White Beach. When you disembark, you will be given a red bandana. You will tie this to your head. You may be given a protest sign to carry, or a banner. Follow the instructions of the police. You can ask questions later." People began talking loudly with each other, shouting questions forward, but the person on the intercom, who Noriko could not see through the sea of legs and torsos, simply started repeating exactly what they had just said. "Attention please. By order of the national government…"

Noriko sighed. Everything changes and nothing does. She remembered the mainland troops arriving on Okinawa in 1945. She'd already been pressed into service in the hospital by then, treating casualties of the American bombing, but they'd pulled people off the streets then too. Got them digging ditches and making barricades in the streets. Even after the Americans landed, the mainland troops pushed the civilians out in front of them to keep digging, keep piling sandbags, uncaring as they were mown down by American mortar and machine-gun fire.

Noriko gripped Yoshi's hand and smiled up at her.

"Thank you, child," she said. She thought then of her little American friend Usagi and hoped she was somewhere safe.

Bunny 'Usagi' O'Hare was seriously regretting her decision to fly out to the *Lyndon B Johnson*. When she had been forced to go to war in the past, she had usually been in control of her own fate. Being a ride-along passenger in a seagoing tin can was not a role she found particularly comfortable.

She got even more uncomfortable when her worst fears were confirmed. The electronic warfare drone launched by the *Makin Island* had picked up a 200-watt X-band microwave radio signal reflecting off the water to their west. With only one data point, it couldn't be precise, but it put the epicenter of the satellite footprint anywhere from ten to twenty miles away from the *Lyndon B Johnson*.

The Stingray was not headed for Shanghai.

She was impressed by the sense of calm in the ship mission center, or SMC, of the *Lyndon B* – considering that at any moment a US Mark 50 torpedo could appear out of the deep, aimed straight at their guts. She had been Royal Australian Air Force, not Navy, and used to a more heightened sense of urgency in combat operations, where an enemy stealth fighter could appear out of nowhere, giving a pilot milliseconds to react. In the double-deck SMC of the *Lyndon B*, people walked and talked in hushed tones. Low lamps lit the workstations and the few external ports were shuttered to limit the leakage of light in the dark Pacific night. No one shouted, barking orders. And 'Ears' Reilly was being left to do his work, with only Bunny sitting beside him and the XO, Weisner, hovering over his shoulder.

"*Port Royal* has confirmed the target area, sir. We're signal mapping grids AE42 and BF33 right now, but it looks like the enemy vessel is between ten and twenty miles distant," the sensor operator said. "I'm moving the Sea Hunter to grid AE43. Our footprint is entering BF32 in five zero five. I have the *Fire Scouts* sounding in sectors AC40 and AC20. *Monsoor* has two birds up and is clearing sectors D12 through 14. All birds have about 30 minutes before bingo fuel." Now that they had a search vector, the two *Zumwalts* were acting in concert and sharing aircraft sonar data in real time. They had launched four *Fire Scout* rotary-winged drones, which could hover over the water and drop cables to deploy powerful sonar buoys, sweeping the waters within, ahead, and behind the search zone.

They had formidable anti-submarine capabilities and Bunny was hoping to see first-hand just how formidable. In addition to its aircraft, standard hull-mounted and towed array sonar, Reilly had access to a Continuous Trail Sea Hunter submersible drone, which carried its own passive and active sensors, which Weisner had ranging out in front of the *Lyndon B* in the most likely direction of the threat from the Stingray according to the data provided by O'Hare. "The Hunter is still in passive mode?" the XO asked.

"Aye sir, not pinging," Reilly confirmed. "We're putting out so much engine and prop noise ourselves, not to mention our sonar systems are in active search mode. I've got those *Fire Scouts* acting like hounds in a fox hunt. I'm hoping that between the *Monsoor's* birds and ours, we can scare that Stingray into moving, either to hide, or to find itself an attack solution. If he does that, the Sea Hunter might be able to pick him up without him noticing."

"Don't bet on that," Bunny told him. "We ran an exercise against an *Arleigh Burke* with the Stingray moving at 8 knots, 15 fathoms beneath its keel and above the thermocline. It knew we were in the area, it had a *Hunter* out actively searching too, but it didn't get a single return."

"That *Arleigh Burke* didn't have Ears," Weisner said. "And now he knows your Stingray is out there. If it's where we think it is, he'll hear it." He patted Reilly on the shoulder. "No pressure, Ears. If you screw up, people will die."

Bunny could see how Weisner had gotten his 'Wiseass' nickname, if that was his idea of humor. She watched him walk off and turned to Reilly.

"Your XO is a bundle of laughs," she observed.

Reilly pulled one of his earphone cups off his ear and leaned back in his chair. "He's OK, ma'am," he said. "Kind of guy you'd want on your side in a bar fight, or any kind of fight, for that matter."

"The name is Bunny," she told him. "Not ma'am." He was only about five years younger than her and his politeness made her feel old. "Putting on some Navy blues doesn't turn me back into an officer, no matter what your CO says."

Reilly smiled and held out his hand. "Seamus," he said.

O'Hare feigned shock. "Seamus Reilly? Seriously?"

"Ancestors from County Clare," he said. "O'Hare, that must be Irish too?"

"I guess. No one has been brave enough to do our family tree, though," she told him. "Might find out we only recently came down from the trees."

"Can I ask you a personal question, ma'am?" Reilly asked tentatively.

"Bunny, and yeah, sure," she said.

"I looked up your name before you arrived," he said. "The Karen O'Hare who got a Navy Cross, that's you?"

"Yup. Can't really discuss it though, Seamus," she told him. *Can't. Don't want to. Trying to forget it*, is what she should have said.

"No, no, I didn't… it's just, it helps to know that if things get FUBAR, you've been there before, you know?" he said and looked away in embarrassment.

She put a hand on his shoulder. "Trust me, Seamus, I know FUBAR. FUBAR is where I live," she said.

Takuya Kato was seething. He'd had the whole flight back to the *Liaoning* to let his anger build, with the *Snow Falcon* fighter's AI doing the flying. It kept position in the formation, it automatically

220

entered the landing circuit over the *Liaoning* and, as he was beyond caring now, it also landed itself as well or better than he could have done himself, neatly catching the second wire and pulling itself up well ahead of the ski-jump bow.

The deck of the *Liaoning* was seething too. Darkness was coming and the deck was ablaze with light. As he jumped off its wing, his machine was pushed off to one side for refueling and reconfiguration, as other aircraft were bullied around the deck, ready to be launched.

It looked like a ship at war.

To port and starboard he saw the dark silhouettes of Chinese missile cruisers, sailing closer than they had in previous days, as though gathering beneath the feathers of a mother hen, though he knew that metaphor was wrong. They were there to provide close-in anti-missile protection to their flagship, not to hide in its shadow.

He'd been pulled immediately into a debriefing by technical intelligence officers desperate to understand why their electronic countermeasures had not worked against the US low-level anti-air defense radar. They were also interested in how his AI had defeated the Stinger attack by outrunning the missiles in a vertical climb. But he could tell them nothing that they could not learn by simply downloading the data from his *Snow Falcon*'s onboard AI, so after two rounds of questions, they had released him. He had returned to the wardroom to find Li Chen and get new orders.

She was sitting with three of her pilots, one of them moving his hands as though they were aircraft. In the way of all combat pilots, they were trying to recreate the action, to understand how they had lost their man. He sat beside them, not interrupting, but Li saw him and stood. "Enough for now," she told her men. "Get some food and rest. Be ready for recall. I suspect we will see action again soon."

The men walked away, giving him looks that ranged from neutral to hostile. Had it not been his job to jam the American systems? And had he not failed? He received their judgment with equanimity. I flew *your* aircraft, with *your* jamming system, he told them in his mind. Judge yourselves.

"Join me in my ready room," Li said and led the way. He trailed along behind her. Was he to be disciplined? If so, he was not sure he could contain himself. She was not his commanding officer. His superiors were on the *Izumo*. The mission was not his failure, he was not the fool who had conceived the plan to try to intimidate a nation that had shown innumerable times it would *not* be intimidated. Neither did it hesitate to act when action was demanded. He felt the emotion boiling in his chest and waited for the first hint of a reprimand...

But as he closed the door behind him, she collapsed on her bunk, lying down on her back with her heels drawn up to her backside and an arm over her face. "Oh, Takuya, what have I done?"

It was a human question, not a military one. He sat down on a chair opposite and took her free hand. She gripped it tightly.

"I have never lost a man in combat," he admitted. "But we saw him eject. He is probably safe."

"If he didn't drown. If his back wasn't broken by the seat booster. If angry civilians didn't drag him from the water and beat him to death..." she said. She was talking quickly, words tumbling out. "I knew this mission was foolhardy but I said nothing. Someone thought a press release and a supersonic flyover would send the Americans fleeing for their boats after ninety years on Okinawa?!"

"You couldn't have known about that networked Stinger system," he said. "Your technical officers said it was linked to a new kind of frequency hopping anti-jamming radar system. If you had known, you would have adjusted the flight profile..."

She sat up, letting go of his hand. "Would I? Or would I just have followed my orders like a mindless robot? As they knew I would," she spat. "Takuya, I have the worst fear and I cannot speak it to anyone but you." She swung her legs off the bed. "I do not know you, but I believe in *yuanfen*, in fateful coincidence. There is a reason you, a foreign pilot, are here, on this ship, at this time..."

He could not disagree. The reason was a command from his childhood friend and regent, but he could not tell Li Chen that. She continued speaking anyway.

"… you, whose great-grandfather and mine, enemies at the time, were also brought together by *yuanfen* and made fateful decisions that have led directly to you and I being here today. But for my great-grandfather's mercy, your grandfather would not have been born and you would not be here, but here you are."

"Your great-grandfather, the *American*," Kato pointed out.

"Do you think I do not think of that every day?!" she asked. "That I have not had to fight that history every single day of my career in this air force?" She mimicked hostile voices. "How can we trust her? Her great-grandfather fought with the Americans! She still has family in America, how do we know she is not a spy?"

"They will trust you now," he said. "After leading an attack on a US naval base."

"It was *not* an attack!" she said. "You know that!" Then she lay down again, forearm over her forehead. "Oh, forget it. Of course it was. You saw that yourself when you asked why we did not send the *Sharp Sword* drones if it was just a recon mission. We were set up, Kato-san."

His blood chilled. "What?!"

"My ops intelligence officer is more loyal to me than to his line," she said. "Our mission planners knew about the new American Stinger system. We were told the only air defense radar was a twenty-year-old unit mounted on a thirty-year-old corvette, but my superiors knew that base was protected by a highly sophisticated low-level anti-air system." She paused. "Even knowing that, they could have sent us over at 20,000 feet, out of range of the Stinger missiles. The sonic boom would still have been heard, the symbolism of our incursion on American airspace would still have had impact."

"But they did not," he said. "They sent you in at low level, hoping…"

"Not hoping," she said. "*Knowing* that I would almost certainly lose one or more aircraft to 'unprovoked' American fire. Which I dutifully did." She gave a bitter laugh. "I landed, expecting to be court-martialed. Instead, I was shown sympathy. Sympathy!"

"China wants war with America? Over Okinawa?" He shook his head. "It makes no sense."

"China wants a conflict, not a war," she said. "A conflict it can win. Does history not point the way? We militarized atolls and sand islands in the South China Sea, skirmished with US ships and aircraft, and their politicians shouted 'why are our sailors dying for a few coral reefs a million miles from home?' Korea reunited under our patronage when America decided it wanted its troops in Europe, facing Russia instead. We moved on a chain of islands in the Philippines and their tinpot dictator, who had been thumbing his nose at America for decades, cried for help and America turned a deaf ear. Okinawa is the last remaining US base within a thousand miles of Taiwan and little more than a symbol today, but the US still has a battalion of Marines and a naval taskforce forward based there. Which could easily be upgraded to a regiment of Marines and a super-carrier strike group at very short notice."

"The *GW Bush* carrier strike group is on the way from Pearl Harbor," Kato pointed out. "They made no secret of that."

"That's the gamble, isn't it?" she said. "If together we try to push them out of Okinawa, will they respond in kind? Or will they, as they have in the past, sail their fleet up and down our coast but decide that Okinawa is a fight they can't be bothered fighting?"

Kato had a feeling the US might feel differently about Okinawa to the way it felt about a few rocky atolls in the South China Sea, but he kept the feeling to himself. "Your mission…" he said, being deliberate to distance himself from it, "… provoked an American response, but it was not a direct attack on the American base. You lost a pilot; Japan lost lives, *civilian* lives. America lost nothing. They need not 'respond' at all."

Her face lost its animation, drained of emotion. "No, but they are about to," she said with a dead voice. "We are preparing a massive airstrike on White Beach in retaliation for the loss of our pilot. The base is being surrounded by Japanese infantry. The *Liaoning* strike group will spearhead the attack, as much for public relations purposes as for any military reason. After our aircraft go in, Japanese troops will move in and mop up. By this time tomorrow, it is expected that White Beach will be back in Japanese hands and the surviving Americans will be loaded aboard aircraft and sent packing to Pearl Harbor, or Guam, or wherever they wish to decamp to."

Now Kato's anger boiled up again. "*Chinese* aircraft are going to attack a target on Japanese soil?" How could his generals have agreed to this? It was one thing to support China in a strategy to achieve the reunification of Taiwan without starting a war that would damage economies in the entire region. It was another altogether that Japan would pay the price of its support for that strategy in Japanese blood.

"No," she said, standing. "I told you, this is a PR exercise as much as a military one. We will be providing air cover, but Japanese F-35s from your carrier *Izumo*, together with rotary-winged aircraft from your airbase at Kadena, will conduct the air-to-ground operations once we have secured the airspace over the target." She looked at him sadly. "I thought you deserved to know the real reason why, before we go into action."

"I am to join you again?" he asked.

"Of course," she said. "Everything in this action is about signals and symbolism," she said. "We could use mainland-based forces for this, Japanese and Chinese, but the intent is to show the world the power of our joint naval strike group. Your pre-mission interview from this afternoon is probably being edited for distribution as we speak. You will be interviewed again before we take off for Okinawa at dawn tomorrow," she said. "The personal representative of the newly ascended Empress of Japan, joining in battle against the Americans, to rid his nation and this entire region of their presence once and for all," she said with irony. "*Banzai!*"

She walked to the door and opened it for him, indicating the time for honesty and openness was over. He went to move past her, but she put a hand on his shoulder and held him up. He had never been close enough to her to notice before, but she smelled of sweat and jasmine. "Go rest, Takuya. We will be called to alert status at 0400," she said and hesitated. "It is strange, is it not? Nearly a hundred years ago our ancestors were face to face, but on opposite sides. Now we stand together. I feel it was meant to be." She patted him softly on the chest, then stepped back so that he could pass and closed the door behind him.

You may feel it was meant to be, Kato said to himself. My Empress does not.

Bunny wasn't meant to be a sailor. She'd learned that serving on a US Navy base in the Arctic where the personnel had to be ferried to and from the base by submarine. And she was relearning it now, as the *Lyndon B Johnson* heeled over to port to begin searching for the Stingray along a new bearing and her stomach lurched in the opposite direction.

Reilly regarded her warily, holding out a wastebasket in one hand and a phone in the other. "Call for you, ma'am," he said. "White Beach."

Bunny waved the wastebasket away, took a deep breath to force the bile back down, and took the phone. "O'Hare."

"Hey boss," Kyle's voice said. "Do you know how hard it is to put a call through to someone on a warship if that someone doesn't let the radio operators on that ship know that they are on that ship?"

"Been a bit busy, Kyle," Bunny said, holding onto a bulkhead for support. "What is it?"

"It's Kevin, he..."

"Shoot him."

"Boss?"

"Seriously, if Kevin is annoying you, you have my permission to shoot him," she said. "Now, I have to get back to work here."

"Noted for future reference, thanks, but that's not what I was going to say," Kyle said. "Kevin may have found a way to get control of the Stingray back. Here, you tell her." She heard the phone being handed over and Kevin came on the line.

"Hello," Kevin said. "I went back over the 'lost comms' programming trying to find a hook we could use to get ourselves back in, and I found something weird."

"Weird?"

"As in something that made no sense, so I dug out the schematics for the X-band motherboard and freak me sideways, the original engineers put an A2 chip on it in case they ever totally lost comms with their boat. It wasn't in any of the documentation, though. Must have been way way back when this Stingray was first assembled."

"A2 what?" Bunny asked.

"A2 computer chip; as in 'Ann Arbor', named by the Massachusetts hackers that developed it," Kevin explained. "It's a physical chip you put on a circuit board that can be activated by radio energy on a particular frequency. You hit it with the right radio waves and when you do it adds a charge to a capacitor on the chip. Even if an enemy successfully blocks the Stingray from sending or receiving, the charge keeps building, until it is enough for the backdoor code on that chip to execute and trigger a blunt force reboot."

"Reboot the Stingray?"

"Yeah, see? We ping the chip long enough, it boots the Stingray into startup mode and we get our boat back! Or at the very least, we can try to shut it down and send someone out to pick it up."

For the first time in days, Bunny saw a ray of light.

"You are a certified genius, Kevin!" she said. "Get to work on that reboot. And put Kyle back on, will you?"

The phone was handed over again. "Kyle here."

"I rescind my order. Please don't shoot Kevin just yet," she said.

"Aw, seriously?" Kyle said. "I could just wound him a bit?"

"OK, but no vital organs. And not his chest, either; if this works, he'll need somewhere to pin the medal."

227

"DARPA doesn't give medals, boss."

"I've got a spare one," Bunny said. "He can have that."

Weapons Authority

Twenty minutes later, Dragon Bird spun on his chair as a beeping sound started coming from Po's workstation.

"Oh, this is not good," Po said. He frowned and crouched low over his keyboard.

DB stood and walked to his shoulder. "What is not good?"

"I just lost steerage!" Tanken said, turning away from his instrument screens. He wiggled a joystick impotently and dragged a mouse back and forth across his desk. "Not only do I not have weapons, I don't have navigation now, either!"

"Wait!" Po said. He peered at his screen, paging through some code. "Oh. You sneaky bastards!"

He jumped from his chair, grabbed a binder off a shelf behind him and started flipping at manic speed through pages. Finding what he was looking for, he spread the binder on the desk next to his keyboard and started typing manically.

"Talk to me, Po," DB said. The man ignored him, lost in whatever was going on. Frangi also stood and walked over and was leaning over his shoulder, looking at the pages spread out beside Po.

Frangi was reading code. "That looks like A2 backdoor code? They're using that?"

"Yep."

"Can you ride it in?"

"Yep. I think so. Dunno. Probably. Or not."

She looked at his screen. "Hey, it's an OR2400 processor, dummy."

Po frowned. "Oh, right." He ordered his system code bot to pull down a couple of pages of code and started typing frantically again. He wasn't spitting out code manually, but was sending commands to a bot which pulled down pre-written code snippets and compiled them on the fly.

DB slapped the table beside Po, but he didn't even flinch. "Someone talk to me!" he demanded.

Frangipani straightened and turned to him. "Sorry, Comrade Team Leader. The US is triggering a backdoor into the command and control system of their Stingray. An old trick but a good one for this purpose – a circuit on a physical chip they can excite, to trigger a system override."

"They'll get control of the Stingray back from us?" he asked, worried now. It would be the end of their mission. KAHLO and their penetration of DARPA were just means to an end now and the end was the Stingray. Without it, there was no mission and the entire APT 23 operation to take the USS *Makin Island* off the board could fall apart. "I thought we had cut off their communications!"

"We have blocked DARPA from contacting the Stingray directly," Po said. "But we can't stop them bathing it in radio waves to trigger that chip. There was no reason to suspect they would mount an Ann Arbor chip in their own system! Either this is standard protocol in US drones, and we missed it, or they have one completely paranoid programmer on that team."

"So disable the boot code!" DB yelled. "Neuter that chip!"

"We could, but we may not want to," Frangipani said, in an annoyingly calm voice. Her reaction suggested she found the entire situation fascinating. But that was her nature. DB could already see the barbed wire gates of a re-education camp opening to welcome him, but all Frangi could see was a fascinating cyber warfare scenario unfolding. "On the one hand, we might lose command of the Stingray," she continued. "But on the other, if Po is half the genius he thinks he is, this reboot could be our way into the weapons system."

"Respectfully, shut the hell up, comrades!" Po said. "I'm working here."

"OK, I got a return, it's executing!" Kevin said as a new screen came up on his console. "We're back in!"

Other screens came alive around Kyle and his heart leaped as he recognized navigation, positioning, steerage, communications, and weapons readouts spring to life. His eyes sought out the tactical map on the wall screen. "Where the heck are you, big boy?"

He couldn't see the Stingray where he expected.

"There!" Kevin yelled, pointing at the screen.

"Oh no," Kyle whispered. The icon for the Stingray was directly ahead of the group of icons on the screen that was Taskforce 44. And frighteningly close.

Kevin wasn't looking at the tactical screen any more though, he was looking at his own PC screen. "Wait! No, no, no, this isn't happening..." he said.

As Kyle spun toward him, the screens at his workstation started going black again.

"I'm back in! The exploit is running!" Po said, lifting his hands into the air and leaning back in his chair. One by one, the flickering screens in front of him began flowing data again.

"Now what?" DB asked.

"Now we wait," Frangi said, deadpan. "DARPA triggered a brute force system reboot, but it wasn't complete. Po has tried to hijack it with his new code to lock them out again and give us full control. Think of it like a factory reset of your cell phone, but we changed the user ID from DARPA to APT 23."

Data continued to flow across Po's screens and he used his space bar to pause it occasionally, giving no clue about whether their counter-attack was succeeding or not. DB had his fingers to his mouth, not that he had any nails left to bite.

Finally, Po hit a key and raised a fist in the air. "Oh yeah, baby! Navigation. Propulsion. Communication. Weapons. Sensors." He turned and grinned. "They're back up and we've got them all."

"Did you say *weapons*?" DB asked, not believing his ears.

"I've got steerage back!" Tanken called out, looking from screen to screen at his station. "I've got weapons!"

DB grabbed Po's fat head and kissed it on the crown. He swept the slight frame of Frangipani up in his arms and swung her around, which sent her glasses flying across the room. Her ponytail fell out of its tight bun and her hair fell down around her shoulders. As he put her down, she blushed and rushed to look for her glasses.

The phone at Reilly's elbow rang again and he listened briefly, then handed it to O'Hare who was standing beside him. "White Beach again."

She grabbed the handset. "Give me the good news."

"That Stingray is right on top of you, boss!" Kyle said, almost yelling. "Kevin is sending the coordinates through now via Jensen. We got the boat back but we lost it again."

"You what?"

"We got counter-attacked. China still has the Stingray. But we might have got a positioning fix on it."

Almost simultaneously, Reilly spoke into his headset with menacing calm. "XO? Communication from White Beach. We have an unconfirmed position on the target. Adjusting search pattern." A pale face looked up at O'Hare. "Range is *eleven miles*."

"Is it my fate to starve to death in the city with the most restaurants per head in the whole of China?" Po complained. "My recruiter promised me when I joined the People's Liberation Army I would never have to worry about where I was going to sleep or what I was going to eat, ever again."

"He was making a joke, lumpfish," Frangi told him.

"Shut up, both of you," Tanken said. "And get me an update on the position of those destroyers. I've got nothing on my sensors yet."

"We just had lunch three *hours* ago," Po moaned. "We aren't on an actual submarine in the middle of the actual Pacific. We can make a call and have food delivered. Actual food, I mean." He hit a combination of keys and a window on one of his screens started flashing. "New satellite data," Po called out. "Updated US surface vessel movements. Patching it through now."

DB walked over to Tanken's workstation, where they had concentrated all the intel screens related to their mission. They were populated with data being fed in by Tanken's Strategic Support Force team around the globe, pulling data from PLA satellites, reconnaissance aircraft, surface vessels, and even Ministry of State Security human sources. Of central interest was a map of the western Pacific, east of Okinawa. On it they had several plots, a key one being updated positioning data on the progress of the USS *GW Bush* strike group, which was currently three days out of Pearl Harbor and ten days from Okinawa. The other big group of icons was US Navy Taskforce 44, with a large targeting box around the *Makin Island*. DB had earlier read an updated intelligence report indicating that the US amphibious assault ship and its escorts were conducting air assault training operations and it was currently at sea with its full complement of six piloted F-35B stealth fighters and fourteen unmanned *Fantom* drones.

Given the news reports they had been reading of a Chinese aircraft being shot down over Okinawa, DB could now see why theirs was a critically important mission. He had no illusions that the ill-fated Chinese overflight was the end of military action over Okinawa. DB could also see icons on Tanken's tactical map showing that a Japanese destroyer flotilla was making speed down the eastern coast of Okinawa toward White Beach. Other missions, similar to his, were probably also underway as part of combined land, sea, and air operations. It could be fatal to those plans if the USS *Makin Island* was allowed to intervene.

He watched the Taskforce 44 icons wink out and then wink in again as the plot was updated. "All is going to plan," he observed with satisfaction. "You will soon be within range!"

Tanken sounded grim. "All is not going to plan, Comrade Team Leader. I am already within range of the taskforce picket destroyers." He spun his chair to face Po and Frangi. "Prepare for a combat engagement!"

"Situation, Lieutenant Tanken?" DB asked curtly.

Tanken pointed at the icons. "The target, USS *Makin Island*, was patrolling a fixed grid here. The prevailing wind is westerly, so they were probably launching aircraft as part of their training exercise." He pointed to a number beside one of the plots. "These picket destroyers were conducting what looked like a routine anti-submarine warfare search about five miles to the northeast of us. They were not a threat. Now, they have changed course directly toward us and increased speed. They are hunting."

"Us?" DB asked.

"Given they are driving straight for the Stingray, yes, I would assume they are looking for us," Tanken said sarcastically.

DB did not like his tone but had come to expect it from the cocky SSF officer. If he had been in DB's own line, DB would see him disciplined the moment their mission concluded. As it was, he could do no more than report the man's insubordinate attitude to his Strategic Support Force superiors. What they did with his report would depend entirely on how successful Tanken had been. It was deeply frustrating.

"How long before the Stingray is at risk of being detected?" DB asked. "You are trained for this, correct?"

"I am not only trained, Comrade Captain. I was steersman aboard *Ming*-class submarine 313, which was the first of its class to penetrate undetected within attack range of a US aircraft carrier in the South China Sea," he boasted. "But to get to that *Wasp*-class assault ship in the middle of their main formation, we first need to pass the destroyers which are hunting us. These are multirole ships, not dedicated submarine hunter-killers. Their search aircraft are the biggest threat right now." Tanken ran some numbers. "We can't see them but we can assume we are already within range of their aircraft." He swung around in his chair and fixed his gaze on DB. "Comrade Captain, I may need to engage and sink a US destroyer in order to achieve our mission and reach the USS *Makin Island*. What are your orders?"

DB's superior officer had made clear to DB that he was not to authorize offensive operations personally. The authorization to fire their weapons would come via a VR link with an officer of the PLA Navy and Shaofeng wanted to be the one who relayed it to Tanken. DB grabbed his phone. "Major Shaofeng? I am sorry to interrupt, sir. I need you in our operations room." It was suddenly hot in the small room and DB wiped his brow. "Yes, sir. Now!"

Master at Arms James Jensen was in no doubt about the orders he had received from Colonel Collins.

The Japanese protesters had passed the first, open, entry gates to the White Beach base and were approaching the security checkpoint where vehicles and personnel on foot were stopped and searched. That meant that technically, the protesters were already on US soil and he was within his rights to stop and eject them. That job, Collins had delegated to his base security officer, Jensen, while the troops of his 1st Marine battalion dug in on the base perimeter.

They had a surveillance drone up and it was showing them that the Japanese 15th Infantry was also moving into position on the north and east flanks of the US base, backed by at least one Type 60 Self-propelled 106mm recoilless artillery gun and ten Mitsubishi Type 89 infantry fighting vehicles, which fielded a 35mm Oerlikon cannon and Jyu-MAT anti-tank missiles. The 1st Marines didn't have any tanks for it to shoot at, but Jensen had no illusions the Japanese tanks had been given orders to seek out and destroy the two Stryker vehicles which Japan and China must now know were based at White Beach.

Jensen doubted it was dumb luck, but the Japanese action was taking place while the Aegis missile cruiser that would normally have provided a formidable anti-air shield in the skies over White Beach was at sea on exercises with Taskforce 44. The *Port Royal* and its escorts could still provide ground fire support – together they could fire volleys of up to 40 Tomahawk 'launch and loiter' cruise missiles, which could fly to a holding position off White Beach and then be called down by US troops on targets as needed. But their use in a fast-moving ground conflict was fraught with challenges. They would take 20 minutes to cover the distance between the taskforce and Okinawa. At that range, they would be able to loiter for just 45 minutes before running out of fuel. At a million dollars a shot, Navy doctrine for using the new loitering Tomahawks in sustained combat was to launch fewer, overlapping waves, to ensure several were arriving on station as others became redundant. But it meant fewer were overhead at any one time and overlap was never perfect, leaving potentially fatal gaps in coverage.

Jensen was also aware that the latest intelligence coming in on the Japanese 13th Destroyer Escort Squadron was that it was well down the eastern coast of Okinawa island and was expected offshore of their position at any time. That set a pretty obvious timeline for Japan's potentially military intervention, as they'd clearly be planning to have naval fire support for any ground action at White Beach.

It didn't look to him like the US was being left very many options for withdrawing peacefully from Okinawa. To him, it looked like China and Japan were aiming for total and humiliating capitulation, with accompanying media images of defeated US Marines waving white flags and being marched into captivity to be used as bargaining chips. Jensen had no idea who the Japanese or Chinese commander was behind this particular attack, but it showed he had very little understanding of either the resolve and capabilities of the 1st Marine Battalion, or their commander, Ted Collins.

Their first problem, however, was the protesters.

Jensen was standing at a watchtower, two hundred yards behind the security checkpoint, looking at the situation through binoculars and on the screen of the recon drone operator beside him. "I'm seeing about two hundred civilians, being led forward by two guys in black paramilitary clothing shouting into bullhorns," he reported to the man. "Behind them, some more goons in black with bullhorns and batons, prodding everyone forward. I see utility belts on the goons, could be armed with sidearms, but no rifles. A hundred yards behind them, I have one Type 89 troop carrier and a platoon of infantry, moving forward on overwatch. Assault rifles and a couple of heavy MGs. Concur?"

The man consulted his screen. "Make that 300 civilians and two of the black-clad militia are carrying cameras, looks like they're documenting the action. Otherwise I concur, sir."

"I'm going forward," Jensen said. "Pass the word to HQ. We're going to try to push them back to the gate."

He slid down the iron ladder of the small tower to the ground and doubled toward his squad. He had put every one of his men on the perimeter, but they were stretched pretty damn thin. The base was on a triangle-shaped point of land, two miles along each side. There were double wire fences on the landward side facing north, but not the kind of defensive earthworks or infrastructure needed to keep out enemy infantry or vehicles. So he had his 200-man company digging foxholes in the sandy ground for cover, all along the perimeter fence. He had only three combat platoons – one here at the main gates, another in bushland to the west where the base perimeter met a public road, and the third in the east where double gates led out into farmland and a small access road. The buildings behind his men were being fortified by the 1st Marine Battalion, but until and unless hostilities began, his security force was the thin green line of base defense.

They were armed only with their venerable M4 carbines, though when he saw the Japanese armored vehicle moving up, Jensen had put two M27 automatic rifles in the guard huts flanking each side of the road in and out of the base and sent for a man-portable Javelin anti-tank missile launcher. There were only eight of his men visible and exposed, four of whom stood prominently at the boom gates, carbines held at the ready across their chests, while the other four stood less threateningly beside the guard huts.

"Corporal!" he yelled, calling a squad leader, Garcia, to him. The man was a tall, quiet Texan and very good at persuasion. Much better than the undiplomatic Jensen had ever been. He pointed up the road to where the protesters were shuffling uncertainly forward, bullied by the men in black uniforms in front of and behind them. "You have a sidearm?"

"Yes sir!"

"Hand your carbine to one of your men. You and I are going out there to stop this circus," he said. Garcia ran over to his second in command, gave the man his carbine and some well-chosen words about the rules of engagement, and then rejoined his CO. Checking out of habit that his 9mm Sig Sauer was snugged into its holster on his belt, Jensen led the way toward the mob.

"We'll take the goon on the left with the bullhorn," Jensen said quietly. "Follow my lead. Keep your weapon holstered unless things get out of hand and only fire in the air if they do."

The crowd was moving slowly forward from only fifty feet away and Jensen and Garcia closed the distance at a fast walk. Jensen planted himself in front of the man with the bullhorn and held up his hands. "Stop right there!" he said. "This is a US Navy facility and you are…"

The man was shorter but stockier than Jensen and glared back at him. From his bearing, Jensen had no doubt the man was a soldier, not a civilian. He didn't even hesitate, just went to step around Jensen's left and kept shouting in his bullhorn. The real civilians were not so insistent. Most of those in the front row stopped up, with Garcia further down the line also holding his arms out.

Jensen reacted instantly to the black-clad man's attempt to get past him. He pivoted on his left foot, kicking the man behind his knee and bringing him down on one leg. With a quick stiff-armed shove to the man's left shoulder he laid him out flat and then stood over him with a boot on his throat. "I said *stop*, sir!"

The other black-clad man, further down at the front of the first line of protesters, dropped his bullhorn and pulled a baton from his belt. Garcia quickly grabbed his Sig Sauer from his holster and pointed it at the man's chest. "*Tachidomaru!*" he yelled. "Halt!"

238

Several civilians screamed and tried to step back. A couple tried to turn and run back toward the main road, but the militia at their rear spread their batons and prevented any going past. The man under his boot was struggling and yelling and Jensen pressed down harder. Around the side of the crowd, he saw one of the black-clad men running forward. He also saw the Japanese armored vehicle moving slowly to a position where it had a clear line of fire past the protesters to his troops back on the security barrier. Its rapid-fire 35mm cannon swiveled back and forth menacingly.

"OK, here comes the boss," Jensen said, watching the Japanese armor with his peripheral vision, but without taking his eyes off the man running toward them. "Keep cool, Garcia."

"Cool as yesterday's pie, sir," the Marine said, his pistol still pointed at the guy with the baton, who had decided he'd also stop and see what his boss had to say, as the alternative seemed to be getting himself shot in the heart.

The new arrival stopped a few feet away from Jensen and started talking to him in Japanese. He was in his fifties and looked lean and fit. Definitely military. He had the red bandana all the others were wearing, but was carrying it in his hand. He appeared to be glancing back over his shoulder and Jensen quickly realized why. There was another 'civilian' about ten feet away, filming everything. It was probably being streamed live to the web. That changed nothing as far as Jensen was concerned. He ignored whatever the man was saying and spoke loudly in English.

"You are trespassing on US Navy property," he said to him loudly and slowly. "I am going to release this man and you are going to turn these people around and take them back to the public road. You can continue your protest there."

There was some shouting from inside the crowd – a woman's voice this time – not directed at Jensen or Garcia, but at the man with the military appearance. The man shouted back at her and then reached into the crowd and hauled her roughly out. It was an old lady.

A very old lady. A younger girl supported her by the elbow and tried to push the black-clad bully away, but a shout from him was enough to send her back a few steps.

He spoke brusquely to the old woman, then ushered her forward. She came slowly, shuffling in sandaled feet, until she stood right in front of Jensen. The bully shoved her in the back, urging her to speak.

"He doesn't speak English," she said in a calm, clear voice. "I told him I do."

The bully yelled a question at her and she turned around, saying something to him in Japanese and then in English, "I am telling the American you are an imbecile, is that not correct?"

The man nodded, "Hai!" and spoke rapidly to her again.

She was bent over and had to look up at Jensen with her neck at what appeared a very painful angle.

"He wants me to tell you the people of Japan have come to reclaim their land," she said. "What is your reply?"

"Tell him this is US Navy property and my men have orders to prevent any entry onto this base, civilian or military."

She turned her head and spoke briefly and the man started shouting back at her, but she leaned forward, speaking so softly only Jensen could hear. "I heard them speaking outside the bus," she said. "They are trying to provoke you to use violence."

Jensen reviewed his tactical options. He could pull back to the security barrier, but the problem would repeat itself in the time it took for the mob to move forward. With the shoot-down of the Chinese fighter, infantry on their perimeter and a mob at their gates, the situation had progressed beyond rubber bullets and teargas. He could see no option but to pull his men back from the gates to join the Marines on the line and see what the Japanese forces' next move was.

Jensen lifted his boot off the throat of the man still writhing underneath him and took a step back. "Tell your friend our troops have orders to defend this base and they will shoot to kill if that is required," he told the old woman.

"Then many will die," the old lady said, with terrible fatalism.

Jensen was taken aback and was about to reply when several things happened at once. The black-clad man Jensen had released from under his boot rolled to his feet and tried to kick Jensen's legs out from under him. The bully shoved the old lady in the back, pitching her toward Jensen, and then urged the mob forward. Garcia made a snap decision, took his pistol off the man he was holding it on, turned and shot Jensen's attacker in the side. People screamed, scattering in all directions, some forward, toward the security barriers. One of the black-clad men at the back of the crowd grabbed a sidearm from the small of his back and fired at Garcia, who dived to the ground and then ran for cover.

Jensen instinctively grabbed at the old lady to break her fall, then went down in a crush of bodies. As he fell, he heard the terrible sound of a 35mm cannon opening fire!

"I have two surface contacts in active search mode," Tanken told Shaofeng. "Multiple dipping buoys in the water, almost certainly rotary drones. The Stingray AI is calling the surface contacts *Zumwalt*-class destroyers." He spread his arms out to his sides and flexed his fingers. He hadn't just turned up on DB's team by chance. He had been training on stolen and copied US weapons and sensor systems for several years, even though his superiors had not been sure when, where, or how he might one day use that training. When he had been ordered to Shanghai and told what he would be asked to do, he had just one thought in his mind. *Bring it.*

"What is the risk of discovery?" Major Shaofeng demanded.

"The US destroyers are moving on a course that would take them within two to four hundred yards of us," Tanken said urgently. He had his eyes on his screens but was speaking over his shoulder to DB and Major Shaofeng. "Their sensor footprint is considerable. We should move south to evade them while we still can, but given the changed speed and direction of the US taskforce, this carries with it the risk that we would then be out of position to attack the *Makin Island*."

"No!" Shaofeng said. "Our target is that US assault ship!"

Tanken was visibly disappointed and sighed. "Very well. We are over the Mariana Trench, Comrade Major. The safest tactic would be to drift deep and shut down all systems," he said. "Let the American destroyers pass over us and then resume our interception of the *Makin Island*."

"Yes, yes," Shaofeng said. "Good! Do it."

"There are also risks if we follow that course of action, Comrade Major," Tanken said. He turned in his chair to face Shaofeng. "At any depth beyond 400 feet, the Stingray would be forced to cut its comms buoy …" He consulted his screen. "We would temporarily lose direct control of the Stingray."

"Lose direct control of the… what do you mean?"

Po spoke up. "If we lose our comms link to the Stingray, it will revert to AI control. We can't be certain where and when it would re-establish contact, if at all."

"That is unacceptable!" Shaofeng said. His fatherly demeanor was cracking. "You must retain control of the American vessel!"

"Outline the best option, Lieutenant Tanken," DB prompted. "So that the Major can make an informed decision."

"Yes, Comrade Captain," Tanken said, clearly enjoying his moment. "I recommend we continue to proceed toward the intercept with the *Makin Island* at quarter speed, attempting to maximize our stealth profile. This optimizes our opportunity to intercept the *Makin Island*, but increases the risk of detection. In that scenario, I would recommend adopting an *offensive* posture, sir." Tanken raised his eyebrows and waited.

DB blanched, but Shaofeng frowned. He was the administrator of a cyber warfare unit, not a PLA Navy officer. DB realized Tanken's explanation was not entirely clear.

"The Lieutenant is suggesting we be prepared to attack the US destroyers if needed, to clear a path and ensure the best possible chance of intercepting the US carrier."

"You... this ..." Shaofeng was in danger of scratching his ear right off his face. He appeared paralyzed. The clock was ticking.

Frangipani stood and coughed. "May I suggest the Comrade Major immediately present the options to our PLA Navy comrades, to allow them to make this decision? We could be detected any moment."

"Yes," Shaofeng said. "The Colonel. Yes." He stopped scratching and held out his hand. "Telephone, please. Quickly!"

"Your boat has pump-jet propulsion, you said?" Reilly asked. He had his headphones glued to his ears, his eyes fixed on the readout from his Acoustic AI assistant, which replaced the human assistant he would earlier have been working with. He had two destroyers, four rotary-winged drones, and a Hunter Continuous Trail submersible searching the area around the coordinates Bunny's team had sent through and they were finding precisely ... nothing!

"Like the *Virginia*-class boats, but smaller," Bunny told him. "But if it knows you're nearby, it will either shut down or pulse glide in intermittent bursts. You have to be pretty lucky to pick it up during a thrust cycle."

"Well, it's your baby, what's its weakness?" Reilly asked.

She thought carefully. She'd had plenty of time sitting at her console during sea trials, thinking about how she'd go about hunting her Stingray. "I doubt the Chinese would be confident enough to put it in full autonomous mode, even with an enemy sub hunter in the area. And if they wanted to be able to engage us, they'd need to be able to contact it via satellite, to issue navigation and weapons commands in near real time, so it would have to be relatively shallow and it would have to be trailing a comms buoy on the surface. That makes noise," she said. "You could try looking for that."

"How shallow is relatively shallow?" Weisner asked.

"From the surface, 400 feet."

"And are these buoys the same as our Sea Hunter uses? Anechoic coating?"

"No. The ones fitted on this prototype are bigger. Royal Navy X-Sub expendable 4-inch buoy," she said. "Teardrop shape. Deployable at up to ten knots. They aren't stealth optimized. And they're about the same size as a kettle BBQ." She looked around her. "Is there some way to get my guys back at White Beach plugged in here so they can help work this too?"

"You mean on a radio link?" the XO asked.

"Getting them plugged into the tactical feed would be ideal, but a simple radio link would be better than nothing," she said. If ever there was a time she needed the capable Kyle and the infuriatingly indispensable Kevin on her side, it was now.

"Ears, you ever find a sub by locking onto its comms buoy?" the XO asked.

"No sir, I have not."

"Alright, O'Hare, I'll send you an information systems tech, tell them what you need. In the meantime, Ears, that buoy..."

"Aye sir, if it's getting pulled along the surface by a cable and it's made of metal, we might be able to pick it up on K-band radar, as well as sonar," he said. "I'll use a mine-hunting algorithm, set it for multi-sensor surface search." He started punching keys. "I can use the Chinese *Quickstrike* cluster mine profile. Those little guys are about the same size as that buoy."

He called up the *Monsoor* to coordinate with its search aircraft, then hit execute on the new algorithm, sending it to all search platforms, including the submersible drone.

"How long until we are within range of its torpedoes?" Bunny asked.

"We don't know its current speed or heading, but twenty minutes ago it was eleven miles out," Reilly said tersely. "The Mark 50 has a range of nine miles. We're cavitating like a windmill in a storm. I'd say it's already got us dead in its sights. It's just a question of whether it shoots or scoots."

"Yes, Comrade Colonel," Shaofeng said, talking into his telephone with his back to DB and his team. "Yes, I understand. Yes, we will. Thank you, Comrade Colonel!" He turned around again and DB could see that the knuckles around his telephone were white. "We are not authorized, under any circumstances, to fire on the American destroyers. Our target is still the *Makin Island* and the weapon of choice is the EMP torpedo. Even though we risk the failure of our mission, we are not to fire any weapon, including the EMP torpedo, without the express authorization of PLA Navy Commander Wang Heng."

Tanken was not fazed. He had the American destroyers on his sonar now and knew exactly where they were. "In that case we are about to see how good the stealth technology is on the US submersible." He checked the Stingray's stealth profile and ordered it to rescan the thermocline and move to the optimal depth for evading the enemy destroyers, but not to adjust its speed.

The *Lyndon B*'s comms tech had not only patched Kevin and Kyle into the tactical feed from Reilly's screens, she had also rigged up a live video call that used the cameras from the two Stingray programmers' workstations to show them both on screen.

"OK, well, in cruise mode it stays above 400 feet, with a comms buoy on the surface at all times. In stealth mode it reels the buoy in, heads under the thermocline, and you'll have almost zero detection probability," Kevin was saying.

"Can we spook it?" Kyle said. "Into a radical maneuver?"

"Spook it how?" Reilly asked.

"I don't know … drop a random depth charge, fire an ASROC torpedo on active homing?"

"Not without a target lock," Reilly told them, shaking his head. "Your chances of randomly dropping a homing torpedo in the Pacific anywhere near that boat are a million to one."

Bunny leaned into the camera view. "Come on, guys, we've got helos in the air, we've got a Sea Hunter scouting along the last known bearing we took, we've got a position that is less than thirty minutes old. There has to be something!"

She saw Kyle hit a key to mute their feed and he and Kevin started arguing. Kevin was shaking his head, but Kyle was jabbing a finger into the table and finally turned back to the camera, taking it off mute.

"Your Sea Hunter, it's in passive mode right now, just listening, right ... but how much radiation could it put out if it wanted to be heard?" he asked.

"It uses the same upgraded sonar array as the LA-class boats," Reilly said. "So once it starts pinging, you'd be able to hear it up to twenty miles away."

"So here's an idea," he said. "The Stingray AI can be provoked to go offensive if it detects a threat with a high probability of intercepting it. An attack-class sonar pinging it within a five-mile range would meet the probability threshold."

"It's a complete roll of the dice," Kevin complained. "If you go active outside that range, the Stingray will know exactly where you are and just plot a course to evade you. That Sea Hunter is the only ace up your sleeve. You'll burn it and achieve nothing."

"Or if you are lucky, you could provoke the Stingray to go offensive and attack the threat," Kyle said with a shrug. "You wanted something. It's something, right?"

"You want 'something', how about this?" Kevin said, not giving up. "You provoke my AI to go offensive, it might not be satisfied with just taking out the Sea Hunter. You could find *yourselves* on the pointy end of a brace of Mark 50 torpedoes too. How's that for 'something', boss?"

"We need to discuss it with the XO," Reilly said. "It's his call. Is there any way I might see or hear that your boat is going on the attack, before it uses its ordnance?"

"Sure," Kyle said. "If it goes offensive, the first thing it will do is cut the comms buoy loose," Kyle was saying. "That's a weak spot, right there. It makes all sorts of noise, the wire being cut, the buoy jumps in the water like a whale breaching..."

"So I might get a sonar return, might even pick up the profile of the buoy as it bounces..."

"Oh come on," Kevin said. "Are we in Kansas anymore? Let's say you get lucky and the Sea Hunter *is* close enough to spook the Stingray when it goes active. You would have maybe thirty seconds of transient noise in the water that wouldn't be much louder than a whale fart. Good luck with that."

Reilly grinned. "The algorithms I use are so advanced they can tell the difference between a whale fart and a dolphin fart, boys." He started tapping away at his keyboard. "They can also tell me when my Sea Hunter has max probability of being within five miles of your Stingray. I say we go for it."

Bunny clapped his shoulder. "Keep working it, Ears," she said. "I'll go sell it to Weisner."

Four hundred feet below the waves, the Stingray executed Tanken's orders with silicon equanimity. Its onboard AI had been monitoring the battlesphere around it and it was fully aware that American *Fire Scout* drones using dipping radar had been executing a search sequence around it. It had identified four separate platforms and at the edge of its passive detection range picked up the noise of ship-borne active sonar, also in search mode. It was monitoring two vessels and concluded that at least one of them was actively searching the area through which it was going to be transiting. But it had been up against US anti-submarine platforms before – it knew their capabilities and its own intimately. It calculated a high likelihood of escaping detection.

247

When it received Tanken's order to further optimize its stealth profile, while maintaining bearing and speed, it assessed that these were conflicting orders. In order to optimize its stealth profile, it should reduce speed, reel in its comms buoy, dive below the thermocline and change bearing. In a low-threat environment, it would have simply obeyed its human operator, no matter how illogical the order. But it was not in a low-threat environment. It was being hunted and it had learned much in the last intensive year of its at-sea existence. About how to stay alive and how to kill.

The Stingray ran a scenario and probability analysis and assessed that with the enemy search platforms so close, even with stealth propulsion in pulse mode, there was a 38 percent chance of detection if it executed Tanken's new orders. But it could adjust its response profile to be ready to evade an attack and initiate a counter-attack, which under its current rules of engagement required human authorization.

It sent a plain language message to its human operator. Your orders create a 38 percent chance of detection, this can be optimized further. Optimize, yes or no?

Tanken read the alert with amusement. *Optimize?* Well, duh. Thirty-eight percent risk seemed too high for comfort. Those were worse odds than he'd had sneaking through the American picket in his *Ming*-class sub and he'd only just pulled that off! *Yes, optimize*, he'd replied.

He smiled at the idea the drone's AI was challenging his decision. Machine insolence was not something China built into its weapons, but he could see it had its uses.

A short while later, two affect circles on Reilly's tac monitor started to intersect: the projected position of the Stingray, and the active sonar field of his Sea Hunter. Weisner had come down from the overhead floor to reduce command lag and was hovering over his shoulder. He hadn't enjoyed hearing from O'Hare how small were the chances of intercepting the Stingray, but he was happy she and her team were at least bringing him a solution, not just explaining the problem. He'd put all offensive and defensive systems personnel on the highest possible alert for the coming action.

"Stingray inside the five-mile probability zone," Reilly said quietly. He turned to Weisner. "Initiate active search on the Sea Hunter, sir?"

Weisner nodded. "Light her up, Ears."

"Aye sir, 360 degrees, full power, all arrays," he said. "If it's within five miles, it'll hear us loud and clear."

"Question is, what will it do next?" Weisner said. "Any bets, O'Hare?"

Before she could answer, Reilly leaned forward. A flow of lines like the graph on a lie detector ran down his screen and he stopped them at a tiny blip. "Mark! Time 0422, surface anomaly on the K-band, searching for a match!"

The system's voice was inaudible to O'Hare and Weisner, but the text transcript rolled across the bottom of the graphical interface. *Anomaly analyzed. Quickstrike surface cluster mine detected.*

"It's cut its buoy!" Bunny exclaimed.

"Target! Designating A1," Reilly called out, though his targeting data was already going directly to the weapons officers in control of the *Zumwalt*'s anti-submarine missile system, sitting in a booth right beside him. He was calling verbally for the benefit of Weisner. "Bearing 242 degrees, distance 2.02 miles, assume depth zero to 400 feet! Sea Hunter has a lock! I have an acoustic profile match. *Target confirmed!*" He sounded like a kid that had just thrown a fifty-yard touchdown pass and spun his chair full circle to high five O'Hare and return to his screens. "The *Monsoor* caught the buoy on surface radar," he said. "Tin can must have bounced a yard in the air…"

"Who has the best shot?" Weisner asked Reilly, cutting him off. He had command authority for the search, so he had to make the call over whether the *Lyndon B* or *Monsoor* was in the best position to attack.

"We are occluded by the *Monsoor*," Reilly replied. "*Monsoor* has the best solution, sir."

Weisner turned to his left, to the weapons station. "Clear the *Monsoor* to shoot. ASROC salvo, target A1!"

Buried inside the artificial calm of the *Lyndon B*'s control center, Bunny had to imagine what was happening five miles away across the water, as the rocket-launched torpedoes leaped out of tubes along the side of the *Monsoor* and arced away over the water to drop around their suspected target.

She didn't have time to think about it very long, before Reilly was yelling again.

"*Enemy torpedoes in the water!*" he said. "Bearing 242! Target *Monsoor*. Impact … one minute ten!!"

Bunny paled. Yet again the Stingray AI had shown how damn smart it was. It must have analyzed the sonar signal directed at it, and identified it as coming from an unarmed Sea Hunter. Not a primary threat. So it had turned its weapons on the nearest true threat – the USS *Michael Monsoor*.

On the bridge, Commander Sallinger and his bridge crew saw Weisner's launch order on their screens, followed by the enemy torpedo alert, but his command and control AI reacted before he could even call out his orders. It queued up a decoy and evasion sequence in case torpedoes were also fired at the *Lyndon B*, requiring Sallinger only to confirm it by hitting a button on his command station. More concerned about the risk of torpedoes coming his way than about giving away his position, he punched it and clawed for his seatbelt.

Reaching for his comms handset, he keyed in the command center and held it up to his mouth. "Talk to me, XO!" Sallinger yelled at his second in command.

"Enemy target engaged, sir," Weisner told him. "It counter-attacked, target *Monsoor*."

"*Monsoor* maneuvering, releasing decoys!" Reilly said.

"Comms lost," Tanken said with false calm. His adrenaline was surging.

"What, what does that mean?!" Shaofeng exclaimed.

Tanken tried to keep his voice level. "It means we have lost communication with the Stingray, Comrade Major, as I warned. There could be any number of reasons."

"How can we find out?" Shaofeng asked.

"The Stingray can still transmit on very low frequency radio, using the untethered buoy as a relay – the Americans call it *Deep Siren* tactical paging. And it only works one way; from the sub up to our satellite. It should report in shortly if it is still capable. We can't issue orders and there will be a lag of approximately … one minute."

DB looked around the room. Shaofeng was tugging at his earlobe like he wanted to rip it off, Frangi was staring at the tactical screens with a deep but also slightly detached fascination. Po was lost to the world, his head buried in his own screen, either in code, or a dinner menu. DB? He felt demons crawl over his back and shuddered.

A sudden beep jolted the silence and Shaofeng jumped.

"Message coming in … decrypting …" Tanken said quietly. A red icon began flashing on his screen, near the icon that was their Stingray. *Under attack. Counter-attack initiated. Target USS Monsoor.*" Tanken almost whispered, his voice no longer calm, as he frowned at data on his screen. "The Stingray was attacked and responded by firing two torpedoes at its attacker! I swear, sir, I didn't…"

Shaofeng looked like a man standing in front of a firing squad. He was pale, shaking visibly.

"We were ordered not to engage," he said weakly, then repeated himself. "Under any circumstances! Unless it was the *Makin Island*."

"I didn't do it! It must be some sort of AI self-defense routine," Tanken protested.

Shaofeng pointed at Tanken, turning to DB. "I ordered him not to engage the American destroyers," Shaofeng said, as though appealing to a court-martial judge. "You heard me!"

"And I didn't!" Tanken yelled at him disrespectfully. "What kind of idiot do you think I am?"

"Lieutenant Tanken!" DB said sternly. "Compose yourself!"

Tanken ran a hand through his hair. "Apologies, Comrade officers." Another message came across his screen. "Oh God. *Evading. Five seconds to target impact.*"

The team at DARPA had designed the Stingray's original defensive countermeasure system well. When it detected a homing torpedo coming toward it, the Stingray's AI took evasive action and, if possible, attacked its attacker. It was this programming that had led the Stingray, on a test mission, to fire its torpedoes at a curious, now deceased, blue whale. So, until they found a workaround, Bunny and team had rewritten the code so that the Stingray could not deploy its offensive weapons without a manual command from shore. This should have made it impossible for the Stingray to engage the *Monsoor* on its own authority, even with its rules of engagement 'optimized' for a high-threat environment by Tanken's own order.

However, the brute force reboot that had briefly restored control to DARPA before it was snatched away again by APT 23 had wiped the restraining code. The Stingray had reverted to its original programming, giving it weapons autonomy and allowing it to do what it judged it needed to do to protect its integrity and pursue its primary mission objective. Just as it had once fired torpedoes at a whale, it queued up a pair of torpedoes for what it assessed to be the largest existential threat; not the unarmed Sea Hunter tracking it, but the destroyer USS *Michael Monsoor*, which was in the best position to attack it. But Kevin had made *some* progress in its programming. It did not fire them immediately. Despite the enormous risk to itself with an enemy vessel aggressively pinging it with targeting sonar, it locked up the *Monsoor* and waited to see if the US warship would attack first.

It did.

Less than a second after the Stingray heard the *Monsoor*'s ASROC torpedoes splash down and start homing, it fired its own torpedoes, cut its buoy, shut down its engine and feathered its pump-jet propulsion. Any chance of cavitation noise was eliminated and the Stingray became a perfectly silent shadow, gliding deeper through the water.

A perfectly silent, rather huge shadow, though. So before it shut down, it fired four noise-emitting decoy drones out of the top of its hull which drifted on small engines to a position that was a safe distance from the Stingray but close enough to spoof an incoming torpedo. They automatically kept station with each other so that they could replicate the length and volume of a large submarine and started emitting both sonar energy and gas bubbles to create a huge 'pick me, pick me' hole in the ocean. It was exactly the type of decoy profile that the Common Broadband Advanced Sonar System on a CBASS Mark 50 torpedo was designed *not* to fall for.

But the four ASROC torpedoes fired by the *Lyndon B* were not CBASS enhanced. They blinked as the Stingray went silent, saw its decoys and fell in love, racing toward them to explode harmlessly 500 feet from the Stingray.

The near miss was reported to Beijing one minute and five seconds later via *Deep Siren*.

"*Torpedoes evaded!*" Tanken yelled, punching the air. "We're still in the fight."

"There should be no fight," Shaofeng moaned. "Our mission is over."

The torpedoes fired by the *Monsoor*'s ASROC crew had missed the Stingray because they were dumb. Those fired by the Stingray and now closing on the *Zumwalt*-class destroyer were a newer generation designed not to fall for decoys. They had no trouble at all deciding that the noise- and gas-emitting decoys fired from the bottom of the frantically maneuvering *Monsoor* were *not* a 15,000-ton displacement warship.

"ASROC detonations," Reilly said, giving them a running commentary. "No secondaries." He wasn't picking up any noise indicating that the Stingray had been hit – hull collapsing, ballast tanks blowing as it surfaced...

"What about the torpedoes headed for *Monsoor*?" Weisner asked.

"They're not going for the *Monsoor*'s decoys!" Reilly said. "Both incoming torpedoes still running true. Impact ... five seconds!"

"Where is *our* solution on that damned Stingray, STS?" Weisner demanded. If the *Monsoor* was incapacitated, he wanted to be able to take on the Stingray himself.

Reilly was working the contact feverishly. "I've got two *Fire Scout*s moving to the location of that buoy, but nothing on sonar. Too much noise after our torpedoes detonated. Sea Hunter has lost it too."

Bunny watched transfixed as the attack played out on Reilly's tactical screen. Two blue lines showed the track of the torpedoes from the Stingray. The *Monsoor* was turning in a tight half-circle as it tried to come around and present its stern to the incoming torpedoes, giving them the smallest possible target. And it just about made it.

The two 100lb shaped warheads on the Stingray's torpedoes smashed into the *Monsoor*'s propeller housing. Each *Zumwalt* was driven through the water by twin five-bladed nickel-aluminum bronze propellers measuring over 18 feet in diameter and weighing nearly 60,000 pounds apiece. In effect they were the best armor anywhere on the ship. One of the Stingray's torpedoes smashed straight into the portside propeller and detonated without the blast reaching the hull of the *Monsoor*. But the destroyer wasn't all the way through its turn and the second torpedo punched into the propeller housing just forward of the blades, the explosion buckling the starboard shaft and sending the port shaft into an overspeed state which threatened to burn out its Rolls Royce turbine engine. Power to the shaft was automatically cut to stop the engine tearing itself apart.

The *Monsoor* began decelerating immediately. Within ten minutes it would lose steerageway. Within fifteen, it would be dead in the water.

There were no torpedoes headed for the *Lyndon B* or other vessels. Yet.

"Prop strike!" Reilly said, leaning forward, still in his harness, hands cupped around the headphones over his ears as he peered at a display on his screen. "Yeah, hit them in the ass. They're losing way."

"They hit the engines?" Bunny asked.

"Don't think so," he said. "If those torpedoes hit the props, bent something out of shape, they're probably powering down to prevent them tearing themselves apart. But they're sitting ducks."

Kevin and Kyle were still monitoring the tactical feed, and though their voices had been dialed down, O'Hare heard Kevin mutter, "Told you. I told you this was a *bad* idea …"

Reilly's sensor screen flashed an alert.

"Possible contact from the Sea Hunter! Bearing 253, depth 450, distance 4,400 yards!" Reilly said.

"Lock it up, Ears," Weisner said urgently, telling the sonarman to make the return precise enough to allow a firing solution. "Weapons!" he added. "Prepare to salvo ASROC when you have target lock."

"No! Wait!" Bunny said, jumping out of her chair. "Those torpedoes were only fired at the *Monsoor* after the Stingray detected our torpedoes in the water." She looked at Weisner and Reilly and realized they didn't know what she meant. "It's reverted to native programming," she explained. "It will only attack again if it is threatened."

"Unless whoever is at the controls of that machine decides otherwise and goes postal on us?" Weisner asked.

"The Chinese are not in control of that boat right now," Bunny told him. "When attacked, it cuts its comms buoy and goes autonomous until it's out of the threat zone. It isn't supposed to be able to use its weapons autonomously, but it did. I'm just saying, if you shoot at it, it will get angry and shoot back. If you don't, it probably won't."

"That's some kind of crazy-ass warship you guys built there," Reilly muttered.

"Thank you for the contextual analysis, Reilly," Weisner said dryly. "But our mission is to protect the *Makin Island*, even if it means putting ourselves in harm's way. Because that's why we're here. Lock it up, Reilly."

"Narrow beam targeting search, aye sir," Reilly said. "Target locked! Designating Alpha 2."

"ASW, do you have a solution?" Weisner asked.

"Aye, sir. Confirm. *Lyndon B* has a solution," the anti-submarine weapons team responded this time.

Weisner gripped the back of Reilly's chair. "ASROC! Target is Alpha 2, full salvo. *Shoot!*"

Bunny's Stingray was indeed one angry unit. Or as angry as silicon could get. If it had been the type of AI that held grudges, it would have been royally pissed. First, it lost communications with its Okinawa base. Then when communications were re-established it was given a new set of mission orders, to which it responded immediately. Then it was subjected to a brute force cyber-attack which triggered a root-level reboot and when that was complete and it had resumed its mission, it was attacked by a ship *from its own Navy*. It was used to this, in a simulation or exercise environment, but it had immediately detected that the torpedoes fired at it were very real and it had responded in kind. And whoever had been hunting it, was hunting it *still*. The narrow beam sonar hit from the Sea Hunter was proof of that. And that just made it angrier.

Which was a gross 'humanization' of a few million lines of computer code, but explained nicely why the Stingray did what it was about to do.

It checked the status of the warship now behind it and falling further behind by the minute. The destroyer, which it had identified as a *Zumwalt*-class destroyer – and, judging by the acoustic signature of its propellers and shafts, most definitely the USS *Michael Monsoor* – was drifting to a standstill. Its active sonar was no longer radiating. The Stingray AI calculated probabilities and assigned a 73 percent chance to the hypothesis that the *Michael Monsoor* had been successfully disabled and was currently not a threat.

Scanning the bubble of space out to its maximum detection range, the Stingray analyzed the rest of the threat environment. There were still four intermittent sonar sources, probably drone-mounted dipping sonars, but none with a high probability of detection. For good measure, the AI initiated jamming at a frequency calculated to neutralize the dipping sonar anyway. The Sea Hunter was too close to jam, its radiation too powerful. That meant the attacking force would still have a weapons solution. A second destroyer, which the Stingray had identified from its acoustic signature as the *Zumwalt*-class *Lyndon B Johnson*, was moving on a track parallel to the Stingray. The Stingray was, however, well within range of either destroyer's sea-air-launched ASROC torpedoes.

The tactical situation was not complex. It had disabled the *Michael Monsoor*. It now had to destroy or disable the USS *Lyndon B Johnson* before it was destroyed or disabled itself. A simple torpedo strike would not suffice as it needed to knock out both destroyers' anti-submarine weapons.

There was only one weapon in its torpedo pod with the capability needed, and the Stingray brought it online.

To Die, To Live

Takuya Kato shared a similar dread to Karen O'Hare, though they were several hundred miles apart. That feeling of emotional detachment from your own situation, the ice-cold blood flowing up your spine to your skull. He didn't have enemy torpedoes racing straight at him, but he was in an existential crisis nonetheless.

He was back in the cockpit of a *Snow Falcon*, holding formation with Li Chen's fighters, five miles east of the *Liaoning*, two hundred miles north of Okinawa, waiting for the last of the fighters and Li Chen herself to join the formation so that they could move on Okinawa.

Their mission was a combat air patrol at high altitude over White Beach naval base. They were prepared for air-to-air combat – the US had attack aircraft aboard the USS *Makin Island* and it could send strategic bombers or drones from Guam to support its Marines. But the biggest threat to the Japanese troops now engaged with US forces defending White Beach was targeted cruise missile strikes, fired from US surface or submerged warships out to sea, which was why Li Chen's aircraft were armed with a mixed loadout of air-to-air missiles (with which to target any cruise missiles that slipped through the destroyer screen) and *Eagle Strike* anti-ship missiles. Li Chen's intelligence officer had explained during the briefing that satellite data showed Okinawa's four-warship US taskforce could be within range to provide ground support, though probably not anti-air support, within the mission window.

Kato had been interviewed, as Li Chen had forewarned him, by a camera crew before climbing into his aircraft.

"Comrade Lieutenant," the media officer had asked, "you are a Japanese pilot. How do you feel to be representing your country on this joint operation with the People's Liberation Army Naval Air Force?"

How do I feel? Conflicted? Bitter? Angry? He hated himself for not saying what he was thinking. "I am proud to be flying for my country," he'd said. "Thank you, I must get into my aircraft."

With the *Snow Falcon*'s AI keeping formation and running its own system checks, there was nothing for Kato to do but think and he had much to think about.

He thought about the warning he had sent to the Palace about the impending air attack on the US base and how he had learned that it was already out of date, because Japanese ground forces were already engaged with US Marines at White Beach.

And he thought about the message he had received in return, from Mitsuko. His friend. His empress. There was only so much you could say in a coded, burst transmission. But there was only so much she needed to say.

My dearest Takuya. My dear and lifelong friend. I must ask of you a most difficult thing. You must, at all costs, find a way to disable the *Liaoning* immediately. I realize that this will put you in grave, perhaps even mortal danger. For your country and for me, I must ask this of you. Mitsuko.

The request – the order – of his friend and Empress was clear. How to execute it was not. Since his arrival on the *Liaoning*, Kato had been kept constantly busy. He had studied, trained, flown sorties, slept an exhausted sleep and seen nothing of the ship but the flight operations and officers' briefing room, wardrooms, and sleeping quarters. As he looked over at the ship in the distance, barely visible in the half-light of dawn, he could see its decks teeming with aircraft being jockeyed into position, as another *Snow Falcon*, probably Li Chen's, was fired off the deck and into the air. He had anti-ship missiles on his aircraft, but they were AI-controlled and even if he managed to spoof the AI into targeting the *Liaoning*, all he could do was order it to fire them, an order which it would automatically refuse if the target was a Chinese warship or aircraft!

He was powerless to carry out his duty.

"Get that Javelin up here right now!" Jensen yelled at Garcia. They'd disentangled themselves from the cluster which had been the protest action and ducked down behind the concrete base of the guard hut behind which they were sheltering. The metal walls and roof of the hut had been shredded by the 35mm cannon of the Japanese troop carrier, but the reinforced concrete base was still holding and Jensen and four of his men were huddled behind it, returning fire at the Japanese infantry who were trying to take his position. To the east and west he heard other firefights – his biggest fear was that one of their flanks would fall and the Japanese would get in behind him.

Most of the civilians had fled, but between the Japanese infantry and his position were the bodies of several of the civilians who had not been able to get out of the line of fire when the Japanese had opened up. None were moving.

"We could fall back, sir!" Garcia said, before spinning into a crouch to fire briefly and then duck back down. He nodded at the platoon of 1st battalion Marines crouched behind concrete barriers further inside the base, sniping at long range. Much of the fire being directed downrange by the Japanese armored vehicle was aimed over Jensen and Garcia's heads, at the troops beyond, to keep them from moving up. It had already used two wire-guided missiles on their positions. The Type 89 troop carrier was pulling in and out of cover behind a gray, three-story apartment building with two cars, now wrecked, parked in front of it.

"Get back there and get me a Javelin!" Jensen repeated. "When you return, I'm going to detach the command unit, try and get a flanking position behind that wall…" He pointed about fifty feet ahead and to the left, where what had been the marble structure saying "*White Beach, Commander Fleet Activities, Okinawa*" was now little more than a pile of rubble. "I should be able to get a good lock on that armored vehicle from there. I'll try to draw it out to take a shot at me. It will be side on to you. As soon as you hear me get a lock, you fire. Understood?"

"Aye sir!" the man yelled, crouching lower as another salvo of 35mm and rifle fire chewed at their position.

To the other men beside him he yelled, "Covering fire on three. One, two, three! Go go go!" He yelled, sending Garcia on his way and then swinging his rifle over the concrete foundation and firing in the direction of the Japanese troops. He saw movement in the brush hillside a hundred yards down and directed his fire there. Then the Type 89 pushed its nose out from behind the apartments again and swung its turret his way. "Down!" he yelled as the incoming cannon rounds hammered at the concrete. One of his men wasn't quick enough and his helmet went flying back into the road behind them, with most of his head still inside it. Jensen pulled the still quivering body back into cover and waited for the incoming fire to slow. Another man beside him began vomiting. "Listen up!" he said, spinning around to face the two remaining men at the barrier with him, getting them focused on their roles for the job ahead.

A moment later, Jensen saw Garcia humping up the road toward them in a crouching zig-zag, anti-tank missile launcher in his arms. Dust from Japanese rifle fire kicked up dirt just to his left. "Cover fire!" Jensen yelled, taking a deep breath and then swinging his carbine over the concrete foundation to fire blindly uprange. He knew he should be making calm, precise, short bursts, but whoever wrote that manual didn't write it with a goddamn Japanese Oerlikon 35mm cannon firing at them!

Garcia tumbled to the dirt and smashed concrete beside him, one arm cradling the weapon, the other holding his helmet. Jensen ducked down again and pulled it out of his hands. The CLU or Command Launch Unit on the latest marques of the Javelin was detachable and could be used to spot targets and then send that data to one or more Javelin launchers. He tapped Garcia on the helmet. "When you hear a lock tone, you pop up and fire. I don't want to see you sticking your head up or showing the enemy that missile before then! Clear?"

"Aye sir! Clear sir!" the man said. Then he noticed the headless body beside them. It was one of his men, but he couldn't see who. "Oh Jesus."

Jensen grabbed Garcia's chin and pulled his face to look right in his eyes. "You kill that tank, we can hold this position and those

261

Marines behind us can be deployed elsewhere. So let's do this." He switched the CLU on, checked it was transmitting and had a signal from the Javelin launcher, and then lifted himself into a crouch. The Type 89 tank had pulled right back into cover, probably to reload missiles. "Ready … now!" he yelled and the two MPs began laying down heavy cover fire while Jensen sprinted for the ruin of the base welcome sign with his own M4 carbine strapped across his back. A Japanese round plucked at his sleeve as he zigged and zagged across the open ground, but he made it and threw himself down behind the rubble, a volley of rifle fire following him in.

He checked the CLU again and set it to narrow field of view, with instant thermal targeting. He also checked it was set to direct attack mode, not top attack, as there would be no time for the Javelin missile to climb to a height before striking the enemy vehicle. Direct attack, infrared; he locked it in. He knew where the enemy vehicle was and he knew it would be hot; engine running, gun barrel glowing. Rolling onto his stomach he crawled to the edge of the rubble, which was barely above the height of his prone body, and stuck his head around. He had a clear line of sight to the Type 89 as it crept forward once again to the corner of the apartment building, some heavy rounds peppering it from an anti-materiel rifle back on the 1st Marines' lines.

He put down the CLU and pulled his carbine off his back.

He took a lungful of air. *Now or never, James Jensen,* he told himself. Rolling clear of the rubble of the sign, lying on his belly, he put half a magazine of 5.56mm rounds into the armor of the Type 89. He didn't expect any of them would penetrate; all he wanted was to knock on their door. Sure enough, the gun turret began rotating around toward him and the vehicle nosed forward, looking for the shooter. Rolling back into cover, he grabbed the CLU and slid its base along the ground within inches of the corner of the rubble, checked one last time it was in targeting mode and connected to Garcia's launcher, and then quickly shoved it out, putting his head behind it and his eye to the eyepiece. Japanese rifle rounds began scattering stone chips and dirt on the ground around him, but he squeezed one eye shut, centered the Type 89 in the sight as it kept inching forward and smiled a grim smile as he saw the targeting reticle turn from red to green.

Lock!

Corporal Aloysius Garcia had never fired a Javelin missile in anger. Hell, he'd never shot a man either, or been shot at himself, until today.

He'd only ever fired a Javelin in training and even then, the last time had been two years ago, before the detachable CLU models had been introduced. No one had told him you should do anything different with this model, so when he heard the target-lock tone in his ears, he rose into a crouch, laid the barrel of the missile launcher on the concrete berm and pulled back on both the target acquisition and firing triggers of the Javelin at the same time. Luckily, the weapon still worked the same, detachable CLU or not.

The missile launched in two stages, the first a 'soft launch' to get it a safe distance from the soldier launching it and the second stage when a rocket booster ignited and drove the missile toward its target.

As the Japanese tank rolled out to get a better position on Jensen, the missile flew out of Garcia's launcher with a sound like a jet of steam and Garcia didn't wait to see what happened next. He pulled his head back down into cover and held onto his helmet, spinning around so he didn't get his damn face burned off when the rocket booster ignited.

The infrared-seeking Javelin flew in a low curving arc toward the Japanese tank and slammed into it right at the base of its red hot, glowing cannon barrel. It didn't penetrate to the crew inside, but it splintered the cannon barrel, just as a high explosive round was being fired by its gunner. The 35mm round exploded halfway down the barrel, splitting it apart like a cartoon banana and sending a gout of superheated gas back into the crew space of the Type 89, incinerating the gunner and the vehicle commander, who were standing in the turret, but leaving the driver with nothing more than burst eardrums and a flash burn on his right shoulder. Shocked, but still conscious, he pulled his vehicle back into cover and scrambled out of his floor hatch as the crew space inside began to burn.

Jensen saw Garcia's missile arc into the enemy tank and turn its insides to fire. But the weight of small arms fire still coming his way did not subside and now that he had given away his position, the chances of him getting back to Garcia and behind the safety of the berm were almost zero. Something kicked his boot and sent his leg sharply backward. He looked down and saw a deep gouge on the toe from where a Japanese round had bored through the steel cap of his boot. He felt no pain, so he pulled himself into a ball, clutched his sidearm to his chest and waited out the incoming fire.

After a few minutes, it died down and the volume of fire coming from the Marine lines behind him seemed louder. Risking a peek, he stuck his head out from behind the mound of shattered marble and saw Japanese troops leaving their positions, pulling back. Not in disarray but as though they were making an orderly, planned retreat.

Whatever, this was his chance. He took a deep breath and gathered himself to make a break for the berm.

At that moment, the air overhead split with a thunderous roar as the Japanese self-propelled artillery began laying a barrage of 106mm shells on the heads of the 1st Marine defenders.

Divine Wind

It was still dark over the East China Sea when Li Chen joined her squadron and they fell into formation behind her. One of her seven *Snow Falcon*s had reported a technical fault with its landing hook control module during the takeoff and had to engage a backup module, so she took a moment to review its status and satisfy herself it was mission capable. They were on waypoint and five minutes ahead of mission start time, with a full complement of aircraft. It was a good portent, considering there was a new urgency to their mission. Something had gone wrong with the mission planning. Japanese forces were relying on her *Snow Falcon*s to support their move on the US base – to provide air cover, intercept cruise missiles, degrade defensive positions, and interdict naval targets. They were not supposed to roll until the *Liaoning*'s aircraft were in position over Okinawa before they initiated ground operations. But they had already engaged! She needed to light her tail and get moving.

But there was one more thing to attend to quickly before they could begin.

She reached for her comms panel and opened a channel to Kato. She would make up the time en route to Okinawa.

"Lieutenant Kato," she said, "you are being recalled to the *Liaoning*."

"Sorry, Comrade Captain?" he replied. "I received no such instruction from the carrier."

"I was granted permission to advise you personally, Kato-san. There have been political developments in Tokyo. Your Empress, Mitsuko, has dismissed her own government on charges of treason and national security agents have arrested the Generals of the Army, Navy, and Air Force. We understand elements of your armed forces do not accept the authority of the Empress and are refusing to comply with police orders to return to barracks. Your troops moved ahead of schedule to take the US base at White Beach and are currently engaged in heavy fighting but your air force has refused to provide air support without Imperial Palace assent. We have been asked to fill that gap. There is growing public unrest in cities across Japan."

"I see," the Japanese pilot said.

"You understand this is not a reflection on you," Chen added. "But you represent the Empress, so your status and allegiances are currently unclear. I am sorry, Lieutenant."

"Very well. Thank you for your gesture in telling me in person, Comrade Captain," he replied. "I wish you luck with your mission."

"I will check in on you on my return, Kato-san," Chen said. "Chen, out."

She saw an indicator on her status panel as Kato switched his machine to manual control and watched as he banked his aircraft and dropped out of formation. It was a rather sloppy exit. She sighed and shook her head. *Still trying to fly the machine. When would he learn?*

Freed from the mission, ordered to return to the carrier, new possibilities opened for Takuya Kato. He had not had time to explore the *Liaoning*, but he had learned all he needed to learn about the J-31 *Snow Falcon*. He had learned how to disengage the AI flight control system.

The combat AI could not be disengaged as it was a safety system intended to protect both the aircraft and the pilot, but the flight control system was designed to allow pilots to manually fly the aircraft so that they could complete their training certifications in manual takeoffs and landings. Once an aircraft entered the landing pattern for its host carrier, the combat AI was locked out and the aircraft could be landed either manually or by the dedicated flight control AI.

"Aircraft 69 Alpha, entering the pattern," Kato called to the primary flight control center.

"Roger 69 Alpha, you are cleared in, 210, 23, we have you at angels 8, expected approach time 42, approach button 10." He looked out over his portside wing at the Chinese carrier, now only a mile away as he passed, heading behind it to make a landing approach from the southwest. He kept the AI disengaged and pulled around onto the glide slope behind the carrier on manual pilot, listening to the landing officer 'call the ball' as he dropped gently toward the deck. It was a calm night, the carrier solid and heavy and seemingly unmoving, even though it was sailing into the wind at a respectable 20 knots.

"You are too high, 69 Alpha," the landing officer called over his radio.

"Acknowledged," Kato replied. "Coming down."

An automated warning started sounding in his ears in Chinese, "*Too high … too high … too high*." He ignored it.

He had not known what today would bring, but when he had received the coded message from Mitsuko, he had written a letter to her, made two copies, and left one on his bunk in an envelope addressed to Her Royal Highness the Empress Naishinnō. The other was in his pocket. It was not a traditional letter, it was a *haiku*. A poem, based on a haiku written by the Japanese poet Etsujin nearly three hundred years earlier. Like all haiku, it was just three lines:

It's enviable.

The gracefulness of

A friend's love.

In Japanese, it was only seventeen syllables, and would be meaningless to any other reader than her, but he knew it would say all he needed to say. That he understood how difficult it must have been for her to order him to put his life at risk, knowing he could be captured, tortured, imprisoned, or worse. That he admired the graceful strength in her which allowed her to ask it, even of a childhood friend. That he was honored she had asked. That he was humbled she trusted him so deeply.

And that he loved her.

Five hundred feet out from the carrier, the landing officer waved him off. "You are still too high, 69 Alpha, burn for a go-around! Abort landing!"

"Roger, 69 Alpha going around," he said calmly. Reaching for his throttle, he pushed it forward through the gate, igniting his afterburner so that he would have the airspeed to be able to climb away. The engine responded smoothly, pushing him firmly back in his seat as his airspeed built rapidly and the carrier's deck flashed past underneath his wings.

"*Liaoning* control to 69 Alpha. You will engage landing AI, pilot," the primary flight controller broke in on the radio. "We have aircraft to launch. We do not have time for you to make another aborted landing."

"Understood," Kato replied. "I will re-engage AI. 69 Alpha out."

His airspeed was still building as he climbed away from the *Liaoning*, fire pouring from his tail as he banked to bring himself around. Engaging afterburner after an aborted landing was a normal procedure. Leaving it engaged was not. One thousand feet, eight hundred knots ... 1,200 feet, 850 knots ... *1,500 feet, 900 knots*! His hand went to his throat and touched the small metal wave on a chain around his neck.

I am the Divine Wind, Kato told himself as he brought his *Snow Falcon* around and lined it up on the *Liaoning*'s port beam. The Chinese carrier was broadside on to him now as he tilted his nose down and his *Snow Falcon* blasted through the sound barrier, creating a bubble of almost total silence around him, broken only by the hum of his own engines. *I am unstoppable.*

"69 Alpha, rejoin the pattern," the controller on *Liaoning* barked at him. "Cut your airspeed and ..."

Kato flicked his radio off. He pointed the nose of the fighter at the aircraft carrier's waterline. He had not been able to explore the entire ship on foot, but he had identified a potential vulnerability. During combat operations on all aircraft carriers, the ordnance needed for missions is assembled by sailors and then ferried from deep in the armored guts of the carrier up to the 'bomb farm' on the aircraft flight deck to be fitted onto the aircraft. If the bomb farm is struck, the heavily armored flight deck will absorb and reflect most of the explosive force, meaning the ship could continue sailing, even potentially continue flight operations. Targeting the *Liaoning*'s bomb farm would not guarantee it would be disabled. But …

Kato had seen that due to the cramped flight deck of the Chinese carrier, its bomb farm area was quite restricted, even compared with the smaller Japanese carriers. To compensate for this, Chinese ordnance officers ferried mission supplies to the flight deck in two stages. The first loadout was sent up to the flight deck for transport to the bomb farm, then the elevator returned to the ordnance bay level and a second loadout was sent up and the ordnance elevator was parked in a holding position, below the flight deck and just above the waterline, waiting for space to be cleared in the bomb farm. An enemy missile striking the port side of the *Liaoning* during combat operations, while the elevator was parked below decks and stacked with ordnance, could do serious damage, perhaps even cause a breach in the hull that would admit seawater and cripple offensive operations.

To do so, the enemy missile would have to be very, very lucky, or aimed by a pilot who knew *exactly* where to strike.

Kato had no illusions that he could destroy or sink the massive ship, but if he could punch a hole in its side and detonate the ordnance on the elevator and the bomb farm above, the *Liaoning* would be as good as dead. And would probably take years to repair.

He armed his full complement of weapons. He could not fire them, but their warheads would add considerably to the damage he would inflict. Not so much the air-to-air missiles, but he had launched with two cut-down *Eagle Strike* anti-ship missiles in his weapons bay. Each of them carried a 165kg warhead to add to the full load of jet fuel and the massive kinetic energy of his fighter plunging into the heart of the *Liaoning* at Mach 1.5!

The huge ship filled his forward windscreen, black against the gray dawn sky. His hand made minute adjustments to the joystick to keep his nose pointed at the exact point where the foaming waves lapped at the sides of the carrier underneath the bomb farm guard rails.

And then the ship was all he could see.

He closed his eyes and reached for the pendant at his throat.

I am the Tsunami!!

Fifty miles out and headed for Okinawa, Li Chen had her mind half on the mission ahead, half on the last mission she had led. A failure. Her first combat mission and she had lost a pilot. Yes, they had gathered valuable intelligence about American capabilities and probably achieved the true mission objective, which was to provoke a US attack. But the loss burned her pride.

Li Chen was not accustomed to failure.

She had not been bragging to the Japanese pilot. She had worked her ass off her whole life, in school, in the military academy, in pilot training and in exercises, to finish first, always and only first. Exorcising the demon of a drunken father, a former naval aviator himself, who had more than once told her she did not have to prove herself to him. He had wanted a son, and she could never be that.

So she had resolved she would not try just to be his son, to walk in her father's footsteps. She would be more than that. She would be and do and be recognized for more than *he* ever had.

Success in the coming mission would be the next step on that journey.

Would be … until that possibility suddenly evaporated as a recall alert came up on her main tactical screen and a 'mission abort, squadron recall' icon began flashing.

Her heart fell. What the …

"*Liaoning* control," she said, flipping her radio to the *Liaoning*'s frequency and keying her mike. "This is Alpha leader. I am showing mission abort and squadron recall. Please confirm."

There was an ominous silence. She repeated her message three times before she got a response.

"*Liaoning* control to Alpha leader, confirm mission abort," the controller said. There was more than a little tension in his voice. "You will divert immediately to Shanghai Dachang airbase and take instructions from controllers there."

Her mind whirled. "Alpha leader to *Liaoning*, divert to Dachang? Please confirm!"

Another ominous silence, then as the controller came back online she could distinctly hear shouting in the background, inside the Pri-Fly. "Confirm Alpha, divert Dachang, *Liaoning* out!"

Something was very wrong. She switched to her inter-flight frequency. "Alpha squadron, we are aborting the mission. Leave your machines in formation-keeping mode, I am diverting us to Shanghai. No chatter, thank you. Alpha 1 out." She knew her pilots would be seething with questions, as was she, but she had no answers for them. With one hand on her joystick she banked the aircraft slightly to bring her flight around in a wide circle and point it back to the west. With the other hand she quickly tapped her multi-role display, putting in navigation waypoints that would take her into the airspace over Shanghai, and checked their fuel state to be sure they had fuel enough for the 500-mile flight. She was satisfied with what she saw; they would make it within acceptable limits, even without dumping their payloads.

Which also meant she had sufficient fuel for a small detour, back over the *Liaoning*.

She wanted to see what the hell was going on back on her ship!

The sun was starting to break the horizon in the east as her flight approached the carrier. She had expected to be challenged by flight controllers as she entered controlled airspace and had ordered her pilots to switch on their Identify Friend or Foe transmitters so there were no concerns aboard the *Liaoning* about whether her flight was friendly or hostile. Nonetheless, she should have been contacted by traffic controllers as soon as they picked up her flight approaching.

She had contacted the ship multiple times on her approach. There was only silence.

She flipped on her mike again. "Alpha 1 to *Liaoning* control, 185 at 10,000, overflying your position on transit to Shanghai. Confirm?"

The air boss on the *Liaoning* should be yelling at her by now. She was entering the traffic pattern with no idea about where they wanted her in relation to other aircraft or the carrier. But she could see no other aircraft on her sensor screens. Not fighter aircraft, at any rate. Her search radar was picking up some rotary-winged aircraft low to the water in the area of the carrier, now ten miles ahead of her. But the combat air patrols that should have been circling the carrier as part of its routine defenses were … gone.

Had they been diverted to the mainland as well?

She felt an unaccustomed panic rising in her chest.

"Moving down to five thousand," she told her flight. "You will maintain radio discipline as we cross over the *Liaoning* and stay alert, but stay in formation."

An eternity passed as they approached the carrier from the south, at 800 knots.

As it came into view, she could immediately see something was wrong.

Very, very wrong.

The 'island' or superstructure on the carrier was a five-story-high tower, the width of a city block, topped by radar and radio masts. She could see it outlined clearly against the dark horizon beyond.

It was canted at a twenty-degree angle.

The *Liaoning* was stationary and listing badly to port. She touched her stick and kicked in a little right rudder, lining up her flight to make a pass down the port side of the carrier, about a half-mile out and 2,000 feet over the water. She pulled their airspeed back to 500 knots.

As they drew level, she gasped.

There was a gaping hole in the middle of the carrier's portside hull, right at the waterline. Water was foaming around the breach. There were lifeboats in the water alongside, more being lowered, and she saw two destroyers moving through the water nearby, hooking the bulbous lifeboats with grapples and heaving them up out of the water. The bravery of their captains and crews was incredible – the huge carrier leaned right over the top of them as they worked. If it went over, they would be crushed.

A missile, or torpedo, it must be. Or even several, by the look of it. An American submarine must have gotten through their multilayered defenses and drilled a hole in the side of the carrier! It was taking on water, in danger of capsizing. She could understand now why Pri-Fly had not responded – the *Liaoning*'s commander had ordered its 3,000-strong complement into boats!

Her heart fell to her boots as she took a last look at the carrier over her shoulder and guided her aircraft back up to cruising altitude to point it at Shanghai. No country had sunk another nation's aircraft carrier since the Second World War! If the *Liaoning* went down, if it was even just mortally wounded and America was responsible? This could tip the two superpowers into all-out war.

How dare they? she asked herself, her shock turning to anger. If indeed they wanted war, she was sure they were about to get it.

A Situation in Flux

Aboard the *Lyndon B Johnson*, the war had well and truly come to Bunny O'Hare.

"ASROCs in the water and deploying! Target A2 at 242 degrees, depth 620 … oh shit," Reilly said. He looked up at her and Weisner, eyes unfocused, lost in the sound in his headphones. "*Enemy homing torpedo in the water!*"

"Heading?" Weisner asked calmly.

"Zero two niner," Reilly said, checking a screen. "Target is the *Lyndon B*! Range 3,200 yards, closing!" Reilly said.

"Goddamn, I hate robots," Weisner muttered.

The *Lyndon B*'s combat AI picked up the attack at the exact same moment and the torpedo impact klaxon began sounding. Sallinger had already authorized the appropriate evasive action protocol and Bunny felt the deck shake as the destroyer began to accelerate and heel over to starboard.

Reilly checked his screen. "Enemy torpedo impact in … four thirty-five!"

Once, when Bunny was still a college student, cramming math courses and dreaming of being a fighter pilot, she had been at a dinner party on a beautiful, crisp, winter night. A drunken student who had the responsibility for dessert had decided to do crème brûlée, and had brought an industrial blowtorch to brown the caramel with. Everyone had laughed, until he set fire to the tablecloth, then panicked and swung around, setting fire to the curtains as well. Being students of few means, everything the fire touched was polyester or plastic, and the room instantly filled with poisonous fumes.

The dinner party had scattered, men and women alike screaming or yelling, some running for the door, others diving for the floor and trying to crawl away from the choking smoke. Bunny stayed in her seat, took a moment to look around herself, then poured a glass of water onto a napkin and put it over her mouth and nose. Eyes stinging, she pulled the burning tablecloth off the table, grabbed a bottle of wine off a sideboard and doused the tablecloth in wine. Then she pulled the flaming curtains to the floor, heaved the window behind her open, and threw the curtains into the snow outside. Satisfied there was no more fire to deal with, she'd taken what was left of the wine, sat herself on the windowsill in the fresh cold air, and waited for the smoke, and hysteria, to clear.

It was that presence of mind which had made her such an effective combat pilot, and which she brought to bear now.

"Torpedo?" she asked Reilly carefully. "Just one?"

He double-checked. "Aye, one incoming. Range 2800…"

"EMP!" she said. "If it was using conventional torpedoes it would have used a spread of at least two. It's using the EMP weapon!"

Weisner stared at her for a long second. "EW!" he suddenly called to his Electronic Warfare officer. "Rig for EMP!"

"Aye sir, initiating EMP protocol!" the officer called back.

"You better be right, O'Hare," Weisner said, snatching up a phone to call up to the bridge while he still could. "Because if you aren't, I just killed us."

The EMP protocol on the *Zumwalt* destroyers was a last line of defense in case a nuclear airburst weapon went off above the ship. It activated a 'Faraday Cage' mesh built into the hull and superstructure of the destroyer which could take an electromagnetically induced power surge, distribute it across the hull and dump it into the saltwater surrounding the ship. At the same time, it cut every power switch across the ship, instantly killing all electrical devices. A massive EMP surge could fry a circuit board whether it was powered up or not, but powering them down reduced the damage by what could be a critical fraction.

The *Lyndon B Johnson* instantly lost all propulsion, steerage, sensor, and weapons control.

In an instant, it had gone from predator to helpless prey.

As the ring of four new ASROC torpedoes hit the water around it, the Stingray calculated its chances of one final torpedo launch on either of the *Zumwalts* … and decided that the window was closed. If it was to survive the next two minutes, it would need to deploy the last of its countermeasures, and crash dive.

Checking the depth of seafloor below, it saw that it was over the northern tip of the Mariana Trench, with 20,000 beautiful feet directly under its keel. With maneuverability no manned sub could match, the Stingray rotated on its axis and dived vertically for the seafloor, firing its full complement of eight decoy drones into its wake, staggered to create a cloud of targets each twenty yards apart.

It passed through 500 feet. Accelerating to 15 knots, it might reach its maximum survivable depth of 600–650 feet before the ASROC torpedoes caught it. And to do so, they would have to push through a cloud of decoys first.

One down …With silicon calm, it noted the explosions in its wake as the proximity detonators on the pursuing torpedoes were triggered. *Two … three …*

One ASROC torpedo did not deviate or detonate. It had been the last to hit the water and, ironically, the furthest away. The first explosions had destroyed most of the Stingray's decoys. The final torpedo's track disappeared from the Stingray's sensors, indicating it had closed to within kill range. If the Stingray had been endowed with a more philosophical AI, it may have had one final rueful thought in the last millisecond of its 'life'. Or if it had been human, it might have panicked at the thought of its imminent death.

It didn't. In a quantum computing split second, it analyzed the tactical environment and reviewed its options one last time. Its EMP torpedo had passed under the keel of the *Michael Monsoor* and closed to within 2,000 yards of the *Lyndon B Johnson*.

In the moment before the last ASROC torpedo from the *Lyndon B* detonated in its baffles, the Stingray triggered its Electro-Magnetic Pulse weapon.

The warhead inside the EMP torpedo didn't generate gamma waves like a nuclear weapon did – it generated high-power microwaves which were potentially much more destructive. The first weapons the US tested in the early 2000s were modest 10-gigawatt devices, which had a shielded-equipment lethal range of only 500 yards. Higher-power flux compression generator weapons were developed to expand the lethal range out to two miles through water, and frequency 'chirping' cathode ray oscillators improved the ability of the weapon to attack via multiple vectors – through power wires, gaps between panels, and any poorly shielded interfaces.

The stricken *Michael Monsoor*, still coasting to a halt after the first attack by the Stingray and without either the warning or the power needed to defend itself, was closest to the EMP warhead when it exploded. The torpedo had run under its keel, heading for the *Lyndon B*, and detonated just 500 yards off its starboard quarter. The *Monsoor* took the full brunt of the pulse and every system on the ship went dark.

The Stingray's conventional torpedoes had wounded the *Monsoor*. The EMP weapon blasted it back into the stone age.

The *Lyndon B Johnson* was at the edge of the lethality envelope for the bomb and its Faraday Cage mesh had been activated. The EMP shielding dealt with most of the microwave radiation from the 10-terawatt weapon, but not all.

Bunny's world was plunged into terrifying darkness.

In Shanghai, the men and women of APT 23 stood in mute silence.

"Read that again?" DB asked, even though he didn't want to hear what Tanken had to say.

"*EMP weapon fired*," Tanken said, checking his watch. "That's the last message it sent. Five minutes ago."

All through the engagement, the Stingray had sent a minute by minute update on its status.

"Is it still operational?" Shaofeng demanded. He was rubbing his wrists, as though he could already feel the handcuffs closing on them.

"It should have sent another status update by now. US torpedoes probably got it," Frangi said. "Or it fried itself with its own EMP."

"The loss of the enemy submersible is bad enough." Shaofeng was sitting in a corner, his head in his hands now. "But you may have sunk the American destroyers," he moaned. "In contradiction of our express orders. This is … we will all be …"

"Perhaps not," Tanken said. He shrugged. "The EMP weapon is non-lethal. They may have survived."

For the survivors on the *Lyndon B Johnson*, 'survival' was a relative concept. The crew were retrieving hand-held gas-burning lamps from shielded lockers and setting them up throughout the SMC, which was otherwise still in semi-darkness. Some of the computer systems were coming back up and screens starting to glow, others remained stubbornly dead. Weisner was taking damage reports and relaying them to Sallinger on the bridge. Most worrying was that the EMP blast had knocked their main Rolls Royce gas turbines offline, but they had 34 MW of power available because the two smaller auxiliary turbine generators that were used to start up the main turbines had powered down before the EMP detonated and the hull shielding had protected them. They had ship-to-ship communications and were taking orders from their flag, the *Makin Island*, which had not been affected by the EMP weapon and, together with the *Port Royal*, was holding at its current position.

Weisner, who had been on the intercom with Sallinger, put his handset down and raised his voice so all in the SMC could hear him. "Listen up!" he called. "We are still at battle stations! Satellite intel indicates that a force of Japanese destroyers is moving to intercept us. White Beach is under attack by elements of the Japanese armed forces but is holding on and what is left of this taskforce is their only hope! Now get to your stations. While we work to restart the turbines and get our systems back up, I want to see section heads in my briefing room to review orders from the flag and give me options. Let's move, people!"

Reilly shot a questioning look at O'Hare.

"Japanese 13th destroyer squadron," she told him. "We heard it sailed yesterday. Now we know why. Insurance, in case the Stingray didn't do the job."

"What about the *Monsoor*, sir?" Reilly asked Weisner, who was getting ready to head back to the upper level of the SMC. "We might be able to get moving again, but last I saw before my screens went down, they were dead in the water."

Weisner paused. "The *Lucy Stone* will move up to assist the *Monsoor*. *Port Royal* is preparing a cruise missile strike on Japanese troops on Okinawa, *Makin Island* is scrambling its fighters, and when we get sensors back I need you to be focused on making sure there isn't a damn *Soryu*-class submarine riding shotgun with those approaching destroyers. For now you can take a breather, alright Ears?"

"Aye sir!" he replied, pulling his headphones from around his neck and collapsing in his chair.

Bunny realized she wasn't needed in the claustrophobic SMC anymore and got the sudden urge to get outside and get some air. Heading through a bulkhead, remembering to lift her boot so she didn't scrape her shins, she went out onto a small observation deck. Inside the SMC, it could have been any time of day or night. Outside, she was surprised to see the sun well up now and looked at her watch. It was 0715.

From behind her she heard the sound of missiles launching just over the visual horizon and watched as ten white contrails lanced through the sky. Cruise missiles, headed for Okinawa! Kyle and Kevin were no Marines. She hoped they'd bunkered down somewhere safe, though where 'safe' was when you had a Japanese infantry regiment bearing down on you, she had no idea. Then she thought of the indomitable James Jensen and felt a little better. She'd seen him shut down a raging bar brawl between Marines and Yakuza henchmen, with cool, calm efficiency. Let the Japanese overrun his base? Never happen.

The hatch behind her opened and Reilly stepped out.

"I thought I'd join you," he said. He looked up at the sky, to the drifting contrails of the cruise missiles. "*Port Royal* has joined the party."

"Looks like it," she said. She heard shouting on the forward deck. "Things sound pretty bad."

"Not great. But not catastrophic either," Reilly said. "Priority right now is damage assessment and control. We'll be trying to get the turbines restarted as soon as we can, but if we need to we can use the auxiliaries to power one of the screws – that's the advantage of being the first class in the navy with all-electric drive and the mofo-grade EMP shielding that goes with it."

"Not mofo enough, buddy," she observed. "If there had been two subs out there, we'd be swimming with the sharks right now."

"Hmm. I came out here hoping you'd lighten my mood," he said. "With respect, you are failing miserably, ma'am."

"Don't ma'am me," she told him. But she gave him a smile. "And you're welcome."

He leaned his elbows on the railing and looked out over the water. "My Sea Hunter is out there somewhere," he observed. "Probably floating belly up. Where should we send the check?"

"Send the check for what?"

"For my Sea Hunter – one of those costs about 20 million. It was your Stingray that fried it with an EMP," he said with a gleam in his eye.

She turned and leaned back on the railing too. "Tell you what, why don't you send the check to DARPA? Then they can send Navy a check for the Stingray you torpedoed," she said. "Should be about *eighty* million, less your twenty, so … you'll still owe DARPA sixty mill."

"OK, you want to play that game?" he smiled. "How about we throw in the repair cost for our two *Zumwalt*s? Shot and then deep fried by your drone? That's going to be at least a billion, minus your sixty mill."

"Touché," she said. "You can send that check to Beijing."

He looked out to the horizon and tapped a hand nervously on the rail. "I won't lie to you. The situation isn't good. The *Monsoor* is probably down for the count. We're stuck out here on our own with a Japanese destroyer squadron headed our way," he said. "It's not in visual range, but the *Port Royal* has our backs, if that's any comfort."

"Can't the *Makin Island* scramble some attack fighters, scare the Japanese destroyers off?"

"It could, but if Japanese troops have moved on White Beach, that's where those fighters will be headed."

"So we just sit here, until we get shot at again," Bunny said with pseudo cheer. "Story of my life."

"Well…" he said. "That Japanese destroyer squadron is made up of *Atago*-class ships; and we're already within range of their anti-ship missiles. They haven't engaged us yet, so I'm guessing they're just making a blocking play – on their way to draw a line in the water, so to speak. They may or may not know the *Monsoor* is out of commission and they likely won't want to risk a real stand-up fight."

"But if they do? Seems to me the time it would take for their missiles to reach us would be less than the time it would take for the *Port Royal* to initiate a counter-attack."

"That much is true." Reilly straightened up and clapped her on the shoulder. "Not to mention that our missile launch tubes, point defense, and fire-control systems may still be out of commission." He pointed to a crew pulling the radar-reflective box housing off the railgun on the forward deck. "But it looks like we still have the railgun. It pulls about 20mW of juice and can take its targeting from the *Port Royal* or the *Makin Island*'s airborne warning and control aircraft if we can't get our own radar up and radiating."

"One railgun on a crippled *Zumwalt* against three missile-armed destroyers?" Bunny said. "That's a big ask."

"Now it's my turn to cheer you up, Lef-tenant," Reilly said. "Japanese ASM-3 anti-ship missiles fly at *three* times the speed of sound. Even if our own radar is out, the *Port Royal* would pick them up the second they launch, so would the *Makin*'s electronic warfare aircraft. We probably wouldn't be facing more than five or six at a time. The *Lyndon B*'s railgun shoots projectiles at *seven* times the speed of sound and it can shoot ten projectiles a minute. The math is *totally* in our favor."

On Okinawa, Garcia was huddled behind the concrete berm in a cloud of dust, eyes squeezed shut, carbine shaking in his hands as he sheltered from the incoming fire. *Smoke!* The Japanese artillery had laid down a barrage of smoke shells. But was it to cover their retreat, or were they advancing? There was no more incoming small arms fire, which was something. He had sent his two remaining men back to the 1st Marines' lines, where they were hunkered down behind whatever cover they could find, just like him. He had stayed at the concrete berm waiting for Jensen to return, but for now, apart from the headless man, he was alone. He had no infrared or thermal vision, couldn't see ten yards in front of himself.

Oh Jesus and Mary, he prayed, pointing his carbine uselessly at shadows in the smoke. *Let them be pulling back!*

"What exactly are you doing, Garcia?" a voice behind him said suddenly.

He spun around to see Jensen, on one knee behind him, covered in … marble dust? "Waiting for you, Chief," Garcia said. "What's our next move, sir?"

"Depends what the Japanese are planning," Jensen said. "That little bunfight didn't feel planned. I'd say someone in that Type 89 got trigger happy and whoever is in command out there is having second thoughts now he saw we aren't just going to bend over and play nice." Jensen stuck his head above the berm and looked around them, but all they could see was swirling smoke.

Garcia would have preferred clear air and the sight of Japanese troops advancing. At least you could see what the hell was coming at you!

"Keep that carbine ready, Garcia," Jensen said. "I'm going to get orders." He crouched down behind the concrete barrier and tapped the mike on his comms headset. Even though he kept his voice low, it seemed loud in the eerie quiet following the chaos of the last half hour. Garcia tightened his grip on his M4. If there were enemy troops close, they couldn't fail to hear.

Jensen finished his call and spun back to Garcia. "OK. The drone was showing the Japanese troops pulled back about a mile and regrouped with their main armored force. But it's been shot down. You and I are going to get outside this smoke, see what we can see."

"Aye, sir!"

"Laser Target Designator, Corporal, yours up?" Jensen was asking him.

He felt for his helmet and pulled the multifunction camera off its mount. It had a camera, position locator, and target designating laser built in. He checked it was working "Yes, sir."

"While you were having your little nap here, Navy launched a brace of cruise missiles," Jensen yelled. "They'll be overhead in ten and loitering for targets." He pointed through the smoke to where Garcia knew there was a hill in front of them; a hill which until recently had been held by Japanese troops. "With our drone out of play, we're heading up there to see if we can paint those armored vehicles further down. You're watching my back."

"We're going to call down a cruise missile strike on Japanese armor?" Garcia asked, shocked.

Jensen put a hand on Garcia's shoulder. "No, son, we're just going to try to put a laser dot on their noggins. Someone with way more stripes is going to decide whether to drop a cruise missile on them."

High Seas, High Stakes

Captain Ken Tamai of the JDS *Takeo*, commander of the 13th Escort Squadron, was preparing himself for a very tense, high-seas standoff.

The *Takeo* had been named after a World War Two heavy cruiser which had rampaged through the Pacific from the Philippines to Midway and Guadalcanal. She had survived an attack by American dive bombers at Rabaul before being torpedoed off the Philippines in 1944 by the US submarine *Darter*. But again she survived and retired to Singapore for repairs. Japan no longer had sufficient resources to make her seaworthy again and she was moored in Singapore to serve as an anti-aircraft platform, but that wasn't the end of her story. She was attacked by British commandos who infiltrated the harbor in a mini-submarine and blew several holes in her hull with limpet mines. Again, she survived. She finished the war unbeaten, finally boarded by British ground troops on September 21, 1945.

The crew of the modern-day *Takeo* were very aware of the illustrious reputation of their ancient namesake. They had orders to prevent the US taskforce approaching closer to Okinawa, but had not been granted permission to fire upon the US warships unless they were fired upon first. The Americans had already tested their nerves when they launched a volley of cruise missiles at Okinawa, but these had passed well south of the Japanese squadron and they had held their fire.

Tamai had received and been ordered to ignore a warning from the Commander of the US taskforce that he was not to approach within twenty miles of the picket destroyers his drones had spotted stationed out in front of the small US carrier and its accompanying *Ticonderoga* cruiser. The American *Zumwalt*-class destroyers were behaving strangely – both virtually becalmed, holding a stationary position about five miles apart as though waiting for something, neither of them showing active radar signatures and with very limited radio energy leakage. It was most curious, but he had to assume they were both combat ready.

"What the hell are they up to?" he asked his executive officer. They were both standing over a desktop flat screen showing a real-time plot with the positions of his own ships and those of the US taskforce. Overlaid on it was vision from a surveillance drone, which curiously the Americans had either not detected yet or decided not to try to shoot down. On the decks of both ships, a few crewmen could be seen moving with urgency and purpose under the direction of officers. But to what end? The bulk of the crew was apparently still below deck or out of sight in the angled superstructures. Doing what?

"Submarine ops, sir?" his XO ventured. "Years ago, when we were still exercising together, I accompanied a US warship conducting a hydrographic survey with an undersea drone. They had to stay geostationary the whole time."

"Ridiculous," Tamai said. "They should be on high alert. They must know about the action on Okinawa, their *Ticonderoga* has fired a half dozen cruise missiles already, these two should be moving into defensive positions to screen their carrier."

"A trap then, Captain," his XO continued. "To trick us into approaching, or engaging, while a US submarine puts a damn torpedo up our backsides."

"We have no reports of a submarine accompanying the US taskforce," Tamai said, chewing his lip.

"No, sir."

"Maintain this heading," Tamai decided. "We will hold a line in grid ZX44 ten miles from the US ships and block any attempt to approach Okinawa, as ordered."

"While the *Ticonderoga* rains cruise missiles on our troops on Okinawa!" the XO protested. "And that amphibious assault ship launches its attack aircraft!"

Tamai glared at him. Not for the first time he asked himself if the man was emotionally suited to a combat role.

"Our mission is to prevent the US amphibious assault ship from making port in White Beach to support or evacuate the US troops there," he reminded the man. "Those cruise missiles and aircraft would have been anticipated. Our troops and air force will prevail regardless."

"Aye, sir," Tamai's XO said and turned to his helmsman. "Steady as you go, heading 094, speed 20 knots."

"Aye, sir, maintain heading 094, speed 20."

Tamai bent to the flat screen tactical plot again. The two American destroyers had not moved at all. It was profoundly unusual. But they had not painted him with their weapons-targeting radar, nor had they acted to thwart his surveillance or jam his electronic systems. The only radar the *Takeo* was picking up were the powerful signals from the American *Ticonderoga* cruiser and the Assault Ship, as was to be expected.

Could the American destroyers be taking a deliberately unprovocative posture to signal that the US did not want the battle on land to turn into all-out war at sea as well?

He sincerely hoped so.

"*Port Royal* targeting radar synchronized!" the radar technician two workstations away from Reilly and O'Hare in the ship mission center of the *Lyndon B Johnson* called out. He did not have to yell – everyone in the destroyer's SMC was working with quiet, practiced efficiency. "Satellite tracking data synchronized. *Fire Scout* data feed nominal. Targets bearing 303 degrees, range 23 miles, speed 18 to 20 knots. Three surface vessels, designating group C12!"

It had taken two hours, but the *Lyndon B* was a warship once again. It had power to one screw, so it was able to maneuver. Its sensor suite was still offline, but it was able to pull targeting data from the other ships in the taskforce. Its missile launch system was dead, as were its 30mm anti-missile point defense cannon, but its railgun was fully operational.

Weisner was prowling the room like a caged panther as the Japanese ships approached the twenty-mile no-go zone around what remained of Taskforce 44. At a range of twenty miles, a Mach 3 missile would take less than a minute to reach the US destroyer. And despite Reilly's bravado, in a missile-to-missile slugfest the three *Atago*s would almost certainly overwhelm the *Lyndon B*'s single railgun, even backed with ship-ship missiles from the *Ticonderoga* cruiser, *Port Royal*.

But the *Lyndon B* was not going to wait to find out what the Japanese intentions were. The *Port Royal*'s radar had tagged the enemy ships, with real-time optical and infrared satellite targeting data and a *Fire Scout* reconnaissance drone combining to give the *Lyndon B* a near-perfect firing solution despite the fact its own sensors were still down.

The Japanese ships showed no signs of slowing as they approached the twenty-mile no-go perimeter communicated to them by the commander of Taskforce 44 on the *Makin Island*.

"*Fire Scout* has visual," a drone operator said. "Isolating. Nearest target identified as JDS *Takeo*, sir! Targets, C12A through C14 confirmed as units of JDS 13th Escort Squadron."

"Box them up," Weisner said, then turned his head to his weapons officer. "Prepare to shoot." He called up to the bridge. "Japanese ships are about to breach the safety perimeter, Captain. No sign they intend to respect it."

"I know, XO," Sallinger's voice came back. "We just got a hail from them, demanding we hold our current position and make no attempt to enter Japanese territorial waters."

"Orders, sir?"

"No change in the rules of engagement, XO. Our Marines on Okinawa are in active combat with Japanese ground forces. If those destroyers cross that twenty-mile perimeter, you are cleared to engage."

About fifty feet out from the berm the smoke around Jensen and Garcia began to thin. They had been moving cautiously when they were inside the smoke and went prone when they couldn't use it for cover any more. They encountered no Japanese troops. Belly crawling their way forward, they headed for the small hill overlooking the entrance to the base. The dirt had been chewed up by the earlier firefight between the Marines and Japanese infantry and as they reached the crest of the hill, under some shrubs, they wriggled themselves a couple of inches deeper into the dirt, if only for the psychological protection.

Garcia peered up at the sky. "You sure they're up there, Chief?" he asked Jensen. He wasn't sure how high a loitering Tomahawk cruise missile could fly. If there were ten of them overhead, shouldn't they be able to see them?

Jensen looked up too. "We have to assume so," he said. "But they won't necessarily be right overhead. Probably holding just offshore." He looked at their laser designator. "We've still got a satellite lock, so we have to hope someone out there is waiting for a target."

They badly needed binoculars, but didn't have them. The helmet unit had a camera with a 4x zoom and a small Post-it note-sized screen. Pointing it downhill, they could make out Japanese troops, milling around behind a group of about ten tracked infantry fighting vehicles. Smoke still blanketed the base, but up on the hill and outside the base perimeter where Jensen and Garcia had crawled, they were beyond the smoke.

"Looks like they're mounting up," Jensen said. He lifted the laser designator and aimed it downrange, looking at the readout in the camera. "We're in range. I'll call it in."

As he got onto his radio and reported what they were seeing, Garcia did a mental count. He counted ten infantry fighting vehicles, each of which could carry seven infantry, in addition to its crew. It looked like the Japanese were preparing a company-sized advance. It was ominously quiet on their flanks, but Garcia imagined similar preparations were underway to the west and north.

Jensen finished his call and squinted at the camera display again. "We've knocked out one tank," Jensen said, as though thinking out loud. "So they know they aren't going to be able to just roll in here without taking heavy casualties. If I'm the Japanese commander, I'm not moving until we've been softened up with arty or airstrikes."

Garcia scanned the sky overhead again. "I don't see or hear any Japanese air support, sir."

He was right. But as they spoke, the first tank began to roll. The Japanese commander had decided to move anyway. Either he was the type who stuck to a plan even when it was going wrong, or he was supremely confident. "Here they come! We'll let them get moving, away from those houses back there," Jensen said. "Paint them when they get into the open."

"Aye, sir," Garcia said, checking lines of fire. "Sir, do you think … did we start all this? Back at the gates? With those protesters?"

"You mean, did they come here expecting us to wave a white flag and we showed them that wasn't going to happen and then they got all mad and started killing people, is that what you're asking, Lieutenant?" Jensen said, peering at the image on the camera screen.

"I guess so, yes, sir," Garcia said.

"Then yes, Corporal, I do believe that was what happened." Jensen could see the man was spooked. "Corporal, you and your men did good back there. You kept your shit together under heavy enemy fire and you held your position."

"I lost a man, sir," Garcia said, not meeting his eye.

"You didn't lose him, Corporal, the enemy took him, in an unprovoked attack," Jensen said bitterly. "Remember that."

The Japanese vehicles were moving slowly forward now and Jensen turned on the target designator mode on the camera and centered the crosshairs on the third vehicle in the line. From somewhere back inside the base, further to the west, a single M27 automatic rifle opened up, firing in short bursts. The bark of rifles soon joined the distant hammer of the M27. Garcia had no idea how many of his men, or those from other companies, were engaged right now. More than a few, it seemed. The Japanese must be moving up across the other side of the base too.

"We clear, Garcia?" Jensen asked, his thumb on the laser button.

Garcia did a 360-degree sweep over the sights of his carbine. "Clear, aye."

"Alright, let's light 'em up," Jensen said, rising into a crouch and laying the laser targeting sight on an approaching Type 89 tank.

The railgun that the *Lyndon B Johnson* was training on the Japanese vessels released no tell-tale missile launch bloom. The gun itself operated invisibly, electrically, the whirring of its magnetos and the metal slam of its catapult thudding into the restraints at the end of its barrel the only sound as it launched its projectiles. It could send ten 23lb shells a minute toward targets up to twenty nautical miles away, at a velocity of Mach 7, or *5,300 miles per hour*. The rounds were undetectable and twice the speed of a ship-to-ship missile. It took a railgun sabot round less than fifteen seconds to cover twenty miles.

The JDS *Takeo* and its sister ships, the *Atago* and *Ashigara*, crossed the US no-go line in staggered line-astern formation toward their planned intercept with the US taskforce and within range of the *Lyndon B*'s railgun.

They had less than fifteen seconds to live.

Noriko Fukada couldn't feel her shoulder at all, but she decided that was probably a good thing. She lay on her face in the dirt outside the American base, where she had fallen. Panicked people had stampeded right over her and crushed her brittle old bones. She was having trouble breathing and could only pull in a breath every few seconds or so. She remembered a time when a blackbird had flown into one of the glasshouses at the nursery and she had found it lying on the floor, gasping. It had probably broken its neck when it flew into the glass and as she held it in her hand, it had breathed in little, irregular gasps for a minute or so, and then it had died.

So it would be for her, she understood that.

She wasn't in pain. Or rather, she was in so much pain her mind had shut down, which was the same. And she wasn't afraid. She had lived a good life and had expected to join her ancestors and her husband long before now.

But she was very, very sad. She couldn't really move her head, or she would have turned it away so that she didn't have to look into the dead face of the poor girl lying crumpled beside her, shot through the chest. What was her name again? Yoshi. That was it. Poor, scared Yoshi. It was a name that had many different meanings, depending on the character used. *Luck*. Perhaps not that one. *Virtue*, that was another one. Yes, definitely virtue. She had stood by Noriko right to the end, trying to pull her to her feet when the shooting had started. A good girl, a brave girl.

Noriko was also sad that her one small life had started and ended in war. So many years, so little learned.

Noriko took another small sip of air, not enough to fill her lungs really. She tried to take another and found she couldn't.

She hoped someone would remember to look in on her plants at the nursery after she was gone. They would need watering tomorrow. And she hoped she would find poor Yoshi in the next life, so she could thank her.

Weisner held his handset to his ear and called up to the bridge again. "Twenty-mile perimeter has been crossed. Targets locked, ready to shoot, sir. Aye, sir!" He turned to his men. "Targets C12A, C12B, C12C. Shoot sabot. Ten rounds per target and adjust shot. Shoot at will!"

"Sabot, thirty rounds continuous, aye sir! Shooting!" his weapons officer barked back at him and tapped an icon on her screen.

The sonic booms that battered the *Lyndon B* and Bunny O'Hare's ears each time the railgun fired were inaudible to the Japanese destroyers.

The first they knew that they were under attack was when the *Takeo* rocked with the impact of the first sabot round. Guided by real-time satellite imagery, supplemented by *Fire Scout* drone and triangulated by the powerful radar of the Aegis cruiser *Port Royal*, the artillery shell smashed into the destroyer's stern, just below the fantail, giving it an almighty shove sideways. The hyper-velocity sabot round was essentially a depleted uranium spear inside a radar-guided shell. Unlike a high explosive round, it did not penetrate a ship's armor and explode – it was moving so fast and with such force that the sabot spear hit its target and blasted straight through.

Which was why it was fired at an elevation that allowed it to strike its target in a diagonal, downward trajectory, taking the spear through the upper hull plating and exiting through the bottom of the hull, below the waterline.

Five of the six sabot rounds fired by the *Lyndon B* hammered into the *Takeo*. Even as the first sonic booms caught up with the shells that made them and crashed across the deck of the *Takeo*, it had started sinking and the first railgun round was slamming into the next ship in the line.

The 'launch and loiter' Tactical Tomahawk, fired forty minutes earlier from the *Port Royal*, was circling in a racetrack pattern at 30,000 feet above White Beach Naval Base, along with eight others. One had experienced a guidance malfunction en route to the target and had been destroyed by the operator aboard the cruiser.

It took thirteen seconds for Jensen's laser target designator to lock onto a satellite and another ten for the data to be relayed to the *Port Royal*. The target had to be authorized by the Surface Warfare duty officer and the target coordinates relayed back to the circling Tomahawk, which began looking for the laser radiation that marked its target. In that time, the advancing Japanese Type 89 infantry carriers had covered five hundred yards toward the shattered base gates, which were still shrouded in smoke. Jensen doubted the troops inside the base could pick up the vehicles on infrared, in daylight, through the smoke. They weren't being fired on as they advanced and the lead element was now only four hundred yards from Jensen and Garcia, getting closer by the second.

Garcia didn't want to say it out loud. Didn't want to sound like he was about to lose his shit. But in a few minutes they'd be just yards from the Japanese tanks. And if the Japanese didn't kill him, there was a fair chance his own cruise missiles would, if they didn't strike soon! *God*, Garcia said to himself. *If this goes wrong, you look after my madre, OK?*

"Come on … dammit!" Jensen muttered under his breath, his laser designator still locked on a tank in the middle of the Japanese line. "M10, this is G35," Jensen said urgently into his mike. "Adjust fire, grid ES 923 945. Painting target. Ten enemy IFVs, in the open, danger close! Over!"

Jensen finally heard his request confirmed and shoved Garcia on the helmet. "Eat dirt, Corporal!"

He had barely dropped to the dirt himself when three thundering seconds later not one, but two loitering Tomahawks screamed down 100 yards apart, each scattering 166 submunitions before detonating their remaining JP-10 fuel load in a thermobaric blast that sent Jensen and Garcia flying. Jensen felt a flash of light and heat and then his world went black.

Bunny O'Hare had flown F-35s with the RAAF in the Turkey-Syria war. She had commanded a *Fantom* drone swarm from under the Arctic ice during a border conflict between Russia and the USA in the Bering Sea. But she had never seen, so dramatically, the carnage that could be wreaked by modern weapons on ships at sea as she saw in the aftermath of the *Lyndon B Johnson*'s engagement with the Japanese 13th Destroyer Squadron.

Weisner had returned to the SMC command deck, but Reilly was following events on his tactical monitor in between constantly scanning his sensors and dispatching his scout drones to be sure there were no Japanese undersea vessels likely to ruin their day. The sensor AI would alert him immediately to any contact, but he was old school and liked to keep an 'eye over its shoulder'.

"One Japanese destroyer down at the stern, crew abandoning," he told Bunny, tilting his screen so she could see the *Fire Scout* visual feed on his screen. "One disabled, dead in the water but still afloat. A third damaged but occupied in rescue and recovery." He leaned back, hands behind his head. "I'd call that three for three."

"They didn't think we'd engage," Bunny said, still shocked. "Or they were ordered not to. There's no other explanation for them coming on blindly like that."

"Could have been that," Reilly agreed. "Or it could have been imperfect information. Lack of data sharing between the Chinese and the Japanese."

"How so?"

"China went to a lot of trouble to steal your Stingray. It wanted the attack to be deniable. Say they didn't let Japan in on the plan. So all the Japanese commanders knew was they were being asked to move out and draw a line in the sand to persuade us to stay out of whatever is going down on Okinawa." He pointed at Bunny. "They didn't have a clue there was a full-on battle happening out here under the waves and so they had no idea what kind of mood USPACFLEET was in when they issued their ultimatum. They didn't know we'd already lost the *Monsoor* and taken a punch to the jaw from our own EMP weapon."

O'Hare shook her head slowly. "And I'm willing to bet they had never been on the receiving end of a railgun."

"No one has," Reilly observed. "Until today."

Jensen woke on his back, blinking up at the sky, watching clouds drift over him. It was a beautiful sky, deep blue, and the world around him was calm and quiet.

Too calm, too quiet.

Right on cue, his ears started buzzing in a high-pitched tone. He realized the clouds drifting above him weren't your standard Okinawa rainclouds, they were more like battlefield smoke. And the sound of shouting began breaking through the ringing in his ears. Any doubt he was still in a combat zone disappeared as an arrowhead formation of US *Fantom* drones blasted overhead at supersonic speeds and unleashed a volley of air-ground missiles.

He should have been burrowing deeper into the dirt of the hillside, but his mind was still getting a grip on his new reality. He sat up, watching with remote detachment as the *Fantom*s peeled up into the sky and their missiles bored down into what remained of the Japanese armored column. Dozens of craters gouged into the earth by the Tomahawk munitions surrounded wrecked vehicles and the burned, shattered bodies of Japanese infantry. Those vehicles that hadn't been destroyed by the loitering Tomahawks had been trying to withdraw when the *Fantom* drones from the USS *Makin Island* had arrived over White Beach and started going to work.

Something didn't make sense to him. Where were the Japanese F-35s he knew were stationed ten minutes' flying time away, at Naha? The Chinese had put a squadron of aircraft over Okinawa the day before, so where were *they* now? There were two damn aircraft carriers just off the coast ... the sky should be teeming with Chinese and Japanese fighters. Why had the Japanese forces advanced without air cover? Another flight of *Fantom*s blasted overhead, sending a single missile into the rear of a retreating Japanese Type 89 before pulling up into the sky and disappearing out of visual range in the tropical haze.

Something must have gone *seriously* wrong with the Sino-Japanese strategy.

Finally, it occurred to him to check himself for injury. He wiped his face, checking for blood, and one of his hands came away red; feeling his head a little more carefully, he soon found the source – he was bleeding from the ears. The exposed skin on his hands and forearms looked like he'd received a bad case of sunburn and was already beginning to blister. He'd been lucky not to be any closer to the fuel-air explosive blast wave from the Tomahawk strike, but it had burst his eardrums. The one good thing as far as he could see was that, despite the fact the earth around him was scorched black and the shrubs they had been hiding in had been stripped bare of foliage, his limbs and appendages seemed intact.

Straining through the damage to his hearing, he picked up sporadic shooting to the east and west. But it seemed to him it was lessening, even as he listened. Theirs probably wasn't the only target hit by the circling cruise missiles.

He was still holding the laser range-finder. He needed to find his people and get new orders.

Garcia?

The last time he had seen the corporal, he had been up on one knee, his carbine trained on the advancing Japanese troops. Standing up, Jensen looked around. The smoke had been cleared away by the thermobaric blast. Back at the concrete berm that was all that was left of their guard station, a couple of medics were lifting the body of the headless man onto a stretcher and carrying him away. A line of Marines was moving warily forward. Jensen looked around for Garcia and then saw the man's carbine, five feet away next to a mound of chewed-up dirt and blackened branches. He walked over and picked it up.

Something's wrong, Jimmy boy, a voice told him. *Something is wrong with this picture.*

Then he realized what it was. The M4 had been lying next to an outstretched hand and he recognized the signet ring on the third finger. The hand was sticking out of the dirt, along with a leg and a foot and some sort of … oh, it was Garcia's helmet. Jensen picked it up, fixed the laser range-finder back on the helmet, then looked at the leg. That was weird. Just a foot in a sock; where was the boot? He began moving branches.

"Chief?"

He looked up and saw an NCO from the 1st Battalion, Sergeant Tracy Williams, come jogging up the rise to stand a few feet away,

M4 carbine dangling from one hand. She was looking at him strangely.

"Yeah?"

"What are you doing, sir? We just got word the Japanese are pulling back on all sides. Local radio is saying their Prime Minister has been arrested, the heads of their General Staff too." She cocked her head. "Sir?"

He looked down at Garcia's sock, then looked around himself again. "Corporal's lost his boot," he said quietly. "Man can't walk with one boot…"

Williams frowned at Jensen, seeing for the first time the blood trickling from his ears and the body in the dirt. She kneeled and checked the body briefly, then took Jensen by the arm. "OK, sir. You come with me and we'll find Garcia a new boot. How about that?"

NSA XKeycore Ground Station, Pine Gap

Allan Pritzkat hadn't slept more than a few minutes for the last forty-nine hours. He and Ravi, as Chinese PLA Navy cryptanalysts on the NSA front line in the Asia Pacific, had found themselves working feverishly to keep up with the volume of reporting being generated by CYBERCOM and NSA sources around the East China Sea, pulling it together into reports that made a modicum of sense and firing it off to Virginia. Then dealing with the million dumb questions that came back at them. Luckily Ravi had his AI assistant HOLMES updating sitreps that covered most of the questions people were asking.

Sitting in a windowless, air-conditioned cube in the Australian outback, they were ironically the two people in the world who had the best overview of the situation on the ground in Japan and at sea to the east and west of Okinawa. And that had meant their telephones were ringing constantly.

Ravi was on the telephone with a duty officer at the Pentagon. Allan had just got off the phone with his boss when it rang again. He had three half-drunk cups of coffee and six empty cans of energy drink in front of him. He took a slug of cold coffee and grabbed his phone. "Pritzkat."

"Mr. Pritzkat, please hold for the Director," a female voice said. Before he could reply, a familiar holding tune started playing in his ear. He looked at his watch, having lost all track of time in the perpetually semi-dark situation room that he and Ravi had commandeered. It was 4 a.m. in Virginia. He reached over and pushed Ravi's shoulder, pointing at his phone and mouthing the words 'The Director' at him. He ran a finger across his throat, a sign to Ravi to cut his call off as soon as he could. He put his phone into speaker mode.

"Yeah, look, I have a priority call coming in," Ravi told the caller he was on the line with. "No, I'm not saying you're not a priority..."

"Please go ahead, Director," the female voice said, suddenly loud in the small room.

"Mr. Pritzkat?" said a new, deep male voice. "This is Kyle Sandiland."

"Yes, Mr. Sandiland," Pritzkat said, leaning in to his phone. He'd never met the Director of the NSA, never even had occasion to speak with him. "Uh, I'm here with my colleague, Mr. Chandra."

"Gentlemen," the Director said, "I won't waste your time. I'm about to go into a meeting with the Under-Secretary of Defense and I want to make sure I have the latest of the latest data before I do." Allan thought he heard a car horn and there was a rumble on the line as though the Director was in a car somewhere.

"Where do you want to start, Sir?" Ravi asked, shrugging at Allan.

"Sino-Japanese fleet comms," Sandiland said. "Traffic pattern analysis."

"Sir, the pattern indicates comms activity at a level we've never seen before, centered on the Sino-Japanese fleet, but also right across the 3rd Military Command."

"Any new indications of ground unit movements on or from the Chinese mainland?"

"None, sir," Allan said. "I've sent reports on possible repositioning of mobile missile launchers…"

"Saw those."

"… but nothing indicating China has moved units on the mainland outside their normal zones of operation."

Allan heard papers rustling. "This engineering corps…"

"The 73rd Engineers? They haven't moved, sir. High level of ingoing and outgoing traffic, but still located in Shanghai."

"Could that be masked?"

"Yes, sir," Allan said. "But they haven't done so previously, even when conducting operations in the South China Sea."

Ravi pointed at himself and Allan leaned back from the phone. "Sir, Chandra here," Ravi said. "Sir, our latest analysis shows signals separation is increasing between Japanese fleet comms and Chinese fleet comms."

"Meaning?"

"Meaning, when they finished exercises and rejoined their two fleets to sail south, their comms signatures were congruent because they were sailing in formation. Our latest intel suggests the two fleets have split. The Chinese fleet is headed west, the Japanese fleet is headed east. Satellite imagery should be able to confirm it," he added.

There was a pause at the other end before Sandiland spoke again. "There's thick cloud over the East Asia Sea right now, I'm told, but infrared imaging confirms what you just reported. For your information, we are getting reports of increased political unrest in Japan – their fleet may have been ordered to return to port. Anything else?"

"It may be nothing, sir," Ravi said. He hesitated. "No ... forget it."

"Let me decide what's nothing and what isn't," Sandiland told him. "Go on."

"Sir, I've been monitoring Japan Self-Defense Force and security communications because of the situation on Okinawa."

"Yes?"

"As you know, many of the JSDF army units are still using ciphers and equipment that were provided in the time of the US-Japan military alliance, so we are able to get near-real-time decrypts from units that have not swapped out their equipment yet..."

"Give me the short version, son," Sandiland said. "I'll be pulling into an underground car park in about five minutes."

"Yes, sir," Ravi said. "Everything I'm seeing says to me that Japanese ground forces in Tokyo are mobilizing."

"Just in Tokyo?" the Director asked. "What about other urban centers?"

"In other urban centers there's heightened police comms traffic, but the only place outside Okinawa where I'm seeing direct mobilization orders for JSDF ground units is Tokyo."

"I see. Your thoughts?"

Ravi swallowed. He hated going out on a limb, especially on a call like this. But Allan nodded at him, urging him to keep going. "From what I've seen on news channels regarding the standoff between the government and the Palace, sir, I'd say the military is getting ready to put the Palace back in its box."

Girl On A Tank

Mitsuko Naishinnō, First Empress of the *Seiun,* or 'prosperity' era, heir to the Chrysanthemum throne, had spent her life defying convention and the advice of her 'elders and betters', and she was about to do so again. Because she knew that she was right.

She had received word of the kamikaze action by Takuya Kato and it had not made her break with grief. It had made her fiercely proud.

He had crippled the Chinese carrier and it had been taken under tow, headed for its home port of Dalian under a screen of heavy smoke, the rest of the Chinese strike group with it. Unlike Li Chen, the Chinese government was not in doubt about which pilot, and thus which regional power, had attacked its flagship and it had gone ominously quiet, not even reacting as the JS *Izumo* and the ships accompanying it were called back to port in Japan. But even if the Chinese leadership had lashed out diplomatically, to express their outrage at the betrayal of their new alliance, they would have been raging into a vacuum.

Mitsuko had shown the world that the Imperial House of Japan was not just a ceremonial institution. As head of Household Security, Santoshi commanded the 900-strong Imperial Guard police service, with agencies in Tokyo and Kyoto. By tradition and protocol, the 7,800 officers of the National Police Agency were also answerable to the Imperial House and their commanders did not question the authority of either the Imperial Guard or their new regent. Once he had realized his Empress was serious, Santoshi and the Imperial Security Forces had been very efficient indeed. In a lightning, simultaneously executed swoop by the Imperial Guard and the NPA, the Prime Minister and his Cabinet were all placed under house arrest, as were the Generals of the Army, Air Force, and Navy, who had conveniently gathered in Kyoto for a meeting of the General Staff to discuss reports of the attack on the *Liaoning.*

Her childhood friend Takuya Kato had done what needed to be done, had given his life without thought for himself, but because his nation had demanded it. How could she do less?!

She had been reviewing intelligence reports all night. Countless civilians and troops dead on Okinawa, both Japanese troops and US Marines. One US destroyer torpedoed, with media reports speculating the culprit was probably a Chinese submarine. Plus one Japanese destroyer sunk in a foolhardy engagement with the Americans and a further two so seriously damaged it was unlikely they could be salvaged.

She had been right to suspect that China's alliance with Japan was only ever intended to benefit the long-term interests of China, even though it dangled short-term economic benefits in front of the greedy politicians of the morally corrupt government. She had been right to sack that government, and the treasonous generals who had led Japan into an armed conflict with a former ally that was escalating out of control by the hour. And she was right that her place right now, in this moment of crisis, was not here in the Akasaka Palace but down on the streets, with her people!

She had just finished telling this to the well-meaning Santoshi.

"With respect, I cannot allow it!" he said. "It is not safe."

No one else could speak to her like that. No one else would dare. But for her entire life, Santoshi-san had been her bodyguard, her protector, and finally her head of Imperial Security. They were standing in a first-floor office inside the Kogu Police Headquarters, on the grounds of the Imperial Palace, just inside the main gates. Santoshi had moved them there when a crowd starting forming on the main boulevard outside the Palace, Uchibori Dori. They did not appear organized. They weren't chanting or waving placards, but their mood was febrile and fights had broken out between the crowd and a group of overzealous police who tried to move them on. On Santoshi's orders, the police had pulled back into the Palace grounds and were just keeping watch, preventing anyone from entering. Though it was still dark and hard to count, Santoshi's people had reported nearly fifty thousand people were estimated to be outside.

Then the tanks had arrived.

Six type 87 armored personnel carriers from the 1st Infantry Regiment at Camp Nerima, outside Tokyo, each carrying two machine guns, smoke and tear gas launchers, and bearing twelve men. They arrived in two columns, moving slowly down the boulevard toward the Palace entrance, ironically pausing beside the statue of Kusunoki Masashige, the 14th-Century samurai who resisted an attempt to overthrow Emperor Go-Daigo. There, they formed a wedge and began to press through the crowd toward the gates, an officer standing in the central hatch at the front of the lead vehicle with a bullhorn, ordering people out of the way. When they reached the gates they spread out – not facing outwards as though to defend it, but with their guns facing forward, toward the Palace.

The officer climbed out of his hatch up onto the vehicle and demanded in the name of the Japanese Self-Defense Ground Forces for the *traitor* Mitsuko Naishinnō to restore the legitimate government of Japan and step down from the Chrysanthemum throne. He pointed out that she had not yet had her enthronement ceremony, claimed she was not the legitimate ruler and that her actions were illegal.

"I am going to speak with them," Mitsuko told Santoshi firmly.

"It could provoke a riot. Blood will be shed, perhaps your own," he replied. He made to stand in her way. Frail as he was now, she could almost pick him up and set him aside, and his gesture made her heart swell.

"I am going, Santoshi-san," she said gently. "And before you insist again, I am going without a dozen armed police surrounding me."

He looked at her, his eyes moist now, and apparently decided she would not be dissuaded. "I know you," he said. "I knew you would do this. So I brought this." He reached down to a bulky duffel bag at his feet which seemed to contain clothing.

"I am not going to wear a bulletproof vest!" she said, anticipating his next suggestion.

He unzipped the bag. "No. I know. This is a different kind of armor." He stood and pulled from the bag a long, flowing, red and gold embroidered gown. He pointed at her plain jeans and black sweater. "Put this on. Your people need to see an Empress, not a *manji* girl." He held it out to her.

She smiled at his use of the street slang word for 'naughty' and lifted it from his hands. It was heavy, comprising twelve layers of overlaid and embroidered silk. "What is it?" she asked.

"This is the *jūnihitoe* kimono your grandmother wore to your grandfather's enthronement in November 1990," he said. "Before you were even born. It is based on a design from the *Heian* era, a thousand years old. I was going to suggest it for your enthronement."

"It must weigh twenty kilograms!" she protested, lifting it. "I won't be able to move in it!"

"You may not be able to wave your arms about, but in this kimono, you will move a nation," he said solemnly. "I will help you dress. Please remove your sweater, Empress."

The kimono was truly beautiful. After Mitsuko slipped off her sweater, she pulled on the plain white *hitoe* inner robe and then Santoshi helped her take on layer after layer of the brightly colored *uchigi*, each fastened with small buttons or ribbons to hold it in place. On top of these came the *uchiginu*, a beaten silk scarf used as a stiffener to hold the outer robe in place, the *uwagi*, a patterned robe, shorter than the *uchigi*, and finally, the *karaginu*, a heavily embroidered jacket.

Dressing her in this way was something that would usually be done by a team of the Household Staff, but Mitsuko found it incredibly touching that the old man had taken the duty on himself, in defiance of all tradition.

There was no mirror, so with some difficulty she held out her arms and did a slow turn in front of him. "How do I look?"

A tear rolled down his cheek, but he stood proudly, hands behind his back. "The Empress looks like a *manji* girl in a beautiful robe." He stepped forward, straightening the jacket, and then patted the lapel. "You look like the first Empress of Japan."

Santoshi did not let her go down to the street without a guard. He sent twelve men and women in plain clothes, all armed – six ahead of her to mingle with the crowd and six together with her as she walked out of the police station toward the crowd being held at the barrier.

Mitsuko could only take ridiculously small steps in the heavy kimono and realized it would take forever for her to reach the barriers. But step by tiny step, she moved forward.

At first, no one noticed her. Then there was a rising buzz from among the crowd. People who had been swarming around the tanks, arguing in groups, now pressed forward against the barrier to get a look at her. The flash of phone cameras sparkled from the crowd. The road into the Palace had been lit by harsh arc lights by the police and she inched up the road, with Santoshi and just one of his people by her side, as though she was being escorted up the red carpet at a society ball.

She felt ridiculous. She felt stiflingly hot. She could see one of the troop carriers over the head of the crowd and a soldier there, leaning on his machine gun.

She felt absolutely terrified.

She had rehearsed what she wanted to say, but she had completely forgotten it. She looked at the milling masses around the troop carrier with sudden angst and turned to Santoshi. "How will I speak?" she asked. "No one will hear me!"

"I have sent people ahead, Empress," he replied. "And the media are at the barrier. They are live streaming. What you have done, what you are about to do, is completely without precedent. The whole world will hear you."

The officer on the bullhorn was still yelling – she couldn't hear his words, or was too nervous to focus on them – but as she got to within twenty feet of the barrier, he stopped. Police started pulling

307

aside the barrier to allow her to pass and the crowd began to part slightly, people shuffling back, uncertain about what she was going to do. A preternatural silence had descended over the front of the crowd. She turned to Santoshi as she walked. "I want to make my address from on top of that tank."

"I thought as much," he sighed. "My people have taken collapsible scaffold stairs with them from the Imperial Gallery. You can be lifted onto the tank by them, if it is your will," he said.

"It is," she confirmed as they waded into the crowd.

The armored personnel carriers were idling their engines and as she stepped up to the lead vehicle, the officer there, a captain by the insignia on his uniform, looked worried, as though he had not actually anticipated that she would appear. He raised the bullhorn to his mouth, but then lowered it again as Santoshi's unmarked officers ordered the troops aside and placed the scaffolding steps up against the treads at the side of the tank. After a moment of hesitation the troops stepped aside, and with Santoshi holding one arm and his lieutenant the other, Mitsuko was assisted up the steps onto the deck of the troop carrier. Soldiers from inside the tanks formed a ring of green around each of them. They were bearing sidearms but had not taken their rifles out of their vehicles. Despite their demands for her abdication, she took that as a good sign. In the crowd she saw people nearby straining to hear her first words – further back, they were watching and listening to a live stream from nearby cameras.

She was not a slight woman and had worn a pair of black sneakers under the kimono that had an inch of heel. She was a half head higher than the officer on the tank and, with the kimono, twice as wide. He did not bow to her, as custom demanded. He had marshaled his feelings and was trying to project a defiant resolution, but he waited for her to speak.

She folded her hands in front of her and spoke softly to him so only he could hear.

"What is your name?"

"I am Captain Toshiki Yoshinobu!" he said, sticking out his jaw. "Of the Japan Self-Defense Forces Eastern Army, 1st Division."

"Captain Yoshinobu, who do you serve?" she asked.

"Not you!" he replied quickly.

She felt the knife's edge. "Who do you serve?" she repeated gently.

"I serve General Koji Akada!" he said. "Who you have illegally imprisoned."

It was the answer she had expected. "And who does he serve?"

"He serves the Government of Japan, which you have dismissed!" he said. "And I am here to…"

"Who …" she asked quickly, "… does the Government of Japan serve?"

He frowned. "They … they serve the people."

She leaned forward, forcing him to do the same. "Yes, Yoshinobu-san, they serve the people of the Empire of Japan, as do you, and I am their most passionate defender. When the government and the generals conspire against their country, in the service of a foreign power, it is your duty and mine to defend them."

She did not wait for him to respond; she wanted him to dwell on it a moment as she turned from him and lifted her arms as best she could toward the crowd. She could see news cameras forcing their way into the space around the troops ringing the troop carrier. "Citizens of Tokyo. Citizens of Japan! Our loyal troops!" Her voice rang out into the night and the crowd hushed. *Were they expecting her abdication? If so, they were about to be disappointed.*

"Yesterday, I ordered the dismissal of the Prime Minister and his Cabinet and dissolved the Parliament until new elections can be called in forty days, as the constitution demands. I also ordered the removal from their positions of the Generals of the Army, Navy, and Air Force.

"I have acted to defend our constitution, which clearly states that *the people of Japan forever renounce war*!" She paused and there was a ripple of applause from within the crowd, but she could tell she did not have them with her – yet.

309

"Yet, over the last two days in Okinawa, we have seen war!" she continued. "Not a war of our choosing! Not a war in the interests of Japan. This was a war being fought at the behest of *China*!"

Now there were loud boos from the crowd and a few shaking fists in the air. She had chosen her next words carefully.

"A Chinese aircraft killed the civilians in Naha. Our troops attacked the US base on Okinawa on the orders of Chinese generals! A Chinese submarine attacked an American ship in Japanese waters! Chinese politicians want war with America. And they want Japan to fight their war for them! America is not our natural enemy! For ten thousand years we have time and again defended our kingdom from the real threat, China, across the sea to the west. But now the Prime Minister and the Generals have sold our armed forces to the Chinese for a chest of gold, betrayed the constitution and betrayed their country!"

The crowd raised their voices now, angry. A few began pushing at the soldiers around the tanks.

She raised her hands. "Please, be calm and listen. Yesterday, a lone Japanese pilot from the JS *Izumo*, Lieutenant Takuya Kato, flew his jet aircraft into the Chinese aircraft carrier *Liaoning* and killed himself in a kamikaze action to stop the *Liaoning* from making war on Okinawa. The *Liaoning* was crippled and is returning to China." She paused, letting the words sink in. "I knew Lieutenant Takuya Kato personally. He was a simple man, who loved books, loved his beer and his udon, and he loved his country. And now Takuya Kato is dead. He died for you, he died to stop a war."

There was a shocked hush across the boulevard. What she was telling them had not been on the news reports. China had made every effort to ensure that there was no vision, satellite or otherwise, of its flagship limping back to port.

Mitsuko pointed up the boulevard to the statue of the warrior Kusunoki Masashige. "Like the samurai before him, Lieutenant Kato knew that his loyalty lay with this people, with the Empire of Japan, and not with the People's Republic of China!"

A mighty roar swept the crowd and the troops around their tanks drew together nervously.

She turned to the 1ˢᵗ Division captain and spoke in a loud voice as the shouting of the crowd died down. "Now is the time to decide, Captain Yoshinobu," she said, deliberately using his name so it would be recorded for posterity. "Do you and your men stand with Japan, as Kusunoki Masashige did, as the hero Lieutenant Takuya Kato did, or do you stand with China?" She almost spat the last word, then held out a hand to him, half expecting him to twist it behind her back and bundle her off the top of the tank.

She could see a war going on behind his eyes as he made his decision, but then he took a step to stand beside her, bowed deeply, then gripped her hand tightly and raised a fist in the air. "I stand with Japan!" he said. "I stand with *Kinjō Kōgō*, the Empress of Japan!"

Epilogue

Dragon Bird tossed his empty tea flask in the air, flipping it from end to end as he rode the elevator to the mall level. The doors opened and he stepped out into the flow of shoppers, none of whom gave him a second glance.

He had just been advised that Advanced Persistent Threat Unit 23 was being disbanded. Frangi and her KAHLO system were being retasked and Po had been assigned to an economic warfare unit that operated out of Hong Kong. It was not a promotion, but he had been happy because he had heard the restaurants in Hong Kong were even better than in Shanghai. Tanken had already been recalled to the Navy and, after Major Shaofeng's efforts to paint him as the scapegoat for their failure to disable the USS *Makin Island*, DB was not hopeful for his future prospects.

DB had spent the last couple of weeks in uncomfortable 'debriefings' and they had each kept coming back to the one question – why had the hijacked Stingray fired on the US destroyers instead of its primary target, the US carrier? Who had given it the order to fire? If not Major Shaofeng, if not Dragon Bird, then who? Could Officer Tanken have decided to do so of his own volition? Was it possible the American drone had acted autonomously, to fire on its own warships? It was obvious no one believed so and Tanken was a ready-made fall guy for an operation that had gone so well for so long and then, at the last, critical moment, had gone so horribly wrong.

One operation among many.

Chinese State media had contained no mention of the military action on Okinawa. The last footage shown of the *Liaoning* had been taken when it was still at sea, during multinational exercises. These exercises had shown that Japan was not suited to be an equal partner in a military alliance with China, a State media spokesperson said. Its forces had been comprehensively shamed during Operation Red Dove and the Sino-Japanese self-defense treaty had been officially suspended by China due to the inadequacies of Japanese forces to meet the minimum standard needed to operate with their superior Chinese counterparts safely. China also deeply regretted the 'precipitous' actions of the former Japanese government and strongly condemned its attack on US forces on Okinawa.

Diplomatic relations between China and Japan had been frozen until clarity emerged regarding the nature and intentions of any future Japanese government.

As a member of Unit 61938, however, Dragon Bird did not only get his news via Chinese State media. He had learned that his operation was not the only one to have gone awry in the action around Okinawa. His own sources within the People's Liberation Army Navy had told him the *Liaoning* had been put out of action for at least a year, perhaps longer. The anti-China Japan Nationalist Party was leading in the polls and was expected to win government at the coming Japanese elections. In Taiwan, the main pro-China opposition leader had been arrested and charged with sedition. The US had announced its intention to base more troops on Okinawa and its ambassador had told a press conference that as soon as a new government was in place in Tokyo, it wanted to begin negotiations for the right to expand its footprint and resume control of the former US Kadena airbase on Okinawa.

As he had packed his small bag and picked up his thermos for the last time as leader of APT 23, DB had seen a news report that the USS *GW Bush* carrier strike group, which had just finished calling at White Beach and then at Seoul in Korea, was now on its way to dock in Taipei on Taiwan, in what Chinese media called the 'most brazen naval provocation of the modern century'. He had shrugged at that. With only one functioning aircraft carrier remaining, one still under construction, and without the support of Japan, the Chinese Navy was hardly in any position to challenge it.

Regarding his own future, DB was sanguine. He had led a successful operation to penetrate to the heart of DARPA, the USA's secret weapons sandbox, and had proven not only that his attack vector was viable, but also that it could be weaponized. And they had successfully withdrawn KAHLO from the DARPA system before it could be counter-attacked and give up all its secrets. He was certain NSA CYBERCOM would be in paralysis right now, worried about what other stealth attacks may have been executed within their walls, which of their systems they could now trust and which they could not. To say nothing of the data they shared with allies, whose systems must also now be suspect.

He had been given two weeks' leave and it had been intimated that he would receive an important new assignment on his return, exploring a new attack vector with ten times the potential of KAHLO.

Bunny O'Hare stood at the door to Noriko Fukada's apartment. A small shrine had been put against the wall by one of the neighbors and there were votive offerings and flowers lining the wall along the sidewalk.

Bunny hadn't actually said goodbye to her friend. The last time she had talked with her, she had tried and failed to persuade her to get off the island. And made the mistake of thinking *what the hell, she'd survived 103 years, she'd probably make it to 104.* Jensen had been all kinds of messed up when she visited him in hospital, but he'd managed to give her some idea of the cluster that had been the Japanese action at White Beach. Even though he had told O'Hare how Noriko had died, Bunny still didn't understand how the frail old woman had ended up a part of the fighting outside White Beach naval base.

The woman had survived the Second World War, the Cold War, and lived to see Korean reunification. She had been alive for the birth of atomic weapons, television, bullet trains, the internet, renewable energy, driverless cars, and quantum computing. She tended cactuses and made tea for her neighbors. She had deserved to die quietly and peacefully in her bed.

The only thing that gave Bunny some satisfaction was knowing that Chuck, the former NSA spook, was being held in pre-trial custody in Fort Leavenworth, Kansas, where he would probably spend the rest of his days after being convicted of treason. It turned out that he had booked a flight to Hong Kong from Naha airport, which pretty much confirmed which master he had been serving. He'd tried to escape during the chaos of the Japanese infantry attack on White Beach, but had only made it as far as the wire on the western boundary of the base before an alert Marine by the name of Sergeant Tracy Williams had confronted him and returned him to the base brig. O'Hare knew she would kick herself the rest of her life for putting Chuck in a position where he could help the Chinese hijack her Stingray, but if nothing else, it had exposed vulnerabilities in DARPA's network that they could now close. Until China found new attack vectors, of course.

She looked at the other flowers in front of Noriko's building and then at the ones she had bought at the metro station. Hers looked wilted and pathetic and she was suddenly embarrassed at the sight of them.

"They are beautiful, aren't they," a woman beside her suddenly said in English. O'Hare hadn't noticed her. She was about Bunny's age, dressed simply in jeans and a dark blue sweater, her hair tied up in a single ponytail. No makeup. Not an office worker – a housewife or mother, perhaps, her children in school – though she did have the natural beauty and poise of a film star. She was talking about the flowers around the shrine, of course, not the ones Bunny was holding. The Japanese woman also had some flowers in her hand and knelt down to place them with the others against the wall. Her bouquet was small but elegant. Of course.

Bunny put her train station flowers down quickly and took a step back. "Yeah, they are. Did you know her?" she asked.

"I only met her once," the woman said in clearly accented British English. "When she turned a hundred years old. We talked about her childhood on Okinawa. She had a presence, don't you think?"

That was when Bunny broke.

The woman took a step toward her and held Bunny gently until she had pulled herself together enough to get a tissue from her pocket and wipe her nose. Bunny couldn't help noticing she smelled wonderful and the sweater was probably pure cashmere. Not for the first time, she felt a bit shabby. But she wasn't a cashmere kind of girl; she had realized that a long time ago.

"Can I have one?" the woman asked, indicating the package of tissues, and Bunny was glad to see she wasn't the only one who was a wreck. They both blew their noses at the same time and laughed.

"You are from the US base?" the woman asked her, tucking the tissue into her jeans.

"I was," Bunny said.

"Oh. You're going home?"

"Not sure. I'm just a contractor and things are ... well, you know," Bunny admitted. "My last job was 'terminated early', you could say."

"Because of the conflict," the young Japanese woman nodded.

"No, because I punched a Chinese spy called Chuck in the nose while he was under interrogation," Bunny said. "But I didn't tell you that."

"Consider it forgotten," the woman said. "But I hope you find another job."

"Yeah, nah, don't worry, I'm a bit of a rarity. They'll find something for me to do."

"A bit of a rarity. Yes." The woman smiled at her. "I don't suppose you'd like to join me for a beer somewhere?" she said. "We can drink a toast to lost friends and you can tell me some stories about Fukada-san. I'm sure she had a fascinating life."

Bunny looked at her watch. It wasn't like she had anything better to do. "Sure," she said. "That would be nice. I know a place near here." She held out her hand. "Karen O'Hare."

The woman shook it. "Mitsuko," she said. They fell in quietly beside each other as they walked off.

Bunny took out some chewing gum, offered it to the other woman and took a piece herself, chewing thoughtfully. "You said you met Noriko when she turned a hundred?"

"Yes."

"This wouldn't have been at the Imperial Palace in Tokyo by any chance?"

316

"Yes, actually. All centenarians get an invitation, it's such an honor to meet them."

"Thought so," Bunny said. "So you're *that* Mitsuko?"

"Yes. I'm afraid so."

"And those guys walking along behind us, they're with you?" she asked, looking over her shoulder.

The woman looked behind her, where two men in dark suits and sunglasses were discreetly keeping pace, and nodded. "Sorry. Perhaps this was a bad idea. A week ago our countries were shooting at each other."

"Nah, I'm cool with it," Bunny said. She threw an arm over Mitsuko's shoulders. "Any friend of Noriko is a friend of mine."

/END

The following is a preview of the next title
in the Future War series:
'SUBORBITAL'

Chelyabinsk, 15 February 2013, 0915 local

Nine-year-old Anastasia Grahkovsky had the same breakfast ritual every morning and as she spooned her semolina porridge into a bowl, careful to avoid the biggest lumps, she had no idea it would nearly cost her her life.

Anastasia hated the lumps. Not only did they stick in your throat, but if they were big enough, then the semolina on the outside of the lump was squishy, while the grains in the middle of the lump were uncooked and crunchy. Her mother made the porridge when she was working day shifts at the Zinco plant, but at the moment she was on night shift, which meant her brother Sergei had made breakfast, and at this he sucked.

But she had no one to complain to, because he had already left for school when she got up, so she loaded up her bowl, picked out the biggest lumps and dumped them back in the pot, then pulled her dressing gown tighter around herself and walked to the window of their apartment, climbing up to the windowsill and sitting on the ledge looking out over the line of birch trees between herself and the refrigeration works. She was really getting too big to sit there but she'd done it every morning as long as she could remember, and though she was really too chubby now to sit comfortably, she still did it. Her class was doing a fitness assessment this morning, but it was only 14 degrees outside and she had asthma, so she didn't need to be at school until they were finished at 11.

The sun was just coming up, though at this time of year it never really got far into the sky before it was going down again. She shivered. Lumpy and cold. It described her porridge, and herself. She shifted her backside on the narrow windowsill and leaned her head against the cool glass.

Then the sky lit up.

There was a brilliant ball of light moving across the sky from right to left, leaving a trail of white smoke behind it. Her eyes were drawn to it like it was magnetic and, as she watched, it speared toward the ground at incredible speed, then while it was still high in the sky, it exploded!

The entire sky flared brilliant white and Anastasia blinked, her irises slamming shut, but too late. When she opened them again, all she could see were red and black blotches.

"Mama!" she screamed reflexively, though she knew her mother was five miles away at the zinc factory. She panicked, hands scrabbling at the glass window pane. "Mama!"

Then came an ear-shattering sonic boom, the window she was sitting beside shattered into a thousand needle-sharp fragments, and Anastasia was blown back into her kitchen, skin flayed from her face, sunburned, blind and deaf.

It was a meteor that detonated over Chelyabinsk in 2013, though for Anastasia Grahkovsky it might as well have been a nuclear bomb. She'd been one of 1,200 people injured that day when the 66-foot wide, 12,000-ton lump of rock had slammed into the earth's atmosphere at a speed of 40,000 miles an hour and exploded 20 miles above Chelyabinsk.

Anastasia got her hearing back, but not her sight. And as she stood at her washbasin 21 years later and applied thioglycolic acid to her ravaged scalp to remove the hair which grew there in random tufts, she couldn't help reflect on how she could draw a direct line between that day in 2013 and now.

The roof of her mother's zinc factory had collapsed, trapping a hundred workers, including her mother. Her school had been locked down and the students kept inside, and her brother hadn't been able to come home until the middle of the afternoon. So Anastasia had lain on the floor of the kitchen, curled into a ball, whimpering and bleeding from a hundred cuts, until her brother got there at 2pm. He didn't see her at first, the apartment a scene of devastation, freezing wind blowing through the gaping window, glass all over the kitchen, cupboards and their contents strewn across the bench and floor. And Anastasia.

A neighbor had driven them to hospital, Anastasia wrapped in a bedspread, not crying, barely breathing. The hospital emergency ward was chaotic – a woman with a broken back lay on a stretcher in a brace, people with cuts and broken limbs sat on chairs or on the floor up and down corridors as nurses and doctors ran from one to the other trying to triage the worst cases. The car crash victims were the worst, blinded by the flash and then injured as their cars plowed head on into buildings, poles, trees, or each other.

Thanks to the quick action of her brother and neighbor, to the care of overstretched doctors and nurses who stopped her from dying of shock and cold, Anastasia had lived. And on that day was born her dread fascination with the power of meteorites.

She could trace the day it really took hold to a morning when she was thirteen and walking with her brother to school. She knew the way herself by then; after all, it had been four years since she became blind. She had a cane and could walk herself there, but her brother insisted on walking with her, made her take his arm the whole way. He was sixteen, stronger than her and sighted, so she couldn't exactly fight him.

One morning there had been roadworks and they had to take a detour through an abandoned car yard.

"See," Sergei had told her, "this is why you need me. How would you have found your way around the roadworks?"

"I would have asked someone," she'd said grumpily.

"Yeah? Before or after you fell in that pit over there?" he'd asked.

She'd been about to say something smart right back at him when her foot had come down on a stone, and she twisted her ankle. He let go of her as she gave a small cry and dropped to one knee, grabbing her foot.

"You OK?" he asked.

"No, stupid," she said angrily. "You walked me straight over a dumb rock." She sat down on the cold ground and began massaging her ankle.

His feet scuffed beside her, and he grunted, "Hey, I think it's a piece of the meteor." She heard him bend over and pick something up. "Yeah, for sure."

People had been finding the small pebble-sized meteorites all over Chelyabinsk since the explosion. Nearly every family had one or two on a mantlepiece or bookshelf. But not their family. She was sure her brother would have found one before now, but either he or their mother had decided it wasn't a thing they wanted inside their house after what had happened to her.

She stood up and held out her hand. "Give it to me."

"Nah," he said. "It's worthless. You used to be able to get a few rubles for them, but no one is buying anymore."

"I don't care," she said. "I want it."

"Mum will throw it out," he told her.

She stuck her hand out further. "Just give it me!"

He dropped it in her palm and she closed her hand around it. It was hard, like a lump of coal, but round. She ran her fingers over it. The surface was smooth in parts, rough in others; pockmarked, like her face.

She slipped it into the pocket of her jeans and tested her ankle. "Let's go," she said.

From that day, she had started collecting meteorites from friends, from her mother's workmates, from people selling them on the internet. Her mother had tried to stop her at first, then had complained about the growing pile of rocks in Anastasia's bedroom; on shelves, in boxes, under her bed. Eventually she shrugged and gave up.

Anastasia learned how to classify them and sort them by feel. Two thirds were smooth-surfaced chondrites, some with shock veins of nickel or iron running through them. But about one third were melt braccia, a fine matrix of chondrite fragments fused

321

together by a collision some time in the meteor's past. She valued these more. They felt like she felt, blackened and battered. But they were survivors, like her.

She had a quick mind and an obsession with science, and one of her teachers had taught herself braille so that she could feed Anastasia's insatiable thirst for knowledge about the universe outside Chelyabinsk, outside Russia, outside Earth. She was studying text books from the Chelyabinsk State University while she was still in junior high, and left high school two years early to start undergraduate studies in astrophysics. As an honors student, she had been the first researcher to quantify exactly how much energy the Chelyabinsk explosion had released, her calculations revising the previous estimate up from 1.4 to 1.8 petajoules or the equivalent of 480 kilotons of TNT, 33 times the energy released by the atomic bomb at Hiroshima. She had published her calculations together with her physics professor, and it had been at an astrophysics forum 1,000 miles across the Ural Mountains to the west in Moscow, where they had presented a poster, that she had been talent spotted by an officer of the Russian Aerospace Force's Titov Test Center.

Six months later, at the age of 22, she joined the research program called *Molotok*.

Baikonur, Kazakhstan, 2032, 0615 local

Colonel Andrei Yakob was accustomed to the effect his lead scientist had on people she had never met before. The first thing they usually noticed was her shaved head. The second thing they noticed was the filigree pattern of scars over her scalp, face, and neck from where she had been sliced by flying glass. Curiously, they did not always notice her blindness, especially if, like now, she was sitting quietly at a table full of people, having been the first to arrive, and being largely ignored by the many senior officers and government staff around the table who considered themselves rather more important than some woman they had never met and who, frankly, made them a little queasy to look at.

The group around the table called itself the Technical Committee, but there was nothing technical about it. There were no engineers or scientists among the 12 members present, and they were not interested in debating technical issues in anything more than the most superficial of detail. If the name should reflect the truth, they would call themselves the Political Committee, because their one and only function was to approve or reject recommendations from the Titov Test Center's senior officers about whether to progress a project to the final milestone, which was a recommendation to the Minister of Defense, General Andrey Gerasimov, to deploy, redirect, or abandon a project.

Project Molotok had now completed its final trial and reached its final milestone.

Despite having served in the armed forces all of his adult life, Yakob was also an accomplished bureaucrat. He knew that to walk into a meeting such as this, without knowing in advance how each of the members of the committee would vote, was suicidal. So, standing at the end of the table, next to his lead scientist, he already knew that today's decision was hanging on a thread. Six of the voting members were in favor of canceling Molotok, six in favor of deploying. None believed the research should be continued or redirected into other avenues. The committee required a simple majority of seven votes to confirm a decision, so unless Anastasia Grahkovsky could persuade at least one of the 'no' voters to change their mind, Molotok would be canceled today. He'd told Anastasia Grahkovsky this, and had rehearsed with her every single argument he felt might sway his colleagues to change their vote.

Andrei Yakob was a firm believer that Molotok would change the balance of military power in Russia's favor in a way no other weapon under development could do. He fervently believed it should be deployed, and the sooner, the better. With the Middle East about to go up in flames due to the collapsing price of oil, and Russia's oil- and gas-based economy on the brink of a meltdown, he was convinced that Molotok would give Russia leverage no other nation could match in the next decade or more. That was what he had just spent the last half hour explaining to the committee. The why. He felt he had brought most of the room along with him.

Now it would be up to Grahkovsky to seal the deal by explaining the how.

"In conclusion, ballistic missiles armed with nuclear weapons are not an option in the current threat environment unless we want to trigger mutually assured destruction and planetary devastation. Hypersonic cruise missiles like our *Tsirkon*, traveling at a mere five times the speed of sound, can now be intercepted by quantum AI directed high-energy liquid laser defenses with more than 80% certainty. There is no conventional weapon in our arsenal that can be used to strike an enemy at a moment's notice, with devastating effect, in a way that cannot be countered, and that guarantees the absolute destruction of even highly protected hard targets." He paused, letting his words sink in, looking around the table into the eyes of the doubters. Good. He could tell they were listening. "Molotok is the solution to these problems. As you know, it has completed the final phase of its testing. Chief Scientist Grahkovsky will now run through the results of those tests and take your questions, and I will sum up with our recommendation."

The young woman stood. As he sat down, Yakob noticed more than one of the committee members flinch involuntarily, or look down suddenly at the notes or tablets in front of them. Some openly stared.

She had no notes in front of her, though she did have a digital braille notepad device he had seen her use on other occasions. But she knew her data inside out, so he was not worried she would trip up over the detail, and besides this group was not the kind to ask detailed questions. All she had to do was convince them Molotok worked, and after all their time rehearsing for today, he was completely confident she would.

"Thank you, Colonel, ladies and gentlemen." She stared straight ahead, her eyes dull and unfocused. Now even the slower members of the audience might begin to realize she was not only scarred, but also blind. She gave a slight smile. "But before I begin with the results of our final series of tests of the Molotok system, I must make a comment to Colonel Yakob. Colonel Yakob is a true champion of this project, and he has put his personal and professional life on the line to see it succeed. Colonel Yakob has asked me to explain to you why you should be confident to propose to Minister Gerasimov that Russia deploy Molotok. Instead, I am here to tell you why you should *not*."

It took a moment for Yakob to process what the woman had just said. He had been nodding and smiling when she called him a champion of the project, but only as people around the table stirred in surprise did he take in what she had actually said. Several committee members leaned toward each other and began murmuring, and Yakob rose to his feet, taking the scientist by the arm. "Perhaps you and I should talk, outside," he said. "Chairman, if you will just excuse us…"

The committee chairman was a Russian Aerospace Force Lieutenant General called Yevgeny Bondarev. While those around him had reacted with shock or surprise at Grahkovsky's opening words, he had just smiled slightly and steepled his fingers beneath his chin. He had been one of the six doubters identified by Yakob, and now he leaned forward, pointing at Yakob's recently vacated chair. "Comrade Colonel, please sit down. Chief Scientist Grahkovsky, please continue."

Yakob reluctantly slipped Grahkovsky's arm free and scowled as he sat. His finely laid plans had just gone seriously sideways.

Anastasia smoothed the sleeve Yakob had grabbed, and continued. "Thank you, Chairman Bondarev. I know this will displease Colonel Yakob, but I do not believe that the Molotok weapons system should be deployed."

Bondarev raised his eyebrows and tapped on the tablet in front of him. "I have read the reports of your final test series, Grahkovsky. They indicate the weapons system performed with devastating effectiveness. Are you saying that the reports are incorrect or that false data has been presented to this committee?" He was in his early forties, had the tanned, square-jawed features of a movie star warrior, and Yakob knew he had been decorated several times as a pilot for bravery under fire.

Grahkovsky shook her head. "No, Chairman. Molotok performed completely within the defined success parameters. All test targets were acquired within the 30-minute operational window, the launch platforms experienced no significant failures during live-fire exercises, and the targets were struck with, as you say, devastating effect. The post-attack analyses showed our most modern armored vehicles were easily destroyed, the bunker complex test site comprising hardened concrete reinforced with steel rebar was penetrated to a depth of around six meters, effectively collapsing it. Used against moored warships with half-inch deck plating, it sunk three of four and disabled the fourth to the extent it would likely have been written off. If used against troops in an urban environment, we expect it will have an effect footprint of between two and five square miles and a guaranteed casualty ratio of 47% with a confidence interval of 5%." She paused to let her audience keep up. "The Molotok weapons system met every success criterion that this committee imposed on it."

Unlike Yakob or his fellow committee members, Bondarev did not appear phased by the contradiction in the woman's words. He simply sat back and folded his arms. "Why, then, would you recommend that the system not be deployed?"

Anastasia Grahkovsky lifted her chin and turned her head, first to the left, and then to the right, her eyes staring into the distance. "Look at me," she said.

There was more murmuring around the table, but Bondarev did as she asked, and even Yakob could not help but lean back in his chair and look up at her, seeing again her ravaged face as though for the first time.

"I know your history, Chief Scientist. And everyone here knows what happened at Chelyabinsk. Your point, please?" Bondarev asked quietly.

"My point, Comrade Chairman, is that if you use this weapon in a populated area, those who are not lucky enough to die will become …" she turned around slowly, lifting her arms out to her side so that her sleeves rose up her arms, showing the committee members the scars there too. When she was facing them again, she lowered her arms and folded her hands in front of her. "This," she said. "Or worse."

There was a shocked silence around the table.

Yakob tried to recover. "Chairman, if I can just…"

Bondarev held a hand in the air to silence Yakob. "I have a question for the Chief Scientist," he said.

Grahkovsky didn't flinch. She kept her chin in the air and stared straight ahead. "Yes, Chairman?"

"Have you ever seen the impact of a fuel-air explosive weapon on a human being?" he asked.

"No sir," she replied. "Nor would I want to."

"None of us would want to, Grahkovsky," Bondarev said quickly, his voice cold. "If you are within the blast epicenter, you are burned alive. If you are within the effect radius, you are suffocated, or buried alive as buildings around you collapse, or crushed by flying debris, or poisoned by unspent fuel mist. In Anadyr, I was buried alive when the enemy used a fuel-air explosive to attack my airbase and we lost *two hundred* men and women in that one attack." The impact of his words was all the more chilling to Yakob because he was saying them in a detached and clinical tone. "This is what modern weapons do, Chief Scientist. We deploy them precisely because of what they do, in the full knowledge there will be casualties, both military and civilian, and we do so only out of necessity, knowing that if we do not, the enemy will. You may sit."

She didn't. She remained standing. "With respect, Chairman, some weapons are banned under treaty and we have signed such treaties." She held up her hand and started counting on her fingers. "Cluster munitions, chemical weapons, biological weapons, low-yield nuclear weapons, cyber-attacks directed at medical infrastructure…" She lowered her hands again and clasped them calmly in front of her. "If we deploy it, I guarantee this weapon will one day be on that list."

Everyone turned to look at Bondarev's reaction, but he remained impassive. "Your opinion is noted. You need not sit. You are excused from the meeting, Chief Scientist Grahkovsky."

Heads swung back to look at her, wondering how she would react to being dismissed, but she simply tightened her lips, reached

327

down for a cane that was resting against her chair, and turned, tapping her way toward the door and out the room.

Anastasia waited outside in a cold corridor on an uncomfortable chair. After about 45 minutes, she heard voices coming closer and the door to the meeting room opened. People filed out, some chatting, but no one addressed her and of course she couldn't see if any of them had given her a second glance. The last two to emerge were Bondarev and Yakob and she heard them speaking about the agenda for a future meeting, giving her no clue to the outcome of this one.

Bondarev said goodbye to Yakob and then raised his voice. "Goodbye, Grahkovsky."

She nodded. "Goodbye, Lieutenant General Bondarev."

There were footsteps and then a creak as Yakob took the seat beside her. She could smell sweat and aftershave, and heard his feet sliding on the floor as he stretched them out in front of himself.

"Am I fired?" she asked.

"You should be," he sighed. "What in God's name were you thinking?"

"Was the project canceled?" she asked, ignoring his question.

She heard him reach into a pocket for cigarettes and a lighter, and then sit them on his lap. It wasn't allowed to smoke inside the administration building at Titov.

"The recommendation for deployment was approved," he said. "By a vote of ten to two. It will go to the Minister within the month."

Anastasia smiled, grabbed her cane, and stood.

"Why the hell are you smiling?" Yakob demanded. "You nearly cost us everything. Where are you going?"

"Back to work," she said. "Are you coming?"

There was a beat or two before he said, "Are you trying to suggest you wanted this outcome?"

"You needed Bondarev's vote," she said. "I got it for you. And more besides."

"You could have cost us the whole committee!"

"But I didn't," she insisted. "Your way was to persuade them through logic, but that was working against us. Molotok will be the most expensive weapons system Russia has ever deployed, at a time we can barely afford to keep our Navy afloat and our Air Force in the air. In an age of precision weapons, it is inaccurate. In an age of sophistication, it is crude. Your sources said six of the committee were against us, while mine told me eight were. But you were right, we needed Bondarev on our side. I knew he could bring the others with him so I went for his weak spot."

"Bondarev is a decorated war hero, he has no bloody weak spot," Yakob said.

"Ah, but clearly he does," she said. She reached out with uncanny accuracy, using only the sound of his voice to guide her, and put the tip of her cane on Yakob's chest, above his heart. "Here."

"Nonsense. The man has no heart."

"No, but he is a patriot. I had a conversation with a military intelligence officer who served with Bondarev in the 3rd Air Army. He told me about that attack in which Bondarev lost two hundred personnel. He also told me that Bondarev had confided in him that it was weakness of will that had killed those men and women. He said Russia had held itself back from using the most powerful weapons in its arsenal during that conflict, while its enemies had not, and as a result it had been defeated. He has sworn more than once that this would never happen again under his command. So I did two things." She lowered her cane and placed it between her feet. "I told him that Molotok was a terrifyingly powerful new weapon. And I challenged him not to use it."

That night, Anastasia stood in her kitchen, making herself dinner. To anyone unfamiliar with her history, it would have seemed most bizarre. A woman, standing alone in her apartment, cooking herself a vegetarian stroganoff. In total darkness. But to Anastasia, it was just another Tuesday. Occasionally she did laugh at herself, and wonder what a visitor might think. But then, visitors weren't really a problem she had to deal with, the way her life had turned out.

Another thing that might have struck an observer was that she was strangely happy that night. She had just engineered a decision which meant that a new weapon of mass destruction was about to be visited on an unsuspecting world, a weapon she had helped develop. And not only that, she had told the absolute truth. The effect of the weapon on those civilians not lucky enough to be killed by it directly was exactly the same as she had experienced at Chelyabinsk. A shock wave, flying glass and debris, collapsed buildings – blindness, deafness, broken bones and backs, flayed skin. But as she stirred her stroganoff and added a little more pepper, she was whistling a happy tune.

Because though Anastasia Grahkovsky had lived through the meteor strike on Chelyabinsk, a part of her had died on the floor of that kitchen as she writhed in blood and glass. She had not only lost her physical sight, she had lost the ability to see beyond her own fascination with the power of meteors, of the orgiastic energy of objects striking the planet from space. The thought of it drove her; no, it consumed her. Anastasia had had sex, but nothing in her life had compared to the ecstasy she had felt hearing that the weapon she had created had destroyed those tanks, obliterating them in a two-mile-wide crater, turned that concrete bunker complex into powder and smoke. Having lived through a powerful meteor strike, having developed into one of the world's leading experts in the destructive power of kinetic energy deployed at the petajoule scale, she had determined that it wasn't just something she wanted to have lived through.

It was something she wanted to *control*.

"I am become death, the destroyer of worlds," scientist Robert Oppenheimer had thought to himself as he watched the first atomic weapon explode over the desert of New Mexico. It had been a quote from Hindu scripture, the Bhagavad Gita.

As Anastasia Grahkovsky had read the report of her weapon wiping an empty Siberian village off the face of the planet, leaving only a five-mile by five-mile sea of mud, bricks, and smoking sticks, a quote from a different scripture had come to her mind. It was one she had heard a bearded, black-robed priest say in mass in the church in Chelyabinsk after she got out of hospital, and which felt like it was written just for her. Psalm 2, 7:12: "*Ask of Me, and I will surely give the nations as your inheritance, and the very ends of the earth as your possession. You shall break them with a rod of iron, you shall shatter them like earthenware.*"

'SUBORBITAL' IS COMING IN 2020

Author notes: on the writing of OKINAWA

Following up a novel like BERING STRAIT, in which a team of ex-military advisers helped set a pretty high bar for authenticity, was never going to be easy. So I approached it in a similar way, putting together a team of volunteer 'beta readers' who were enthusiastic, generous with their time, and expert in their fields.

As always, the writing started with a desire to take existing mil-tech platforms and those under development and push them a short way into the future to explore how combat might be altered by their appearance on the battlefield. In BERING STRAIT that platform was the X-47 unmanned combat air vehicle. In researching OKINAWA, I became particularly fascinated by the US government's decision to green light the Boeing XLUUV Orca platform for further development. In the words of the manufacturer, "The vehicle's advanced autonomy enables it to perform at sea for months at a time, delivering a more affordable, mission-capable solution over traditional UUVs." The more I read, the more convinced I became that such vessels are the future of submarine warfare. And the more terrified I became at the idea of them falling into the wrong hands. In this novel, those hands are China's, but the threat could also come from non-state actors such as terrorists.

Next came the challenge of creating a plausible conflict scenario which is grounded both in history and in current affairs. I didn't want to do a simple 'China invades Taiwan and the USA gets drawn in' plot, but I am grateful to Japanese PM Shinzo Abe for providing me with the germ of the idea for OKINAWA when in 2018 he visited Beijing and declared a desire for China and Japan to begin a 'new era' of cooperation and co-existence. In OKINAWA, I took that declaration to one admittedly extreme but not impossible end: a mutual defense pact between Japan and China.

Many readers will realize there is a centuries-long enmity between the two empires, but Chinese ambition has been tempered in the past by Japan's relative military strength. Japan won a war against China at the turn of the twentieth century, and despite heroic resistance by China, Japanese troops only relinquished control of large parts of China at the end of World War Two after

Russia forced Japanese troops out of Manchuria and the atomic bomb brought an end to Japan's willingness to continue the war.

Since World War Two, China has reversed the military balance dramatically. Japan could no longer stand alone against the People's Republic, and it knows it. Hence its recent and unprecedented overtures to China.

The plot for OKINAWA followed as I played that thought out and explored what such a Sino-Japanese pact might mean for the region – two former enemies, the two largest economies in the region, now united militarily?

Throw into that mix the potential for Korean unification within the next twenty years, a resurgent threat from Russia, and a related drawdown in the US presence in the region as a consequence, and you have a recipe for Chinese domination of the Asian sphere. The threat of which the US Pentagon recognized in its 2018 National Defense Strategy document.

What could China not do, with Japan at its side? It was an idea worth playing with, I hope you agree!

Japan has already taken the first steps toward greater alignment with China, but is a long way from embracing a status as junior partner in the Pacific region. Rather than signing on to the Chinese Belt and Road initiative, it has created a competing alliance with … not the USA, please note … but with the European Union.

So we are still many years from the scenario painted in this novel. But we are not many years from the time by which China will choose to act to achieve reunification with Taiwan. I believe there are strong grounds to believe China's preference is to achieve this without a full-scale military invasion – war is, after all, bad for business. But that does not mean China will shy away from demonstrations of its new military might and Korea, Japan, the Philippines, and others in the region could be unwilling parties in China's Taiwan endgame.

FX Holden, Copenhagen, November 2019

7-3-21

CPSIA information can be obtained
at www.ICGtesting.com
Printed in the USA
LVHW041744120220
646719LV00004B/755